C000172569

Mr Bad Face

Mr Bad Face

Mark Morris

PIATKUS

Acknowledgements

Thanks, as ever, to my wife, Nel, for her unflinching support, love and faith in what has been a very tough year.

Thanks also to all the friends who've kept me going - you know who you are.

Especial thanks to Grenville Williams for all his information on how the police go about dealing with a murder inquiry. Any deviations from reality are down to me, not him.

Copyright © 1996 by Mark Morris

First published in Great Britain in 1996 by
Judy Piatkus (Publishers) Ltd of
5 Windmill Street, London W1

The moral right of the author has been asserted

A catalogue record for this book is available from the British Library

ISBN 0-7499-0330-9

Set in 11/12pt Times by Action Typesetting Limited, Gloucester
Printed and bound in Great Britain by
Butler & Tanner Ltd, Frome & London

This one is for my son, David Jack,
dedicated with love so fierce it hurts.
'Fuff'

Prologue: 1943

They each had their routines, their mascots, their talismans. Each morning before an op Straker would look in the cracked mirror above the sink where he was shaving and would see his reflection asking anxiously, 'Am I ever going to see you again?' And then afterwards, when he came back, he'd say, 'Welcome home, me old mate,' and he'd take out the stone Jean had given him – the one where a flaw in the rock had caused crystal deposits to form a white cross in the grey granite – and he'd kiss it and brandish it like a tiny trophy.

He remembered Jean giving him the rock as if it were yesterday. He'd just been accepted by the RAF. They'd driven to Southwold for the day despite the rain and the buffeting wind. They'd been the only people walking on the beach. Jean had stooped, and at first he thought she'd lost her balance and he'd put out a hand to catch her arm. But she had risen with the rock in her hand, shiny and dark in the rain, and she had held it up, showing him the white cross. 'A kiss for luck,' she'd said, her voice cracking, and then had stood on tiptoes to press her warm lips against his cold ones, pushing the rock into his palm.

It was easy to dream when all you had to stare at was a black sky, when all around you was the bellowing din of the engines. You dreamed even though you were fully alert to the merest hint of danger, even though you'd taken your wakey-wakey pills as the Lancaster rumbled down the runway and you were wound up tighter than a coiled spring.

This was Straker's seventy-fifth trip. He shifted uncomfortably in his tiny perspex cabin at the tail of the plane, intermittently fingering the controls of his Brownings. Every trip he'd make the same joke as he squeezed himself into his seat: 'Here I go, into my coffin.' And at the end of each trip, someone, invariably Terry Baxter, would say, 'Bloody hell, 'ere's tail-end Charlie, rising from the grave.'

The worst thing about these trips was waiting for something to happen. And the smell, of course, which could be broken down into its constituent parts – cold sweat, oil, gas, leather, the canvas of the flak suits, the greasy metallic odour of the ammunition boxes – but which taken as a whole seemed to Straker nothing less than the smell of fear.

The intercom had been quiet for a while, just routine stuff coming from the nose of the plane. Now, though, Gibbo said, 'Okay, brace yourselves, fellas. We're twenty miles from the Dutch coast, coming into radar range. You still with us, Terry?'

It was a standing joke. Baxter, in the front turret, born within the sound of Bow Bells and 'prard ov it', always claimed that the best way to get through trips was to sleep through them. Now his dopey voice came through the intercom, making Straker and no doubt the rest of them grin. 'Duh, what's that, Skip? I was having a terrific dream.'

The navigator's report came in, more routine stuff, a bit more banter. Straker joined in with it, though he felt as if there was an expanding hollow in his belly. His arms tensed, fingers flexing and unflexing. Any minute now ...

'There's the coast,' Straker heard Dudley say, and imagined it as a black line, thin but widening, between the dark gleam of water and the endless night sky. Almost immediately Gibbo said, 'Flak ship. Too far away. She won't reach us.'

Straker looked down and saw a necklace of fiery pearls flare and then die in the darkness below. He didn't bother firing back.

Next moment they passed over a pale moving thread that he knew was the frothing surf on Holland's shore. Now they were over enemy territory. This was where things would really begin to hot up.

Dudley, the navigator, said, 'New course, 105 magnetic.' Straker felt the gentle motion like a curling in his belly as all three aircraft in the vic swung to the left in an attempt to weave a path through the flak.

Without warning, there were flashes of fire in the darkness below. At first the flak seemed to rise slowly, lazily, then all at once it was rushing at the plane, bursting and exploding all around like fireworks. This was the moment Straker had been waiting for. He positioned his Brownings and began pumping bullets at the flares below. He knew that from the ground his tracer fire would resemble cannon shells, like spitting angry stars, intended to frighten the flak gunners and put them off their aim.

Suddenly the Lancaster shuddered. Straker felt the shock waves rush through his body. A tinny voice in his intercom yelled above the cacophony of machine-gun fire, 'We've been hit!'

Straker tried to blot out the babble of voices, tried to blot out everything but the job at hand, which was to attempt to counteract the flak below, reduce its effect. He gritted his teeth and continued firing.

Three searchlights converged on them from the ground. Straker concentrated his efforts on them, knowing that on a clear night like tonight they were sitting targets. He hissed in satisfaction as he saw one of the searchlights wink out. He even fancied he could hear the pop of it exploding, though he knew that was impossible.

Seconds later another searchlight winked out. Straker had no idea whether he'd hit it or one of the other gunners had – later, if they got out of this, they'd all take joint credit; they'd all say they single-handedly put out two enemy searchlights. There'd be no arguing, no rivalry. They'd all congratulate each other on a job well done. In this situation, they were a single entity, different cogs and levers, all pulling together to make the machine work.

The flak fell away behind them, sparks and flashes that seemed to recede from Straker's sight as the plane ploughed on through the night. He relaxed his grip on his Brownings. His ears were ringing like alarm clocks. Beyond the clamour in his own head the noise of the four engines seemed unchanged.

The damage report came in. It was all minor stuff. 'You hear that, men? Bumps and bruises, that's all,' said Gibbo.

'Bumps and bloody bruises?' exclaimed Terry Baxter from the top turret. 'I can see a hole the size of me 'ead from where I'm sitting. Another few feet and I'd have been shovelling me intestines back in wiv me 'ands.'

Everyone laughed, more out of relief than genuine humour, and began to take the mickey out of Terry. Gibbo gave them their head for a while and then said, 'Okay, men, settle down. We'll be flying close to a Jerry night-fighter field pretty soon so we all need to be on full alert. I'm going to take us in low, try to duck underneath the little bastards. Don't waste your ammunition, gunners, but the first sign of flak, you give them what for.'

Straker felt it in his stomach once again when the plane began to dip towards the ground. The aim was to duck beneath the enemy night-fighters, which would be buzzing higher above them, and make them harder to pick out. The disadvantage, of course, was that flak from the ground would be able to reach them far more easily and its effects could prove twice as devastating.

Straker shrugged his shoulders, feeling them crunch. Swaddled in his flying gear he felt hot and heavy. When he'd first started using the Brownings, he would ache so much after an op that it would feel as if he'd beeen rodeo riding. Now his muscles, particularly his biceps, were like steel.

'There she is,' he heard Dudley say quietly in his intercom. He looked down, and a moment later saw the flare-path of a German night-fighter field, close to which was the aerodrome, like a scattering of children's building bricks.

'Full alert, men,' said Gibbo quietly, though he didn't really need to say anything; they all knew what to expect. 'Keep your eyes peeled, Terry.'

They flew low over the aerodrome. Straker kept glancing between that and the skies around him. He knew that the night-fighters could come suddenly, whining and roaring from the darkness, spitting fire. Just for an instant, before he started firing back, he would know how a mouse feels when it sees a hawk swooping down on it.

It was Terry who saw them first. 'Bandits, ten o'clock high,' he shouted. Straker swivelled and began firing, gritting his teeth, eyes darting this way and that as the night-fighters buzzed them like mosquitoes. A dogfight like this was a matter of instinct rather than planning and precision. Straker's senses were overwhelmed, filled with chaos, fire, sky, smoke, the ear-splitting cacophony of battle. All you could really do was blaze away and hope that you hit them before they hit you. After a while the Brownings seemed to become a part of you. Feeding and firing the guns felt as though you were spitting the bullets yourself.

Straker saw one of the Jerry fighters suddenly turn its nose to the ground and begin to plunge towards the earth, spinning out of control, a funnel of smoke blacker than the night trailing behind it. He wasn't sure whether he could actually hear the whine of its dying engines or whether he was imagining it.

The fighter took a long time to reach the ground, and when it did its demise seemed oddly insignificant, a small burst of flame that quickly dwindled. As ever, Straker tried to block out the thought that there were people in that aircraft, young men like himself, with families, friends, homes; hopes and dreams; thoughts and emotions. The only time he allowed himself to dwell on such matters was later, when the mission was over and he was tucked up in bed and the war was a day nearer to ending, which he continually assured himself it soon would be. How would he react in such a situation? Would he scream or keep silent? Would he black out with the pressure and the terror or remain conscious? Would he and the rest of the crew be tossed about like peas in a tin, bones breaking like matchsticks, dead from crush injuries long before they hit the ground, or would the aircraft seem stable enough and their heads remain clear enough for them to think about bailing out?

The Lancaster was shuddering as the flak peppered it from below, but Straker didn't think it was causing any real damage. On his port side he could see Jimmy MacDonald, pilot of one of the other Lancasters in the vic, taking evasive action. A couple of night-fighters were skipping round his plane like wasps round an ice cream cornet. Straker would have had a pop at them if it wasn't for the fact that he would have been more likely to have hit his own boys than the enemy. There was so much gunfire, so many frenetic, flickering bursts of light, that it was impossible to tell where most of it was coming from.

And then, quite suddenly, they were through. Straker caught a glimpse of a Jerry fighter peeling away; of the others there was no sign. Evidently there were bigger guns waiting for them somewhere ahead. 'Come back an' fight, ya bleedin' pansies!' Terry Baxter yelled in Straker's intercom.

Everyone relaxed, at least a little bit. The flak had caused minor damage to the plane, but nothing to worry about. Gibbo called up the other two planes in the vic to see if they were all right. Jimmy MacDonald reported minimal damage, but when Gibbo tried to speak to Hutchinson, who was flying P for Polly, all he got was static.

'Flak must've smashed his radio and intercom,' MacDonald said. 'He looks to be flying all right.'

'Hutch, if you can hear me, you might as well turn back,' Gibbo shouted into the transmitter. 'There's no point carrying on without communication.'

They were not sure whether Hutch had actually heard them or whether he was at that moment reluctantly coming to the same conclusion. Whichever, Straker looked out and saw the Lancaster on his starboard side dip its wings slightly in order to peel away and execute the large arc that would point it back towards home.

He felt envious, though he knew the boys in P for Polly would be frustrated, disappointed, would even feel, unjustifiably of course, that they had let their comrades down.

'See you back at base, Hutch. Get the drinks in,' Gibbo shouted as a parting shot.

The two Lancasters flew on into the darkness, engines beating like the wings of a thousand birds.

For a while the planes flew unimpeded. Below and all around them was blackness. They saw no lights on the ground, no sign of anything moving. In a way this was worse than the fighting. It was hard to shake off the notion that you were heading straight into the vast jaws of a trap. The two Lancasters were flying close, as though for comfort.

'We're over the border,' Dudley announced. 'In another few minutes we should see the Rhine.'

'Okay men, get ready,' Gibbo said. 'We're approaching our target. Terry, are you awake?'

'Leave it out, Skip,' Terry said, relaxed as ever.

Straker slipped his hand into the pocket of his flying jacket, squeezed the kiss-stone for a brief moment and thought of Jean sitting in front of a log fire at home, reading a book or listening to the wireless.

All at once four or five searchlights lit on them from below, opening like huge eyes, their beams converging. Almost immediately the air was full of flak and the aircraft was shaking. Straker fired back, and was heartened to see one of the searchlights blink out. In the dying glow he could even see the gunners on the ground, running for shelter like insects from beneath a rock.

The barrage of flak was fierce but brief. 'Everyone okay?' Gibbo said when they were through.

Everyone was, and a few minutes later the Rhine came into view, a silver thread glinting occasionally in the meagre moonlight. A boat on the river opened fire on them, blips of white in a thin, almost ruler-straight line, but they were out of range before the bullets could reach them.

That was the problem with being in the leading group. You could guess where the flak was going to come from, but you didn't really know for sure. Straker knew Chocky Young would be tapping out a flak warning now for the chaps at base to pick up. They would then re-broadcast the message on the group radio so that all the other aircraft would hear it and take precautions.

In his intercom Straker heard Dudley telling Gibbo, 'We have our sighting, sir.' He looked down and saw the M-shaped tributary they had been instructed to look for. A little beyond that was the kidney-shaped lake, shining like glass. Everything looked crystal-clear below them now and Straker felt a surge of optimism; perhaps God was on their side for this one.

'Commencing bomb run,' Gibbo said, and Straker felt his stomach curl again as the Lancaster dipped slightly, getting into position.

'Two minutes to target,' said Dudley.

'Open bomb bay doors.'

'Bomb bay doors open.'

'How's it looking, Spud?' Gibbo asked a few moments later.

Spud MacMahon, the bomb aimer, a large, quiet Scotsman with a face lumpy and shapeless as a King Edwards, said, 'Nearly there, sir ... nearly there ... Over the target ... now!' There was a brief pause and then he said, as though commenting on the weather, 'Bombs away.'

Straker looked down. Even in the darkness he could see the bombs dropping, like black eggs laid in mid-flight by a vast bird. His gaze outpaced the falling bombs, alighted on their target below. The pale buildings, like a series of almost-interlocking L's, housed a major assembly plant for German 1-90 fighter planes. Straker knew that during his briefing Gibbo had been warned that the plant was squeezed between a hospital and a large civilian area, which meant that there was no margin for error; the bombs had to be dropped smack on the target or not at all.

Straker held his breath as the bombs fell towards their target with ever-increasing speed. As the Lancaster flew on, prior to making a sweep back, the assembly plant receded, growing smaller and smaller. Straker had lost sight of the bombs now, and so couldn't help blinking when the first of them hit. All at once the assembly plant was engulfed in eruptions of flame that turned the sky a livid orange.

'Right on target!' someone yelled excitedly in Straker's ear.

'Stick that in your pipe and smoke it, you Jerry bastards!' Terry Baxter whooped.

'Well done, men. Good work,' Gibbo said. He radioed Jimmy MacDonald, giving him clearance to commence his bomb run and wishing him good luck, then said, 'Right, lads, let's go home.'

The words were barely out of his mouth when a blistering barrage of flak leapt at them from almost directly below. 'Jesus Christ!' someone yelled. The plane shuddered so violently that Straker's head whipped back, causing his neck to flare with pain. For a few seconds black stars obscured his vision. He groped for the controls of his Brownings, trying desperately to blink the stars away. He could smell smoke; it pricked at his throat, making him cough.

Someone shouted, 'We've got a hole in the left wing, a bloody big one!'

Suddenly the intercom was filled with a babble of voices:

'We're losing fuel.'

'Use the fuel transfer pump.'

'Pump not responding.'

'Near starboard engine's gone! Bloody hell, the wing's on fire!'

Straker tried to blot the voices out, to concentrate on his job. His head pounding, he directed his Brownings at where he thought the flak had come from and opened fire. He couldn't see much – the fire on the wing was producing copious amounts of black smoke – but he hoped his tracer fire was putting off the flak gunners below.

Suddenly Gibbo's voice, admirably calm, came over the intercom. 'Okay men, hang on. The fire extinguisher's damaged, so we're going to have to dive to try and put the fire out.'

Straker squeezed his eyes tight shut as the Lancaster dipped its nose and began to pick up speed. Sitting at the tail of the plane he felt as though he was being scooped high into the air. For a moment he was transported back to his childhood, to the thrill of funfairs and swings and being swept up from the ground and placed on his father's shoulders. Then he drew the stink of cordite and smoke and sweat and oil into his lungs, which instantly obliterated his fragile memories.

The Lancaster was screaming now, and rattling so hard it felt like it was shaking apart. Straker felt as though all the breath was being squeezed slowly from his body. He clenched his hands, his teeth, hunched up his shoulders, screwed up his face. His mind was too frozen to allow him to feel fear, to allow him to feel anything, in fact.

Gibbo kept asking in a steely calm voice, 'How we doing out there?' as if no one would tell him when the fire went out.

Finally Terry Baxter yelled the words that they had all been waiting for: 'Fire's out, Skip. You can take her back up.'

There was whooping and cheering and laughing, a general air of celebration. Straker leaned his head back and expelled a breath that he felt he'd been holding in his lungs for minutes. He reached into his pocket and squeezed the kiss-stone. I'm okay, Jean, he thought, I'm okay.

They turned and headed for home. Straker looked around for his bearings, pain stabbing through his neck and head like broken glass. Far below him, to his left, he saw the German assembly plant, white flames leaping from it, the cluster of buildings glowing orange as embers in its centre. He looked around for the other Lancaster and saw it high above them, on his starboard side. It seemed almost to be waiting for them to catch up. Gibbo was speaking to Jimmy MacDonald, telling him what had happened. It was only now that Straker realised flak was still flying up at them from below. He positioned his Brownings and fired back.

They were halfway home when the second engine failed. MacDonald had flown on ahead by this time. They'd been bombarded by flak now and again, but Dudley had done a good job plotting a course through the worst of it. All of a sudden the Lancaster gave a lurch and then seemed to jerk forward in a series of bumps as it lost height. Straker thought of a ball bouncing slowly down a set of wide stone steps. The initial lurch was so violent and unexpected that he bit his tongue, drawing blood which flooded his mouth like liquid iron. At first he thought they'd been hit by flak which he had somehow failed to see, and then he realised that the timbre of the engines had changed.

Next moment his worst fears were confirmed. Jack Hunt, the engineer, announced, 'Far port engine's gone, sir. Must've been damaged by flak.'

Gibbo swore briefly, then said, 'Okay, we'll reduce speed and take it easy. We're over water now anyway and out of the worst of it. We could probably guide this crate in on one engine if needs be, but check your life jackets and parachutes, men, in case we have to bail out.'

The remaining two engines, to Straker's ears at least, seemed to whine with the strain of supporting the huge aircraft. After the initial series of lurches, Gibbo had brought the Lancaster back under control and it now seemed stable again, though it was flying at a reduced height and speed. Below him he could see the black water of the North Sea, white slivers of shattered moon cresting the swells. He'd heard stories of pilots who'd flown their aircraft over vast distances on one engine, but he'd never actually met anyone who'd done it. Gibbo's words, he suspected, had been spoken to keep up morale as much as anything else.

For a while, however, things went fine. Straker was grateful that they had managed to dodge the night-fighters on the homeward route, even though they had had to go a long way round to do it. The two remaining engines were still chugging away. They were only twenty minutes from the coast now, nearly home. They were all well aware that fuel was dangerously low after the earlier leak, but Gibbo was a skilful flyer and had used every trick in the manual to try to conserve as much as possible. The pain in Straker's neck had well and truly settled in by now; each time he moved his head, even minutely, sharp red stabs of agony entered the back of his skull, sometimes making his vision blur and jitter.

'There's the coast up ahead,' Dudley announced, trying to stem the excitement in his voice.

'I hope Hutchy's got the beers in,' Terry Baxter said. 'I'm bleedin' parched.'

The atmosphere was more relaxed now. Dudley started singing a dirty song about a girl called Mary Lou that the Yanks had taught them earlier that week, and after a few moments a couple of the other men joined in. Straker grinned, though he couldn't sing because his neck hurt too much. Suddenly there was a phut-phut sound and the noise of the engines was momentarily reduced by half before picking up again. The Lancaster dipped, seemed as though it was going to roll right over, before Gibbo brought it back under control. The singing was replaced by swearing, confusion, consternation.

'What's going on?'

'It's another bleedin' engine, innit?'

'You're joking!'

'Jack?' said Gibbo.

'It's the far starboard engine, sir. It's on its last legs. Probably finding it hard to take the strain.'

'Dudley, how far to home?'
'On one and a half engines? Forty-five minutes? An hour?'
'Right,' said Gibbo calmly, and then said nothing more; there was nothing more *to* say. They would either get back or they wouldn't. It was in God's hands now. At least if we die, thought Straker, we'll die on home soil. He took the kiss-stone from his pocket and pressed it to his lips. A kiss for luck, he thought.
The failing engine held for another half an hour and then began to play up again – cutting out and picking up, as though it was a light switch someone was flicking on and off. The Lancaster was lurching, shuddering; at one point Straker felt sure the aircraft dropped like a stone for long seconds before Gibbo managed to bring it back under control. Jack Hunt suggested bailing out, but Gibbo was adamant he was going to stay with the plane. If they deserted it they would lose it for sure, and what was worse, it might crash down in a civilian area.
'You can bail out if you like, Jack,' he said icily, 'but I'm going to land this crate.'
There were a few seconds of tense silence, then Terry Baxter, evidently feeling he was speaking for all of them, said, 'We're with you, Skip. You know that.'
Death before dishonour, thought Straker bitterly. At that moment the old adage seemed ill-conceived, though he didn't voice his opinion that seven lives were more important than a piece of machinery. He was certainly no coward, but he didn't want to die for nothing. He was wondering whether to suggest turning the plane round, aiming it back towards the sea and then bailing out, when Dudley called excitedly, 'There she is, there's the airfield.'
Despite the situation, optimism was suddenly high again, and Straker knew his moment had gone. They couldn't die now, not this close to home, not when they could almost smell the bacon and eggs, imagine themselves downing pint after pint of cold beer.
'Okay, men, we're going down,' Gibbo said. 'Assume crash landing positions.'
Straker did so, drawing himself into as tight a ball as possible, protecting his throbbing head with his hands.
'Get the landing gear down,' Gibbo ordered.
Straker couldn't decide which was worse, having the responsibility of bringing the crippled aircraft down safely, or just curling up here and waiting out these last few minutes, unable to affect the outcome.
At least the engines seemed okay for the time being, if the ratcheting, whining, straining roar of them could be termed as such. The Lancaster began to shudder and rattle as it descended. Straker

squeezed his eyes tight shut and began to murmur the words to the song about Mary Lou that Dudley had sung earlier. He promised himself that he'd sing them with gusto later in the bar if his aching neck allowed him. He tried to blot out the voices coming through on his intercom. He didn't want to know how well or how badly Gibbo was doing, how close to the ground they were, how the remaining engines were holding up. He didn't want to know anything until they were safely down and the plane was stationary, and he could scramble out of his seat into what at first would seem like ear-ringing silence. After an op, for a little while, the voices of everyone around him would seem small, far away, as if he was half-asleep and they were speaking to him through a dream. He wanted to hear Terry Baxter say, 'Here's tail-end Charlie, rising from the grave,' and he wanted to look at himself in the mirror and welcome himself back, and hold up the kiss-stone in celebration.

Try as he might, however, he couldn't blot out the moment when the crippled engine failed again. Suddenly the intercom was filled with shouting voices. Gibbo, normally so cool, was yelling, 'Not now, not now! Come on, you bitch, come *on!*'

Someone started to yell wordlessly, though not really in terror; more than anything it was a bellow of rage.

The sound persisted for what seemed to Straker like minutes, but could have been no more than seconds ...

And was superseded when the stricken bomber hit the ground.

The noise alone, like a thousand earthquakes, seemed enough to blot out consciousness. Straker had a brief though vivid impression of being plucked from his seat and lifted high into the air, the straps and buckles that held him in place tearing like wet paper. And then he was being bombarded by hard, sharp, flying objects, or perhaps it was he that was bombarding them. He knew he was in appalling trouble, but as before had no time to feel fear or even pain. For a fleeting instant, he felt nothing but a white, all-encompassing sense of disbelief, and then, like the Lancaster's engine dying in mid-air, he simply switched off, stopped working, tumbled into a blackness so profound it was like nothing.

Just as suddenly, flickering white light woke him. He opened his eyes and was immediately blinded by it. As consciousness rushed in, so too did agony, of such intensity that he almost blacked out again at once. He could see nothing but a wall of white light, blurring and dancing. The pain engulfed him so completely that he could neither move nor make a sound, could barely even think. He realised he was still alive, that he had survived the crash, but if this was life then he wanted no part of it; he wanted to slip back into oblivion.

The thought came suddenly, a hot knife sliding through the membrane of confusion. *Fire! The white light is fire! The plane's burning! I have to get out!*

Trying to deny the pain, he lifted an arm, intending to crawl forward, to look for an exit, which he had a vague idea would be a patch of darkness amidst all the light. He saw that rising in front of his face was something shapeless, something red and bubbling, dribbling like a melting candle. For a few seconds he was confused, and then realisation slammed into him and he felt an overwhelming urge to scream, but try as he might could make no sound.

What was wavering in front of him, what was even now charring black in the incredible heat, was his own hand.

Part One:

Stefan's Big Picture

Monday 21 November

1

Carl Pryor, more commonly known as the Creep, hailed Chloe the instant she walked into the classroom. He made it obvious that he fancied her like mad, but if he thought that embarrassing her in front of her classmates was going to make her feel the same way about him then he was even sadder than his taped-up spectacles and disgusting BO suggested. Chloe was kind-hearted enough to put up with Carl's moronic comments, though she certainly didn't encourage him. Mind you, to someone like Carl, not telling him to go play in the traffic was probably akin to blowing him a kiss and flashing a bit of leg.

'Hey, Clo,' he barked today, 'someone's left a present by your desk.'

Tanya Roberts, Chloe's best friend, whom she had met up with ten minutes earlier on the way to school, was neither kind-hearted nor tolerant, particularly not on Monday mornings.

'Get lost, slug features,' she retorted on Chloe's behalf. 'Why don't you go and look for your breakfast in a bin or something?'

For an instant Carl looked almost comically hurt, then the shutters clanged down behind his eyes; you could almost see the thick skin forming over his body in readiness for another long week of insults, threats and just plain indifference.

'I wasn't talking to you, Roberts, I was talking to Clo,' he said in his foghorn voice.

'That's Chloe to you, Creep,' said Tanya, undeterred. 'And when will you get it into your thick skull that she's not interested in a maggot like you? You should hang yourself and do us all a favour.'

Carl was grinning and shaking his head as if to imply that Tanya's outburst was so childish she was humiliating no one but herself. He looked around at his classmates, raising his eyebrows and pulling faces as if he honestly believed himself the popular choice here.

'Come on, Tan,' Chloe murmured, embarrassed at being the centre of attention, 'let's sit down. He's not worth it.'

Tanya shot Carl a look of pure malice, then turned away. 'Yeah, you're right.'

The two girls crossed the classroom, Chloe all too aware of the admiring glances they were attracting. Or rather, she reminded herself, of the admiring glances *Tanya* was attracting. Although Chloe was frequently asked out, she genuinely found it hard to believe that boys actually fancied her. Okay, she might have fine dark hair and smooth skin, but whenever she looked in a mirror all she saw were lips that were too big and eyes that were too small. Tanya, on the other hand, was truly gorgeous. She was tall for fourteen and looked a bit like a young Cybill Shepherd. Already she had a figure to die for, a mane of blonde hair and big blue eyes with long lashes. She wanted to be a model, and had got her cousin's friend's brother, who was a professional photographer, to take some photos of her which she had started sending out to agencies and magazines. Chloe turned down most of the boys who approached her for a date, and although she told Tanya it was because she didn't fancy them, or because she was saving herself for Ben Wyatt, the real reason was that she could never shrug off the suspicion that boys were asking her out simply as a stepping stone to Tanya. Tanya didn't exactly help matters either by flirting with every boy who came within ten feet of her. She had a different boyfriend every couple of weeks and had already been the cause of a number of fights in the school - much to her delight, of course.

Carl climbed up on to his desk. 'It's by your chair, Clo!' he shouted.

'Drop dead, you little twat,' Tanya snapped.

Carl did a spastic dance, screwing up his face, which was evidently supposed to resemble Tanya in a rage.

'Creep's probably left you one of his turds he's saved from the weekend,' Tanya muttered.

Chloe winced. 'Urgh, don't. The thought of it. Hey, no, look, there *is* something.'

The two girls had adjacent desks on the far side of the room. They were in a prime spot here, next to the radiator, which ticked and burbled companionably on cold winter mornings, and right by the window, out of which they could stare longingly during boring lessons.

Propped between the radiator and the side of the desk was a brown cardboard tube about two feet long. A piece of white paper had been Sellotaped to it on which the words CHLOE KNIGHT had been printed in black biro.

'Creep must have come right over to my desk to see this,' Chloe said, 'unless he put it here himself, that is.'

'He's probably came in early to lick your chair. Feel it to see if it's wet.'

'Tanya!' Chloe gave her friend an admonishing slap on the arm. As Tanya giggled, Chloe hefted the tube in her hands. 'I wonder who it's from?'

The tube had been well-secured at both ends with brown packing tape. Tanya dumped her bag and sat down whilst Chloe began picking at it, trying to get her fingernail under a loose edge.

'Come on, hurry up,' Tanya urged. 'Bell'll be going in a minute.'

Chloe succeeded in lifting an edge of the tape and began peeling it off.

'What have you got then? Who's it from?' demanded Carl, who had jumped down from his desk and sneaked up behind the girls.

Tanya swung round on him. Up this close they could both smell his pissy odour, see the rash of yellow-tipped pimples on his chin, the ingrained dirt in the creases of his neck.

'None of your business. Piss off!' Tanya said.

Carl leaned forward, enveloping them both in a cloud of BO. 'Make me.'

'Jesus, Creep, you *stink!*' Tanya declared, loud enough for everyone to hear. 'Don't you ever have a bath?'

As derisive laughter filled the classroom, Carl stuck out his front teeth, crossed his eyes and waggled his head in another wildly inaccurate impersonation.

'Who's that? Your mother?' said Tanya.

Carl was about to reply when a voice rang across the classroom: 'Pryor, what are you doing out of your seat?'

Carl hunched up his shoulders as if the voice had been carried on a gust of freezing cold air. The anguished expression on his face almost made Chloe feel sorry for him.

'Nothing, sir,' he said pathetically, turning slowly to face the teacher who had just entered the room.

Mr Holbrook was everything that Carl was not – smartly dressed, tough, athletic, self-disciplined. He taught Geography and ran the school rugby team, and made no secret of the fact that he favoured pupils who were like himself, and treated those that weren't with barely concealed contempt. Some pupils, generally those who found least favour with Holbrook, were of the opinion that he was a closet gay, or perhaps a wife-beater. Whether or not either of these was true, it was certainly plain to all in 3W that he conducted his campaign against slovenliness in the pitiful shape of Carl Pryor with an almost pathological zeal. It was as though Holbrook believed Carl, by turning up looking like crap every day, was wilfully, even contemptuously, trying to undermine all that he held most dear. Indeed, the level of victimisation might have sent one of Carl's classmates scuttling to have a quiet word in the Year Head's ear if the boy had not been so unpopular.

'Nothing,' Holbrook repeated now, lips curling within his trim beard. 'I'd say that just about sums you up, Pryor. You're a big nothing, and nothing is what you'll amount to. *Now sit down!*'

Everyone jumped as Holbrook's bellowing voice reverberated around the room. Carl sped back to his seat in such panic that once again Chloe couldn't help feeling sorry for him. She knew that if Holbrook had found anyone else out of their seat, if it had been her for example, he would simply have muttered, 'Back into your seat, Chloe. Bell's about to go.'

Chloe's next lesson was French with the po-faced Mr Milton, and it wasn't until morning break that she was able to turn her attention back to her gift. She met Tanya by the girls' toilets and together the two girls trudged out into the playground.

It was cold and windy, the sky grey and blotchy as drying cement. A group of boys some thirty-strong dominated the main playground area, chasing a football around with apparently little effect. Girls and smaller boys huddled resentfully on the periphery of the action. In the corner of the playground, beside a high chain-link fence, first and second years swarmed over a geodome which resembled the exposed nub of a vast skeleton.

Tanya noticed Chloe scanning the group of yelling footballers and sang softly, 'I know who you're looking for.'

Chloe blushed. 'You're just jealous.'

'Of Ben Wyatt? Oh, yeah.'

'What's wrong with Ben?' Chloe asked indignantly.

'Nothing's *wrong* with him. He's just not my type. I prefer older men.'

'Oh yeah, since when?'

'Since I met Nick in Mr B's at the weekend.'

'You went to Mr B's? You never told me about this. Did they let you in? And who's Nick?'

Bickering good-naturedly, the two girls made their way over to the grassy area beside the tennis courts. During the summer term they would lounge on the grass, ties and blazers off, soaking up the sun, but today it was too cold and the grass too damp for them to sit.

'Go on then, open it,' Tanya said, indicating the cardboard tube. 'I've been dying to know what it is.'

'Not as much as I have. I've had to sit through Milton's boring French and then Talbot's boring Physics, just staring at the thing.'

As she spoke she was peeling the packing tape away from one end of the tube, scrunching strips of it up in her hand and stuffing them into her blazer pocket. Finally she revealed a plastic lid which she popped off.

The two girls pressed their heads together, looking eagerly inside.

'It's a scroll or something,' said Tanya.

'It's a poster,' said Chloe.

It was indeed a poster, and as Chloe pulled it from the tube a piece of paper fluttered out and settled on the grass, only to be instantly twitched away by the wind.

'Hey!' shouted Tanya and pursued the paper as it danced across the grass; she finally caught it attempting to sidle round a sapling.

When she returned to Chloe she had a big grin on her face.

'What does it say?' Chloe asked, trying to sound cool but unable to stop her stomach fluttering with anticipation.

Tanya opened up the paper, which was nothing more than a lined white sheet from a notepad, perforated raggedly along the top edge where it had been torn from a ring binder.

In block capitals the note said:

TO CHLOE
FROM AN ADMIRER
AND NOW IT BEGINS

'An admirer, hey?' said Tanya. She was still grinning. 'Who might that be then?'

'How should I know?' said Chloe. She could feel her cheeks burning and placed her cold hands on them in the hope it would make a difference.

'And what has this *admirer* bought for you, I wonder?'

Chloe still had not unrolled the poster, but she did so now. It was a glossy photographic print of Stefan Edberg, the tennis player, in mid-serve. He was in sharp focus in the foreground, up on his toes before a Wimbledon crowd of blurred faces, many of which were half-hidden by dark glasses and sun hats. Edberg was bringing his racket round to strike a ball which he had evidently just tossed into the air. His blond hair was dark with sweat, strands of it sticking to his forehead; the muscles were standing out on his serving arm.

Tanya curled her top lip. 'Bor-ring,' she pronounced disgustedly.

'What do you mean, "boring"? It's Stefan.'

Stefan Edberg was Chloe's idol. The walls of her bedroom at home were plastered with pictures of him. In the backs of most of her exercise books were doodles of hearts and flowers intertwined with the words: 'Stefan 4 Chloe' or 'CK + SE = True Love'. Admittedly Chloe had linked her name similarly with that of Ben Wyatt's, but this was merely because she felt it prudent to hedge her bets. Stefan was the impossible dream, Ben merely the lofty ambition. In fact, if truth be known, the main reason she fancied Ben was because he looked a lot like Stefan: slim, nice face, blond hair ...

'Who do you reckon it's from?' Tanya asked.

Chloe looked at the note again as if there was some clue to be found in the arrangement of the words or the slant of the handwriting.

'I don't know. Someone who knows I like Stefan. What do you think this means – and now it begins?'

'Maybe he's planning on giving you loads of presents. Aw, it's probably just Creepy, after all.'

'No it isn't.'

'How do you know?'

Chloe wrinkled her nose. 'I just do. He wouldn't send me a present, would he?'

Tanya shrugged. She seemed oddly resentful of Chloe's gift. 'Who then?' she said almost sulkily.

'I don't know,' said Chloe, and then added hesitantly, 'Maybe it's from Ben.'

Tanya hooted with laughter. 'Ben! No chance! Why would he send you a picture of his greatest rival?'

There was malice in Tanya's voice – only a little but it was definitely there. Though Chloe had a slow fuse, it had now almost burned down, and she snapped, 'Oh, stop being such a bitch, Tan! Just because no one's bought *you* anything!'

Tanya blinked, her blue eyes wide with surprise. Then those eyes narrowed and her lips set in a terse line.

'All right,' she said, 'let's go and ask Ben, shall we?' She swung her bag viciously on to her shoulder so that it spun on its strap and bounced against her thigh, then turned impressively and stormed off.

Faced with this prospect, Chloe's irritation turned to alarm. She hurried after her friend, hampered by her efforts to roll up the poster and slide it back into its cardboard tube.

'No, Tanya, don't,' she pleaded. 'Tanya!'

But Tanya would not be swayed. She strode around the playground, mockingly calling, 'Benny-wenny, where are you?', stopping whenever she saw anyone who might know Ben to ask if they'd seen him.

If Chloe had been thinking logically, she would have realised that Tanya was only persisting with her crusade for the simple reason that Chloe was trailing after her, pleading with her not to. If Chloe had simply let her friend get on with it and walked away, Tanya would have run out of steam soon enough. Chloe was not thinking logically, however, though even so the friendship might still have been unharmed if the girls had not spotted Ben hanging out with his cronies by the science block, just as Chloe was beginning to think she was about to be saved by the bell.

Ben was fifteen, blond and athletic-looking. He was cocky and arrogant, well aware of his good looks, and although he was no troublemaker, he was tough enough that not even the sixth formers messed him around. He had a number of admirers among the school's female population, though as far as Chloe was aware he didn't have a steady girlfriend at the moment. For a while he had dated Kristen Williams, who was in the fifth year and had the biggest boobs in the school. Although this had mortified Chloe at the time, she had now managed to convince herself that Ben's finishing with Kristen indicated that he was a sensitive soul to whom physical attributes were not the be-all and end-all.

Over the past few weeks Chloe had been making steady progress in getting to know Ben. She had started by smiling at him when she passed him in the corridor or the playground, which she had made a point of doing often, then she had begun saying hello to him, as a result of which she had spent most of the rest of the day basking in the glow that his half-smile and his murmured reply of 'All right?' produced in her. Last Wednesday had seen the most wonderful development thus far: when she had smiled and greeted him as usual, he had asked softly, 'Hey, aren't you Knighty's daughter?'

Chloe instantly felt as though her stomach was oozing into her shoes. 'That's right,' she had barely managed to say.

Ben had produced that slow, mysterious half-smile of his and had murmured, 'Thought so.'

As opening exchanges go, it hadn't been the most earth-shattering, but it had been enough to encourage her to seek out Tanya frantically, to run up to her squealing, 'He knows my name, he knows my name!'

Now, though, it looked as though Chloe's best friend was about to undermine all that carefully laid groundwork. As Tanya marched up to Ben, who still hadn't seen her approaching, Chloe caught hold of her arm and attempted to pull her away.

'Please, Tan, don't,' she begged.

Tanya half-turned. 'I thought you wanted to know who the poster was from.'

'I do.'

'Well, you'll never find out if you don't ask, will you? I'm doing you a favour.'

She pulled her arm free and continued her march towards Ben. He had seen her coming now and so had his friends; Chloe saw them unconsciously adopting cooler poses against the wall of the science block.

She felt as though Tanya had now crossed a line which she dared not cross herself. She could only stand and watch with a kind of horrified compulsion, as if viewing a car accident too ghastly to avert her eyes from. She saw Tanya walk right up to Ben, saw Ben incline his head towards her as she spoke to him. Chloe felt as though she was shrinking with shame and embarrassment when Tanya turned and made a vague gesture in her direction, prompting Ben to accord her no more than a perfunctory glance before turning his attention back to Tanya and shaking his head.

The look on Tanya's face as she walked back towards Chloe was one of barely concealed triumph.

'Well, *he* never sent you the poster. He didn't know anything about it.'

Chloe was trembling with rage and betrayal and humiliation. When she spoke her throat felt fragile as an egg, threatening to crack and flood her voice with tears.

'I hate you, Tanya,' she said, spitting the words as though they were a curse. 'You're a bloody cow, and if you think I'm going to be your friend after this, you can forget it!'

2

At the same time as Carl Pryor was receiving a tongue-lashing from Mr Holbrook, Oonagh Walsh was being introduced to her new classmates. She felt like a freak show exhibit standing in front of 4T, Miss Paget's hand resting lightly on her shoulder. She moved nervously from foot to foot, her eyes flickering across the rows of faces in front of her. She saw distrust on those faces, even hostility. She wasn't imagining it; she was used to it. 'Dislike for the unlike' – that was what Mrs Cantleigh, who'd been travelling with them for as long as Oonagh could remember, called it. She tried not to let the belligerence she sensed get to her, tried to focus on what Miss Paget was saying.

'I hope you're going to make her feel very welcome,' the teacher said, and squeezed Oonagh's shoulder to show that she certainly was. Oonagh could see, however, that her words were having little effect. Although it felt as though the entire class was generating ill-will, Oonagh had learned from experience that in general it wasn't the boys she had to worry about when she joined a new school, but the girls. A clique of them in particular, sitting in the top left-hand corner of the room, she just knew were going to be trouble. She could see them sizing her up, leaning across desks to whisper to each other, all the time casting her baleful glances. This performance continued all the way through the first two lessons; though Oonagh tried to ignore the girls, she felt their eyes on her back like hot coins.

It started at morning break as she knew it would. Oonagh made no attempt to avoid the girls. Something else she had learned over the years was that there was no point running away, because if you did you'd just be running for ever.

The instant she stepped out on to the playground, feeling the cold wind on her hot face, a voice came from behind her:

'Oi, you.'

It was the biggest of the four girls; she would have been pretty if meanness hadn't tightened her features. Her name, Sue Kuznitsky, sounded Russian or something, though her Yorkshire accent was almost as broad as the farmer's whose field Oonagh, her parents and their friends were staying in.

Oonagh composed herself and turned round. Keeping her voice level, neither friendly nor unfriendly, she said, 'Were you talking to me?'

Sue swaggered forward, her cronies trailing her like a three-pronged shadow. 'What's your name again?' she demanded.

Oonagh recognised a leading question when she heard one, but decided to play along for the time being.

'Oonagh.'

Sue cast a glance back at her friends and sneered. They reciprocated obediently. 'What kind of a name's that?'

'It's Irish, I think,' Oonagh said, still keeping her voice neutral. She knew that any hint of either defiance or weakness would incite these girls. She was not exactly scared, but she was wary.

'Is that where you're from then?' said one of the other girls, her red crimped hair pushed back from her forehead by a wide black headband, 'Ireland?'

'No,' said Oonagh.

'Why have you got an Irish name then?'

'I don't know. My parents must just have liked it, I suppose.'

'So where *are* you from?' Sue said, making it sound as though Oonagh had been trying to mislead them.

'I was born in Camberley. In Surrey.'

'Is that why you talk funny?'

Oonagh shrugged and said diplomatically, 'It's why my accent's different to yours.'

'Where do you live now then?' said a third girl, dumpy with black hair cut in an unflattering bob.

Here we go, Oonagh thought. It was a point that was always

reached sooner or later. In the early days she had lied or tried to prevaricate, but had quickly learned how pointless that was. Nowadays she told the truth for a different reason, which was simply that she had gradually come to realise that she had nothing to be ashamed of.

Nevertheless she braced herself before replying, 'I live with my parents. At the moment our trailer's parked in a field near to the woods.'

'You mean you live in a caravan?' Sue scoffed.

'A trailer. It's bigger than caravan.'

'You're still a gypo, though, aren't you?'

Oonagh bridled, but tried not to show it. If there was one thing she hated it was prejudice born of ignorance. However, she tried hard never to take the kind of bait that was being dangled in front of her now. Her parents, Graeme and Linda, were both pacifists, and since she had been very small had impressed upon Oonagh their belief that violence solved nothing, that it was ugly, hateful, undignified, and brought only misery.

Therefore, in answer to what had been little more than an accusation, Oonagh replied evenly, 'I'm not a gypsy, I'm a traveller. Gypsies are different. They're —'

'Don't get fucking smart with me, bitch,' Sue said, taking a step closer.

'I wasn't getting smart, I was just trying to explain.'

There were sneers on the faces of all the girls now. The dumpy one with the bob said, 'She couldn't get smart even if she wanted to. It's a well-known fact that all gypos are stupid.'

It was a dumb comment, and plainly intended to goad Oonagh. She ached to tell these girls that her parents had taught her to read and write by the age of three and that she had found the lessons she had shared with them that morning ridiculously easy, but she kept her mouth shut.

'Yeah, and dirty,' said the girl who hadn't spoken yet, a long-haired brunette with a short skirt, thick black tights and Doc Marten boots.

'Yeah, don't go near her, Sue, she's probably crawling with nits,' said the redhead. The girls all giggled nastily, and spent a few seconds making disgusted noises as if Oonagh was something vile they had found in a gutter.

'Why are you in *our* class?' Sue said when the joke had begun to flag.

'I don't know,' Oonagh said. 'It's just the class I was put into. It was nothing to do with me.'

'You should be in 4P with all the thickos,' said Sue.

'Yeah, you can't even afford a proper school uniform,' said the redhead as if clothes and intelligence were intrinsically linked.

'You can't stay at our school if you haven't got a proper uniform,' Sue said.

'Yeah, we don't want people turning up in rags at *our* school,' said the girl wearing the Doc Martens.

They were closing in on her now. Although Oonagh's instinct was to run, she had learned over the years that the best thing to do if physically attacked was not to fight back, but to go down quickly and try to protect as much of her body as possible. This generally attracted almost immediate attention, and sometimes even earned her a fair bit of sympathy afterwards.

Of course, a far better alternative was not to get attacked at all, and sometimes Oonagh had managed to defuse a potentially dangerous situation by remaining calm and talking in a reasonable voice.

'We travel around so much that it's not usually worth my parents buying me a uniform,' she said, ready now for the first fist or the first kick, bracing herself to drop to the ground.

Just then the brunette with the Doc Marten boots seemed to stiffen, then nudged the redhead with the headband and muttered what sounded to Oonagh like, 'Nightie.'

Instantly the girls began to peel away. Sue stuffed her hands into her blazer pockets and turned to follow her friends. Just before doing so she delivered a parting shot, sotto voce: 'We'll see you later, gypo.'

'Not unless I see you first,' murmured Oonagh when Sue and her cronies were out of range. She wondered what had frightened them away, and then noticed that a man in a brown corduroy jacket and thick green sweater had appeared from the door to her left, the one she had come out of a few minutes before. This was evidently 'Nightie', a teacher on playground duty. He was tall and thin, with glasses and a receding hairline. He was sipping from a cup of tea he held in his right hand, holding a saucer under his chin with his left to catch the drips.

Oonagh looked to make sure Sue and her friends really had gone, that they weren't just standing watching her from some distance away, and then she turned and walked in the opposite direction.

After break they had double art. Oonagh sat as far away from Sue and her friends as possible and studiously avoided eye contact with them. However when someone knocked over a jar of cloudy water, Sue said loudly, 'It's all right, Miss, you can mop it up with that rag the new girl's wearing.' Some of the class laughed at this, but the teacher, Miss Jephcott, was not amused.

'That's enough, Susan,' she snapped. 'As you seem so keen on offering advice you can stay behind afterwards to help me tidy up.'

Later, Oonagh was engrossed in her painting when she felt a sharp nudge in the back. Before she could turn, Sue hissed into her ear, 'I'll get you for that,' before moving on to the sink in the corner of the room to wash her brushes under the tap.

Oonagh made no particular effort to avoid the girls at lunchtime, but was nevertheless relieved when the hour passed without her encountering them.

It was a different story at the end of the day. Oonagh noticed that as soon as the final bell went, Sue and her three friends gathered up their belongings and rushed out of the classroom before she had even finished closing all her books.

Sure enough, she saw the girls the instant she set foot on the curving path that led up towards the school's main entrance. They were leaning against the railings by the bus stop just outside the gate, scanning the crowd as they came through, like border guards.

It was the redhead who saw her first. Oonagh saw her nudge Sue and nod in her direction. She averted her eyes and pretended she hadn't seen the girls turning to stare at her. However, her heart was thumping as she came level with the gates, and then passed through them. She turned her back on the girls and began to walk in the opposite direction, but almost immediately Sue Kuznitsky's voice, rising above the crowd, said, 'Where do you think you're going, bitch?'

Oonagh kept walking, didn't even half-turn. 'Home,' she said firmly.

'Back to your shitty little caravan,' one of the others said (Oonagh thought it might have been the dumpy one).

She didn't reply, just concentrated on putting one foot in front of the other.

'Oi, bitch, don't you fucking ignore us. Look at me when I'm talking to you.'

Oonagh stopped, sighed and slowly turned round. Although kids were streaming out of the gates, and queuing up at the ice cream van and the bus stop, she couldn't help feeling that she was on her own here.

Sue had her head cocked on one side, her jaws working at a piece of chewing gum. The sneer on her face seemed as permanent as a tattoo.

'You got me into trouble with Jephcott, you fucking gypo.'

Oonagh could see the grey wad of gum in Sue's mouth when she spoke. 'No, I didn't,' she said evenly.

'You calling me a liar, you gypo bitch?'

This time Sue's voice was loud enough to make heads turn in the bus queue, cause kids who were walking past them to glance around curiously. However, no one moved to intervene; Oonagh knew she would have to get hurt before that happened.

'No,' she said, 'but you know what happened. I didn't do anything.'

The attack came with shocking suddenness. Sue closed the distance between them in less than a second, and before Oonagh could react had curled her hand into a fist and punched the smaller girl in the face.

Oonagh staggered back, red stars exploding across her vision. She felt as if she'd been hit with a brick; her nose was a hot stinging hole in the centre of her face. Her ears filled with ringing static; one of the girls shouted excitedly, 'Go on, Sue, kick her face in!' To Oonagh the girl's voice sounded muzzy and booming.

She made her knees buckle, which wasn't difficult, and tried to fall to the ground, but Sue had hold of her hair and was yanking on it hard. Oonagh knew that if she dropped now her hair would feel as if it was being torn out at the roots. She reached up, not to fight back but to try to disengage Sue's hand, and she screamed as loudly as she could, knowing that this often brought people running to break up the fight all the sooner.

And then her scream was abruptly cut off as something that felt like a sledgehammer but was more likely a boot or a fist slammed into her stomach. For a few terrifying seconds she couldn't breathe; it was like being underwater.

This time she had no choice. Her legs turned to jelly and she went down. She felt an intense flare of pain as a clump of her hair took all her weight for a second, and then the hard cold pavement tilted up to meet her.

It was almost comforting feeling the concrete beneath her body. She had to open her mouth to breathe; her lungs felt like bleeding wounds. She still couldn't see anything, was so woozy she wasn't even sure whether or not the girls were still attacking her. Instinctively she curled into a ball, one hand covering her face, the other holding her stomach.

She wasn't sure, but she thought she might actually have blacked out for a few seconds. Certainly she had the impression that a chunk of time had gone missing, like a needle skipping a couple of bars on a scratched record. When she came to, it was to hear one of the girls saying, 'Bloody hell, Sue, you've knocked her out.'

The girl's voice was still booming and distorted, as if she was shouting into a well and Oonagh was standing at the bottom of it.

Then Oonagh heard Sue Kuznitsky say, 'Serves her right, the silly cow.' However this time there was uncertainty in her voice.

Then Oonagh heard a new voice, a male voice. She thought it was a boy rather than a man, and he was shouting, 'Oi, leave her alone.'

Good advice, Oonagh thought. Great advice. The best advice ever.

'Get lost, Knighty,' she heard Sue say. 'This is none of your fucking business.'

Knighty. Oonagh pictured the tall balding teacher with the horrible corduroy jacket, speaking with a boy's voice. It didn't make sense. She tried not to think about it too much.

The argument raged on above her head, like one of those Radio 4 plays Linda liked listening to.

'I've just made it my business.'

'Why don't you just fuck off. This is between me and her.'

'Between you and your three mates and her, you mean. Really tough, that is.'

'It was a fair fight, one on one.'

'I don't give a shit. She's smaller than you are. And what's she supposed to have done anyway? Looked at you funny or something?'

'She was giving me a load of lip.'

'So you gave her a bust one?'

'Ha, ha, you're about as funny as cancer.'

'Come on, Sue, let's go. He'll only get Daddy on to us if we don't.'

'I'm not going. Why should I?'

'I reckon you ought to take your friend's advice.'

'Oh yeah, or what will you do?'

'It's not just me who doesn't like bullies, Kuznitsky. There's all this lot as well.'

There was a pause, then Sue said disgustedly, 'For fuck's sake, she's only a bloody gypo.'

'Yeah, and you're just a piece of slime, so I reckon that makes her better than you.'

'Come *on*, Sue.'

There was another pause, then Sue said, 'You're in for it, Knight, I mean it. You and that fucking wimp of a dad of yours.'

'I'm really scared. I'm trembling.'

'You fucking well should be.'

Oonagh heard movement, footsteps scuffing the ground, and pictured Sue and her friends moving away, pushing through the crowd that she imagined had gathered around her. She heard Sue a little further away telling someone to, 'Get lost,' then she felt a gentle hand on her shoulder and the boy said, 'It's all right, they've gone.'

Oonagh moved her hand away from her face and turned over, and was immediately struck by how intensely bright everything was. Ninety per cent of what filled her vision was sky; then her squinting eyes swivelled down and round, and she saw legs, both male and female, like a forest of trees around her.

Then she became aware of someone bending over her, the boy's voice asking her if she was okay. She tried to speak, but her mouth felt as though it was clogged with soft metal. Something white flapped in front of her. 'Here, use this to wipe your face.'

Carefully Oonagh pushed herself upright. The world tilted dizzyingly, then steadied. She felt bits of grit popping out of the craters they had made in the flesh of her cheek. She took the handkerchief and wiped her face, then gasped, 'Oh!'

The handkerchief was no longer white, but smeared with redness so vivid it was like a slap.

'Your nose is bleeding,' said the boy as if in apology. 'It's all down the front of your jumper.'

Oonagh looked down. Her grey V-neck jumper, which Linda had bought from a jumble sale as a kind of generic school jumper, was splashed with dark stains, the main one as big as one of those squashed tomato car noses that had been on sale a year or two ago for Comic Relief. It was always a shock seeing so much of your own blood, and that must have shown in her face because the boy said, 'Come on, I'll help you get cleaned up.'

He put out a hand, which Oonagh automatically took. There were still people around her, though most were beginning to drift away now. The boy pulled her to her feet, Oonagh all too aware, despite the pain and shock of her attack, of the soft warmth of his hand clasped in hers. Because of the nature of her lifestyle – moving from town to town, never staying in one place for too long – she had had little physical contact with the opposite sex, and at the age of fourteen and three-quarters holding hands with a boy was still a pretty big deal for her. She felt excitement and embarrassment in equal measure, and desperately hoped she wasn't blushing – or if she was, hoped the boy would think it a consequence of her ordeal. She released the boy's hand at the earliest opportunity and made a big show of dusting herself down.

'You've still got blood on your face,' the boy said, taking the handkerchief from her free hand and holding it out to her. 'Here, spit on this.'

'I can manage,' Oonagh said, more brusquely than she intended. As she cleaned her face she looked at the boy properly for the first time.

He was quite tall, gangly but already starting to fill out. He had dark straight hair, cut short around the ears and at the nape of the neck, but with a long fringe; brown almond-shaped eyes; freckles. He offered her a hesitant smile and asked concernedly, 'Are you sure you're all right?'

Oonagh nodded, and then wished she hadn't. The movement made it feel as though bits of bone in her nose were grating together. She blinked back tears which sprang instinctively to her eyes. 'Ow. My nose hurts.'

'It's still bleeding a bit,' said the boy. 'Do you want to go back into the school and wash your face properly?'

Oonagh had always thought herself pretty tough and independent, but just now all she wanted to do was go home to her parents.

'No,' she said, 'I'll be all right. Can I borrow your hanky? I'll wash it and give it back tomorrow.'

'Course,' said the boy, 'but how are you getting home? On the bus?'

'No, I'll walk.'

'Well, I'll get my dad to give you a lift if you like. He's a teacher here – Mr Knight. My name's Tim. I'm in 5X.'

'Knighty,' Oonagh remembered.

The boy smiled. 'That's right. Some of the kids call him Dirty Knighty. I don't know why, cos he's not – dirty, I mean. He's just a bit scruffy, I suppose. A bit of an old hippy.' There was a pause, then he said, 'Look, I'll go and ask him. He won't have left yet.'

He looked all set to scamper off, but Oonagh said, 'No, it's all right. I'm fine, honest. She only hit me once, just caught me a lucky one on the nose, that's all.' Anxious to avoid any fuss, she didn't mention the kick in the stomach.

Tim was evidently reluctant to let her go. 'Well, maybe I can walk home with you then? I mean, Sue and her friends might be waiting in ambush somewhere.'

Touched by his concern, Oonagh said, 'I probably go a different way to you.'

'Which way do you go?'

'I'm living up near the woods at the moment.'

'Well, that's the way I go,' Tim said, sounding genuinely delighted. 'I always walk through the woods. It's a short cut.'

Oonagh hesitated a moment longer, then smiled and said, 'I suppose we might as well go together then.'

As they walked she dabbed intermittently at her nose, which was becoming more tender and still leaking blood.

'What's your name?' Tim asked.

'Oonagh.'

'You're new, aren't you?'

'I wouldn't say that. I've been on this planet nearly fifteen years.'

He glanced at her, grinning when he realised she was teasing him. 'You know what I mean. You're new to the school.'

'How can you tell?'

'I just haven't seen you before. Besides, you haven't had time to get a uniform.'

'My parents can't afford to buy me a uniform,' she said a little defiantly.

'Oh,' said Tim, and looked so uncomfortable that Oonagh was immediately sorry for her gruffness and felt compelled to add, 'We travel around too much for it to be worthwhile.'

'What do your mum and dad do, then?'

'They're musicians. My father plays the guitar and my mother plays the flute.'

Tim's eyes lit up with interest. 'Are they famous?'

'No,' said Oonagh, smiling. 'They just get work where they can – in pubs mostly. If there isn't much pub work going, they busk, or try to find something else. My mother sometimes makes jewellery which she sells door to door or down the markets.'

Tim looked impressed. 'That sounds pretty cool. My dad's just a boring old teacher and my mum – well, she's my step-mum really – owns a flower shop in the village. My real mum lives in Nottingham, but she's travelled all over the place. She lived in New York for a bit.'

'Well ... that all sounds good too.'

'Yeah, I suppose it's all right, actually. I never went to New York or anything, though. I didn't even meet my real mum until she came back, when I was six. Well, I did meet her, but I don't remember it. She and my dad split up when I was born.'

They walked down a steep hill, through an area of housing which Tim knew would eventually peter out into farmland beyond which rose the dark mass of the woods. He had lived in Bramwell most of his life. It was somewhere between a large village and a small town, affluent and picturesque. Although only a dozen miles from the outskirts of York, the fields and woodland which surrounded it gave it a sense of drowsy isolation.

On a map Bramwell most closely resembled a fat croissant, or a crab with the woods to the north an emerald teardrop pooled between its outstretched claws. The main street ran like a grey thread through its centre, a thread which frayed at both ends, forming tributary roads which meandered through the countryside, and led to larger roads, and eventually to motorways.

The town's only secondary school, Bramwell Comprehensive, at which Tim and his half-sister, Chloe, were pupils, and his dad a teacher of English and Drama, was large enough to accommodate all the local children aged between eleven and sixteen who weren't sent away to private schools. Whilst this undoubtedly consolidated the town's sense of community, the disadvantage for Tim and Chloe was that the school was a long way from home. It was situated in the south-east corner of the town whilst the house on Stonecroft Avenue where they lived was over two miles away in the north-west corner.

This meant a long walk to and from school every day, a walk which was lessened considerably if they took the short cut through the woods, which Annette had forbidden them to do ever since that business with the flasher in the summer. Chloe had little argument with her mother's orders – she didn't like walking through the woods anyway – but Tim was of the opinion that what Annette didn't know wouldn't hurt her. If the flasher appeared to him, he had every intention of making sure the guy never sang baritone again. Of course, one way of getting home quickly would have been to cadge a lift off his dad, but Tim would rather stick needles in his eyes than do that; it was bad enough your dad being a teacher at your school without having to acknowledge the fact in front of your friends.

It was unusual actually for Tim to be on his own at this time, but his two best friends, who lived near him and whom he normally walked home with, were otherwise engaged. Andy Soper was at computer club and Steve Collins, together with the rest of the first team, had been called in for extra football practice after their 9–0 thrashing against Appleden at the weekend.

'Big houses here,' Oonagh said, indicating a stone-built place they were walking past. It had an adjoining stable block and a large paddock, and they could just glimpse an orchard beyond a sweeping gravel drive on which were parked a red Porsche and a four-wheel drive Mitsubishi.

'Yeah,' said Tim. 'Some of the people who live here have got massive wads of dosh.' Oonagh looked at him, and he said hastily, as if being rich was akin to having a transmittable disease, 'We haven't, though. We live at the other end of town. Our house is much smaller than this.'

The houses were getting further and further apart now, often separated by ploughed or open fields. The road was narrowing, and all at once the tarmac came to a crumbling end at a right-hand turn, and Tim and Oonagh were suddenly trudging along a bumpy dust track which led past a farm with corrugated iron sheds and a few acres of fields before dipping down to the edge of the woods. They could see the woods below them – from here the tops of the trees resembled a greeny-brown carpet, lumpy and threadbare beneath the drab autumn sky.

'How do I look?' Oonagh asked a little anxiously, turning to Tim.

Tim was glad of the chance to appraise her without making her think he was staring. She was an extremely pretty girl, small and slight with a sharp chin and dainty features. Her thick honey-coloured hair was pushed back from her face and tied in a loose ponytail. The bridge of her nose looked a little swollen and discoloured and there was a pencil-line cut across her right cheekbone. Apart from this she looked fine, and he told her so – except for the blood on her jumper, of course. She looked down at herself and grimaced.

'Maybe I'd better take this off. I don't want Graeme and Linda to get too big a shock.'

'Graeme and Linda?'

'My parents.'

'You call your mum and dad by their first names?'

'Yeah, why not?' Oonagh said, her voice hardening with defiance once again.

It seemed strange to Tim, but he decided to let it go. He called both his mothers 'Mum', which would have been awkward if they were ever to be in the same room, but fortunately they never were; it was like an unspoken rule, even a taboo. Tim himself had no problem with not only calling them both 'Mum', but also thinking of them as such. Annette had brought him up for all but the first six months of his life, and to regard her as anything but his mother would have seemed like a snub. But by the same token he couldn't call his real mum 'Jackie' either, not when she had actually given birth to him and was ever-eager to make up for abandoning him as a child. Neither of his mothers ever asked him anything about his relationship with the other, which he put down to the fact that they each wanted to avoid the hurt they'd feel if they construed something he said to mean that he loved the other more. The only time he himself felt awkward about the situation was when he was talking on the phone to Jackie and Annette was nearby, or when Jackie put 'Love From Mum' on the cards and (usually over-the-top) presents she bought him for his birthdays and Christmas.

Oonagh was hauling the jumper over her head, taking care to hold the bloodstains away from her face. Her hair crackled with electricity as the fabric passed over it.

It was a cold day, and now she was wearing only a thin white T-shirt on to which the bloodstains had soaked in stippled pink patterns. Already goosebumps were rising on her arms.

Tim put his bag down and pulled off his blazer. 'Here, have this.'

She rolled up the jumper and stuffed it into the battered canvas knapsack she'd swung from her shoulder. 'No, don't be silly. Then *you'd* be cold.'

'I'm all right. I've got a shirt and a jumper.'

'Ooh, big macho man.'

'Honestly, I'm fine. Look, take this and give it back to me tomorrow with the handkerchief.'

'How do you know I won't just keep it?' Oonagh said.

'I trust you,' Tim replied. 'You've got a nice face.'

Oonagh looked away as if she was suddenly interested in the view. When she turned back her lips were curved in a smile. 'I suppose you won't shut up unless I take it, will you?'

'No,' said Tim, also smiling. 'I'll go on and on and on and on and on and on and —'

'All right, all right, I give in,' she said. She took the blazer from him and put it on. It was big and baggy on her. She had to roll the cuffs back to find her hands.

They resumed their walk down towards the woods. 'Whereabouts is it that you live?' Tim asked for the second time.

Oonagh surprised him by suddenly stopping and pointing. 'There.'

He followed the direction of her finger. In a fallow field away to his left he could see a cluster of mud-spattered vehicles: trailers, caravans, camper vans, Land Rovers. A couple of dogs, one a big yellow mongrel, the other a Collie-type thing with a black face, were chasing each other in and out and under the vehicles whilst a toddler watched them with delight and clapped his podgy hands. A man with a dark beard, wearing an overcoat, fingerless gloves and a trilby hat, was feeding fuel into a glowing brazier from which smoke curled like a giant black cobra from a snake charmer's basket.

Tim looked at Oonagh and saw she was looking back at him with that familiar defiant expression, her lips pursed, her sharp chin thrust out.

'So you really are a gypsy,' Tim said, remembering Sue Kuznitsky's earlier comment. Before he could even blink, Oonagh's face had curled into a scowl and she had turned and begun to stomp away from him, down the lane.

'Hey, what's the matter?' he called, hurrying after her. She was heading towards a five-bar gate set in a dry-stone wall from which a muddy trail led up to the encampment.

Without turning she snapped, 'You're just as bad as the rest of them. I suppose you can understand now why those girls were attacking me?'

Tim caught up with her by the gate, considered reaching out to take hold of her shoulder, then decided against it. In the end he just said, 'Why? What did I say?'

She stopped dead, but remained with her back to him for a moment as if deciding whether or not to answer his question. In the end she swung round, her face like thunder. 'You just don't understand, that's all.'

Tim grimaced, half apology, half bewilderment. 'I'm sorry, but I don't know what I've done. Whatever it was, I didn't mean anything by it.'

She was still scowling, though not as fiercely. 'I'm not a gypsy,' she said.

'Oh,' said Tim. 'What are you then?'

'A traveller.'

'Oh,' said Tim again and shrugged. 'Okay.' He glanced across at the camp; the motley assortment of vehicles and mobile homes were stark against the sky in the encroaching twilight. After a moment he asked tentatively, 'So what's wrong with gypsies?'

Oonagh gave a hard half-laugh and said, 'Nothing's *wrong* with them. I'm just not one, that's all.'

'Okay. Well, I won't call you one again then.' The two of them hovered for a moment by the gate like first-daters at the girl's front door uncertain how to say goodbye. Then Tim asked, 'So how long have you been a traveller?'

'All my life. I was born on the road. My parents became travellers in the mid-seventies. They both had good jobs – Graeme was a manager in a tinned food company, Linda sold air freight space or something. They had a car each, a house, a mortgage, all that stuff. But they weren't happy. Linda says they were drowning in materialism, accumulating wealth for the sake of it. So they quit their jobs, sold up and got out. For a while they lived on their savings and then they started to busk and to look around for bits of work here and there. They never earn much, but we don't *need* that much, just enough for food and essentials.'

Tim thought of all the things he spent his money on, most notable of which were art materials and comics. He was a good artist, easily the best in his year, if not in the school, and his ambition was to become a graphic artist, and perhaps one day to illustrate a graphic novel scripted by Alan Moore. But art stuff wasn't his sole expenditure: he also bought computer software (he and his dad had sent Mum crazy just recently trawling the Internet for hours on end), and CDs (*What's the Story*) *Morning Glory*? by Oasis, which he'd bought last week, was brilliant, even if his dad did keep saying that they sounded like the illegitimate children of the Beatles and the Sex Pistols). Then, of course, there was the throwaway stuff – visits to the cinema, bus fares into Leeds on a Saturday, chocolate and crisps and the occasional McDonald's, Cokes at Bertolucci's, where he also played songs on the jukebox at 10p a time, 50p's for the pool table in the sixth-form common room which he sneaked into with Andy sometimes when it was quiet ... He couldn't imagine life without such luxuries.

'I was born in 1981, right there in our trailer,' Oonagh was saying, and then added with some pride, 'Linda refused to go in to hospital. She didn't want to be pumped full of drugs.'

Tim refrained from asking whether that wasn't a big dangerous, and instead said, 'So what about these other people? How did you all get together?'

Oonagh shrugged. 'We just meet up with people on the road. If they want to join us, they can. There's a few – the Cantleighs and Mrs MacEvoy – who've been travelling with us for as long as I can remember, from before I was born. Other people come and go.'

'But you don't just let anyone join, do you?'

'Yeah, why not?'

'Well, how do you know some of them aren't murderers or child molesters or ... or escaped convicts on the run?'

Oonagh said, 'How do you know your neighbours aren't?'

Tim frowned, frustrated by her argument. 'That's different.'

'Why is it?'

'Well ... what if someone wanted to join who looked really shifty?'

'We don't judge by appearances. We leave that to ignorant people like Sue Kuznitsky.'

'Okay then, what if somebody joined and started making trouble?'

'Then everyone would get together and ask them to leave. I mean, we don't judge people before we've got to know them, and we don't lay down any heavy rules or anything, but if someone causes hassles for somebody else, or makes trouble for the group, then that's not on.'

Tim shrugged. 'It all sounds so simple.'

'It *is* simple. Life's simple when you think about it. It's only authorities and governments and things who make it complicated.'

'But they're only trying to protect people, surely? I mean, we need organisation and laws and stuff, otherwise there'd be chaos.'

Oonagh shrugged and smiled. 'That's your opinion.'

Tim felt frustrated, but he didn't want to get bogged down in an argument and part on bad terms. To change the subject completely he said, 'Which trailer's yours?'

Oonagh pointed to a large brown and white trailer parked beside a chunky Daihatsu van with rust-speckled chrome work. She pushed open the five-bar gate. 'Actually, I'd better get home and get cleaned up.'

'Oh, yeah,' said Tim. 'Me too – get home, I mean. See you tomorrow?'

'You'd better hope so, or you won't get your blazer back.'

'Shall I call for you in the morning? About half-eight?'

'If you like,' she said, trying not to look pleased.

'Right. Great. Well ... see you then.' He turned abruptly, swung his bag on to his shoulder and began to trudge down the lane towards the darkening woods.

Oonagh watched him for a moment and then called, 'Tim.'

He turned round. 'Yeah?'

'Would you like to come in for some tea or something? Graeme could give you a lift home. You could take your blazer back.'

Tim grinned as if he'd been hoping she'd ask him. 'Yeah, great,' he said, and began to jog back up the lane towards her.

3

Those bastards! Who the hell did they think they were?

Jackie was still fuming when she arrived home. She screeched her Golf into its space, jumped out as if the seats had caught fire, and shoved the door so hard that the choppy slam of it seemed to echo and echo in the chill air. Her heart was beating much too fast, and she forced herself to stand still for a moment, one hand resting on the car roof, the other clutching her briefcase. She took a few deep breaths, the cold air rushing into her skull and making her forehead ache. But at least after a few moments she felt calmer. She turned and climbed the stairs to her apartment block.

She swiped her identity card through the electronic lock and pushed the heavy door open before the buzz of the disengaging lock mechanism could cut out. The reception area was light and airy, very modern, very clean. Eric was always telling her that she ought to buy a house, that the exorbitant rent they charged on this place was just money down the drain. She could picture him now, so earnest, so sensible: 'You could get a house twice as big in a decent area, and still save on monthly mortgage payments.'

'What does it matter to you?' she'd reply. 'It's my money.'

'I know, but I just want to see you happy and settled.'

'I *am* happy. I like my apartment. And I'm not interested in being settled. That was always your thing, not mine.'

It was true. Even now the permanency, the responsibility, of having a house scared her. She'd always hated being tied down, though she had to admit that as she got older, she found herself envying Eric more and more for the life he had carved out for himself. Sometimes, in more maudlin moments – when she was watching an old film alone in bed, for example, having drunk one glass of wine too many – she actually found herself thinking that she'd made a mistake, that she should have stuck at her marriage, made it work. If she had, she'd be truly happy now, content in the way that she always thought of Annette as being. Eric was a sweet man, safe and reliable and public-spirited. He'd only turned to Annette in the first place because Jackie had made it impossible for him to love her any more. She'd go to sleep with these thoughts circling sadly in her head. But in the morning she'd wake up and think: How ridiculous! She had never wanted that kind of stifling sameness and she never would.

She crossed to the lift and pressed the button for the third floor. There was no one around, no sound from anywhere. This place often seemed more like a plush office block early in the morning before the workers arrived than a place where people actually lived.

She felt calmer now, watching the lights come on in the buttons as the lift climbed, able to think more clearly. She considered her options, of which there seemed to be several. Either she could back down quietly and leave Rebecca to sort out her own problems; or she could stick by her and see this thing through to the end, however bitter that might be. *Or* she could do what she had done so often in the past, which was to walk away when things got too tough, start afresh somewhere else.

Ten years ago – maybe even five – she would have gone for the third option like a shot. But nowadays ... well, the opportunities in front of her didn't seem quite so bountiful any more. And she *did* like her apartment, enough to want to stay here for another two or three years, at least.

Maybe the situation would resolve itself without her having to become too heavily involved. Maybe old Hopkirk would have a word with his son-in-law, tell him to keep his hands to himself in future (although he had warned Jackie, when she'd complained on Rebecca's behalf earlier that day, to mind her own business and get on with her job whilst she still had one). Or maybe Rebecca would find the courage to kick up enough fuss to make Peterson stop.

The worst thing, of course, would be if things just went on as normal, Peterson getting his kicks by groping Rebecca half a dozen times a day, she suffering in silence, and retreating every so often to the toilet to lock herself in a cubicle and sob her heart out – which was exactly what Jackie had stumbled across her doing earlier that day.

If that happened, Jackie wouldn't be able to keep quiet. She had never been the sort of person to stand by and let things happen. Her dad had described her as 'feisty', her mum as 'strong-willed'. Sometimes Jackie just thought of herself as dumb, the kind of girl who fought lost causes, who made snap decisions and regretted them later.

The lift doors opened on to what looked like a small version of a hotel corridor: plush carpet, gold and white striped wallpaper, bland, vaguely arty floral prints, pot plants with polished green leaves in copper pots. There were four doors on the landing. Hers was the one closest to the lift. Outside her door was an intriguing-looking parcel, about the size of a shoe box, wrapped in brown paper and lots of thick brown tape which she guessed she'd have to take scissors to.

She unlocked her door and went in, pushing the parcel over the threshold with her foot. There were a couple of letters on the doormat, one which she knew without opening was from her friend, Lisa, in New York.

Her apartment (she always thought of them as apartments rather than flats, another hangover from her New York days) consisted of a wide-ish corridor with two rooms leading off on either side. On the left was the bathroom and bedroom, on the right the kitchen and sitting room. All the rooms were large, and the building was constructed in such a way that each room had its share of natural light. The sitting room had bay windows opening on to a balcony, which was where she spent much of her spare time in the summer – sunbathing, drinking wine, eating barbecue.

She slumped down on the creaky chair beside the bamboo telephone table and pressed the playback button on her answering machine. There was only one message – from her hairdresser, Philip, who wanted to re-arrange the appointment she'd booked for next week. When the message clicked off and the silence set in, she found herself wishing there was someone here for her – someone to make her a cup of tea and listen to her problems. She picked up the phone, intending to ring Gareth, her latest friend (could you call a man a boyfriend when he was forty-seven and you were forty-one? It seemed so juvenile somehow). Phone pressed to her ear, she was just punching in the last two digits when she realised what she was doing. She put the phone down, annoyed with herself. She'd been punching in Eric's number by mistake. She hated to admit it, but he was still the one she first thought of when she had a problem, even after all these years. He was the only person she knew without a doubt would be sympathetic and understanding, would listen to her and provide her with the kind of measured responses she needed.

It was tragic in its way, but perhaps not altogether surprising. After all, he'd been there for her thirty years ago, and she for him; they'd got through that dreadful time by relying on each other, forming a tight bond that back then had seemed permanent, unbreakable. And afterwards, once the traumas had begun to ease, they'd found that they still wanted to be together, that mutual reliance had become mutual love.

As teenagers they'd driven their parents to distraction by throwing themselves headlong into the Summer of Love. They'd smoked a lot of pot, listened to a lot of psychedelic music, gone on protest marches against war and tyranny, and tried to find truth in Eastern religion. But despite this, Eric had always been the same – steadfast and sensible. He maintained that he marched against war because he wanted to live in a world of peace, find somewhere to settle down and bring up a family in safety and comfort.

Back then he had been her rock, her safe harbour. She was the flighty, adventurous one. She wanted to change the world by shaking it up, shouting at it, making it take a long, hard look at itself.

And if she couldn't change it, then she wanted to explore it, to see it, smell it, taste it, cram herself with the highs of life until she was intoxicated. Eric always told her they were the yin and the yang, their characters opposing but complementary.

They married in the spring of '71. They were both eighteen and it seemed like an adventure. They found a place, did it up, and for a while they were happy.

But their happiness didn't last. Whilst Eric became more and more settled, comfortably entrenched in his rut, she started to feel stifled and suffocated, weighed down by routine and responsibility. She tried to explain this to Eric, but she could no longer seem to make him understand what she wanted.

'You can't just travel around like a nomad for ever,' he'd tell her.

'Why not?' she'd reply.

'You just can't. It wouldn't work. It isn't practical.'

'Who cares about practical?' she'd say. 'Practical's for squares. It's for commuters in suits and bowler hats, doing the same thing day in, day out. I don't want to get like that, stuck on the production line of humanity.'

'It doesn't have to be like that,' he'd say. 'Life's what you make it.'

'Exactly. And I want to make it more exciting than it is. I'm rotting away here, Eric. I'm turning to stone. I don't want to put down roots. I want to keep moving.'

Gradually, inevitably, they had begun to drift apart, to find that, wanting different things, they no longer had much to say to each other. Eventually they had begun to snipe and bicker as if scoring points off one another. It was a miserable time for them both, but they couldn't seem to help themselves; each time they tried to make up, they were like repelling magnets, veering apart before they could make contact.

And yet even at this stage, Jackie had been horrified at the thought of their going their separate ways. She and Eric had been through so much together that she couldn't conceive of life without him. It would be like cutting off a leg that was giving her pain. Without it the pain would be gone, but would she ever be able to walk again?

In the end, one of them - she couldn't remember who - came up with the idea of having a baby. Maybe that would mend things between them, bring them back together.

Looking back, she couldn't believe how foolish she'd been, couldn't imagine what she must have been thinking of. She knew now that marriages had to be strong to survive children. Babies in particular, however much you might love them, were disruptive and demanding, liable not to seal rifts in a relationship but to make them yawn ever wider. But in her early twenties she had been naive, and far more prone to whims than she was now, and perhaps a baby had seemed like a romantic idea, or at least like a possible solution to a desperate situation.

And so she got pregnant. And in October 1978, when she was twenty-five years old, she gave birth to Tim.

It was a mistake. Almost from the start, from when the pregnancy test came out positive, she knew it. But she tried to deny her doubts to herself, tried to convince herself that she was happy, that it was her hormones making her feel miserable and scared, trapped by her own body, resentful of the thing growing inside it. Once the baby actually arrived, she would love it, she felt sure; everything would change. It would be the making of her and Eric. A new start. A new challenge.

She was wrong.

First of all, the pregnancy was a nightmare. She was so sick that her oesophagus split and she had to be rushed in to hospital. And then she kept bleeding: her body was trying to reject the baby because their blood groups clashed. And there were a hundred and one other things - chronic backache, swollen ankles, mood swings that would take her into blacknesses she never even knew existed. She spent a large part of the nine months cursing Eric and cursing the thing inside her.

And when Tim finally arrived, he did so in trauma and blood and thirty-five hours of the most unbelievable pain.

Afterwards she didn't want to look at her baby, didn't want it or Eric anywhere near her. She hated them for what they'd done to her, what they'd put her through. She just wanted to close her eyes and sleep and forget. The midwife, the nurses, the doctors, all told her that that feeling was natural and that it would pass, but it didn't, not really. She couldn't shake off the awful dark resentment she felt towards her child and her husband, couldn't stop herself feeling she'd somehow been duped into a situation she wanted no part of.

Post-natal depression set in, and if anything that was even worse than all that had gone before. Jackie had never believed it possible to feel so utterly dreadful, had always thought of depression as a finite thing, but this seemed bottomless, an awful black pit into which she fell, deeper and deeper and deeper, never touching the bottom.

She had blazing rows with Eric, which degenerated into screaming fits. She was terrified by the extent to which she lost control of herself. She threw things at him, became totally unreasonable, calling him all sorts of names, accusing him of trapping her deliberately. She couldn't bear to have him near her. For a while the sight of him, the sound of his voice, made her feel physically sick.

Throughout this time she cared for Tim, albeit in a dutiful, mechanical, sometimes lackadaisical way. She was never able to conjure up even the faintest stirrings of love for him, which in turn made her feel even more wretched with guilt and inadequacy. As far as she was concerned he was nothing but a squalling, demanding parasite that tied her to her life with Eric.

As for Eric himself, he tried to be patient, as he always did, but sometimes his patience snapped and he yelled right back at her. She knew he resented the fact that she was spoiling what should have been a precious time – caring for their first child together – and eventually, inevitably perhaps, he began to seek solace elsewhere.

He found it in Annette Butler, an art teacher at the school where he taught English and Drama. For a long time their relationship was platonic. They went out for drinks together, and then for meals, Eric pouring out his heart, she listening to him, offering support, advice, comfort, whatever she could. But as the situation at home got worse, Eric and Annette's relationship became deeper, more intimate, until finally one night, after Jackie had picked up a knife and threatened to kill him, Eric had left the house with Tim and hadn't come back until the following morning.

Jackie still remembered that day so clearly, still remembered the look on Eric's face. There had been a determination about him, a quiet resolve. She had known even before he said anything that something momentous, far-reaching, was about to happen. His mood had rubbed off on her, and for the first time in weeks, maybe months, they had sat down and talked, quietly and calmly. Eric told her about Annette, holding nothing back, and for the first time he voiced what they had both known for a long time: their relationship had become irretrievable. After fourteen years together, they had finally come to the end of the road.

They had both cried. They had even hugged one another. Indeed, now that it finally looked like ending, Jackie had clutched Eric as if she never wanted to let him go and sobbed, 'Oh, Eric, what's happened to us? Why couldn't we just have been happy?'

Eventually, once the dust had settled, once they had both cried themselves out, Eric said to her quietly, 'Are you sure this is what you want?'

She felt shattered and confused. Uncertainly, she said, 'I don't know if it's what I *want* exactly, but I think it's for the best.'

'And what about Tim?' he said. 'Do you want me to keep him?'

'He's your son.'

Eric frowned. 'He's your son too.'

'Yes, but you love him.'

There had been a silence then, and then Eric had released a long, sad, deep sigh. And soon after that he had left. He had packed Tim's stuff, and some of his own, and he had driven away in his car.

And apart from the loose ends, and the actual divorce, which neither of them contested, that was that. They sold the house quickly, and less than two months later, she was in New York.

Like many turning points in her life, it was a spur of the moment decision. Her friend, Lisa, whom she and Eric had met during a brief sojourn at a Buddhist commune seven years earlier, rang Jackie to ask her if she could use a holiday after all that she'd been through. Jackie said yes, and the very next morning she was sitting on a plane looking down at the Atlantic ocean.

She left for a few weeks break, and ended up staying for six years.

She lived with Lisa for three months, during which time she found a job waiting tables in a pizza parlour, and then a better one as a receptionist in a publishing company. She found her own apartment, made a bunch of new friends, and had the kind of wild, exhilarating time that she believed human beings were put on this earth to have.

She knew she was running away, but she knew also that she had been running for a long time, constantly trying to outpace the ripples of guilt that lapped at the edges of her life. She had been running ever since she was twelve years old, when she and Eric and Andrew Dullaston and James Keeve had done that terrible thing. The guilt wasn't easy to live with, but she could cope with it; it didn't engulf her as it had once done. She didn't feel as though she were drowning in it.

She wrote to Eric, telling him where she was, what she was doing, and he wrote back with reports on Tim's progress and accompanying photographs. Every two months or so she'd get new pictures, and she'd be constantly amazed at how quickly Tim was growing up, changing from a tiny baby to a toddler to a little boy. And with each letter, each new batch of photos, she'd find herself becoming more and more wistful, thinking about what might have been. When Eric wrote to say that he and Annette had got married, she had a little weep to herself, but sent them a Congratulations card. And when, in January 1981, Eric wrote to tell her that Annette had given birth to a daughter, Chloe, she cried again, and for the first time since she had arrived in America, she felt lonely and unloved.

It was when Eric sent her a photograph taken at Tim's sixth birthday party that the realisation hit her like a thunderbolt. This is my son, she thought, I gave birth to him. And then, following that: It's not too late to get to know him. She was astounded by the almost epiphanic nature of the thought. It was as though a cloud had finally shifted from her mind. She received Eric's letter on a Friday, and spent the weekend in a state of nervous excitement. By Sunday she was thinking: I could see Tim in two days if I wanted to.

By Monday afternoon she was on a plane back to England.

The moment she touched down, she hired a car at the airport and drove the two hundred miles to Yorkshire. Even now she could recall the dream-like, almost surrealistic nature of the journey – the weirdness of driving on the left-hand side of the road once again; the way everything seemed so small and quaint and peaceful, as if, during her absence, England had somehow slipped back in time. Jet-lagged, she found a pub about ten miles outside Bramwell, and crashed out for the night in their only guest room. The next day she embarked on what felt like the last lap of her odyssey, her stomach churning at the prospect of seeing her son.

She timed it so that she would arrive late afternoon, when the family were back from work and school. When she saw the house for the first time, she got the shakes, almost convinced herself she'd made a mistake and that she should turn back. She sat in the car for a long time, until eventually, trance-like, she made herself get out, open the garden gate, walk up the path to the front door and ring the bell. It was a nice house in a leafy suburban street, just the kind of place in which she imagined Eric living.

It was Eric himself who answered the door. His hair was receding, he had lines around his eyes and mouth that hadn't been there when she had last seen him, and he had new square spectacles that made him look like an accountant, rather than the round ones that used to cause people to remark on his amazing likeness to John Lennon.

To say he was surprised to see her was an understatement. His expression was almost comic – eyes widening, mouth dropping open, colour draining from his face. He took a step forward as if to fill the doorway so that she couldn't get past, or perhaps to shield her from sight like a guilty secret.

'Hi, Eric,' she said, feeling as though her stomach were unravelling, 'I'm back.'

He closed his mouth, swallowed. 'So I see,' he rasped. 'My God, I don't believe this. Why did you ... I mean ... when did you get back?'

'Yesterday. I decided to hire a car, drive up to see you.' She didn't mention Tim. She wasn't sure how it would be construed if she were to admit she was desperate to see him.

He stood there, shaking his head, looking stunned. 'This is incredible. Why didn't you let us know you were coming?'

'You know me. It was a spur of the moment thing.'

He invited her in, albeit a little reticently. She could tell he was worrying about the consequences of his wife and ex-wife being in the same room together. Jackie had never met Annette, had never even seen a photograph of her. She had a mental image of a small, mousey woman, vaguely pretty, calm and sensible like Eric. She followed him in to the lounge, and suddenly there was the woman whose name she had known for over six years, sitting on the settee with her legs tucked beneath her, body inclined towards the TV which she'd been watching before turning to see who Eric had brought in to the house.

She looked nothing like Jackie had imagined. She was edging towards dumpiness, though was not unattractive, her chestnut hair cut in a demi-wave, her eyes large and brown, her mouth wide and generous. She looked like the archetypal mum – warm, friendly, homely. Even sitting there on the settee, watching the early evening news, she gave the impression of being utterly suited to her role in life, content and comfortable with her lot. The impression was accentuated by the presence of her children – or rather, her child and step-child. There was little Chloe sitting on the rug in front of the fire, gleefully slamming Stickle Bricks together. And on the far side of the room, sitting at the dining table in front of a window that looked out on to a large back garden, there was six-year old Tim, the fringe of his then-blond hair hanging over his face, his tongue sticking out with concentration as he bent forward over a pad, the green felt tip pen in his hand squeaking as he coloured in some picture he had drawn.

It was an idyllic scene. Family life through rose-tinted spectacles. Jackie was unable to take her eyes off the little boy as Eric explained to Annette who she was, how she had driven all this way to see them.

Tim didn't look up from his pad at first, didn't acknowledge her. Jackie felt an urge to call out his name, but restrained herself. She heard Annette say, 'Hello,' and forced herself to tear her attention away from her son.

The greeting had been cool. Eric's new wife looked wary now, suggesting by her stance that this was her territory and that she considered Jackie a threat here, or at least an unwelcome visitor. Jackie smiled disarmingly to reassure her. Eric made coffee, and they sat around, making small talk, which seemed ridiculous and false after the number of years that she and Eric had known one another, the chatty letters they'd exchanged.

After fifteen minutes of terse, polite conversation, Jackie finally plucked up the courage to say, 'Actually, I wanted to talk to you about Tim.'

Annette tensed, her shoulders coming up as if someone had opened a window on a bitterly cold day. 'What about him?'

'Well, I just wondered, now that I'm back, whether I could get to know him a little bit.'

Annette's reply was measured. 'Why would you want to do that?'

Jackie smiled as if it was obvious, and looked to Eric for support or understanding, but his pinched, tight-lipped expression was not encouraging. 'Well,' she said, glancing at Tim who was still drawing his pictures, oblivious, 'I *am* his mother.'

To her credit, Annette remained calm, though perhaps it wasn't in her nature to lose her temper; during her time in New York, Jackie had forgotten exactly how repressed English people could be.

'No,' she said, '*I'm* his mother. You're just the person who gave birth to him.'

Jackie laughed in an effort to lighten the mood. 'But I'm his real mother.'

'Who turned her back on him when he was six months old, and hasn't thought about him since.'

Jackie flushed then, feeling the first stirrings of anger. 'How would you know what I've been thinking?' she said. 'You don't even know me.'

'Hey, hey,' Eric intervened, 'calm down.' He glanced meaningfully at Tim, who had looked up from his drawing now, alerted by Jackie's raised voice.

'Go and play upstairs, Tim, and take Chloe with you,' Annette said.

Jackie felt a flash of anger but suppressed it, knowing it would be counter-productive. She couldn't believe that the woman was sending her little boy away after she had waited all this time and come all this way to see him.

'Aw, Mummy, do I have to? I'm drawing,' Tim said.

'Take your drawing stuff with you,' Eric told him. 'Go on, Chloe, go with your brother. Look after her, Tim.'

Tim grumbled, but complied. He had to pass where Jackie was sitting to go out into the hallway. As he passed her he asked tentatively, 'Who are you?'

Jackie didn't know what to say. She had no idea how much Tim knew. In the end she said, 'I'm a friend of your daddy's. An old friend. I've just come back from America.'

The little boy wrinkled his nose. 'Where's that?' he said.

'It's on the other side of the world.'

'It's where Superman comes from, Tim,' Eric added.

Tim's eyes widened. 'Wow!' he said, looking at Jackie with new respect. 'What's your name?'

Jackie glanced at Eric and Annette. Eric's expression was oddly unreadable, though Annette's was not; it was clear that she wanted this conversation to end as soon as possible.

'Jackie,' Jackie said.

'Mine's Tim.'

'I know that.'

'How do you know?'

'Your daddy told me.'

'Tim' Annette said, more sternly than she needed to. 'What did your daddy tell you?'

Tim scowled – much to Jackie's satisfaction, she had to admit. 'All right, I'm going,' he said. 'S'not fair, though. I haven't done anything. I was only drawing.'

After the children had left the room, Jackie said, 'Look, guys, I don't want to rock the boat here. All I want is a chance to get to know my son.'

'Why now?' Annette said. 'Why have you suddenly decided, after all this time, that you want to get to know him? You were never interested before.'

'It's not as sudden as all that,' Jackie said. 'It's been a gradual thing. Every time Eric sent me a new photograph, I felt more and more like I wanted to come home, see him for myself. And now I have.'

'You could at least have prepared us for this, Jacks,' Eric said, 'given us some advance warning.'

'I know, I'm sorry,' she said. 'But it's not really my style, is it? Never has been.'

They spent over an hour talking, discussing, trying to find some middle ground. Eric was not opposed to Jackie's seeing Tim in principle, and to be fair, neither was Annette. Though she was evidently more suspicious of Jackie's motives than Eric, her real concern was for Tim himself. Annette didn't want Tim upset or confused. At this stage neither she nor Eric had told him that Annette was not his real mother; they had been planning to leave it until he was a little older and able to understand the implications. Now they agreed, reluctantly, to break the news to him sooner than they'd planned, and Jackie in her turn agreed to give them a few weeks in which to do so. The last thing she wanted was to see Tim upset, she said. Annette didn't reply, but gave her a look that would have withered dahlias at forty paces.

In the end, things had turned out all right. Tim accepted the news with astonishing ease, even being overheard by Eric announcing proudly to a neighbour that he now had two mummies. He was a little shy of Jackie at first, but quickly became used to her, and within a few weeks was treating her as though he had known her all his life. Jackie, for her part, found that the so-called instinctive motherly emotions she had been unable to muster within her after Tim's birth were now abundantly present. She quickly grew not only to love Tim, but also to like him. He was a happy, funny, lively little boy, and in the ten years that followed, their relationship continued to strengthen.

After that first time, she never went back to Eric and Annette's house, and never saw Annette again. When Tim was small, Eric either brought him round to wherever Jackie was living at the time, or they met at some mutually agreed rendezvous, like spies exchanging merchandise. More often than not these days, Tim travelled up to Nottingham alone, which saddened Jackie a little, though she still saw Eric three or four times a year, and spoke to him at least once a week on the telephone. They had an easy-going relationship – no hang-ups, no undercurrents, no hidden agendas. Jackie had no idea how Annette felt about the situation. Whenever she saw Eric, she would say, 'How's Annette?' and Eric would say, 'Oh, fine,' and that would be the end of the conversation.

Jackie's mind drifted back to the present. It had become dark in the hallway while she'd been sitting there, thinking, so she got up and turned on the light. The parcel was still on the floor just inside the door. She picked it up and carried it into the kitchen. She switched on the kettle and dumped two scoops of coffee into the cafetiere, then took a pair of scissors out of the cutlery drawer and began slicing away at the tape that bound the parcel. It took her no more than thirty seconds to cut through the tape, and as the pressed-down cardboard flaps rose a little, she immediately became aware of a sickly, rotten odour that caused her stomach to roil. Holding her breath she put down the scissors and cautiously pulled aside the flaps of the box to see what it contained.

Sitting in a wad of newspaper, soaked brown with blood, was a sizeable chunk of meat so rotten it had turned green. Bloated white maggots crawled over and around it. The stench was so overpowering it was as if stinking, invisible hands had risen from the box and clamped themselves over her face.

Jackie recoiled, her stomach clenching. She began to retch, and rushed to the sink. She had never smelt anything so utterly vile. Everything she had eaten and drunk that day erupted out of her, splashing the stainless steel. The reflex was so violent it felt as if she was being punched repeatedly in the stomach. Knees buckling and eyes swimming, she turned on the tap.

Who could have sent her such a disgusting thing? Was it someone's idea of a joke? As her retching subsided, she glanced at the box, and for the first time noticed that something was written on the underside of one of the upraised cardboard flaps. She wiped her eyes with the back of her hand to clear her blurred vision, and looked again. The four words had been written in block capitals in red marker pen. As she read them she murmured them aloud:

'And now it begins.'

4

Kicking off her shoes, Annette flopped back on to the settee. She would dearly have liked to have drifted off to sleep, but this time before Eric and the kids arrived home was the only time she got to do her aerobics video. It was her own fault really. Last December she and Eric had set each other New Year's Resolutions which each of them had vowed to stick to. Annette had challenged Eric to give up the twenty roll-ups he'd been smoking daily for the past quarter century, and he had told her to stop moaning about the fact that she was a stone and a half overweight and actually do something about it.

A fair enough arrangement, and for the first couple of months things had gone well. Both had set to their tasks with vigour and resolve, Eric planning a twenty-week programme, whereby he would cut down by one cigarette a week until he had given up, and she setting herself a diet and exercise regime, which involved cutting out desserts and the stodgy comfort foods she'd indulged in far too much over Christmas, swimming in her lunch hour, and leaping about to the aerobics video the kids had bought her as an incentive. By March she had lost ten pounds, and Eric was down to around twelve a day. But then, somehow, things had gradually begun to turn around.

She supposed it was a question of willpower and temptation. The problem was, neither she nor Eric had enough of the first, which in turn made it increasingly difficult to resist the second. All at once she found that she was skipping exercise sessions because she was 'too busy', and beginning to crave the Danish pastries and chocolate biscuits she'd been denying herself. And Eric managed to get down to ten a day, but then seemed to stick there, though sometimes he confessed to smoking as many as fifteen if things were getting stressful at work.

Now, almost a year after the bet had been made, Annette was only two or three pounds lighter than she'd been at the beginning of the year. And today she was feeling particularly guilty, because not only had almost a week passed since she had last donned her baggy pink tracksuit, but at noon her friend, Beryl, had appeared in the shop, proposing they have lunch together. It hadn't taken much persuading on Beryl's part for Annette to say yes. They had gone to San Marco's, the only Italian in the village, where Annette had been unable to resist chicken in a cream and butter sauce with pasta, followed by banoffi pie and coffee with chocolates.

Still lying back on the settee, she held her watch up in front of her face and groaned. It was almost ten to four. The kids, and perhaps Eric if he didn't have one of his NUT meetings, or if he wasn't overseeing that Student Council thing he had helped the pupils set up, or if he wasn't trying to get one of his plays off the ground, would be home in half an hour. If she was going to do her tape she ought to do it now.

Her feet throbbed from standing up all day and she felt listless, with the threat of a headache hovering in the back of her skull. She had had her flower shop, Bloomers, for seven years, and had built it up into a thriving business, despite the fact that she closed every afternoon at 3:30 so that she could coincide with Eric, Tim and Chloe getting home.

She dragged herself upstairs, splashed cold water on her face in the hope it would shock her awake and changed into her tracksuit. She had grown to hate the woman who presented the video with a passion. She was too young, too trim, too energetic and too bloody cheerful. However, Annette followed the woman's movements doggedly and only lost her temper towards the end when the woman chirped, 'Come on, let's see you really stretch.'

'I *am* bloody stretching, you silly cow,' Annette grunted.

She was sprawled in a sweaty, panting but self-satisfied heap on the settee when the lounge door opened and Chloe stomped in, all leggy nervous energy, unconscious beauty, scrambled hormones.

'What's wrong?' Annette asked, struggling to raise herself on her elbows.

'Nothing,' said Chloe, flopping into an armchair, though from her tone of voice and the scowl on her face it was obvious that something was.

'Is it a problem at school?' Annette asked.

Chloe shrugged.

'Oh well, if you don't want to talk about it.'

Chloe looked up at the ceiling, released a theatrical sigh, then stood up and walked out of the room.

'Where are you going?' Annette called.

'To get something.'

Ten seconds later Chloe was back, holding a cardboard tube.

'Someone gave me this today,' she said, taking the poster out of the tube and unrolling it.

'Very nice,' said Annette. 'So what's the problem? Have you moved on to Agassi now?'

'Mum,' Chloe said, scowling, 'this is serious.' She told Annette about how Tanya had made her look stupid in front of Ben. 'And now I've fallen out with my best friend and the boy I like probably thinks

I'm a complete crud, and everything's just horrible,' she concluded, close to tears.

'I'm sure things aren't as bad as that, love,' Annette said.

'They are, they are!'

'But if this boy really likes you, then he's not going to change his mind just because of what Tanya said, is he?'

Chloe shrugged. 'I don't know.' But it was obvious to Annette that this was what her daughter wanted to hear.

'Of course he isn't. I mean, it doesn't sound as though Tanya actually said anything bad about you. She just asked this ... Ben if he was the one who'd given you the poster.'

'But Ben might think I've got another boyfriend and lose interest.'

'How do you work that one out? If he's got anything about him, and is as interested as you say he is, then something like this ought to give him a kick up the backside, don't you think?'

Chloe thought about it, then wrinkled her nose. 'I suppose so,' she said doubtfully, 'but what about Tanya?'

'What *about* Tanya?' Annette almost said, but stopped herself. She didn't like the girl. She was arrogant and self-centred. But she certainly wasn't going to pick and choose her daughter's friends for her. Chloe was old enough and intelligent enough to do that herself.

'Oh, Tanya'll come round,' she said airily. 'You know what she's like, she always wants to be the centre of attention. She's just had her nose put out of joint, that's all. I wouldn't be surprised if she comes up to you at school tomorrow, wanting to be friends again.'

'You really think so?' Chloe said.

'I'm sure of it,' said Annette, crossing her fingers.

'Thanks, Mum,' Chloe said, 'you're a pal.' She jumped up from the chair, scooped up the poster and headed for the door.

'Where are you going?' said Annette.

'To put my new poster up.'

'What about this rubbish that you've left lying around?'

'I'll clear it up later.' Chloe's voice receded as she ran up the stairs.

A cup of tea revived Annette, and she had restored all the furniture to its rightful place and was making a start on the evening meal when Eric arrived home. With his thin face he looked cadaverous when he was tired, blue veins standing out on his temple and around his eyes.

'You all right?' she asked, kissing him.

'It's been a long day. Union nonsense. I could do with a coffee.'

As she chopped onions and he made coffee they chatted about their day. Eric told her about the idea for a new play he'd had coming home in the car. 'It'd be a political satire with an ecological message, and hopefully lots of laughs. It's about this union rep who's really an alien. I might get the sixth form to do it for the younger kids if our esteemed head doesn't deem it too politically biased.'

As he quoted her lines he'd formulated in his head, adopting various roles and silly accents, making her laugh, Annette was overcome with a flush of well-being. Eric was a lovely husband, her children were growing up into the kind of happy, thoughtful, well-balanced people she'd wish them to be, she loved her house and the village they lived in, and she had a successful business. Sometimes she worried that she had it *too* good, that something terrible was just certain to be waiting around the next corner. But for the most part her problems were small ones.

Pools of light marching towards the open kitchen door announced the arrival of Chloe, who was switching on the trio of lamps in the living room as she approached. She caught her parents having a cuddle, Annette giggling and claiming her hands were all oniony whilst Eric rained kisses on the side of her neck, making a sound like a pig grubbing for truffles.

'Oh, for God's sake,' said Chloe, rolling her eyes, 'aren't you two a bit old for all that?'

Annette looked indignant, though she knew that just lately it had started to embarrass Chloe when she and Eric openly displayed affection for each other. She remembered finding a packet of condoms in her father's bedside cabinet when she'd been a teenager, and being horrified at the thought that her mother and father still had sex.

Eric, however, was in a silly mood now. He released Annette, took hold of Chloe's hands and attempted to spin her round the kitchen in a sweeping ballroom dance step, warbling, 'You're never too old for love.'

'Stop it, Dad,' Chloe said as if he was showing her up in front of her friends.

He released her with a sigh and said, 'That's the problem with the younger generation. No romance in their souls.'

'What's for tea?' Chloe asked, looking over her mother's shoulder.

'Wait and see.'

'Didn't we have that yesterday?'

'Talking of the younger generation,' said Eric, 'where's my son and heir?'

'Probably playing computer games at Andy Soper's,' said Annette.

'Computer games,' Eric said, pulling a face, though when he and Tim got on the Internet together, Annette wouldn't see either of them for hours. 'When I was a lad we had to make do with a load of old socks rolled up into a football that we used to kick about between us.'

'Yeah, yeah,' said Chloe, poking about in the biscuit tin until she found a custard cream. 'You used to live in a cardboard box and you got up two hours before you went to bed, and all you had to eat was the grit that you licked off the roads.'

'Don't mock, young lady,' said Eric. 'You don't realise how lucky you are nowadays.'

'Things change, Dad. You've got to move with the times. It's called progress.'

'Progress? Pah. We might not have had much, but things were much better back in the good old days when I were a nipper.'

'Like what? Rickets? Whooping cough? TB?'

Eric had now lapsed fully into his comic Yorkshire accent. 'Aye, well, at least those were diseases you could rely on, not like these new-fangled germs they've got now.'

Annette was shaking her head and smiling. 'Listen to the ancient one. He was only born in 1952, he wasn't exactly a war baby.'

Eric blinked behind his spectacles and said haughtily, 'I'll have you know, I didn't taste a banana until I was eleven.'

'There's no answer to that,' said Chloe, grinning.

'Chloe!' Annette said, trying to sound shocked but spoiling it by laughing.

'Sorry, Mum,' said Chloe. 'Hey, listen, what's that?'

They all heard the rumbling of a larger than average engine in the street outside.

'Sounds like a lorry pulling up,' Annette said.

Chloe wandered back into the living room, still nibbling her custard cream, and looked out of the window. 'No, it's not,' she called, 'it's a van. Tim's getting out of it.'

'I didn't know Andy Soper's dad had a van,' Annette said two minutes later when Tim walked into the kitchen.

'Neither did I,' said Tim.

'So who was that giving you a lift home?'

'Graeme,' Tim said.

'And who might he be when he's at home?'

'Oonagh's dad.'

'And who's Oonagh?'

'Ooh, my big brother's got a new girlfriend. I hope she's brainier than that last bimbo you went out with,' Chloe called from the living room.

'Shut it, Zoo-Breath. Mum and I were having a private conversation, if you don't mind.'

'Tim, don't call your sister such repulsive names,' Annette said firmly.

'Come on, Mum, she started it.'

Chloe cackled, then licked her finger and drew a stroke-mark in the air.

'And Chloe, don't be so rude to your brother.'

Tim grinned, and said scathingly, 'Talking of bimbos, isn't it time for "Neighbours", mastermind?'

'Not for another ten minutes yet,' Chloe said brightly and leaned over the settee. 'Come on then, Tim, tell us all about her.'

'Yes, spill the beans, Tim. Who is this mystery woman of yours?' Eric said from the armchair in the living room, lowering his paper. He reached for the remote control of the TV that Chloe had put on and pressed the Mute button in anticipation.

'I didn't expect the Spanish Inquisition,' Tim said.

Eric laughed at the Monty Python reference and offered a blood-curdling, 'No one expects the Spanish Inquisition!'

'If she's not your girlfriend, why have you gone red?' Chloe said, also grinning.

'I haven't!'

'Yes you have. Face like a beetroot.'

'At least it's better than having a face like an armpit,' Tim retaliated.

'For God's sake, will the two of you stop bickering,' said Annette. 'If you don't want to tell us, Tim, that's fine. I was only showing an interest.'

Tim shrugged, glanced at Chloe who was still leaning over the back of the settee, grinning, and then said casually, 'It's no big deal. She's just some girl I met at school, that's all. She was new, so I walked home with her.'

'Oh yeah?' said Chloe. 'Walk all the new girls home, do you?'

'For your information, Gonzo, the reason I walked home with her was because I saw a gang of other girls beating her to a pulp. I scraped her up off the pavement and took her home, all right?'

'Who were these girls?' Eric said, suddenly serious.

'Oh, look, this is why I didn't want to say anything. I knew if I did you'd put your teacher's hat on and want me to start naming names.'

Eric folded his newspaper into his lap. 'If there's bullying going on in the school, I really ought to know about it, Tim.'

Tim sighed. Sometimes his dad could be so earnest. 'It's not bullying, Dad, it's just a one-off. It won't happen again, I've sorted it out.'

'Ooh, what a hero,' Chloe said.

Tim rounded on her. 'You think it's funny, do you? A girl getting her head kicked in for no reason?'

'Of course Chloe didn't mean that,' Annette said sharply, wiping her hands on a tea towel, 'did you, Chloe?'

Cowed, Chloe said, 'No, course I didn't. I was only having you on.'

'I still think you should have informed me, or at least a member of staff, though, Tim, and not tried to handle it yourself,' Eric said.

'There wasn't time, Dad. I did offer to try and find you so that you could give Oonagh a lift home, but she wanted to walk.'

'So why was this girl being picked on in the first place?' asked Annette. 'Just because she was new?'

'Well, partly that, and partly because she's a traveller.'

'A traveller!'

'You mean a gypsy?' said Chloe.

Tim looked at his sister condescendingly, even though he had made precisely the same mistake. 'No, she's not a gypsy, she's a traveller. They're completely different.'

'So where's this ... traveller girl living?' Annette asked.

'There's a load of trailers up in one of the fields near the woods.' Before anyone could say anything he added hastily, 'They've got permission from the farmer to be there.'

'Oh, Tim, you know I don't like you going up there,' Annette said. 'Especially not when it's getting dark.'

'Is that because of the flasher or because of the travellers?' Tim said as if challenging her.

'I didn't like you going up there before the travellers came, you know that. But now you come to mention it, well ... I mean, you never know with people like that, do you? Some of them can be a bit ... well, funny.'

'Like Vic Reeves, you mean?'

'Don't be facetious, Tim. You know perfectly well what I mean. Some of them can be a bit ... rough, can't they? Getting into trouble with the police, taking drugs. I'm not saying they're all like that, but you can't be too careful.'

Tim shook his head. 'I don't believe what I'm hearing. Oonagh's a perfectly nice girl. She's intelligent, friendly, she doesn't take drugs, and you should see her trailer, Mum, it's lovely. And her mum and dad, Graeme and Linda, are really nice. In fact, Graeme gave me a lift home because they didn't want me to have to walk through the woods in the dark.'

'All the same,' said Annette, 'I don't like the thought of you hanging around there.'

'Well, tough,' said Tim, 'because I'm calling on Oonagh for school in the morning.'

'You're not,' said Annette.

'I am. I promised her. She'll be waiting for me.'

'Tim, don't answer your mother back like that,' said Eric.

Tim flushed, and for an instant Annette thought he was going to retort, 'She's not my mother!' It was one of her constant fears. But instead he said, 'Well, it's not fair. She's just being prejudiced. It's as bad as hating people because they're black.'

'No, it isn't,' said Annette, flushing now too, 'it's completely different.'

'*How* is it different? I mean, what do you think the travellers are going to do to me? Sell me into slavery? Feed me to their dogs?'

'Oh, don't be silly,' snapped Annette, masking her agitation with anger.

'I'm not the one being silly,' Tim said, and thinking of something Oonagh had said earlier added, 'You shouldn't judge by appearances, you know.'

'Don't get clever, Tim,' Eric warned.

Chloe, who since her comment about gypsies had been listening to the exchange in silence, now suggested tentatively, 'Why don't you ask Oonagh to tea or something? Then we can all meet her.'

'Vet her, you mean?' Tim said sourly.

Chloe pulled a face. 'I was only trying to help.'

Tim was still scowling, though he realised Chloe had been trying to make amends for her earlier comment. 'I don't know,' he said, 'I might.' He nearly added, 'If Mum can stand having her in the house, that is,' but saw no point in perpetuating the argument. 'I'm going to do some drawing,' he said, as much as an excuse to get out of the room and allow himself to cool off as anything.

'What about your homework?' Eric said.

'I did that at school, in my lunch hour. Want to check it?'

Eric pulled a face to show Tim how childish he was being. Tim sighed and went upstairs.

For a while peace descended. Chloe became engrossed in her daily soap fix, Annette went back into the kitchen, and Eric unfolded his *Independent* and sat there tutting and shaking his head at the latest government initiatives.

Just as 'Neighbours' was finishing, the phone rang. Eric answered it. Afterwards he wandered into the kitchen to find Annette at the sink, head down, washing the blades of the food processor in hot, soapy water.

'Who was that?' she said in a slightly muffled voice.

'Oh ... nobody,' said Eric, sitting at the big kitchen table.

'It must have been somebody.'

'Well, actually it was Jackie. She was rather upset.'

Annette still had her back to him. Eric saw her shoulders stiffen. 'Why? Has she been dumped by one of her latest boyfriends?'

Eric frowned. 'This is serious, Net. Someone sent her some rotten meat through the post, with a note attached which said, And now it begins. Does that sound like a threat to you?'

Annette shrugged as if she didn't know or care. 'Don't tell me, I suppose she wants you to go up there?'

'No, no, nothing like that. She's called the police. It's rather worrying, though, isn't it?'

Annette turned on the tap and began rinsing the food processor blades underneath it. 'I expect some jilted boyfriend sent it to her. I'm really not that bothered. I've got my own problems, thank you.'

Eric looked at her. 'Are you all right, Net?'

She shrugged, still with her back to him.

Eric stood up, walked across, took hold of her shoulders and tried to turn her round. For a moment she resisted, then she turned and he saw the distress on her face.

'I'm not prejudiced, am I?' she asked in a small voice.

He put his arms round her and kissed her forehead. 'No, of course not. You're just concerned for your son's welfare, that's all. It's understandable.'

'It's just that ... well, I don't like the thought of Tim hanging around that camp. I mean, I'm sure most travellers are perfectly nice people, but ... you read such terrible things.'

'Don't worry about Tim,' Eric said, 'he's a sensible lad. He knows what he's doing.'

Annette hugged her husband, resting her cheek against his left shoulder.

'I don't mean to sound narrow-minded,' she said. 'It's just ... I have to say what I think, but sometimes I listen to myself and I sound like such a fuddy-duddy.'

'You're not a fuddy-duddy,' said Eric soothingly.

'I bet Jackie'd love him having a traveller girlfriend, wouldn't she? She's into all that, freedom and everything, not living by the rules. I'm afraid I'm a bit more strait-laced.'

'It doesn't matter what Jackie thinks,' Eric said.

'Yes it does. She's his mother, so it'll matter to Tim. I don't want him to side with her against me, Eric.' She paused, and then said, as if the words were difficult to release, 'I couldn't bear the thought of losing him.'

Eric hugged her tighter. His voice was gentle. 'Don't be silly, Net, you're not going to lose him. You're getting this all out of proportion. Tim's not going to turn against you, just because of one silly argument.'

'He might, one day.'

'No he won't. He loves you, Net. He'll always love you. You're his mum.'

She blew out a long, deep sigh as if trying to rid herself of her anxieties. 'I hope so,' she said.

5

'Tizer,' James Keeve shouted. 'Tizer, here boy.'

The collie, a whitish blur in the darkening field, sprang to attention, pricking up its ears. Its tongue lolled from its grinning mouth and it wagged its tail briefly before bounding towards its master.

James drew back his arm and hurled the stick he was holding as far as he could. As it left his hand, spinning end over end, he couldn't help but think of how the other boys had laughed at him at school because he 'threw like a girl'.

Tizer didn't care about such things, though. The dog simply barked joyfully and bounded after the stick, mock-snarling as he snapped it up as though dissuading it from offering any resistance. It was a murky evening, the house lights clustered at the far edge of the school playing field, so far away that they seemed like ships on the ocean, smeared and dulled by mist. Tizer streaked away towards the pale, spindly legs of the nearest goalposts, James following at a more sedate pace, swinging the dog lead in his right hand. As ever, he glanced around as he walked; the dark was just one of the many things that made him nervous. As a boy, his small stature and timidity had made him a natural magnet for bullies, but he didn't think his nervousness would ever have become pathological if it hadn't been for the events of 24 July 1965.

More than any other, it was that day that had moulded his future character. For thirty years now, he had honoured the agreement he had made with his friends and kept what had happened a secret. He had remained silent even though he had been plagued by nightmares and crushed by guilt and shame for months afterwards. Even though he had suffered panic attacks, bouts of depression, a gradual erosion of what little self-worth and confidence he had had.

Back then, no one had ever thought to wonder whether there could be a root cause for such a rapid deterioration in his state of mind. Certainly no one seemed to realise that the onset of his real problems had coincided with the events that had taken place at number 39 Jasmine Road. It was thought simply that his symptoms were an escalation of his natural timidity, perhaps brought on by puberty. 'Poor lad suffers with his nerves,' his mother would say as if that explained everything. The family doctor prescribed him anti-depressants which only seemed to work because they dulled his brain to the point of inertia. In the end it was nothing more than time that healed him, though not entirely and not without leaving a great deal of scar tissue.

Indeed, in the years following his initial recovery there had been many occasions when the scar tissue had split and fresh blood had welled from the old wounds. James had been on almost constant medication of one form or another; he had had to take time off work, and he had even spent a few weeks in hospital to recover from a bout of depression so bad that he had stopped eating, stopped washing, stopped sleeping, stopped doing everything except sitting on his bed in his rented flat and staring at a particular patch of damp on the wall.

And then, one incredible Christmas nearly eleven years ago, he had met Marjory. A work colleague's flatmate, she had tagged along to the office party to keep her friend company. James had been standing alone cradling a glass of wine and wondering when he could leave without seeming like a party pooper, when Marjory had sidled up to him and said, 'You look as bored as me.'

James had laughed politely, wishing he could think of something witty to say, wishing he could think of even *something* to say.

Marjory had stuck out her hand and introduced herself as 'Isobel's friend'. 'What's your name?' she had asked brightly.

'James.'

'Not Bond by any chance?'

He had smiled. 'No.'

James was so tongue-tied around women that it wasn't usually very long before those that did speak to him gave him up as a bad job. Marjory was different, though. She didn't appear to notice how chronically shy he was, or if she did she chose not to regard it as a problem. Indeed, as the evening wore on she succeeded in prising James further and further out of his shell. For him, it was an exhilarating experience. He began to relax, to think of things to say, to ask questions, to make jokes, until by the end of the evening – the time having flown by – he was positively gushing, speaking quickly and breathlessly in an attempt to clear the conversational backlog jamming his brain.

Of course, he and Marjory saw each other again. This second date led to a relationship, and from there to engagement, and from there to marriage, and then finally, seven years ago, to the birth of their daughter, Sally. Happy ever after, James thought, shoving his hands into his pockets. Well, not quite, but it was as close as he was going to get.

He still suffered bouts of depression now and again, still slept fitfully, still spent the occasional week off work 'with his nerves', as his mother would say, but his problems were nowhere near as overwhelming as they used to be. He had Marjory and Sally to thank for that, of course. Marjory was his strength, his pit-prop. In all their years together, she had never used his weakness against him, had never become angry or contemptuous or impatient. And Sally ... well, she was just Sally. Funny, loving, bright, thoughtful; when he called her his 'little ray of sunshine' he truly meant it. Whenever he was 'sick', she would make him something – a card, a cake, some biscuits.

Yes, despite everything he was a lucky man. All in all, life was good.

He blinked, emerging from his daydream to realise he could no longer see Tizer. James had wandered into the middle of the field by now. The mist was all around him, so thick and chill and damp that he felt as though he were drowning in it. The mist and the encroaching darkness made his surroundings indistinct, the charcoal-grey field merging with the plum-coloured sky. A black blur in the distance was the school, a watery glow far away to his right the lights of the houses which bordered the school grounds.

'Tizer,' James shouted, his voice immediately deadened by the mist. There was no answering bark, no swish-scurry of paws in the damp grass. For God's sake, where *was* that dog? James felt uneasy, but then that wasn't unusual for him. The mist made him feel deaf and blind, vulnerable. He tried to tell himself that there was nothing to be afraid of, that any potential assailant would be as hampered by the conditions as he was.

What assailant? he thought, annoyed with himself. Why should anyone want to attack him? 'Don't give in to irrational fear,' he muttered. 'There is nothing to fear but fear itself.' Such pep talks, however trite, were usually of genuine help in damping down his anxieties. Nevertheless, when he called Tizer's name again there was a raw edge to his voice.

That was when his inner voice started up, and as always it was the voice of the scared little boy he had once been that he heard speaking in his head. *Don't shout, you'll draw attention to yourself*, the voice told him fearfully. *The dog'll come back when he feels like it. He'll pick up your scent or hear you moving, however quietly.*

James hunched his shoulders, glanced around once more, and then, gripping the dog lead in a hand that was still stuffed in his coat pocket, began to walk slowly forward. Tizer knew his way home, but James owed it to Sally not to rush back without the dog. He'd walk up to the edge of the field, where a chain-link cage imprisoned a row of concrete tennis courts, and if Tizer wasn't there he'd stroll slowly back. Somewhere along the way, the dog was bound to catch up with him. In fact, he wouldn't be at all surprised if he arrived home to find Tizer snoozing contentedly by the fire.

He was perhaps twenty yards away from the chain-link fence when it seemed to drift up out of the mist like a ghost of itself. Immediately Jame's attention was caught not by the fence itself, but by a glimpse of vague movement at its base. He came to a halt, screwing up his eyes to try and make sense of what he was seeing. He could make out something grey, roundish, bulky. If it had been a blustery night he might have believed it was a discarded sack of rubbish stirring in the wind, but the evening was still as death. Could it be Tizer then, snuffling at something on the ground by the fence – a molehill or a rabbit hole, perhaps? No, it was moving too slowly, too languidly for Tizer. It was swaying almost eerily from side to side, like ... like seaweed beneath the sea, or a cobra charmed by a fakir's music.

A chill passed through James, a sense almost of dread. Whatever this thing was, there was something ... not right about it. *All my past sins are coming home to roost*, he thought, without knowing why he thought it or what exactly it meant. His mouth was dry and he had an urge to move away from this thing, quietly and quickly, before it saw him; no, before it *sensed* him.

Before he could do so, however, the thing began to unfurl, to open up, like a vast flower. It spread its petals wide. Only they weren't petals, they were arms. James saw now that the shape was in fact a man; he had been curled into a ball and now he was stretching out, raising his arms, unfolding his legs. Perhaps James should have felt reassured by this, but he didn't. There was still something inexplicably *bad* about this whole situation, something he couldn't altogether explain. There was an atmosphere, a frisson, a feeling that something terrible was about to happen.

James began to back away, moving slowly, carefully, feeling it terribly important that he make no sudden moves.

Then the man did two things that swept James's caution aside.

He sort of *slid* upright, in a way that seemed to James wholly unnatural, that made him feel almost as if he was watching a piece of film played backwards.

And in a fluid movement that seemed somehow robotic, somehow reptilian, he raised his head.

Something about his face ... something *wrong* with his face. James began to back away, his heart and lungs clenching. The man was big and appeared to be wearing a blue boiler suit, overalls, something like that. In the grey mist his head looked very white, almost as if it was glowing. The man detached himself from the fence and began to move towards James; he didn't walk, he didn't run, he *moved*. There was something horrible about the way he moved, something purposeful, remorseless.

Suddenly James was terrified. Not just scared, but absolutely terrified. Though it felt like the hardest thing he had ever done in his life, he turned his back on the figure with the white, glowing head and he ran.

He heard nothing but his own ragged breathing, saw nothing but fronds of grey mist sweeping across his face, trying to form themselves into a net in which to tangle him. His mind shut down, concentrating only on survival, on keeping his body moving as fast as it could. He refused to acknowledge what that terrible face that he had only glimpsed meant to him, refused to acknowledge it on the surface at least. He wouldn't think about it, he *couldn't* think about it. If he did, he was lost.

He ran and ran. He didn't realise he had run all the way home until he crashed in through the front door and collapsed in the hallway, sobbing. He scrabbled the door shut behind him, locked it with fumbling fingers. Only then did he notice the crumpled sheet of writing paper on the mat by the door that someone had evidently shoved through the letterbox. He snatched up the paper, opened it out. Four words, AND NOW IT BEGINS, were written on it in red marker pen in rather childish capitals. Something of Sally's, he thought. One of her games, but the words seemed like a kind of sinister promise. He shuddered violently and crushed the note in his fist.

Tuesday 22 November

6

'May I see Dancer before I go to school, Mummy?' Felicity said across the breakfast table.

Juliette Dullaston looked up from her *Harpers & Queen* magazine. Her eleven-year-old daughter had a hopeful gleam in her eyes and flakes of pastry around her mouth from the croissants she had devoured. She was wearing the grey and green uniform of the private girls' school she had started less than three months before, her straw hat with its grey and green headband sitting on the dining table beside her plate.

'I expect so, darling. But don't be too long. And put your galoshes on,' she called as Felicity jumped up and scampered out.

Juliette took a sip of Darjeeling tea and looked at her husband, who was buried behind his *Times*. 'Andrew, darling, the Paxtons were wondering if we could make dinner one evening this week.'

Andrew Dullaston lowered his newspaper and grimaced at his wife. Whereas she was slender and graceful and fine-boned, he was square-jawed, heavy-set, with wiry, greying hair and a ruddy, slightly bloated complexion. His doctor had warned him on numerous occasions to cut down on the cigars and the booze and the rich foods, but up to now Dullaston had paid no heed. 'What did you say?'

'Ursula and I thought Thursday might be convenient.'

Dullaston scowled, folded his newspaper and placed it beside his plate. 'Do we really have to see them at all?'

Juliette pursed her lips. 'Yes, I rather think we do. You know perfectly well that Ursula and I are old friends. I don't see why our relationship should suffer just because you can't be bothered to make the effort with Gregory.'

'The man's a complete bore,' Dullaston said. 'I don't know what she had to go and marry him for in the first place.'

'I've always found him perfectly civil.'

'Oh come on, darling, nobody likes him, and you know it. Even Sammy thinks he's a bore, don't you?'

Samuel, their fourteen-year-old son, square-jawed like his father but dark-haired like his mother, looked up from the croissant he was buttering. 'He spits when he talks to you. It's totally disgusting,' he said.

'There, you see,' said Dullaston, waving his hand like a prosecuting lawyer who has just unearthed a vital piece of evidence.

'Oh, stop being so tiresome, Andrew,' said Juliette. 'I've told

Ursula we're coming now, so you'll just have to make the most of it, won't you?'

'No, I won't, as a matter of fact. You can go by yourself, tell them I've got some important work to do.'

'In that case, you can go to Monaco by yourself, and don't expect me to subsidise the trip.'

Dullaston looked at his wife with an expression like a startled bull-frog. 'You're not serious?'

'Oh, I am. If you can't make the effort to spend one evening in Gregory's company for my sake, then I'm certainly not going to spend an entire week in France watching silly men going round and round in their silly cars.'

'But ... look, this is hardly fair, Juliette. You know how much I've been looking forward to the Grand Prix.'

'And you can still look forward to it. Just don't expect me to pay for it, that's all. I mean, good God, Andrew, you're hardly destitute. You have a perfectly good job.'

Dullaston glowered at his wife, bottom lip thrust out like a petulant child's. What she had said was true – he wasn't destitute. But he wasn't exactly rich either. All right, so there was a brand new BMW and a Range Rover parked in front of their Grade II listed Georgian country house, which in turn was set in acres of Kent countryside. And they paid enormous fees to have their children educated; and went on two, sometimes three, foreign holidays a year; and had just bought their daughter a new pony; and were members of a number of exclusive clubs ...

But the thing was, most of the wealth on show here was Juliette's. Her father, who had disapproved of her marriage to plain old Andrew Dullaston was an Earl in Surrey, and lived in a house so big that tourists paid to look round it. Dullaston had a good job, as a leading consultant in a firm that sold computer software to big European businesses, but of the £45,000 he pulled in every year, at least half went straight into a pension fund. Dullaston was only forty-two, but he wanted to retire before he was fifty – indeed, within the next five years if possible. In which case, he wanted at least some independence. He didn't want to be reduced to asking his wife for pocket money every week.

He grunted, picked up his newspaper and began to shake it open before conceding, 'Oh, all right, I expect I can put up with that dreadful man for your sake, darling.'

Juliette gave a prim little smile – which almost immediately changed to an expression of alarm as a series of thin, high-pitched screams cut the silence.

Dullaston's newspaper jerked away from his face once again. 'What in God's name is that?'

The screams came again, and though still high-pitched, they were no longer wordless. '*Mummmyyy! Dadddyyy!*'

'It's Lissy,' said Samuel.

The door to the breakfast room banged open and Felicity stood there in muddy galoshes, face white and stricken, tears pouring down her cheeks.

'Whatever's the matter, darling?' Juliette said.

Felicity looked at Juliette with wide, horrified eyes as if she were seeing something far more terrible than her mother sitting there. 'It's Dancer,' she wailed. 'He's dead! Someone's killed him!'

'Don't be ridiculous,' spluttered Dullaston.

'*It's true!*' Felicity shrieked, close to hysteria. 'There's blood. He's dead, I know he is.' She burst into noisy sobs.

'There, there, darling,' said Juliette, 'come to Mummy.' She held out her arms. Felicity stumbled into the embrace, burying her face in her mother's chest.

Speaking over her daughter's head, Juliette said, 'Perhaps you'd better go and have a look, darling.'

'Oh, for goodness sake,' said Dullaston. 'Can't a man even eat his breakfast in peace these days? The girl's probably exaggerating.' He almost added, 'She's as highly strung as you are,' but thought better of it. Juliette gave him a fierce stare, which prompted him to sigh heavily, then get up and stomp out of the room.

Bloody horse, he thought, as he made his way through the house, his footsteps echoing on the wooden floor in the vast hallway. There was a trail of muddy footprints leading from the open door in the kitchen that led to the outbuildings at the back. He marched out of the house and across the yard to the flat-roofed stable block, the cold wind snatching at his tie and ruffling his hair. Both the top and bottom halves of the wooden door to Dancer's stable were hanging part-way open. If the horse wasn't as badly hurt as Felicity had claimed, then it had probably bolted by now.

It was a dull day, and at first as he approached the stable, Dullaston could see little inside except gloom and shadows. As he got closer, a smell touched his nostrils which was stronger than the warm, yeasty smell of horse and straw; this was hot and raw and sickly, and quickly became so strong that he had to take his crisply laundered handkerchief from his breast pocket and smother his nose and mouth with it. He was close enough now to grab hold of the bottom half of the stable door and pull it all the way open. Even before doing so, he was aware of the spiky silhouettes of tack hanging on the walls, and, ominously, a dark bulky mound lying motionless in the straw.

Grey light unfolded itself into the stable, and Dullaston saw what his daughter had seen just a few minutes before. He gagged into his handkerchief. She had not been exaggerating, after all.

Dancer was dead, his skull reduced to bloody meat and shattered bone. Bulging eyes and blocky white teeth protruded from the pulp as though even in death the animal was expressing the terror of its ordeal. There was a sledgehammer lying in the straw close to the body, its head coated in gore. But Dancer's killer had not been satisfied with merely bashing the poor creature's brains out. Whoever the madman was, he had carried out a further frenzied attack on the (probably already dead) animal with what appeared to be a very large, very sharp blade. Dancer had not just been stabbed and slashed, he had been eviscerated. His stomach gaped open, releasing a seemingly endless wet rope of purple and grey intestine. This coiled around the creature's legs like a mass of gigantic, suckling eels. There was blood everywhere - coating the straw, dripping from the walls. The killer must have been drenched in it.

Dullaston's first reaction was one of outrage. How dare someone come on to his property and do this! How *dare* they subject his daughter to such an experience! How *dare* they destroy such a valuable possession! And then he thought of the kind of mentality it would take to commit such an atrocity and a tiny sliver of unease worked its way into the boiling flood of anger inside him. *Why* would someone do this? Were they just sick or was it a grudge thing, something more personal?

Gazing at the butchery in front of him, he suddenly realised that the streaks of blood on the back wall of the stable were not merely random splatters but were arranged in a definite pattern. He stepped forward over the threshold, pushing the two halves of the stable door all the way back, allowing a little more of the pearly autumn light inside. The stench of horse's innards made him gag despite his handkerchief. He squinted hard, and little by little was able to make out that the streaks of blood were, in fact, words. Whoever had killed Dancer had written a message in the horse's blood.

'My God,' murmured Dullaston.

Once he had deciphered the message, he read it over and over and over again, as if he couldn't quite believe it.

AND NOW IT BEGINS
AND NOW IT BEGINS
AND NOW IT BEGINS

7

Tim didn't see his mother at breakfast the following morning, because this was one of her early days when she had to go down to the flower market at the crack of dawn. He had thought about what she had said, however, and he supposed in a way her reaction was understandable. The only time you really heard about gypsies and travellers was when they were on TV for breaking the law. More than anything, Tim supposed that he'd been disappointed with her attitude. He'd expected her to be different to everybody else, not as biased. It was only in the last couple of years that he'd begun to realise his parents - all three of them - weren't as perfect as he'd always considered them to be as a child. He supposed in some ways he was still reeling from the shock of that discovery.

At least his dad hadn't repeated Mum's order to stay away from the travellers' camp, or insisted on driving him to school as Tim had half-expected he would. His dad was easy-going and liberal-minded for the most part, but Tim had still been bracing himself for another argument, or at least a discussion, over the breakfast table. Fortunately it hadn't come.

It was a bitterly cold day, frost sugaring lawns and pavements. Tim's breath plumed from his lips and hung before his face as he walked, like a series of silent, unstable speech balloons.

In the woods, every leaf, every blade of grass, was coated with white; it filled every nook and cranny like inverted shadow. On the softer ground Tim's footsteps crackled like fire. He reached out towards a leaf to see whether he could snap it from the stem like a sliver of white chocolate. After a twenty-minute walk along one of numerous meandering paths, the woods ended abruptly, cut back by man, the trees hemmed in by dry-stone walls as though they might spread like weeds if they weren't contained.

Tim had the impression the sky was toppling towards him as he left the trees behind. He trudged uphill, between black stone walls which seemed to be holding back a dark rolling sea of earth. As he crested the rise, he saw the cluster of trailers where Oonagh lived a couple of fields away on his right, the farmhouse and its outbuildings jumbled together a little further up on his left. Chickens strutted about in the frozen mud of the farmyard, pecking and clawing at the ground. A tractor engine started up, bronchial and spluttering, the sound hard-edged in the still air.

Despite the cold, Tim was sweating by the time he reached the five-bar gate into the field where the travellers had made their camp, each inward breath causing an icy stab at the base of his throat. The white trailers shone like ice; between two of them the dark slash of a washing line supported a row of T-shirts whose colours were brighter than seemed possible.

Tim pushed the gate open and stepped into the field. The muddy ridges caused by the tyre-tracks had frozen hard as bone, sheets of ice stretched between them, their edges puckered like scarred skin. Tim picked his way up the track, taking care not to slip and turn his ankle. He didn't realise a man was striding down the slope from the camp to meet him until he was just a few feet away.

'What do you want?' the man barked, making Tim jump and look up from the knobbly ground.

Taken aback, Tim spoke hesitantly. 'I've, er, just come to call on Oonagh. Er ... Oonagh Walsh. To go to school.'

The man was tall and looked as though he might be muscly beneath his heavy grey sweater and black donkey jacket. He had straggly dark hair and a dark beard, a long bony nose and high cheekbones which seemed to squeeze his brown eyes up into slits. He was fearsome enough even without the shotgun, which was broken open and cradled across his right arm. Tim didn't think he had ever actually encountered anyone carrying a gun before.

The man shook his head and glanced up at the sky as if gauging the likelihood of a storm. 'No,' he said almost distractedly, 'I don't think so.'

'But she's expecting me,' Tim said. 'I was here yesterday. I said I'd call for her at half past eight.'

The man shifted his gaze from the sky and squinted at Tim as if astounded that the boy had actually dared answer him back. 'Read my lips, sonny,' he muttered. 'I said no. N. O. Now piss off.'

'But I'm Oonagh's friend. I'm not here to cause any hassle. You can come with me if you like.'

Tim didn't even have time to put up his arms as the man stepped forward and shoved him hard in the chest. Tim slithered and almost lost his footing.

'You're not listening, boy. We don't want you here. Now if you're not out of this field in ten seconds I'm going to throw you over that fucking wall.'

The centre of Tim's chest throbbed where the man had pushed him, but he was more shocked than hurt. He was also angry. Injustice and frustration boiled inside him. 'This has got nothing to do with you,' he said, hating the lack of authority in his voice. 'Oonagh's my friend. I don't want to let her down by making her think I haven't turned up.'

He wished he'd been more prepared for something like this, but after yesterday he was surprised by the reaction he was getting here. The other travellers he'd met as they had trudged up to Oonagh's trailer - Sara who had a pierced eyebrow and braided dreadlocks and dressed like a punk; Mrs MacEvoy who had been travelling with Oonagh's parents for fifteen years and whose husband, George, had died two years ago; Geoff the former bank manager who did wood carvings of everything from cute animals to *Star Trek* characters and sold them on a trestle table outside the shopping centres of the towns they stopped in - had all been friendly, welcoming, curious, as indeed had Oonagh's parents themselves.

Tim was wondering whether he should make an effort to ingratiate himself with the man by telling him how he had rescued Oonagh from Sue Kuznitsky yesterday when the man did something far more shocking than shoving him in the chest. In one fluid motion he jerked his right arm, causing the hinged barrel of the shotgun to snap into place, then raised it to his shoulder and aimed it at Tim's face.

Tim had never been more terrified in his life. Instantly the moisture drained from his mouth and his heart began to hammer like a piece of machinery operating at a dangerous speed. His thoughts, usually so ordered, broke rank and started scurrying around like a troupe of clowns in his head, crashing into each other, racing in circles.

For a long moment he just stood there, staring into the muzzle of the shotgun. Never before had he felt so helpless, so vulnerable. He had the notion he should be taking some kind of evasive action, but standing in the middle of an open field there was absolutely nothing he could do, nowhere to go. His surroundings seemed to bleed away. He wondered whether he was going to faint.

And then, like a hypnotist's voice waking him from a trance, he heard someone calling his name.

The voice was shrill, insistent. Tim tore his gaze from the gun muzzle and looked beyond the man to see Oonagh bounding down the sloping field towards him. All at once the day seemed unnaturally bright, bleached, as though he had just opened his eyes after snoozing in the sun. The man lowered the shotgun until its muzzle was pointing at the ground a few feet in front of Tim. Tim released a long breath which he wasn't even aware he'd been holding. Immediately it felt as though he had expelled all his strength, for suddenly his legs seemed hollow and wobbly. He began to shake with reaction. Dropping his bag, he doubled over, trembling hands on trembling knees. When he next looked up, Oonagh was beside him, panting from having raced down the hill.

'What's going on?' she demanded. 'Mike, why were you pointing your gun at Tim?'

She was red-faced and wide-eyed, though with anger not fear. The man she had called Mike looked at her in the way a Rottweiler might regard a yapping chihuahua. He shook his head, and without answering her question turned and began to walk back up the hill towards the camp.

Oonagh took two steps after him and shouted, 'I'll be telling Graeme about this.'

Mike turned back, still wearing that same expression, a mixture of amusement and hostility. 'You want to be careful about the friends you choose,' he said.

Oonagh watched him go, looking for a moment as if she was wondering whether to run after him and continue the dispute. Then she turned back and asked Tim, 'Are you okay?'

Tim straightened up and expelled a long breath. 'I feel sick. No one's ever pointed a gun at me before.' He held out his hand and managed a shaky laugh. 'Look at me, I'm trembling.'

'Mike Jordan's a thug,' said Oonagh. 'But he wouldn't really have pulled the trigger, you know.'

Tim crossed his arms tightly across his chest; it felt as though a little icy motor was chugging away in his belly. 'Maybe not, but it's hard to think straight when someone's pointing a gun at your face. I really thought for a minute there I was going to die.'

'Well, I suppose that makes us even now. You've saved me and I've saved you.' She sounded almost pleased, as if the debt had been troubling her a little.

Tim picked up his bag. 'Come on, we'd better get to school. I'll feel better once I'm walking.'

This turned out to be true. He breathed deeply as he walked, and gradually, despite the cold, the shakes began to subside.

'Why do you let that guy travel with you?' he asked as they left the farmland behind.

'I thought I explained all that yesterday. We don't judge people.'

'You said you didn't judge by appearances, but I reckon any bloke who sticks a gun in someone's face has got to be a bit of a loony.'

Oonagh shrugged. 'Mike's only been with us a few months and so far he's not caused any real trouble. Even today he'll probably say he was only trying to scare you off. I wouldn't be surprised if the gun wasn't even loaded.'

'God, I don't believe this. You sound as if you're defending that psycho.'

'I'm not defending him. To be honest, I think he's a creep. But what gives me or anyone else the right to tell him he can't travel with us?'

Tim frowned. In some ways, Oonagh's attitude reminded him of his mum's – his real mum's. She was open-minded and totally non-prejudiced, but if presented with a problem would rather run away from it than face it. She'd admitted as much to him herself, had confessed that that was why she hadn't been around for the first six years of his life – she simply hadn't been able to face the responsibility of having a child. Oonagh and the rest of the travellers were only different in that rather than running away from responsibility they were simply refusing to acknowledge it, burying their heads in the sand. Tim thought that if ever he had a problem, he would face up to it, not run away.

'Yeah, but he's a nutter, isn't he?' he said, pressing home his point. 'I mean, he could be dangerous. What's he like with the rest of the travellers?'

Oonagh picked up a pebble and began flicking it into the air as if it were a coin. 'He's all right. A bit quiet. He keeps himself to himself, but he pulls his weight.' She looked at Tim askance, and as if testing him said, 'You can't tell someone to get lost just because they're a social inadequate, can you?'

Oonagh wasn't that much older than Chloe, but he couldn't imagine his sister, or even any of his own friends, using a phrase like 'social inadequate' in normal conversation. Yet such remarks seemed to trip naturally from Oonagh's tongue. This was one of the reasons he liked her a lot despite their different outlooks – she was like no one he'd ever met before. He shrugged and said, 'I suppose not,' then changed the subject so that the discussion wouldn't degenerate into an argument.

They spent the rest of the walk to school talking about mundane things. Tim told her about his artwork, and about the inspiration for it – comics like *Sandman* and *Swamp Thing*, TV shows like 'Star Trek' and 'The X-Files', films like *Alien* and *Terminator*. He was appalled that Oonagh had not seen, nor even heard of, most of these, and said he would have to educate her. She told him about places she'd visited on her travels, people she'd known, experiences she'd had.

Tim was almost surprised when they arrived at the school gates, he'd been so engrossed in their conversation. He noticed Oonagh looking a little tense, and remembered Sue Kuznitsky and her cronies, of which, thankfully, there was no sign. When she realised he was looking at her, she smiled and said, 'Well, here we are.'

'Yeah,' said Tim. Now they were here, with their schoolmates milling around them, he felt oddly tongue-tied.

'See you then,' said Oonagh abruptly and started to walk away.

Tim was so taken aback he let her get ten yards in front of him before hurrying after her.

'Hey, wait a minute,' he said.

She turned back, her honey-coloured hair swishing. She had a faint purplish bruise across her nose where Sue Kuznitsky had hit her. 'Yes?'

'I was wondering ... would you like to come to tea at our house?'

'When?'

'I don't know. Tomorrow maybe.'

She smiled. 'That'd be nice. I'd have to ask Graeme and Linda first, though. And it'd have to be vegetarian. I don't eat meat or fish.'

'That's okay,' said Tim, hoping Annette wouldn't regard that as another weird traveller thing.

'You're so sweet,' she said, then astonished him by tilting her head and giving him a kiss on the cheek. She turned and walked away as if uncertain how he'd react. A group of girls from Chloe's year went by, giggling and 'whoo'ing, making him blush.

'See you at break?' he shouted hopefully. 'Over by the geodome?'

Oonagh didn't look round but she raised a hand in acknowledgement. Tim watched her until she had disappeared round the corner, and then, stomach twizzling delightfully, he turned and walked into school.

8

As soon as she opened the door of the shop, Annette knew that something was wrong.

She couldn't pinpoint what immediately, though she knew it was something more than intuition. She looked around. The shop was as it should be – the window display which would soon be giving way to Halloween pumpkins and a papier-mâché witch perched on a broomstick suspended on wires from the ceiling; the big white vases full of autumn blooms in cellophane cones; the shelf along the left-hand wall supporting a row of single red roses in tall thin boxes; the door behind the counter which led to the office at the back of the shop, on which a poster declared, 'We Do Interflora'.

Everything seemed normal, and yet Annette found herself licking suddenly dry lips, unwilling to cross the threshold. Behind her on the kerb her van was parked, its back doors standing open. Buckets of flowers, the first of which she held in her left hand, were crowded inside, offering their fragrance to whoever might happen to pass.

Their fragrance! That was it! However many times Annette had opened this door in the morning she had never failed to be captivated by the accumulated perfume that surged out. And yet this morning the perfume was diffuse, partially dispersed by a breeze that was flowing from the back of the shop. The door behind the counter which she always closed at night now yawned a little and then swung back, bumping against its frame.

Someone had been in here, or perhaps still was!

'Mary?' Annette called, but if her assistant was here before her it would be a first. Though the big front windows let in plenty of daylight, the inside of the shop suddenly seemed crammed with shadows. However, there was nowhere in here to hide; even the counter was too small to crouch behind. Annette lowered her bucket of flowers to the floor and walked slowly and deliberately towards the counter beyond which the door stood ajar. Even now it was moving backwards and forwards very gently as though beckoning her. After each step she paused to listen, but could hear nothing. She knew she was doing exactly what she always ridiculed victims in horror films for doing, but she had to know what kind of damage, if any, had been done in the back room. Besides, it was unlikely there would be anyone still here. No one would be stupid enough to break into a shop just before it opened.

Would they?

She rounded the counter, biting her lip as a floorboard creaked beneath her weight. She should have remembered that. She listened hard, but heard nothing beyond the growl of cars passing outside. It suddenly struck her that perhaps there was someone standing on the other side of the door, no more than a foot or two away, standing as motionless as she was. Perhaps someone had entered the shop with the intention of breaking open the safe but had been unable to gain access and had been waiting for her to arrive. Perhaps someone had been monitoring her movements, watching her over the last few days or weeks. The thought made her shudder.

She reached out to place both hands on the door, counted silently to three, and then shoved as hard as she could, causing the door to fly back on squealing hinges. She stepped back instinctively as the office was revealed to her, but succeeded only in bruising a buttock on the corner of the counter. The handle of the door gouging plaster from the wall inside made her wince, but at least proved there was no one behind it. She could see there was no one in the office either, and furthermore the place seemed undamaged. Her eyes moved instinctively to the No Smoking poster covering the safe. It was still in place on the wall.

For a few seconds she stood, rubbing her buttock and trying to control her rapid breathing. She saw immediately where the intruder had got in. At the back of the office was a door, beyond which a short corridor led to another door, this one opening into a high-walled yard that contained a trio of dustbins and little else. Both doors, which should have been closed, were wide open and cold white daylight was pouring through, bringing a breeze that ruffled the papers on Annette's desk. The only other door in the office was the one in the far left-hand corner, behind which was the toilet – a tiny cubicle smelling of damp and disinfectant, and frequently populated by spiders large enough to make Mary prefer to cross her legs all day. This door was firmly shut, as Annette always left it.

It was obvious what had happened. Someone had broken in last night, had found nothing worth stealing, and had left. Although Annette felt personally violated, she knew she was lucky that the intruder had not smashed the place up in his frustration. Abruptly she began to shake with reaction, felt her stomach curl around the coffee and doughnut she had guiltily consumed down at the market. Just for her peace of mind she leaned into the office and glanced quickly left and right to ensure no one was squeezed into a corner, and then she entered and turned on the light.

A hand came down on her shoulder.

She screamed and jumped so violently she felt she'd torn all her stomach muscles. Behind her someone else screamed too, as if in mockery. Annette spun round and saw her assistant Mary cowering in the doorway, hands clenched together against her chest, eyes so wide they seemed to fill her face.

'For God's sake, Mary,' Annette said, terror turning to relief and emerging as anger, 'what did you think you were doing, sneaking up on me like that?'

Mary looked so abject that Annette immediately felt sorry for her.

'S-sorry, Annette, I didn't mean to scare you. I just wondered what you were doing. The van's just standing open outside, full of flowers.'

Annette took a deep breath. 'I'm sorry too,' she said. 'I didn't mean to shout.' She gestured towards the open back door. 'We've had a break-in.'

'Really?' Mary breathed, as if Annette had told her she'd found the office dripping with ectoplasm. 'Oh no. Was anything taken?'

'I don't think so. I was just about to call the police.'

While Annette did that, Mary brought in the flowers from the van. She was pale and thin, and although she was twenty-one she seemed to Annette far too young to have a husband and a two-year-old son. She would have been pretty if she hadn't looked so brow-beaten, which was the consequence of having a domineering father and now a domineering husband. Mary had to refer all decisions to Dale, even down to what clothes to put on in the morning and how to wear her hair. If Annette had a pound for every time she had heard Mary say, 'I'll have to ask our Dale,' she could have paid off the mortgage, retired and be yachting round the Caribbean by now.

After calling the police, Annette helped Mary bring in the flowers and then the two of them did the arrangements, propping the front door open despite the cold. Frozen fingers were preferable to the feeling of confinement Annette felt with the door closed, even if she wasn't alone. Although she was sure the intruder was long gone, neither of the women had ventured further than the doorway to the office yet and wouldn't feel safe until that ground had been covered by the police.

The panda car pulled up at 9:20, and two uniformed constables got out, carrying their helmets. Annette resented their casual manner, the way they swopped a joke across the roof of the car as they locked up. Although this was minor routine for them, it was traumatic for her. She hadn't expected wailing sirens and screeching brakes, but she would have preferred a little more gravity.

The policemen entered the shop, one lanky and sandy-haired, still young enough to be troubled by acne, the other an older, thickset man

with copper-coloured skin, a black moustache and a smudge of beard.
'Mrs Knight?' the older man said. 'I understand you've had a break-in.'
Annette explained what had happened whilst the policemen placed their helmets carefully on the counter like sleeping pets they didn't want to awaken. In their dark uniforms they seemed to fill the shop, blotting out the light from the window. Mary hovered nervously in the background, tidying up shreds of stalk and leaves and mopping up splashes of water.
'May we?' the moustached policeman asked when Annette had finished. She nodded and the two of them stooped through the doorway into the back office like giants.
'Is anything missing?' the younger constable asked.
'Not as far as I know. I haven't really been in here. I was a bit too nervous to investigate in case whoever broke in was – oh!'
Both men turned and looked sharply at her. Annette was standing with her hand pressed against the jut of her collarbone, a look of shock on her face.
'What is it, Mrs Knight?' the policeman with the moustache asked her.
Annette pointed to the open toilet door. 'If that door isn't closed properly it swings open like it's doing now.'
Both men looked at the door. 'What of it?' the younger policeman asked.
'Well, when I came in earlier it was definitely closed.' Suddenly Annette looked very pale. She groped her way to the chair behind her desk and sat down. 'My God. You realise what that means, don't you?'
The policemen looked at her, blank-faced; evidently, they didn't.
Annette took a deep breath. Suddenly she found it a struggle to speak. 'It means that whoever broke into the shop was still here, hiding in the toilet when I came in half an hour ago.'

9

Eric was jotting notes for the play he aimed to begin writing in earnest that evening, chuckling at his own jokes, when the telephone in the staffroom rang. At this time of day only four staff members apart from himself were present. Of these, two were marking work, one was reading *She* magazine, and one, Jim Priest, was trying to stick the broken bits of a fountain pen together with Superglue. Priest looked up. He had dark curly hair and a beard that made him look like the Yorkshire Ripper. 'That'll be Spielberg, wanting me to star in his next movie. I've told him not to pester me at work, but he's desperate, bless him. Get it, Jo, would you?'

Jo Butlin put aside her copy of *She* magazine with a sigh. She was twenty-seven, blonde and slim, with long tanned legs which she seemed to take great delight in displaying. A hefty proportion of the school's male population – both staff and pupils – had spent nights of raging passion with Jo, though only in their dreams. She was the subject of many a frustrated juvenile scribbling on toilet doors and walls, much of which, Eric often reflected sadly, was far more imaginative than the majority of essays he had to mark.

She stood up, smoothing her skirt over her incredible thighs. 'What did your last slave die of?' she said.

'Sexual exhaustion,' responded Jim Priest, raising his eyebrows leerily.

Jo tutted, crossed the room and picked up the phone. 'Hello,' she said, 'Bramwell Comprehensive. You're through to the staffroom. Can I help you?'

She listened for a moment, frowning, then said, 'I'm sorry, you'll have to speak up. I can't hear you very well.' She listened a bit longer, then her face cleared and she said, 'Oh yes, he is. Hang on a sec.'

Cupping the mouthpiece, she held the receiver out and said, 'Eric, it's for you. Some bloke with a terrible sore throat by the sounds of it.'

Eric put down his notepad, crossed the room and took the proffered receiver. 'Thanks, Jo,' he said, then put the receiver to his ear. 'Hello?'

For a few seconds there was silence, and Eric was about to repeat the greeting, when a voice, speaking in a croaking whisper, said, 'And now it begins.'

Eric blinked. 'I'm sorry.'

Again, the silence. And again, the croaking hiss. 'And now it begins.'

Eric felt a pulse begin to beat in his throat. He looked around at his colleagues as if for guidance, but they were all preoccupied with their own tasks once more. 'I don't know what you're talking about, I'm afraid,' he said, managing to keep his voice calm and steady. 'Perhaps you'd like to tell me who you are.'

'And now it begins,' the voice repeated for the third time, the final consonant lingering like the hiss of a snake.

Then there was a click and the burr of disconnection. Eric looked at the receiver for a moment, then replaced it gently on to its cradle. *And now it begins*. The same message that Jackie had received with her parcel of rotten meat. What did it mean? Was it a threat of some sort?

He clenched his hands to stop them from trembling as he walked slowly back across the room.

10

Mum had been wrong. Tanya didn't come rushing over to Chloe at school that day, wanting to make up. In fact, when Chloe walked into the classroom the first thing she saw was Sally Maskell sitting in Tanya's chair.

At first she was annoyed. Sally was not as obnoxious as Carl Pryor, but all the same nobody liked her much – she was a hanger-on and a gossip with a spiteful tongue – and Chloe didn't want Tanya to walk in and think that she had asked Sally to take her place. However, that thought had barely popped into her mind before another scuttled up behind it, and with a sinking heart she turned to look at the place where Sally had been sitting yesterday, on the next to back row beside Fiona May. Sure enough there was Tanya, smirking at her, sneering at her. When Tanya muttered something to Fiona and the two girls began to snigger nastily, their heads together but their eyes on Chloe, it was like a knife in Chloe's heart.

All the same she tried to remain aloof, tried not to let the hurt show on her face. She shrugged as though Tanya's desertion was such a minor thing it barely merited attention and sauntered across to her desk, outwardly calm, in turmoil beneath the surface.

She wanted to speak to Sally, demand to know what Tanya and Fiona had said to her, but she thought that if she did that she would blow her cover. She was sure she could actually feel the two girls staring at her, and it was all she could do to stop herself scratching the fine hairs on the back of her neck which were tickling as though teased by feathers.

Throughout registration and her morning lessons she tried to work out what had put her friend's nose so out of joint, but Tanya's behaviour seemed out of proportion to yesterday's disagreement. Perhaps when Chloe had told Tanya that their friendship was at an end, Tanya had taken her at her word. Did that mean this split was all Chloe's fault? Was *she* the one who should be approaching Tanya, trying to make up with her? Or was it simply that Tanya had just been looking for an excuse to fall out with Chloe and team up with Fiona? After all, Chloe had seen Tanya's fickle side before – girls who one week were in favour and the next, for no apparent reason, were treated like lepers – but she had always thought herself immune from that kind of treatment, had thought that the bond between Tanya and herself was too strong to be broken by such capriciousness.

She gnawed at the problem until her mental teeth were broken and bleeding without really getting anywhere, and by the time the bell rang at the end of the day she was feeling utterly miserable. Mum had told her that in adolescence things often seemed much worse than they really were, but Chloe still couldn't help seeing her life from now on as a horribly empty wilderness stretching endlessly before her.

As she set off for home, the sky seemed to reflect her mood, dark clouds clashing and boiling, expunging the light. She hadn't even seen Ben today, which again seemed like a bad omen. Was it simply an accident that their paths had not crossed or was he avoiding her after yesterday?

Approaching the school gates she saw Tanya and Fiona, arms linked like new lovers, talking animatedly with a group of girls from 3S by an ice-cream van around which children clamoured like autograph-hunters. Fiona threw her head back and laughed shriekingly. She looked, thought Chloe spitefully, like a horse – long bony nose, too many teeth – but the boys liked her because her hair was the colour of cream, and because she flirted with them. ('Fiona May if you give her a quid', they would shout after her in the playground, which actually wasn't that far from the truth).

The girls hadn't seen her yet, but if they didn't move soon then Chloe would have to walk right past them, would have to shoulder her way between them and the scrum around the ice-cream van, in fact. She slowed right down and turned her attention to the gritty ground beneath her feet. She had a feeling that if she looked right at the girls they would sense her observing them, and so she cast them only occasional surreptitious glances, all the while thinking, 'Walk away, walk away'.

They didn't, though. They seemed in no hurry to go anywhere. Indeed, just as Chloe reached the gates a trio of fourth-year boys joined them and the girls really began to tone up their flirting muscles.Tanya reached out and tugged down the brim of the baseball cap that one of the boys was wearing. He pulled it up again, grinning bashfully, then took it off and put it on Tanya's head.

It reminded Chloe of a David Attenborough documentary she'd seen about the mating rituals of African birds. Watching the primping and preening and strutting, she felt scornful, superior, but also excluded. She stepped out of the gates and as she dithered a moment, someone barged into the back of her, shunting her on to the pavement, making her drop her bag. 'You git,' said a first-year boy and ran after the friend who had shoved him. Normally Chloe would have yelled something after them, but today she felt so brittle she just wanted to cry.

And then, to her horror, she saw Fiona start to turn towards her, alerted by the commotion. Instantly she imagined all of them, the boys as well, looking at her, sneering at her, and she suddenly felt horribly exposed, like she'd felt two weeks ago when she'd forgotten to lock the bathroom door and had stepped out of the shower just as Tim barged in. There had been a time when she and Tim had taken baths together, but over the last couple of years Chloe had become excruciatingly shy about revealing her body to anyone, even Mum. She had shrieked at Tim to get out, which was actually unnecessary because he had been as embarrassed as she'd been and had hardly been able to mumble an apology before exiting the bathroom so rapidly he had whacked his shoulder on the door jamb. For two days she and Tim had not been able to look at each other without both of them blushing a deep shade of red.

Chloe wondered now what intimate secrets Tanya had revealed to Fiona about her; she could think of things she'd told Tanya that would make her want to die if she ever discovered that Tanya had spread them around. Scooping up her bag from the pavement, she swung away, showing her back to Fiona, and began to stride purposefully in the opposite direction to that in which she wanted to go. Her body felt robotic, her movements so stiff and jerky she felt sure everyone was staring at her. Every second she expected Tanya or Fiona to shout something out, something vindictive, something deeply personal. If they did that she didn't know what she'd do except flee from the ogling eyes and derisive laughter. Certainly she couldn't see how she'd ever be able to face coming back to school.

But no one shouted anything, and eventually she slowed down, her muscles relaxing. She was walking down the hill that led through the posh houses and thence to the woods, which was not the way she normally chose to go home despite it being a short cut. Earlier this year there had been a flasher in the woods who had never been caught; he had revealed himself on six occasions to girls and women who had been walking on their own. One of the girls had been a second year on her way home from school. When Tanya heard about this she had sighed and said, 'Some girls get all the luck.'

Chloe came to a halt and considered her options. If she walked back up the hill now to go the longer, safer way home and Tanya and Fiona were still there she'd feel really stupid. She supposed she could hang around for a bit and then go back up, but how long should she leave it? It was getting colder and darker all the time, and how could she guarantee that Tanya and Fiona wouldn't walk down the hill and see her standing around like a lemon anyway? They'd know immediately she was trying to avoid them and she'd feel so humiliated.

No, the lesser of the evils was to go through the woods. The chances of encountering the flasher were pretty minimal, after all – he hadn't been seen for a couple of months now – and if she hurried she might catch up with Tim, who walked back through the woods most days, despite Mum's warnings, and never came to any harm.

The first drops of rain began to fall as she headed past the last few houses before the road petered out into a dirt track through the farmland that bordered the woods. The drops were fat and heavy as pigeons' droppings. One splashed across Chloe's cheek, a little shock of wetness. As she wiped it away she remembered a day in London with Mum and Dad and Tim when she was seven or eight. They still had a photograph of Tim standing with his arms outstretched like a scarecrow in Trafalgar Square, covered in pigeons. The birds looked as though they'd swooped en masse and were trying to bear him away, and in fact Mum had labelled the photograph: KIDNAPPED BY PIGEONS. Chloe remembered she had been too scared of the fluttering, cooing creatures to feed them. She didn't like the way they strutted towards her, pecking and jabbing with their beaks, twitching their black studs of eyes.

Although she was getting wet and the ground was speckling to dark mush in front of her, Chloe felt oddly comforted by the rain. If there was a flasher in the woods, surely the weather would send him scuttling off home. Where was the fun in getting your donger out if you were piss wet through? The thought made her smile in spite of herself, and then she remembered how she and Tanya had giggled over the word 'donger' at school, had imagined Ben's willy as a huge heavy bell that chimed in his trousers when he ran, and the smile died on her lips.

The sky was so dark and grainy it was like looking out through a dirty window; when she squinted, the rain looked like thin white scratches on glass. The fields around her were almost black, and the woods below her were black too, the tops of the trees gleaming as though plastic sheeting had been laid over them.

Abruptly the rain eased and then intensified, as though it had drawn breath only to redouble its efforts. Chloe flipped up the hood of her coat and shivered as rain began to patter on it, feeling the delicious ripple of goosebumps on her back and arms. She trudged downhill and only noticed the cluster of caravans and vehicles in the field to her left when she was almost level with them. They looked forlorn, somehow cringing beneath the onslaught of rain, but instantly Chloe felt a little surge of warmth; this must be where Tim's new friend, Oonagh, lived. Somehow she felt as though by realising this she had drawn closer to her brother, and lifted her head, half-hoping she would see him trudging ahead of her, perhaps just about to enter the dripping shelter of trees. Just for an instant she thought she *had* seen someone. She had the impression a figure, dark with rain, had been half-crouching behind a tree, turning its white face towards her. Before she could focus on it properly, however, it was gone.

Immediately unease wriggled its way from her throat to her belly and coiled there like a slow-worm. She thought again of the flasher. Should she turn back? Had she really seen someone? If she turned back now she would have to trudge all the way up the lane and then up the steep hill again; it would take her at least an hour to get home. Was all that worth it just because she *thought* she *might* have seen someone? Just because her imagination was doing a bit of over-time? Even if there was someone in the woods, it might well be another kid from school, or someone taking their dog for a walk.

She had stopped walking, but now she started again, moving towards the woods. There had been no one there, she told herself. The face she thought she'd seen had been a blur of rain, an after-effect of light.

As she approached the first of the trees, deafened and half-blinded by the downpour, she couldn't help feeling that they were waiting silently for her to reach them. She looked up, shivering again, and just for an instant the dark trunks seemed to crawl with movement before she realised it was rain. She thought she could hear a voice, whispering, but when she slowed to listen she realised that that was only rain too, clattering against leaves, hissing in the grass, dripping from branches.

She entered the woods, which at once was like entering a house with a leaky roof. Ahead of her the diminishing trunks seemed to unfold and reform as she walked towards and between them, reminding her oddly of the kaleidoscope she had had as a child. She had loved that toy, the way the colours had constantly seemed on the verge of tumbling into chaos but had somehow always managed to renew themselves before doing so, forming patterns that seemed to hold some meaning she could never quite grasp. She felt somnolent, almost sublime now, cosy and safe beneath her hood. The thought of the hot tea and the warm towel that would be waiting for her at home evoked another rash of goosebumps.

And then, just behind her, fracturing her mood, she heard a mulchy squelch that her mind immediately translated as a footstep. She twisted her head so suddenly that her hood stayed where it was, momentarily blinding her. She clawed it away, but this only caused beads of rain on her fringe to burst and run into her eyes. She fought down panic as she rubbed at her eyes. Her blurred, fragmented vision showed her a wall of bark that seemed to shift and shimmer. She felt vulnerable all over again, no longer secure and warm inside her hood but restricted, suffocated. Her eyes clear of water but smarting with rawness, she stared at the place from where she thought the sound had come.

There was nothing to be seen, not even a patch of grass springing upright after being trampled down. Chloe looked hard at one tree after another, feeling that if someone was hiding behind one of them she'd know – something would give them away – but they stood stoic and silent.

She pulled her hood right down, and immediately, as though it had been waiting for just that moment, a raindrop that felt big as an egg dripped from a leaf somewhere above her and struck the crown of her head. It seemed to burst like an egg too, spreading coldness that seeped into Chloe's hair and skin. She shuddered, and this time the goosebumps were like prickles of ice that found her belly, that even crossing her arms tightly around herself couldn't melt. She was not exactly scared, not just yet, though she felt the threat of fear trying to awaken inside her, like the onset of car sickness.

She turned and began walking, or rather striding, purposefully swinging her arms to deter anyone from sneaking up behind her. There seemed to be movement all around her now, but she ignored it, telling herself resolutely that it was caused by her constantly shifting perspective as she walked, that trees were not really sliding behind their neighbours, keeping pace with her. Her hair was sodden, sticking to her face like wet paper.

This is all your fault, Tanya, she thought bitterly. If anything happens to me ... And then she bit back on the thought. Nothing's going to happen. Don't even think it. Touch wood for luck. She reached out and touched a tree as she passed it. The bark was slimy as slug-flesh.

A whisper. There. To her right. She glanced round, feet sliding in the mud, fear beating at the box in which she was trying to keep it contained. There's nothing there, she told herself angrily. Pull yourself together, you stupid girl. She increased her speed, but her breath was ragged in her throat now, her muscles stiffening like before. Had the voice she thought she'd heard really whispered her name beneath the muttering hiss of the rain? No, of course not. The most frightening thing in these woods is your own imagination, she told herself.

But then it came again, and this time it was as though her imagination had come to life. It was more than a whisper this time, more like a thin moan of autumn wind.

'Chlo-eeee,' it called. The voice was high-pitched and yet soft, teasing yet utterly terrifying.

Chloe began to run, though in these conditions she could manage no more than a stumbling half-jog. Her head thrashed this way and that as the periphery of her vision swarmed with movement, water arcing from her saturated hair.

'Chlo-eeee,' the voice came again. It was a sweet voice, the gentle calling of a father trying to waken a sleeping child. And yet beneath the sweetness there was something dark and mad and wild. Chloe's fear was smashing its way out of the box now, burgeoning to terror, spreading through her like stomach cramps, in jagged, cold spasms. Each breath was a panicked sob; her feet slid and skidded beneath her, as though in a nightmare. The pouring rain made it impossible to tell where the voice was coming from.

'I can seeee yoooou, Chlo-eeee.'

It seemed all around her, a rain-phantom weaving between the trees.

'Get lost!' Chloe screamed, but her voice was more a shrill peal of terror than a defiant retort.

And then, as though her unused voice had been a plug blocking her thoughts, she was suddenly struck by a blinding revelation.

She stumbled to a halt and whipped round, swiping wet ropes of hair from her face. She was shaking and mud-spattered, still scared but angry now too. What she had just realised was this: whoever this was, stalking her through the woods, *knew her name*.

She couldn't believe she hadn't made the connection before. If this person knew her name, then he (or she?) was no casual nutter, no flasher out to show what he'd got to whoever happened to be passing. Which meant that this was some sort of joke, right? Some sort of sick, nasty joke, designed to scare her witless.

Who did she know who'd be sick enough, vindictive enough, to do something like that?

'Tanya!' she yelled, her voice more rage than panic now. 'Tanya, you can come out now! I know it's you!'

More quickly than she could turn there was a rustling behind her, then a soft, lilting voice whispered into her ear, 'Hello, Chloe.'

And Chloe, far too late, realised that it was not a joke, after all.

11

'No,' said Eric, shocked. The expression on his face made Tim grin. Twenty minutes before, Mum had been telling *him* about the break-in, and he had reacted the same way when she had come to the bit about the intruder hiding in the toilet. However, because no harm had come to her, her story could now be seen as exciting rather than alarming. 'I can't wait to see Dad's face when you tell him,' Tim had said.

Annette, though she wouldn't have admitted it, could understand his eagerness. Although the incident had shaken her, as the day had progressed she had actually found herself coming to relish the shocked looks on her customers' faces as she recounted what had happened.

'It's true,' she said to Eric now, trying to keep the satisfaction from her voice.

'My God. So what happened then?'

Annette told him how the policemen had run out through the back door into the yard and down the passageway between the flower shop and the estate agent's next door. 'They didn't find anyone, though,' she said. 'They asked around among the other shop owners, but they hadn't seen anything.'

'Tell Dad about the crowbar, Mum,' Tim urged eagerly.

Eric's face was a picture, much to the secret delight of them both. '*What* crowbar?'

'The police think the man must have used a crowbar to break in with. There wasn't one on the premises or in the yard, so it seems he must have had it with him —'

'When he was in the toilet,' finished Tim.

Eric reached out and hugged his wife as if to ensure she was real. 'Oh, Net,' he said.

Annette laughed and patted Eric's back. 'Don't worry,' she reassured him, 'I've come through my ordeal unscathed. I'm all right.'

'Yes, but you might not have done,' Eric said, and shuddered. 'I dread to think what might have happened.'

'Well, nothing did, so there's nothing to worry about,' she said firmly.

He broke the embrace and leaned back, but still kept hold of her arms as if afraid she might disappear if he let her go. He looked like a concerned owl, eyes wide behind his spectacles, hair sticking up in tufts. 'I'm amazed that you can be so casual about this,' he said admiringly.

'Oh, you should have seen me this morning, I was shaking like a leaf then. I couldn't help thinking of the break-in as a personal attack at first, but I've had the whole day to put things into perspective, and I know now that it was probably just what the police said – an opportunist looking for money, or something to sell.'

'But why break into a flower shop?' said Eric. 'There's plenty more likely targets on the High Street.'

Annette shrugged. 'Well, I haven't got a burglar alarm for one thing. And also there're no living quarters above the shop and it was pretty obvious there was nobody there.'

Eric had adopted his earnest look. 'So what are the police doing now?'

'Well, they did send a man round to look for fingerprints, but he only found mine and Mary's. The fingerprint man said whoever broke in must have been wearing gloves. Apart from that, I don't suppose there's much they can do. I mean, it's not as if anything was taken.'

'Are you sure about that?' said Eric.

'Well, I'm pretty sure.'

'What do you mean, "pretty sure"? You must know if there was anything missing.'

'Well, the only thing that I couldn't find was my new secateurs, but I might just as easily have left them at the market this morning.'

'Did you mention them to the police?'

Annette raised her eyebrows. 'A pair of secateurs? Don't be daft, they'd think I was taking the mickey.'

'You might scoff, but you should never overlook little things.'

'As the actress said to the bishop,' said Tim.

Annette looked at her son, more amused than disapproving. 'If I'd made a comment like that when I was your age, young man, my mother would have made me wash my mouth out with soap and water.'

'It's lucky we live in such enlightened times then, isn't it?' said Tim cheekily, and stood up now that the initial thrill of seeing his dad's reaction to Mum's news was over. 'I suppose I'd better go and do my homework. Promise you won't tell Clo about the break-in until I'm there.'

He trooped upstairs, dragging his bag behind him. As he opened the door to his room, the numerous pieces of paper that were pinned to the walls fluttered and rustled like leaves on a tree. Black-and-white ink sketches were tacked to a large cork board, and on the right-hand wall, above his bed, was a family portrait he'd done in gouache of the four of them dressed as astronauts, holding their helmets under their arms. His parents had been so taken with it that they'd paid £50 to have it framed, though Annette hadn't really wanted it in the lounge because it didn't quite go with the floral patterned suite and the William Morris wallpaper. The majority of Tim's artwork was influenced by his love of science fiction. There were lots of monsters and spaceships, strange planets and futuristic cities in evidence. The bookcase beside his desk was crammed with graphic novels and large hardbacked 'reference' books, which ranged in subject matter from human anatomy to the making of *Star Trek*, H. R. Giger to the history of DC Comics. In the centre of the room was Tim's easel on which his latest masterpiece resided: a large portrait of a snarling Judge Dredd, which he was doing mainly to practise using the top-of-the-range airbrush that Jackie had bought him for his birthday last month.

He dumped his bag on the floor and sat down at his desk, beneath the window looking out on to the back garden. Most of the desk was occupied by an Apple Mac computer and printer, but there was also room for a stack of magazines and comics, on top of which sat a mug in the shape of a skull that was full of pens. As ever, Tim was sorely tempted to lose himself in his artwork until Mum called him down for tea, or to pick up a magazine, or switch on the computer and surf the Internet for a couple of hours. But instead he forced himself to take his History books out of his bag and turn his attention to Barnes Wallis and his bouncing bomb. He'd been up there for an hour, and was just getting to grips with the essay he had to write, when he heard his dad call his name.

'Yeah?' he shouted.

'Would you come down here a minute, please?'

Tim sighed, then did as he was asked. In the lounge, his dad was leaning against the mantelpiece and his mum was sitting a little stiffly on the settee, her hands in her lap. There was a slight but palpable tension in the air.

'What's up?' said Tim, wondering if they had somehow found out about his visit to the travellers' camp earlier that day.

Eric pushed himself gently away from the mantelpiece. 'Have you any idea where Chloe is?'

'No. Isn't she home yet?'

'No, she isn't,' said Annette, her voice edged with anxiety, 'and it's nearly dark now, and raining.'

'She'll turn up,' said Tim. 'She's probably just gone to one of her friends' houses and lost track of time. She'll be all right, Mum, don't worry.'

'Tim's right,' said Eric, walking across and squeezing his wife's shoulder. 'A teenager's main reason for being on this earth is to worry their parents sick. Isn't that right, Tim?'

'Oh yeah. It's Chloe's shift today, mine tomorrow. I'm thinking of getting into hard drugs. What do you reckon?'

Annette smiled weakly. 'I'll kill her when she gets in.'

'That'll be something for her to look forward to,' said Tim. 'Have you tried ringing round her friends' houses?'

'No, your dad was about to, but we thought we'd ask you first. Who is she pals with, besides Tanya Roberts?'

Tim gave them a list of all the names he could think of, and helped them look up the numbers in the directory. Then, as much to escape the tension in the room as anything, he said, 'I'd better go and finish this essay. Give me a shout if she turns up.'

He went upstairs, wishing he'd said 'when', not 'if', but now he found he couldn't concentrate on his homework. In the end he gave up and went back downstairs. His dad was on the phone and his mum was still sitting on the settee, a worried look on her face.

'Any luck?' Tim asked. Annette waved him to silence, shaking her head abruptly.

'Yes, I'm sure she will,' Eric was saying. 'Well, thanks anyway. Goodbye.' He put down the phone and turned to them, shoulders slumping in defeat. 'Well, that's the last of the names on the list. No one's seen her since this afternoon.'

Tim hated seeing the distress on his mum's face. Because Chloe had not been at any of the places he had suggested, he couldn't help feeling he'd let them down.

'Oh, Eric, where can she be?' Annette wailed. 'I mean, look at this weather.' She waved a hand at the window, against which rain was hurling itself as though attracted by the light. Normally they would have closed the curtains by now, but Tim knew that doing so would have seemed like shutting out not just the night but Chloe as well.

'So she'll get wet,' Eric said, trying to sound as if he believed that was the worst that could happen. 'It'll serve her right.'

'Maybe she's been trying to ring while you've been on the phone,' Tim said hopefully.

'Have you any other idea where she might be?' Eric asked.

Tim thought hard. 'She could be at Bertolucci's. Or maybe she's with her new boyfriend.'

'Boyfriend?' said Annette, surprised. 'I wasn't aware she had a boyfriend.'

'Well, I don't think he's *actually* her boyfriend, but there's this fourth-year kid she fancies – Ben Wyatt. She's been trying to get him to ask her out for ages. Maybe she finally managed it.'

Briefly a little scene played itself out in Tim's head: Chloe and Ben Wyatt gazing into each other's eyes over cappuccinos at Bertolucci's; his dad bursting in and causing a scene, then grabbing Chloe's hand and dragging her away like a naughty girl.

Mentally he winced. If Chloe *was* with Ben, she would not thank him for setting Mum and Dad on her tail and putting her fledgling romance in jeopardy. Not that Tim would *really* expect his dad to behave like such a dork, but then again you could never quite tell with parents, could you?

'Be nice to her, Dad,' he said.

A slight frown furrowed Eric's brow. 'All it takes is one phone call, Tim,' he said reasonably, though Tim could tell he was worried. He found the number he wanted and jabbed jerkily at the phone buttons. It was so quiet in the room, despite the rain, that Tim could clearly hear the *brr-brr* of the Wyatts' phone, and his dad's breath reverberating in the mouthpiece like the sound an obscene caller makes.

'Ah, hello,' Eric said suddenly. 'Is Ben Wyatt there, please?' He paused and then said, 'Yes, you can tell him it's Mr Knight, one of his teachers from school.'

Tim looked at Annette and raised his eyebrows. She compressed her lips in a distracted expression of acknowledgement.

Abruptly Eric said, 'Yes it is. Ben, I'd like to know whether my daughter, Chloe, is there with you?'

Tim heard a faint squawk of surprise and moved closer to the mouthpiece, but couldn't quite catch what Ben was saying. 'Well, I was led to believe that you two were, um, seeing each other,' Eric said.

More jabbering from the other end, then Eric said, 'Are you quite sure? Chloe's mother and I aren't annoyed. We just want to know where she is.'

Tim could almost sense the hope draining out of his mum. Ben Wyatt spoke again, this time for a good half-minute or so, before Eric said, 'All right, Ben, sorry to trouble you ... No, no, we're just trying to track her down, that's all. Yes, if you should happen to see her, ask her to give us a call.'

He said goodbye and put the phone down, then turned to his wife and son. 'Well, he hasn't seen her either. He sounded surprised when I asked him if she was there. He says he hardly knows her.' He scratched his head, looking momentarily lost, then said, 'I'll just give Bertolucci's a ring and if she isn't there I suppose we'll just have to wait for her to get in touch with us.'

She wasn't there, as a consequence of which nobody much felt like eating the evening meal – pork casserole with potatoes and broccoli – but Annette served it up anyway, leaving some in the pot for Chloe. Annette pushed her food around her plate and looked up hopefully every time there was a noise outside. Eric kept making reassuring noises, which grew more and more hollow as the evening progressed. Tim munched his way stolidly through his food, even though it got more difficult to swallow with each mouthful, because he felt that leaving some on his plate would be like a confirmation of something none of them was yet prepared to admit. After the main course – dessert wasn't mentioned and nobody asked for any – Eric put the TV on and they all sat staring at it like zombies, as though by pretending it was a normal evening they could make it so.

Time crawled on. Eight o'clock passed, and then nine. When Chloe was going out on a week-night, nine o'clock was her deadline time, but nobody mentioned that. The phone remained stubbornly silent. It got to quarter past nine, then half past. Tim felt something in his stomach screwing tighter and tighter. The longer he sat staring at the TV screen, the harder it became to move or say anything.

All at once, Eric slammed his fist down on the arm of his chair in an uncharacteristic display of frustration and said despairingly, 'For God's sake, where is she?'

His outburst seemed to break some spell that had been keeping them motionless, locking their emotions inside. Tim felt dread curl inside him. Annette looked up, her brown eyes wide.

Eric jumped up, looking upset and so anxious that the curling dread in Tim's stomach clenched like a fist. And then he said something that shocked Tim, because it seemed to bring the seriousness of the situation into sudden sharp focus:

'I'm going to call the police.'

12

Despite being able to see the flashlights of his colleagues winking through the trees like elfin spirits of the forest, PC Robert Backley felt utterly alone. It was not an uncommon feeling for him. For eighteen months now he had been unable to shake off the sense of isolation, of not fitting in, that had been with him since the first day he had donned the uniform he had come to hate.

It was not through lack of trying that he felt like a fish out of water. Indeed, during his training in Harrogate he had made a real effort to join in with the banter and the station gossip, to throw himself into the social whirl of drinking and gambling and womanising. However his heart simply hadn't been in it, and his inability to hide that fact had become apparent to him when he walked into the locker room one day and overheard Sandy Keen say to Kevin Harris, 'I dunno, he's just not one of the lads, is he?' That it was him they were talking about had been obvious, both from the guilty expression on Kevin's face and the way he said, 'All right, Rob?' in a loud and exaggeratedly effusive voice.

Robert had never considered himself a prude or a snob before joining the force, but too often he found his colleagues' behaviour crude and childish. Like the time two of the lads had pulled a new female recruit's knickers down and date-stamped her bottom, or the time Pemberton had got his knob out in a Chinese restaurant and said to the waitress who had come to take their order, 'Get your chop suey round that, missis.'

Robert had been hoping his transfer from Harrogate's busy main station to Bramwell's quieter, more parochial one would make him view the job in a new light, but in fact it had only confirmed his growing conviction that he was not cut out for the force. With only a dozen regular officers to choose from, the atmosphere at Bramwell was more relaxed – no overt sexism, no petty rivalries, no power games – and Robert had been welcomed warmly as a new member of the team. Despite this, however, he soon realised that even if he had been in the friendliest, most relaxed atmosphere possible, it wouldn't change the simple fact that he didn't like the job. He had only joined the force in the first place because it was a family tradition. His dad was a Chief Inspector in Wakefield and his step-brother, Chris, older than him by five years, a Detective Sergeant in Leeds. Robert had no doubt that *they* were both regarded among their colleagues as 'one of the lads'. He remembered how they had both laughed at him when they heard he had thrown up at his first post-mortem.

'Post-mortems are like birthday parties compared to some of the things you'll see in this job,' Chris had told him, somewhat gloatingly.

His father's contribution, in that brusque, dismissive way of his, had been: 'You'll soon get used to 'em, lad. I sit and eat me sandwiches at post-mortems. Only bit o' peace I get.'

But Robert had not got used to them. Nor had he got used to the verbal abuse from schoolkids, the grief of the bereaved, the degradation and social inadequacy he encountered on a day-to-day basis, even in a small, relatively well-to-do area like Bramwell and its environs.

He sighed and looked at his watch: twenty-five past eleven. Any normal person would have been coming home from the pub now, or tucked up in bed with a good book and a cup of cocoa, or watching TV, or spending some quality time with a loved one. And what was he doing? Scouring the local woods in the pissing rain for a schoolgirl who had not returned home. The rain, which had not relented since four that afternoon, drummed on his plastic overcoat, trickled down his neck and up the sleeve of the arm that was holding his torch, and spilled through his torchlight beam like a barrage of tiny silver arrows.

With each slow step he took the ground squelched beneath his feet, water oozing up through the inches-thick covering of fallen leaves. Despite his boots his feet were so frozen he could no longer feel his toes. He imagined himself unlacing and upending his boots back at the station and his toes rolling out and bouncing across the floor like marbles.

How he longed for a hot bath and a warm, dry bed. Twice already he had slipped on the sodden ground, once plunging his left knee into an ice-cold puddle of muddy water and once landing flat on his arse and soaking his underpants right through.

God, he hated this job! He knew he couldn't go on like this for much longer; sooner or later something had to give. The thought of telling his dad and his step-brother that the force wasn't for him actually made his bowels cramp with dread. He could picture their expressions of disgust, could almost hear his father berating him in that gruff, scornful voice of his, calling him a layabout, a wimp, and that old stand-by of his, a woolly woofter. But what was a tongue-lashing compared to the rest of his life? What were a few emotional cuts and bruises if it meant he was going to come out on the other side a free man?

He blinked water out of his eyes and continued moving his torch back and forth in a slow sweeping motion. The four of them, all they'd been able to rustle up at short notice, had been at this for over an hour now and so far had only covered about half the area. In the dead of night, with the rain coming down, this seemed the most inhospitable place on earth. Tree trunks impaled by Robert's torch beam seemed to blanch and swell like mushrooms; dips and hollows were like black mouths of shadow, opening when probed with light.

At the moment he was tramping through a particularly dense area of undergrowth, thick with brambles and scrubby gorse. Progress was slow because you couldn't just wade through it. If you tried that, thorns like fish-hooks snagged on your trousers and you spent most of your time getting your hands torn to ribbons trying to free yourself. Already the barbs had drawn stripes of blood on Robert's hands in half a dozen places. He supposed if he wasn't so numb with cold the scratches would be stinging by now.

Ahead of him, just beyond a tree that was leaning as though trying to haul itself, roots and all, from the earth, the ground dipped into a hollow so black it could have been anything from a sheer drop to a pool of water. He directed his torch at it, but the leaning tree seemed to absorb the light, to shine like wet bone. Robert sighed and edged forward, looking for a path between the brambles, hoping the ground wasn't suddenly going to disappear from beneath his feet. On either side of him blurry discs of light from his colleagues' torches nodded as though egging him on. Away to his left, Sergeant Winslow shouted out, 'Chloe!' as he had been doing intermittently since they started the search, the sound like the braying call of a large and lonely bird.

Robert rounded the tree, but kept hold of it, probing ahead with his feet. His torch beam slid around the tree and illuminated thick coils of thigh-high brambles that made him think of barbed-wire barriers on World War One battlefields. 'Lovely,' he muttered to himself. 'Thank you so much.' Like someone tentatively dipping their toe into a pool to test the temperature of the water, he extended one leg, searching for the ground with his foot.

A couple of feet beneath the brambles his toe touched something solid. However he knew instinctively it wasn't the ground; it was softer, and although it didn't give like mud, it nevertheless shifted a little when he nudged it. He withdrew his leg and holding on to the leaning tree with his left hand, craned right out over the hollow, shining his torch into the brambles. He thought he saw something white down there, but he couldn't be sure. He swore softly, then tucked the torch under his chin and began to pull brambles aside with his right hand, wincing at the hot slivers of pain penetrating the cold numbness as thorns slid into his flesh.

When he thought he had tugged enough of the brambles out of the way, he took his torch from under his chin and shone it back into the hollow. The girl was lying on her back in a couple of inches of muddy water. The white thing he had seen was part of her exposed thigh. He tilted his hand and the torchlight slid up her body and found her face.

The sight of it almost made him drop the torch. He jerked back, making the tree he was holding on to creak alarmingly. He swung back on to the solid ground above the hollow, his stomach performing acrobatics, and squatted down. Despite the cold, sweat sprang up on his forehead; he breathed hard in and out, willing himself not to be sick.

After a few moments his stomach began to settle just a little, and he straightened up. He took a few more breaths, trying to compose himself, and then he looked up and shouted at the top of his voice, 'Over here!'

Wednesday 23 November

13

It was silent in the house, the clock on the mantelpiece showing twenty minutes past midnight. The TV had been turned off, all pretence at normality long since abandoned. It was almost three hours since Eric had called the police, and almost two hours since the police had left the house, their initial period of questioning over, and all the Knights could do now was sit and wait for news.

Tim and his mum were perched at either end of the settee like book ends, his dad in his usual place in the armchair. If this had been a normal evening Tim would have been in bed by eleven, reading comics until his mum walked past and told him to 'turn that light off', or falling asleep listening to Oasis or Blur or Portishead through his headphones (he'd wake in the morning feeling as though his ears had been crushed in a vice). He wished he could curl up in bed now and sleep away the rest of this terrible, interminable night, then wake in the morning to find Chloe back safe and well. He'd give anything for a guarantee that the four of them would be sitting together at the breakfast table in eight hours' time, talking and joking over cereal and toast and cups of tea.

The tension was unbearable, but Tim didn't feel he could do

anything except endure it. He couldn't concentrate on drawing or reading or watching TV or listening to music or mucking about on his computer, besides which it would have seemed indelicate, almost like a display of indifference at Chloe's plight. Even talking seemed taboo – to talk about anything but Chloe seemed inappropriate, but to talk *about* Chloe felt too much like tiptoeing through a minefield. Questions which none of them wanted to speculate upon, fears which none of them wanted to voice, lurked beneath the surface of every potential conversation, primed to explode.

Wind and rain were lashing the house, but to Tim it seemed as though he was encased in a bubble of silence, a bubble whose skin was stretching thinner and thinner as the silence expanded within it. Finally he could stand it no longer, and with a kind of desperation he blurted, 'Does anyone want a cup of tea?'

His voice sounded weak, flat, as though the air in the room, unstirred by the usual flurry of voices and activity, had begun to harden like cement. Annette looked up, slow as a turtle, frowning as if he had interrupted some long and complicated equation she had been working out in her head. Tim had to suppress a shudder at the agony of waiting, dark and depthless, which seemed to be embedded in her eyes.

'No thanks,' she murmured.

'Dad?'

Eric sighed and propped the roll-up he'd been smoking, the latest of several this evening, on the rim of an ashtray. He rubbed both hands over his face, fingers probing beneath his spectacles to rub at the greyish skin around his eyes. 'I'll have one if you're making one,' he said.

Tim went into the kitchen and started making cups of tea that neither he nor his dad really wanted. He was pouring boiling water into a pot shaped like a stack of books with a spout and handle when the doorbell rang. He looked up, slopping water on to the counter where it steamed like acid, then banged the kettle down and rushed through into the lounge. His dad was already disappearing through the door that led into the hallway, his mum still sitting on the settee, hands clasped between her knees, looking terrified and hopeful at the same time. Tim came to a stop just inside the door, as if afraid to venture any further into the room. He heard the front door open, a rumble of voices even above the screaming of the wind, then the rustle of clothing and the soft sound of footsteps on carpet as his dad and whoever he'd opened the front door to approached the lounge.

His dad appeared first, his face set, oddly waxen. Behind him were two police officers, a man and a woman, wrapped in wet blue plastic, their faces just as expressionless.

No one said anything. Eric walked across to where Annette was sitting and sat down, putting his arm protectively around her. The police officers came into the room and stood dripping on the carpet, the man toying nervously with the cap in his hands. Tim knew from the careful, almost reverential way they moved that they had not come here with good news.

'Mr and Mrs Knight,' the man said quietly, 'I'm PC Diamond and this is WPC Kenworthy.'

'Where's Chloe?' Annette said, her voice jagged, almost accusing, as though these two people were representatives of a gang that was holding her daughter hostage.

The two police officers exchanged the briefest of glances, then the WPC, her curly hair frizzy and sparkling with rain, said softly, 'I'm very sorry, but I'm afraid you're going to have to brace yourself for some bad news.'

Tim's head suddenly felt thick and muzzy and he gripped the back of the settee, afraid that he might fall. He felt an urge to hold up his hands, shout at the policewoman to stop, as if by not hearing the words he could somehow prevent their worst nightmare from coming true.

'I'm sorry to have to tell you that we've found the dead body of a teenage girl in the woods, and we have reason to believe it may be your daughter,' the WPC said. 'At this stage it appears that she may have been murdered.'

The words had been half-expected, and yet they were so unbelievable that Tim actually wondered for a moment whether he was dreaming. He'd heard variations on these words so many times in films and TV cop shows that he couldn't believe they were real. Things like this only happened to other people, people you'd never know, people you'd see on the news and feel sorry for and then forget. Something inside him, something intrinsic, seemed to peel away with a painful tearing sensation; it felt like part of his life.

A silence so profound it was like a void seemed to bloom behind the policewoman's voice for a moment – and then abruptly, shockingly, Annette slid forward off the settee, folding at the hips like a puppet with its strings cut. She landed with a thump on her knees, and Tim, afraid she'd fainted, lunged forward at the same time as his dad to prevent her toppling on to her face.

She hadn't fainted. She put out her hands to prevent her face from hitting the floor, and then released a long, bubbling wail of despair. It was a terrible sound; it made the hairs on the back of Tim's neck quill. She began to shake her head slowly from side to side and to moan, 'No ... please no ... please no ...' over and over again.

Tim saw the policewoman swallow. The policeman, who could have been no more than twenty-five, was twirling his cap in his hands, looking as though he desperately wished he were somewhere else.

Eric placed his right hand on his wife's back and began stroking it absently; she didn't even notice. His face looked suddenly old and lined, drawn with shock. He opened his mouth and in a bleak, faraway voice he asked, 'How? How was she murdered?'

The officers exchanged another glance, then the woman said, raising her voice above Annette's denials, 'We think she was stabbed.'

'Think?' Eric said as if he'd never heard the word before. 'What do you mean, "think"? Can't you tell?'

The WPC grimaced. 'I'm afraid tests still have to be carried out, sir. Until we get the results of those we can't be entirely sure.'

Annette had pulled herself up into a ball now and was sobbing wretchedly, her face cupped in her left hand. Tim didn't know whether she was hearing any of this conversation. She seemed to have fallen into her own private pit of grief.

'Was she ... was she interfered with?' Eric said. The question seemed to tear itself from him involuntarily.

'It's too early to say, sir,' the WPC replied in a voice trying hard to remain neutral.

Suddenly furious, Eric shouted, 'Can't you tell us *anything*?'

His anger seemed to pluck Annette back into the real world. Removing her hand to reveal a face that looked raw, she bleated, 'For God's sake, Eric, our little girl is *dead!* What else matters?'

Tim couldn't bear it any longer. He staggered into the kitchen and collapsed on to one of the wooden seats around the dining table. Sitting on the hob was a large cooking pot containing some pork casserole, probably now congealed, which had been intended for Chloe to eat when she got home. Except that Chloe would never now be coming home; she would never eat another meal. She would never sleep in her bed, or go to school, or laugh, or speak, or watch 'Neighbours', or get married, or have children, or anything.

She was dead. Gone for ever. The last words Tim had spoken to her had been, 'Hello, small fry,' when he'd seen her in the dining hall at lunchtime, and she had wrinkled her nose in that little-sisterly way of hers and told him to get lost.

He thought of the family portrait above his bed, and something cracked inside him then – his heart maybe, made of glass, full of ice. He started to cry. He cried and cried. He didn't think he would ever stop.

14

The drive from York took over half an hour, with Lockwood hunched over the steering wheel all the way as though mesmerised by the windscreen wipers' gargantuan tussle with the rain. At the edge of the woods a dark figure loomed in front of the car, face and upraised hand phantom-white in the headlights. As the figure, a constable in helmet and waterproofs, came alongside the car, Lockwood rolled his window down and flashed the man his ID. 'This is DI Farrington, I'm DS Lockwood,' he said, raising his voice above the wind.

Despite his helmet, the constable had water streaming down his face and dripping off the end of his nose. 'Sir, Ma'am,' he said, acknowledging the senior of the two officers with a nod that caused droplets of water to flick in through the window and speckle Lockwood's sleeve. 'If you'd like to park your car just over there, I'll escort you to the murder scene.'

Elizabeth Farrington had never liked being called 'ma'am', thinking it made her sound like a Victorian matriarch, but she let it pass. Lockwood parked the car where the PC had indicated, then unclipped his seatbelt and said, 'Wait there a minute, boss. I've got something that'll save your shoes.' He grabbed his overcoat from the back seat, opened the driver's door and plunged out into the rain. Farrington watched him hurry to the back of the car, a dark fractured blur though the rain-smeared windows. He opened the boot, took something out, and then hurried round to her side. She opened the door and immediately a flurry of rain chilled her, spattering her brown-stockinged legs.

Lockwood was holding out a pair of green Wellingtons. 'They might be a bit big, but they'll keep your feet dry,' he said.

'How very gallant,' Farrington declared, making the second 'a' as hard a vowel as the first, 'but what about you?'

'My shoes are more waterproof than yours. Besides, RHIP – rank has its privileges.'

Farrington smiled. She was a slim forty-one, her arms and legs hard-muscled thanks to a haphazard fitness programme she had to organise around her job, which involved cycling, weight-training, fell-walking and the very occasional game of tennis. She wore her mousy hair pulled back into a ponytail except for a feathery fringe which curled to her eyebrows.

'Just as long as you're not mollycoddling me, Frank,' she said.

Lockwood grinned. 'Mollycoddling *you*, boss? Bloody hell, you've got to be joking.'

Farrington grinned too, accepted the boots from him and pulled them on. Together the two of them followed the constable into the hissing woods.

The scene of crime team had set up arc lamps around the murder site, several of which were directed towards an orange domed tent that nestled in a hollow like a giant glowing pumpkin. Rain drummed on the tightly stretched canvas. Uniformed constables, many of whom had been dragged in from the surrounding towns and villages, were poking about in the bushes, bent double like old men as they painstakingly scoured the area for evidence. By the time Farrington and Lockwood arrived on the scene the rain had soaked right through the shoulders of their coats to the skin. Farrington blew a dewdrop of water from the tip of her nose and pushed wet hair back from her face as a uniformed sergeant hurried across to greet them, hand outstretched.

Lockwood stepped forward like a bodyguard and intercepted the handshake. Introductions were made. The uniformed sergeant was called Winslow. He had steel-framed spectacles and prematurely grey hair beneath his peaked cap.

They were shown towards the orange dome, Winslow pointing out hazards to avoid, pulling up a tree branch for Farrington to duck under. She didn't mind this, but when he took her arm to help her down into the bracken-filled hollow, she snapped, 'I can manage perfectly well, thank you, *Sergeant*.'

'Sorry, Ma'am,' Winslow said woodenly, his eyes betraying nothing and everything. Farrington had seen it all before, had had to struggle through fifteen years of bigotry and chauvinism, of being regarded as either a dominatrix or a dyke just because she wanted to further her career. Even after all this time the attitude still infuriated her, made her feel that as far as women in the police force were concerned, time was standing still.

She picked her way through bracken which snagged at her stockings and dripped water into the tops of the Wellingtons which flapped around her calves. Don't fall on your arse now, Liz, she told herself, or you'll never wipe the smirk from Winslow's face.

The lamps made it feel hot by the tent. The water running down Farrington's face felt like sweat. Winslow, the light on his glasses making the lenses appear white, said, 'It's none too pleasant a sight, I'm afraid.'

'You think it might offend my feminine sensibilities?' said Farrington before she could stop herself. Winslow rolled his eyes and

Farrington, realising too late that the sergeant's warning had been directed at both herself and Lockwood, bit her lip and wondered whether she should apologise. She might have done if she hadn't been so cold and wet, if she hadn't had the beginnings of a headache prickling at her temples, if she hadn't had a butchered teenage girl awaiting her attentions. She was not really the bitch on wheels Winslow had obviously decided she was, but on this occasion she simply said, 'All right then, let's have a look at what we've got.'

She stepped smartly to the tent flap, which Winslow hastened to draw aside for her. With a nod of thanks she stepped inside.

A balding man in his fifties with a downturned mouth – 'face like a bulldog chewing a wasp' was how Lockwood always described him – was crouching beside an open case containing a clutter of medical equipment. He was in the process of peeling off a pair of latex gloves, the fingertips messy with blood, rolling them into a ball like socks fresh from the dryer. It was evident he was not partial to the wet conditions; his shoes and grey suit looked expensive, his yellow silk tie was draped across one shoulder to prevent it dangling in the mud. He peered up at the new arrivals as though they'd blundered into the wrong room.

'It's my bloody wedding anniversary,' he said by way of greeting.

'Congratulations,' muttered Lockwood.

'Twenty-four bloody years! I'd taken my wife to that new French place in town. We were just heading home for a nightcap when your lot called me up.'

Farrington shook her head. 'I dunno,' she sighed, 'Kids today, they're so bloody selfish. Get themselves murdered without a thought for who's got to clean up afterwards.'

The pathologist scowled and sealed the latex gloves into a plastic bag which he shoved into his case. Apart from him and the new arrivals, the only other person in the tent was the scene of crime officer. He was prowling round the body with a ritzy-looking Nikon, taking snaps from all angles. The light from the flash seemed to pierce Farrington's pupils like pins, stimulating the growth of her embryonic headache. She winced and said, 'Excuse me, could you just wait a few minutes, please?'

The SOCO shrugged and nodded, albeit reluctantly. Farrington moved forward to examine the body, which had been extricated from the brambles and laid out on a plastic sheet.

Winslow had been telling the truth. It was not a pleasant sight.

The girl's upper body had been extensively stabbed and slashed. Though the rain had washed much of the blood from her face and other exposed areas, her raincoat, grey jumper and white shirt, all of which had been hacked to ribbons, were soaked with red. The most horrifying injuries, though, were to her face and hands. Her eyes had been punctured and all but scooped from their sockets, the skin of her left cheek from her ear to the corner of her mouth hung open like a flap of raw beef, and every one of her fingers was gone.

Over the years, Farrington had become inured to death in all its forms, though she had to admit that this was one of the worst sights she'd seen. She showed no outward emotion, though deep inside she recoiled from such brutality; she felt horror, grief, despair and a rushing, blazing anger. She straightened up, took a deep breath of the stifling air inside the tent and palmed trickles of water from her forehead and cheeks. Turning to the scowling pathologist and to Sergeant Winslow standing beside him, she said, 'I presume the girl is who we think she is?'

Winslow nodded. 'She hasn't been formally identified yet, but she has a name tag sewn into her jumper. Also there was a school bag nearby. All the exercise books inside it had her name on them.'

'Do we have anything else at this stage?'

'Afraid not, Ma'am. The rain hasn't exactly helped.'

'No sign of a murder weapon?'

'No, Ma'am.'

Farrington sighed and glanced at the girl's face, the flesh like damp white rubber, her hair caked with mud. 'What can you tell me, Doctor Boam?'

Boam moved forward, standing beside Lockwood who was looking down at the girl, his hands in his pockets. Dispassionately the pathologist said, 'All the injuries apart from the removal of her fingers were made by the same weapon, which I would estimate to be a knife with a thin blade about ... oh ... six inches long. We found in excess of forty stab wounds, many of which were inflicted after the girl died. There are bruises on her upper left arm, the position of which seem to indicate that the killer took hold of her from behind and brought his right arm round the front of her body and stabbed the knife towards himself. If this is the case, then the attacker would have been covered in blood.'

He squatted down and carefully pulled aside a little of the girl's shredded clothing, exposing a white bra and whiter flesh. The marks of the knife in the chest and stomach were thin purple slits, like the gills of fish.

'From the angle of these wounds and the damage caused I believe these are the earliest inflicted,' he said. 'They're also the ones that killed her. I think her attacker went straight for the heart and then when she was down and could no longer defend herself, he really went to town on her. The injuries to her face I believe were caused post mortem. He probably went for her eyes because he couldn't stand her looking at him. This wound here —' he pointed to her bisected cheek '— was probably the result of the killer inserting his blade between her lips and slashing sideways. There may have been a latent sexual motive for this, though there's no obvious sign of sexual assault.'

'So you reckon he just killed her for kicks?' said Lockwood.

Boam pursed his lips. 'It isn't my job to establish a motive, Sergeant. It is a slightly odd one, though. If the girls' attacker was a sadist then why make it a priority to kill her? Why not torture her first? Similarly, although the attack was undoubtedly a frenzied one, there is also some semblance of control indicated by the fact that the killer *did* go immediately for her heart.'

'What about the fingers?' Farrington said.

Boam frowned as though he was a lecturer interrupted in mid-flow by a pedantic student. 'I was just coming to that.' He held up the girl's arm, pointing at juts of bone protruding from stumps washed clean of blood by the rain.

'These weren't cut through with a knife or even sawn through. They were removed by a guillotine-like blade, something like a cigar cutter, or perhaps by two blades coming together, as in a pair of garden shears. These wounds were definitely inflicted post mortem and this may well have been the last act that the killer performed before taking leave of the body.' Boam let the girl's mutilated hand drop and almost casually announced, 'It seems the killer took the fingers with him.'

Farrington glanced at Winslow, who nodded. 'My lads haven't found even one of them.'

'You think he was afraid of what we might find under her fingernails?' said Lockwood.

Boam straightened up, brushing his hands together. 'Seems a reasonable assumption.'

'Is this where the girl died?' Farrington asked, glancing around. Much of the bracken and gorse around the plastic sheet on which the girl's body had been laid had been trampled down into the mud.

'More or less,' said Winslow. 'We found shreds of clothing and signs of a struggle just a few feet away, by the tree above the hollow. There were little pools of blood here and there, heavily diluted by rain. It looks as though the guy did her in there and then chucked her down here.'

'Guy?' said Lockwood. 'So we definitely think the killer was a man, do we?'

Winslow shrugged. 'Figure of speech. It usually is, isn't it?'

'Hmm.' Farrington looked thoughtful. 'Any obvious suspects?'

'Not so far, though I thought the travellers' camp would be a good place to start.'

'What travellers' camp?'

Winslow explained about the travellers, who had arrived in the town a few days earlier. 'I wouldn't be surprised if they had something to do with this.'

'You've had trouble with them before, have you?'

'Well ... no, but these people are all cast from the same mould, aren't they? Drug users, layabouts, hippies ...'

'Have you always been so liberal-minded, Sergeant?'

Winslow smiled a little uncertainly. 'Just facing facts, that's all, Ma'am.'

Farrington resisted the urge to shake her head in despair. 'All right, Sergeant. I'll send a couple of my men up to talk to them when they arrive.'

Winslow shifted his weight nervously from one foot to the other. 'There's, er, no need, Ma'am. I've already taken the liberty of sending a few men up there.'

Farrington stiffened. 'You've done what?'

The Sergeant flushed, nervously took off his spectacles, then put them on again. 'Well, as we'd had an influx of extra officers, and you weren't here, Ma'am, I thought it would be a good idea to get things rolling, strike while the iron's still hot, as it were.'

He made it sound as though she'd been dragging her heels. Farrington stepped close enough to him for them to have rubbed noses. Although she was a good three inches shorter than Winslow, the clipped fury in her voice seemed to shrink him down to her size.

'The extra officers were sent purely to help you seal off the area and search for evidence, Sergeant. Weren't you informed that I would be arriving to head the investigation?'

'Well, yes, but I thought that —'

'No. You didn't think. You didn't think at all. If you had done, you wouldn't have abused your position.'

Winslow cleared his throat. 'With all due respect, Ma'am, as I say I was only getting things moving. I didn't do anything that you wouldn't have done yourself.'

'That's a matter of opinion, Sergeant, besides which, as you know all too well, it isn't the main issue here. How many men did you send up there?'

Winslow looked uncomfortable. 'I don't know. Six? Eight?'

'Eight? Jesus! What are you planning to do – challenge them to a football match?'

Winslow evaded her gaze. 'I, er ... well, it was just in case of trouble.'

Suddenly Farrington understood. 'Oh no,' she said, 'tell me it isn't true. You've gone up there mob-handed, haven't you, Sergeant?'

'Of course not!' Winslow snapped, but his denial was a little too vehement to be convincing.

'What were your orders?' she demanded. 'Put the fear of God into these people? Rattle their cage a bit? Am I getting warm?'

This time Winslow said nothing, merely stood and glowered like a suspect pulled in for questioning.

'You idiot,' Farrington muttered contemptuously, then beckoned Lockwood over.

'Frank, I want you to go up there, see if you can undo some of the harm Winslow's mob might have done. Get one of the local PCs to show you the way. I want you to be courteous and, if needs be, apologetic.' Raising her voice she said, 'When did you despatch your riot squad, Sergeant?'

Winslow scowled. 'About twenty minutes ago.'

'Right, get a move on then, Frank. You'll probably be too late, but you never know.'

'Shall I take the car, boss?'

'Whatever's quickest. I'll see you back at the local nick later.'

Lockwood nodded and hurried out. Farrington rounded on Winslow. 'And as for you—'

'Sir, we've found something!'

The shout came from outside. 'Later,' Farrington said, pointing at Winslow, then hurried to the tent flap in her oversized Wellingtons. After the warmth of the tent, the chill outside was like being doused with iced water. She shivered, hunching up her shoulders against the unrelenting rain.

A constable was waiting there, moving from foot to foot to keep warm. He looked surprised to see Farrington, but quickly composed himself when she said, 'What have you got, Constable?'

He drew a plastic evidence bag from beneath his waterproofs and held it out. Speaking more to Winslow who had appeared behind Farrington than to her, he said, 'I found 'em in those bushes over there, sir. I reckon they must have been what he used to cut off the lass's fingers.'

Rain tapped and dribbled on the evidence bag as though trying to get at the contents. Inside the bag, its blades smeared with blood and clots of human tissue, was a pair of shiny new secateurs.

15

Oonagh was woken by shouting.

Her head sprang from the pillow, her heart jumped in her chest. Her little room was pitch black, the darkness stifling; she found herself gulping for air, breathless as if she'd run a race. She felt confused, disorientated. All seemed silent now, and she wondered whether she'd imagined the shouting, whether it had just been part of an instantly forgotten dream. She was about to lower her head to the pillow again when she heard someone shout, 'You've got no right to do this!'

As though the cry had broken down some barrier, other sounds quickly followed. More raised voices, the words indistinguishable; people moving about outside the trailer.

Oonagh sat up and swung her feet out of the camp bed. 'Graeme?' she called, 'Linda?' There was no reply. She fumbled for the lamp beside her bed – a tulip bulb in a wooden base which shone through the stylised figure of a stained glass Japanese lady – and turned it on.

Instantly the light seemed to bring the sounds closer. Oonagh stood up, shivering with cold, and reached for a rust-coloured sweater which she dragged on over her Pixie and Dixie nightshirt. She pulled a pair of thick red socks over her feet, crossed the room and opened the door. Despite the sounds of a commotion outside, the trailer was quiet. She knocked on the door of her parents' room and when there was no reply opened it and looked inside.

The Tiffany lamp beside her parents' bed was turned on, illuminating an empty futon. Their pillows were rumpled and lopsided, and the duvet they slept beneath had been shoved back on both sides as though in haste. Oonagh went out into the narrow corridor which ran the length of the trailer. The corridor widened to a room at both ends – the living room cum dining room at the front end where the door was, a narrow kitchen at the back. In the middle were the two bedrooms and a tiny cubicle containing a shower and a toilet, these three rooms barely more than cabins enclosed by partition walls. 'Graeme! Linda!' she shouted again, though she knew now that the trailer was empty.

She went into the living room, the largest room in the trailer. Everything seemed normal: the plump settee beneath the window covered in brightly coloured cushions, the old rocking chair which Graeme had found in a skip and restored, the Indian tapestries adorning the walls, Graeme's acoustic guitar propped on its stand to prevent it from warping.

The only unusual thing here was that Oonagh could see the room at all. At this time of night it should have been as black as her bedroom. However, screened by the curtains, the window was a rectangle of light. Oonagh crossed to the settee and knelt on it, then ducked her head beneath the curtain and looked out.

The first thing that struck her was the amount of people milling around. It seemed that everyone but her was outside. Lights were on in many of the trailers, and doors open. The strongest light, however, came from the headlamps of cars that had pulled into the field and now stood facing the camp. All that could be seen of the cars themselves were their black outlines. They looked like predatory beasts behind the blazing white discs of their eyes.

The headlights gave the scene a bleached, stark look, like an old movie. Oonagh saw two groups of people, confronting each other. One group was made up of her friends and neighbours, all raggle-taggle, sleepy-eyed, half-dressed. This was the more openly aggressive of the two groups, the one making the most noise, the most indignant. Facing them was a group of perhaps half a dozen uniformed policemen, bulky and intimidating in their waterproofs. Oonagh saw Geoff, the wood-carver, remonstrating with one of the policemen, his thin hair plastered to his head, his beard dripping with rain. It was Geoff's voice she had heard earlier. He was shouting again now. 'You can't do this, not without a search warrant! You can't just barge into people's homes!'

The policeman was impassive, responding to Geoff's anger in a voice so low that Oonagh could only see his lips moving. Mike Jordan, who had tried to scare Tim off that morning, was standing at Geoff's shoulder – minus his shotgun this time, Oonagh noted. Mrs MacEvoy was standing in the open doorway of her trailer, wearing a dressing gown which she was holding across her vast bosom with one gnarled hand. Occasionally she would call something out in her reedy, smoke-scarred voice. 'Leave us alone!' or 'Why don't you go and catch some real criminals!' or 'Haven't you got anything better to do?'

Oonagh saw Graeme and Linda standing talking to Mrs Cantleigh and her daughter, Jewel. Usually the Cantleighs were jolly and rosy-cheeked, but tonight, like everyone else, they looked angry. Jewel, six feet tall and all of eighteen stone, just like her mother, shifted position slightly and Oonagh realised that she had her arm around someone's shoulder. She saw a bowed head of braided dreadlocks, lime green Doc Marten boots. It was Sara, her whole body heaving as she cried. Next moment the door to Sara's caravan – a battered old thing with brightly coloured flowers painted crudely on the side – swung open and two policemen came out, followed by Sara's boyfriend, whose real name was Spencer but whom everyone, even Sara, called Captain.

Captain was angrier than Oonagh had ever seen him. He was flapping his arms as though the policemen were stray dogs he was shooing from his home. Above the rain that was battering the trailer roof, Oonagh heard him shout, 'I hope you're satisfied, you fucking Nazis!'

One of the policemen swung round and raised a gloved index finger, obviously in warning. Captain, however, merely thrust up his middle finger in response and shouted, 'Fuck you!'

The policeman reached out for Captain's throat, and as Captain batted at the black-gloved hand and squirmed away, a number of his fellow travellers, people who'd been milling around aimlessly, suddenly peeled away from the throng and surged forward, roused to action by the flashpoint. Meanwhile a second policeman had joined the one who'd been arguing with Captain, and together the two of them took hold of Captain's waistcoat and hauled him from the step of his caravan so that he slithered and fell on the muddy ground. The policemen jumped on the roaring Captain, twisting his arms behind his back, just as the first of the travellers reached them. The violence had flared with shocking suddenness. Within seconds the simmering situation had degenerated into a melee of flailing limbs and struggling bodies, with those on the sidelines urging the combatants on like an over-excited crowd at a boxing match.

Oonagh watched it all through the window of the trailer, in shock and dismay. The violence was messy, confused, a splintered rush of images. She saw Mike Jordan lashing out with his boot at a policeman who was slithering on the ground, trying to shield his face with one arm; she saw a policeman's helmet fly off; saw Jake, Jewel's boyfriend, duck his blond head as a truncheon crashed down on his shoulder. She saw Sara wailing and shaking, screaming hysterically but ineffectually, 'Stop it! Stop it! Stop it!' Oonagh knew that Sara hated violence because of what her father had done to her as a child; she saw Linda put her arms round Sara and try to lead her away.

She'd lost sight of Graeme by this time, but suddenly she saw him, running after the two policemen who were carrying Captain between them like a large squirming fish towards the line of squad cars. One of the policemen had Captain in a head-lock and Oonagh heard Graeme shouting, 'For God's sake, let him go! You're strangling him!'

'Graeme!' Oonagh shouted as another policeman suddenly appeared behind her father and grabbed him in a head-lock too. Taken by surprise, Graeme lost his footing, his heels skidding away from him. Before he could recover, the policeman twisted his arms expertly behind his back and started to drag him towards the cars.

Oonagh ducked her head back into the room, jumped from the settee and ran for the door of the caravan, feeling as though the darkness inside the room was like treacle, dragging at her legs. When she opened the door, it was ripped from her grasp by the wind and slammed back against the side of the trailer. She wrestled with the door for a couple of seconds, then decided to leave it. Her father was more important than a few bits and pieces being blown around in the living room.

She turned her face into a driving rain propelled by a wind so fierce it felt as though ice-cold blades were slashing at her cheeks. Within seconds she was frozen, her nightshirt sticking to her exposed legs, her sweater saturated and heavy as chain mail. She saw Geoff the wood-carver lying on his front, one policeman sitting on his back and pressing his head into the mud whilst another knelt on his bucking legs and fumbled to lock his wrists together with handcuffs. If the travellers had banded together they could almost certainly have overwhelmed the officers, but Oonagh knew there was no way they could ultimately win simply by retaliation, and most of the others, after the initial flash of violence, seemed to have realised that too. A number of those who had waded in to help Captain were now hanging back, contenting themselves with protesting in colourful language about police brutality and jack-booted thugs.

For the moment, Oonagh was concerned only with the fate of her father. She ran towards the dazzling bank of headlights some forty yards from the camp. She could not see Graeme now. He had been dragged through the chain of light, into the darkness beyond. She had gone no more than twenty yards before she was exhausted, buffeted by the wind and stung by the rain, the mud sucking at her feet as if attempting to drag her down. Behind her she heard people shouting, dogs barking, but the sounds seemed distant now, like something happening on the other side of consciousness. The headlights of the police cars seemed to crackle with rain, to shatter slowly and endlessly. She heard the growl of an engine, and suddenly one of the pairs of headlights was receding, getting smaller. And then the headlights changed from glaring white eyes to funnels of light illuminating their own tyre-tracks as the car swung round.

'Graeme!' Oonagh shouted, trying to put on an extra spurt of speed. All that happened was that the mud sucked her sock from her left foot, causing her to sprawl forwards on to her knees. Her hands slapped into a puddle, and mud oozed between her fingers. She looked up, and in the back seat of the car one of a number of bobbing heads turned towards her and she saw light flash on a pair of round-lensed spectacles.

'Graeme!' she screamed again, but the car was lurching across the field towards the gates now. Oonagh tried to stand, but the rain and the wind and the mud sapped her energy, and she could only flounder like a beetle in a puddle. They'd had trouble with the police before, but never on this scale, never to the extent where people had actually been arrested. The car was through the gates now, gaining speed as it climbed the firmer track towards the town. Oonagh's vision blurred as tears of shock and injustice and rage spilled from her eyes and mixed with the rain on her cheeks.

16

Jackie was swimming with a talking dolphin when the telephone rang.

'Aren't you going to answer it?' the dolphin said.

Jackie didn't want to – the sea was so luxurious – but she said, 'Where is it?'

All at once the dolphin had become Peterson. He was pointing straight up. 'It's there, above the surface.'

He's only saying that because he wants to look up my skirt, thought Jackie, and woke up.

It was pitch black, and the ringing phone sounded insistent, urgent, shockingly loud in the silent apartment. She'd gone to bed at eleven and had no idea what time it was now; she felt as though she'd been asleep for a while. She had a cold, jerky feeling in her stomach. She'd always hated calls late at night, could never equate them with anything but bad news. Feeling as though part of her was still floating in the dream, she jumped out of bed and blundered across the room to where she knew the door was.

She had never been a tidy person, and her feet encountered all manner of unseen obstacles on the journey. Some item of clothing – tights, she guessed – caught round her ankle and she had to pause to shake them off; she stubbed her toe on an ashtray, hearing the dull clunk of it upending, accompanied by the patter of spilling cigarette butts. And all the time the phone rang on and on, the sound drilling into her head, increasing her anxiety with each double-peal. It was never this loud in the daytime, she thought. It was a wonder it didn't wake up the whole apartment block.

Eventually she reached the door, her hand groping for the nearby light switch. She found it, and at once was blind for a different reason, the light piercing her eyes like electric shocks to her retinas. She stumbled into the hallway, shielding her eyes with her hands, misjudged the distance to the telephone table and walked right into it. It began to topple, the telephone, pad and beaker of (mostly empty) pens sliding across its surface. The pens clattered to the floor like a game of pick-up sticks, but she managed to grab both phone and table and steady them.

Picking up the receiver, she snapped, 'Hello.'

The sound at the other end made her think of the sea rushing at the shore; it seemed like a link to her dream, or a mockery of it.

As though it were part of this sound, like the voice a wave might have, she heard her name, the name she had reverted back to after her divorce, the words stretched, lingered over: 'Jackieee Fosssterrr.'

Jackie felt scared and angry at the same time. If it hadn't been God-knew what hour in the morning, the anger would have come out on top, but just at the moment, in her silent apartment, she could do without this kind of weirdness.

'Look,' she said, 'I don't need this shit. Do you mind telling me who you are?'

More rushing sounds. Then the voice again, hissing, sibilant. 'Ask Chloe who I am. She knows me. Soon you will too.'

The line went dead.

It wasn't until Jackie put the phone down that her hands started shaking. She clenched them together, furious. Whoever that wacko was, he had no right to make her feel like this, no right to violate her privacy. His voice on the telephone made her feel as if he had forced part of himself into her apartment. And what did he mean – ask Chloe who I am? The only Chloe she knew was Eric's daughter. What did she have to do with this?

Jackie went back into her bedroom, breathing hard, stepping over clothes and towels that were strewn across the floor. She looked at the time on her clock radio – 1:03. It was too late to disturb Eric now, but she'd ring the police. She was damned if she was going to be persecuted in her own home.

She went back into the hallway and picked up the phone. She still caught occasional faint whiffs of the rotten meat she'd been sent, despite the fact that she'd dumped the parcel, wrapped in several carrier bags, in one of the communal dustbins, and had been keeping the kitchen door closed and the window open. She caught a putrid waft now. It suddenly occurred to her to wonder whether the person who'd sent the meat was also the person who'd called her. She didn't like that idea one bit. She rang the police and told them what had happened.

Then she rang Gareth, her latest, and asked him to come round. He was not happy to be woken up at one o'clock in the morning, and it was only when she impressed upon him how scared she was that he grudgingly relented. She couldn't help thinking that Eric's reaction would have been very different. He'd have been concerned and sympathetic and would have offered to come round before she could even request it. She squashed the thought almost before it could grow legs and walk. No point pondering on such things.

Her desire for something to steady her nerves was greater than the distaste she felt every time she opened the kitchen door and was ambushed by the lingering waft of decaying meat, so she went into the kitchen and poured herself a glass of red wine. She was carrying it back to her room, taking small sips, when the telephone rang again. She was right beside it, and she jumped, slopping wine on to her hand. 'Shit,' she said, and looked at the phone for a moment, wondering whether she should leave it. Then she snatched it up and barked, 'What?'

'Mrs Foster?' said a female voice, trying not to sound taken aback.

'Ms.'

'Sorry?'

'It's Ms Foster, or Miss if you like. I'm not married.'

'Oh,' said the voice. There was a slight pause as if the caller had been knocked off her stride, then she said, 'I'm Detective Sergeant Danby, Miss Foster. I'm ringing in connection to your complaint earlier about a nuisance call.'

Jackie put her glass on the table and sat down. 'Oh yes?'

'Are you sure the caller referred to Chloe Knight, Miss Foster? Did he actually use her full name?'

'No, he just said, "Ask Chloe. She'll know who I am". Or something along those lines. It was my assumption that he meant Chloe Knight, my ex-husband's daughter. She's the only Chloe I know.'

'I see. And could you just tell me again what were the exact words that he used?'

Jackie frowned. 'Can I ask why you're suddenly taking such an interest in this?'

'I'm afraid I can't really divulge that at this stage, Miss Foster. But please bear with me. It is very important.'

'Well, he said, "Ask Chloe, she'll know who I am", and then he said something like, "Soon you will too".'

'And that's all he said?'
'Yes. Then he put the phone down.'
'I see. Just to confirm, Miss Foster, could you tell me your ex-husband's daughter's address?'
'Well, she lives with my ex-husband in Bramwell in West Yorkshire. The address is ... um ... oh, my mind's gone blank. Hang on, I've got it written down in my little book here.' She riffled through the address book beside the phone until she had found it, then read it out to the waiting policewoman.
'Thank you, Miss Foster. Do you think you'd be able to recognise this man's voice if you heard it again?'
'Well, I'm not sure. He was sort of whispering, and there was a funny noise on the line.'
'What sort of noise?'
'I don't know ... a rushing noise. It made me think of the sea, but it was probably just interference. He might even have been crumpling a paper bag by the mouthpiece, for all I know.'
'I see. I won't keep you much longer, Miss Foster. I expect you're eager to get off to bed,' said DS Danby as if suggesting that was what she should do. 'Would it be convenient to call on you tomorrow morning?'
'Well, I go to work in the mornings.'
'What time?'
'I usually leave here about eight-fifteen.'
'Shall we say seven-thirty then? Would that be convenient?'
'Yes, I suppose so. But could you just tell me what all this is about? I'm not going to get a wink of sleep until I know.'
'I'm sorry, Miss Foster, I'm afraid I can't. I'll see you in the morning. Goodbye.'
She put the phone down before Jackie could reply.
Something's happened, Jackie thought. Something serious. Although she had held a perfectly coherent conversation with the policewoman, her mind now felt in such turmoil she could barely think straight. She picked up the phone again and punched in Eric's number. The lateness of the hour didn't seem so important now.
The phone rang three times and then was picked up. A voice said, 'Hello.'
Immediately Jackie felt dread fill her belly. There was something in that voice, some quality that was more than dullness or exhaustion, that seemed to confirm that something was dreadfully wrong.
'Eric?' she said. 'Eric, what's happened?'
There was a pause, then Eric said, 'Is that you, Jackie?'
'Yes it is. Please tell me what's happened, Eric.'

She heard him on the other end of the phone, a series of quick breaths as if he was trying to compose himself. Then bluntly, as though it was the only way he could tell her, he said, 'Chloe's dead.'

Jackie's whole body seemed to freeze, to become nerveless; she almost dropped the phone. For a few moments she couldn't draw breath to speak. Her lungs felt as though they had set like concrete. Then a vestige of sensation came back, and she gasped, 'Oh no, Eric. Oh no, I don't believe it. What ... what happened?'

Eric told her, his voice an odd, zombie-like murmur. When he came to the bit about the police coming to the house to break the news, his voice wound down to almost nothing.

Jackie started crying. She had barely known Chloe, but she knew how much Eric and Tim had loved her. 'Oh, Eric, I'm so sorry, I'm so sorry,' she sobbed. 'I don't know what to say. It's just so awful.'

Eric didn't respond. Silence filled the earpiece. Jackie wanted to offer him comfort, but what comfort could you offer someone whose daughter had just been murdered? Should she simply say goodbye and let him go, or would that seem heartless, as if she was abandoning him to his grieving?

In the end, barely knowing what she was saying, she blurted, 'He phoned me tonight, you know.'

'Who?' said Eric, responding automatically. He didn't sound as if he really cared.

'The man who ... who killed Chloe.' It wasn't until she said it that she realised it might very well be true. 'My God, Eric, he rang me up. He spoke to me. He knows who I am!'

She realised she was getting hysterical, and forced herself to calm down. But she was shaking uncontrollably, and could still feel panic jumping inside her like a bad drug, making her want to do crazy things. She didn't think she had ever felt so vulnerable. Every sound, every shadow suddenly seemed full of menace.

'What do you mean, Jackie?' Eric was more animated now, though cold, interrogative. 'Jackie, what do you mean?'

She told him about the phone call, about ringing the police, and about them ringing her back. The panic was there in her voice, her words shrill, racing. 'Oh God, Eric, what's happening? Who's doing this?'

'Someone who knows us both,' said Eric, his voice lifeless, like a machine. 'Someone who's got a grudge against us both. Someone who hates us.'

'But who?' wailed Jackie. 'There isn't anyone like that. *Is* there, Eric? Can you think of anyone?'

The pause was excruciatingly long this time – minutes long, it seemed – as if Eric was waiting for Jackie to come to her own conclusions. Then he gave a shuddering sigh as if remembering something he'd rather forget.

'No,' he said bleakly.

17

Farrington had torn Winslow apart in his own office and was now feeling a little depressed. The incident at the travellers' camp had been a bloody shambles, a fact which she had brought forcefully to the sergeant's attention. Now, alone, she was wondering what the bollocking had really achieved beyond a fleeting opportunity to vent her spleen. Was it worth making an enemy of Winslow just to see him squirm for five minutes? Was it worth aggravating her headache to such an extent that it seemed to be cleaving her skull?

She looked around the office she'd appropriated, the decor of which was in keeping with her dour mood. Pale green walls, grey filing cabinet, grey carpet. The only splash of colour was the photograph on the desk of Winslow and his family. In it, Winslow was grinning fixedly, an expression in sharp contrast to the one he'd worn when he'd slunk out of the office a few minutes earlier. His wife was plump and mumsy-looking, his sons gangly and toothy, self-conscious with their slicked-down hair and tightly knotted ties. The photographer seemed to have decided to make a feature of their pimples, which were red and shiny as cherry tomatoes. Farrington reached out and turned the photograph on to its face.

Outside the office she could hear voices raised in anger, as the travellers who'd been arrested, plus some who hadn't but had come along to offer support to their friends and neighbours, protested vociferously about the offences they'd been charged with: affray, obstruction, assault, resisting arrest. Farrington had made it quite clear to Winslow that not only was that little lot his responsibility, but also that the slightest hint of it impeding her investigation would bring her down on him like a ton of bricks. Apparently there was some reporter from the local rag out there too, lapping up the dirt; God only knew where he had come by his information so quickly. Well, let Winslow deal with him as well. She had more important things to think about.

'Who is it?' she called in response to a knock on the door.

The door opened and Lockwood's head appeared. 'It's me, boss. Is it safe to come in?'

Farrington smiled weakly and beckoned him inside. By the time Lockwood had arrived at the camp it had all been over bar the shouting. The violence leading to the arrests had apparently been sparked by a couple of officers – without warrants – barging into the caravan of a young couple, and then not only refusing to leave when the girl asked for some privacy to get dressed, but making lewd remarks and leering at her naked body like a couple of dirty old men.

The officers, of course, told a different story. They claimed that the girl was behaving suspiciously, leading them to suspect that her request for privacy might in fact have been a ploy to hide drugs. They admitted keeping an eye on the girl as she dressed, but denied that they had made any obscene remarks, or indeed any remarks that could be construed as such.

Whichever of these versions was true, it couldn't be denied that the girl had left the caravan in tears and that the officers had then, without proper authority, searched the place from top to bottom before brawling in public with the male occupant and causing a near-riot. However you looked at the incident, it was one that was guaranteed to cause the shit to start flying. Farrington was determined that when it did, none of it would stick to her. There were plenty of people in the force all too eager to view a cock-up like this as directly attributable to her gender.

'If you've come to tell me that Winslow's out there bad-mouthing me, I don't want to know,' she said.

'I haven't.' Lockwood crossed the room and tossed a sheaf of notes in a polythene envelope on to the desk in front of her.

'What's this?' Farrington said.

'It's a fingerprint report. Well, a couple of fingerprint reports actually. Makes for very interesting reading.'

Farrington glanced from the boxed smudges on the paper to Lockwood's deadpan face. He was thirty-one – brown eyes with bags underneath, big nose that looked as though it had been broken once or twice, thick-lipped mouth that grooved deep black lines in his cheeks when he smiled.

'Tell me,' she said. 'I've got a headache, Frank, and I'm tired. Explain what we've got here in words of one syllable.'

Lockwood smiled. 'This morning Chloe Knight's mother, Annette, reported a break-in at the flower shop she owns in the town. Apparently nothing was taken, but it seems the intruder was still on the premises, hiding in the toilet, when she arrived to open up at 8:30. Anyway, he got away without anyone seeing him, but the point is a fingerprint man was sent down there, but all he could come up with were the prints of Annette Knight and her assistant, a Mrs Mary Kemp. Now, here's where it gets interesting.' Lockwood opened the envelope and took out the top sheet of paper. 'These are Annette Knight's prints, taken for elimination purposes. And these—' he indicated a second sheet of paper that had been lying beneath the first '—are the prints we've managed to lift from the secateurs found close to Chloe Knight's body.'

Farrington looked from one sheet to the other. The prints on the second sheet were smudged and incomplete, but recognisable.

'They're the same,' she said.

Lockwood nodded.

Farrington looked up. 'So either Annette Knight killed her own daughter, then very carelessly dropped a vital piece of evidence at the scene of the crime, or whoever broke in to her shop this morning stole the secateurs and used them in the killing, then dropped them, either to implicate Annette Knight or to make it clear that he was the same man who had broken into the shop.' She pushed the reports around with her hands. 'Right, well, I think we can safely rule out the possibility that this was a random killing, which is no bad thing. It should make our man easier to catch.'

'Or woman,' said Lockwood.

'Or woman,' Farrington agreed.

'One other thing, boss. Mrs Knight didn't report the secateurs missing.'

'You think that's significant?'

'Well, only in so far as that if the secateurs had gone missing during the break-in, wouldn't Mrs Knight have reported them?'

Farrington pursed her lips. 'Not necessarily. Something like that, it's easy to overlook.'

'In a flower shop?'

'Well, maybe she didn't realise they were missing until later. Would you have made a point of ringing the police just to tell them you couldn't find your secateurs?'

Lockwood thought about it. 'No, probably not. But what if she staged the break-in to make it appear that someone else had been in and stolen the secateurs?'

'Then she'd have made a point of reporting their disappearance to the police, wouldn't she? Besides, that doesn't make sense. If she was that crafty she wouldn't have dumped the things at the murder scene with her fingerprints all over them.'

'Maybe she wasn't thinking straight. Maybe she was so horrified by what she'd done ...'

Farrington shook her head. 'That doesn't ring true either. You'd have to be a pretty cool customer to cut off all ten of your daughter's fingers like that. And remember, Frank, the fingers were taken away. You wouldn't take away the fingers and dump the weapon, would you?'

Lockwood frowned, his dark, bushy eyebrows bristling like a hairy knuckle. 'No, I suppose not,' he said.

'You don't seem too happy about it.'

'It would just have made life easier, that's all, to have thought of the girl's mother as a suspect.'

'We still can. Maybe we're overlooking something. Maybe the two crimes are unconnected and the secateurs slipped out of Annette Knight's pocket as she was leaving the scene.' She leaned back, stretched, looked at the clock. 'You know what this means, don't you, Frank?'

'What, boss?'

'It means we're going to have to talk to Annette Knight now, which, if she is innocent, is an awful imposition to make on a grieving family.'

Lockwood pulled a face. 'This job can be a real bugger sometimes, boss.'

'Tell me about it,' said Farrington.

18

If there was a hell, it couldn't be any worse than this. Annette's grief was more than just an emotion, it was physical pain, it was the most agonising cancer imaginable. It seemed as if there was a bottomless pit inside her, full of poison; no matter how much she cried and screamed, no matter how much poison flowed out of her, the pit would always be full. She clutched to her chest a framed photograph that Chloe had had taken at school just eight weeks before, and she told Eric breathlessly, hysterically, that she didn't see how she could go on, that she wished she was dead too. Eric hugged her and kissed her and tried to comfort her, but it didn't make any difference. Annette felt as though her grief might actually be powerful enough to drive her mad, felt as though her mind would be crushed by the terrible black weight of it.

But if grief was her pain, then memories were the torture implements that inflicted it. The happier the memories were, the more they felt like knives twisting in her gut. She thought back to when she had been pregnant only fifteen short years ago. She had been horribly sick the first few months, and had then developed a craving for tomato sandwiches. Later, she and Eric had watched with wonder as her swollen stomach rippled like a wave machine. On the night of Chloe's birth it had been snowing lightly; Eric had had a cold and had sneezed all the way to hospital. Annette had spent seventeen hours in excruciating agony, bringing her daughter into the world. When her little head appeared, Eric had started crying, had hugged and hugged Annette, whispering, 'Clever girl, clever girl.'

Annette remembered pushing Chloe in her buggy with the squeaky wheel, as Tim, in his reins, toddled alongside. She had nursed Chloe through childhood illnesses, had wiped her nose, put plasters on her scraped knees and elbows, cuddled her until she fell asleep. She remembered the joy of watching Chloe excitedly unwrapping presents on Christmas morning, remembered scouring the streets one rainy day for her favourite panda which she had dropped out of the car window. Miraculously the panda had been found in a gutter and taken home to dry in the oven. Bedraggled and grey though it was now, Chloe had kept the panda all these years, had perched it on the headboard above her bed, where it sat like a tiny guardian angel.

My little girl, Annette thought. My baby. All those years. All that love. And for what? So that her life could be ended by some evil pervert, who had used her to satisfy his own twisted desires before throwing her away like a piece of rubbish.

Tim had staggered up to bed, shell-shocked, some time earlier. His departure had not left her and Eric alone, however. People had been coming and going like wraiths all evening, despite the lateness of the hour. There had been the police, of course, who had stayed for a while and then drifted away; Valerie Jones, who had lived across the road with her husband even longer than the Knights had been here, and who had looked after Tim on the night Chloe was born; other neighbours, who arrived to offer shocked condolences once news had filtered through. All left making the same well-meant but inadequate offer: 'If there's anything we can do.' Margaret Prentiss from number 16 brought a silver crucifix on a chain 'to provide comfort', and a half-empty bottle of Diazepam. Annette responded furiously to the crucifix, shrieking, 'I don't want this! How can you believe in a God that lets something like this happen?'

Eric had seen to everybody, up and down answering the door, making tea, fielding questions, as though on automatic pilot. At one point the phone had rung, after which Eric had told Annette that whoever had killed Chloe had just rung Jackie and threatened her too, which meant that Chloe's killer must have been the same person who had sent Jackie the rotten meat and who had rung him at school earlier that day with the same ominous message that Jackie had also received. Eric had told Annette about that call when Tim had been upstairs doing his homework. The two of them had agreed then that it was best not to tell Tim what had been happening for the time being, because there seemed no point in worrying him. Now, though, Eric said that he would give Tim the whole story in the morning, impress upon him the need to be on his guard. Annette listened to her husband's ramblings, but couldn't quite take in all that he was telling her. Her only clear thought, which she knew she should be ashamed of, but couldn't bring herself to be, was: I wish he'd killed Jackie instead of Chloe.

The visitors had come in a steady trickle until almost 2 a.m., but had finally petered out. The last one had left over half an hour ago now, but Eric and Annette were still up, clinging to each other on the settee like survivors of a sea tragedy, she exhausted from crying, he almost emotionless from shock. Their eyes were open, but they stared at nothing; neither had spoken for perhaps ten minutes, not since Annette had whispered, 'She was only a little girl. Why did it have to happen to my little girl?' They might have sat that way, locked together but alone, all night, if the doorbell hadn't suddenly chimed again, a ludicrously cheery *bing-bong*. Eric got up to answer it.

Annette didn't even seem to notice he'd gone.

When he reappeared, she didn't bother looking up. Whoever had been at the door, it wasn't important; nothing was important any more. It was only when a woman's voice said gently, 'Mrs Knight,' that she raised her head. There was a woman standing there, slim and business-like, quietly attractive, dressed in an overcoat whose shoulders were speckled with rain. 'Mrs Knight, I'm Detective Inspector Farrington and this is Detective Sergeant Lockwood. We're investigating your daughter's murder. I'm very sorry to intrude at this hour, but I'm afraid that we have to ask you some vital questions.'

Annette barely moved her head in response, so Eric waved them to seats and offered them tea, which they declined. The woman, the Inspector, leaned forward a little in her seat, her overcoat rustling.

'Mrs Knight,' she said, 'I understand you had a break-in at your shop this morning?'

Annette blinked at her. With all that had happened in the last few hours she had forgotten about the break-in. It seemed such a trivial thing now.

'So what?' she said, her voice husky and exhausted. 'My daughter's dead. I couldn't care less about the shop.'

The Inspector gave a tight little smile. 'I quite understand your attitude, Mrs Knight, but this line of questioning isn't entirely pointless, I assure you.'

Annette nodded. 'Yes it is. Everything's pointless now. Nothing matters any more.'

Farrington glanced at Lockwood. 'I know how difficult this is for you—' she began.

'How can you know?' Annette snapped suddenly, her eyes flashing as if she wanted to hit out and saw the DI as a viable target. 'Have you ever had a daughter murdered?'

'No I haven't. I don't have any children.'

'Don't tell me you understand then. Because you don't. You don't know anything.'

Annette's anger drained from her as quickly as it had come. The woman was looking at her, not unkindly but neither did she seem especially moved by Annette's outburst. Her eyes were the grey of storm clouds. She had a small mole on the left side of her throat.

'You're probably right, Mrs Knight,' she said levelly, 'but that doesn't mean I don't feel anything. Like everyone on this case, I feel compassion for you and your family, hatred towards the killer, anger and disgust at the crime. We all want to catch whoever killed your daughter, Mrs Knight. We all want him – or her – punished for what they did.'

There was a silence. Annette looked away from the woman's grey eyes. Eric asked, 'What's the break-in got to do with Chloe, Inspector?'

'It's possible the two crimes may be connected,' said Lockwood.

Eric jerked as if he'd suddenly woken up. 'You mean you think the person who killed Chloe was the same person who broke into the shop, as well as making the phone calls?'

Farrington frowned. 'Phone calls?'

'Yes, I told the policeman earlier, but my ex-wife's had one as well now.' He told Farrington about the rotten meat, the message, the phone-calls.

Farrington listened intently, then looked at Lockwood, who raised his eyebrows.

'So was it?' Eric said.

'I'm sorry?'

'The same person?'

'We don't know at this stage, Mr Knight. We're merely exploring various avenues of inquiry.'

'But you must have some reason for asking.'

'As I say, we're simply making inquiries. Now, if you could just bear with me, Mr Knight, while I ask Mrs Knight a few questions. I'm sure you appreciate that the quicker we can complete our initial inquiries, the more chance we have of catching your daughter's killer.'

Eric nodded distractedly and slumped back in his seat.

'Now, Mrs Knight, I understand that you told the attending officers at this morning's break-in that nothing had been taken?'

Annette looked momentarily blank, as if she didn't know what the Inspector was talking about. Then she mumbled, 'Yes ... I ... That ... that's right.'

'And is that still your claim?'

'Um.' Annette rubbed a hand across her face. 'I think so.'

'Well, there *were* the secateurs,' said Eric.

Immediately Lockwood stiffened. Both Eric and Annette noticed it. Annette's eyes widened, and she whispered, 'Oh no. Don't say my secateurs were used to ... no.'

The Inspector leaned forward. 'Used to what, Mrs Knight? Neither the Sergeant nor I have even mentioned your secateurs.'

'We saw how the Sergeant reacted when I mentioned them, though,' said Eric.

Annette put her hands to the side of her head as if there was a pain building there, a horrified expression on her face. 'Oh God, oh God,' she whispered.

'So your secateurs *did* go missing?' the Inspector said firmly, as if to yank Annette back from her inner thoughts.

Annette's eyes focused on the Inspector once again. 'Yes, I ... I realised later that I couldn't find them.'

'Why didn't you report their disappearance to the police?' Lockwood asked.

'I ... well ... it didn't seem important. I wasn't even sure they'd been stolen. I thought I might have left them at the market.' She looked hard at the Inspector, and as if bracing herself said, '*Is* that what happened? *Were* my secateurs used to kill Chloe?'

There was a heavy silence. The Inspector looked about to reply, but before she could, Annette slumped back on the settee, drew a deep shuddering breath and whispered, 'What the hell did he do to my daughter?'

'Could you describe your secateurs please, Mrs Knight?' Farrington asked.

Annette stared at her blankly, her eyes red from crying, set in dark hollows. She looked exhausted, even ill. In little more than a mumble, she said, 'They were brand-new. They had red handles.'

'Are you going to tell us what this is all about, Inspector?' Eric said.

The policewoman looked at him steadily. 'A pair of secateurs were found close to Chloe's body, Mr Knight. They had your wife's fingerprints on them.'

There was a brief silence, then Eric's face contorted from blankness to a horrified disbelief. 'My God,' he said, 'so what are you telling us? You ... you surely can't suspect Annette of killing her own daughter? What about the phone calls? Are you going to ignore those?'

The Inspector's face, like her voice, gave nothing away. 'We don't suspect anyone, Mr Knight. We're simply trying to make sense of the evidence presented to us.' She kept her eyes fixed on Eric for a long moment, and then focused her attention once more on Annette.

'For the sake of our inquiries, Mrs Knight, I'd be grateful if you could take us over your movements since yesterday morning.'

Annette responded dully, numbed by the implications of the policewoman's questioning. The only time she had been alone during the day was the forty-five minutes or so between leaving the shop and Tim getting home from school. Unfortunately, this was also the estimated time that Chloe had been killed, though Farrington made no comment on the fact.

When she had finished listening to Annette, Farrington asked Eric to account for *his* movements that day.

'Why?' he said. 'Do you think I'm guilty as well?' His voice was calm enough, but high spots of colour on his cheekbones showed how angry he was at how they, especially Annette, were being treated.

'As I've already explained, Mr Knight,' said the Inspector, 'this is just routine questioning. If nothing else, we have to ask these questions for elimination purposes.'

Eric was silent for a moment, then he shook his head and mumbled, 'I don't know how you people can live with yourselves, I really don't.' Farrington made no response; Lockwood raised his eyebrows and shrugged. Eric sighed and reeled off an inventory of his comings and goings that day.

When he had done so, Farrington asked, 'Are you a popular teacher at the school, Mr Knight?'

Eric looked surprised by the question. 'I ... I don't know. I wouldn't say I was *un*popular. I helped the pupils set up their own representative body, so that their voice could be heard. Because of that I think they think I'm on their side.'

'And are you?'

'Yes, on the whole.'

'How would you describe your teaching methods? Do you rule with a rod of iron? Are you easy-going?'

'I'd say I'm fairly easy-going, though I like my pupils to work.'

'And are the children you teach frightened of you, respectful, disrespectful, friendly, unruly?'

Eric licked his lips. 'Well ... I suppose I respect them and they give me respect in return. I get on well with my pupils. I think I'm fairly approachable.'

'So you wouldn't say you had a temper? You've never shouted at a pupil? Hit one even?'

Eric frowned. 'Of course I haven't hit one. I'd be out of a job if I had. What are you getting at, Inspector?'

Farrington's face was expressionless. 'I'm simply trying to build up a picture, Mr Knight. What I was actually wondering was whether it's likely you've made any enemies in your time at the school. An old pupil, perhaps, who might want to get back at you for some perceived grievance?'

Eric shook his head. 'I don't think so.'

The policewoman shifted in her seat, smoothing her skirt over her thighs. 'How long have you been teaching at the school, Mr Knight?'

'As long as we've been here,' said Eric. 'It'd be what? Nearly fifteen years.'

'Fifteen years. It's a long time. Are you telling me that in all that time you've never had a problem pupil? Never been threatened?'

'Not seriously. I've had little run-ins from time to time with children *and* their parents. All teachers do. But nothing to merit this.'

The Inspector looked thoughtful. 'Is there anyone else you know who might have a grudge against you and your ex-wife? Anyone who might want to cause you harm? Someone from your past, say?'

Eric glanced at Annette, but she barely even responded to him. 'No,' he said, 'I can't think of anyone.'

'How about you, Mrs Knight? Can you think of anyone?'

Annette slowly shook her head. 'No,' she murmured.

The Inspector sighed. Eric said, 'I can't really believe that Chloe was killed by someone who thought we'd done them wrong some time in the past. I mean, no one in their right mind ...' His voice trailed off as he realised what he was saying.

'People kill for all sorts of reasons, Mr Knight,' said the Inspector, 'some of them extraordinarily banal.' She looked at Lockwood, then stood. 'Well, I think we've outstayed our welcome for now, though I'd be grateful if you would allow us to have a quick look in your daughter's room before we go.'

'Why?' asked Eric.

'Just routine procedure, Mr Knight. You never know what we might find that could be useful.'

'Our son's asleep upstairs.'

'We'll be very quiet.'

Eric looked at Annette as though for guidance, but she was staring into the fire, apparently mesmerised by the red flickering of the artificial flames.

'All right,' he said, albeit reluctantly.

The Inspector offered him a quick, professional smile. 'Thank you, Mr Knight. I promise we won't disturb anything.' She walked to the stairs, followed by Lockwood.

Eric pointed out where Chloe's room was, then went to sit back in the lounge with Annette, who was still staring into the fire. From above came the creak of floorboards, the soft thump of movement. Ten minutes later the two officers reappeared. The Inspector walked into the lounge, buttoning her coat.

'Thank you both,' she said. 'I'm so sorry to have had to put you through this at such a terrible time.'

'Did you find anything?' asked Eric.

'Nothing useful, I'm afraid. Would it be possible, do you think, Mrs Knight, to have a set of keys for your flower shop? I'd like to get a full forensic team down there in the morning.'

Annette looked up as though roused from a daydream. 'Um ... yes. They're in the kitchen. On the hook.'

'Also a photograph of Chloe would be useful. The more up to date the better.' She eyed the framed photograph that Annette had been clutching for most of the interview.

'We've got some copies of that,' said Eric. 'We had a few done to give to relatives and ...' His voice petered out and he looked momentarily anguished, then he said, 'I'll get you one.'

'And there is one other thing,' said the Inspector a minute later, pocketing the photograph and the keys that Eric had handed to her, 'I'll need someone to formally identify your daughter's body in the morning. I'm afraid it won't be a pleasant experience, but it needn't necessarily be either of you if you don't feel up to it. Any other relative would be acceptable.'

'It's all right, I'll do it,' said Eric.

'Fine. Well, if you could be at the station by nine a.m., Mr Knight, I'll get someone to take you over there.'

The two police officers said goodnight to Annette and moved into the hallway, Eric hovering behind them. At the front door Farrington said quietly, 'I probably don't need to tell you, Mr Knight, that in light of all that has happened you and your family should take very special care until this murderer is caught. Try not to go anywhere where you're going to be alone.'

'What about my ex-wife?' said Eric. 'She lives on her own.'

'Is there anyone she can stay with? Friends? Relatives?'

'I'm not sure. Her mother lives in Tewkesbury, so if Jackie was to stay with her she'd have to take time off work. Mind you, I don't think that's likely. The two of them don't really get on very well.'

'Well, we'll sort something out. Try not to worry about it, Mr Knight. You just concentrate on looking after your own family. And if you receive any more threats or strange phone calls, inform us immediately. In fact, if you do get any more calls, we'll put a tracer on your phone, see if we can find out where the bastard's calling from. Oh, and if you see anything the slightest bit suspicious, let us know. It's better to be safe than sorry.'

'Suspicious? Such as what?' said Eric.

'Oh ... a stranger hanging about, signs that someone's been in the garden, literally anything at all that doesn't seem quite right. And perhaps you'd be good enough to draw up a list of people who knew Chloe well: school friends, boyfriends, that kind of thing, and also a list of people who both you and your ex-wife know. I appreciate that this is asking a great deal, but it would be useful to have that information as soon as possible.' She gave a quick smile. 'Well, thank you again for your time, Mr Knight. I promise we'll do our utmost to catch your daughter's killer.'

She opened the door, admitting a flurry of wind and rain that had been waiting in ambush. Turning up the collars of their coats, the two police officers bent their heads and hurried up the path to their car. Eric closed the door after them and was immediately seized by a fit of trembling. Pressing his forehead against the wood of the door, he closed his eyes and waited for it to pass.

19

For a few seconds after he woke up, Tim's mind remained blissfully empty. But then the memories came swarming back, and with them the terrible ache of loss that already felt as if it would grind inside him for ever.

He crawled out of bed, unable to believe his life had changed so irrevocably in the space of a few hours. Was it really only yesterday morning when he had walked to school with Oonagh, when they had laughed at each other's jokes, when he had wondered what it would be like to touch her wheat-coloured hair, to kiss the soft pink bow of her lips? All that seemed as though it had happened to someone else now, someone in another place, another time. Everything that had seemed important to him yesterday, or that had given him pleasure – his artwork, his computer, his burgeoning relationship with Oonagh – now seemed trivial and pointless.

He dragged on jeans and a grey sweatshirt, then tiptoed downstairs, feeling it somehow important that he not disturb the quiet of the house. The thought of bumping into his mum and dad, of being faced with their grief, filled him with dread as he pushed open the door into the lounge. Last night the intensity of Mum's grief had been almost as awful as the actual news about Chloe. Tim had never really realised before just how devastating and final death was, how the loss of someone you loved could make you feel so utterly terrible that you couldn't even imagine carrying on yourself.

The room was empty, the only sign that anything was out of the ordinary being the fact that Chloe's photograph was on the settee, the ashtray was full of dead roll-ups, and there was a plastic bottle of sleeping pills sitting on top of the TV. Tim snatched up the pills, and was relieved to discover that the tube was at least half-full. However he didn't think it a good idea to have pills lying around within reach of someone as wretched as his mum had been last night. He took them into the kitchen, intending to hide them at the back of a cupboard somewhere.

The sink was crowded with mugs. On the hob stood the cooking pot containing Chloe's portion of now undoubtedly dried-up pork casserole. Moving slowly, feeling brittle as old toast, Tim put away the pills, then fixed himself a couple of Weetabix and sat munching his way through them, persevering even though the cereal sat in his belly like wet cement. Afterwards he scraped the pork casserole into a plastic Sainsbury's bag and dropped it into the flip-top bin by the back door. He was washing up the tea things and staring unseeingly out of the kitchen window at the trees beyond the expanse of lawn at the back of the house when he heard the clack of the letter box, the soft slithering thump of post landing on the doormat.

He winced, hoping that the sound had not woken his parents, who he assumed were asleep upstairs. He felt oddly shocked by the sheer ordinariness of post being delivered, perhaps because it brought home to him the fact that in the eyes of the world Chloe's death was unimportant, that elsewhere life went on regardless. Standing with his hands immersed in hot soapy water, he suddenly began to cry, sobs lurching through him. It felt as if he was regurgitating glass. When he was a little kid, not all that long ago, crying used to make him feel better, but now it didn't; now it just made him feel sick and empty.

Eventually the tears stopped. Tim dried his hands and went upstairs. He didn't know what to do with himself. He didn't feel like drawing. Indeed, the picture of Judge Dredd on his easel had sickened him when he'd looked at it twenty minutes earlier. After what had happened to Chloe, the violence that seemed implicit in the figure's body armour and stance, and the way its lips curled in an arrogant snarl, seemed moronic and depressing.

He didn't feel like turning on his computer either, or reading, or listening to music, or watching TV. And he couldn't imagine going back to school. Just at the moment, being surrounded by people for whom life was going on as normal seemed like something he couldn't ever bear to face.

Maybe he'd just go back to bed, try to drown himself in a sea of sleep. He was walking along the landing towards his room when he heard a noise, coming from behind Chloe's door. He froze, then his heart gave a sudden leap. Despite everything, he thought: She's back! The police were wrong! It wasn't Chloe they found, after all!

The door was slightly ajar. Pushing it open, Tim said 'Chlo—'

Then his voice abruptly cut off. His mum was sitting on Chloe's bed, hunched over as though she had stomach cramps, rocking gently back and forth.

Tim was shocked by how awful she looked, her face red and puffy, her eyes bloodshot through crying and sleeplessness, sunk into sockets that looked bruised. In her hands she held Chloe's old panda, the head floppy, the fur threadbare, yellowish stuffing poking through burst seams like clots of fungus. She was holding the panda like a tiny baby, stroking it, caressing it, left hand cradling its head.

The sound Tim had heard had been his mother weeping. It had thrown him because it hadn't sounded like crying; it had sounded like bedsprings creaking gently, little high-pitched whimpers.

'Mum,' Tim said. He took a couple of hesitant steps into the room. He opened his mouth, then closed it again. He'd been about to say, 'Are you all right?' before realising what a ridiculous question it was. Like asking someone who'd been mashed by a juggernaut if they were hurt. He crossed the room and lowered himself very gently on to the bed beside her.

She hardly responded to him, just kept on stroking the panda, as if to draw some essence of her dead daughter from its tatty little body. Tim looked around at Chloe's things, and felt something solid, like a stone, rise and stick in his throat. Her walls were covered with pictures of Stefan Edberg; the new poster she'd brought home from school two days before commanded pride of place on her wardrobe door. It had always been Chloe's ambition to go to Wimbledon, see Edberg in the flesh. Once she had written to Jimmy Savile, asking him to fix it for her to meet the tennis star, but she'd never received a reply.

He looked over at the dressing table beside the curtained window, where a naked Troll with a shock of pink hair grinned and spread its arms above a hairbrush with strands of Chloe's dark hair still clinging to the bristles. Next to that was a pile of plastic bangles in primary colours, a few cosmetics that Mum allowed her to wear at weekends, a tall jar containing seashells that he and Chloe had collected one drizzly day in Robin Hood's Bay.

His gaze drifted to the photographs stuck higgledy-piggledy between the frame and the glass of the mirror, and he felt tears filling his eyes again. Here was a grinning Chloe dressed as an Oxo cube for a fancy dress party; here was Chloe at the age of five, playing Miss Muffet in a school play; here were Chloe and Tanya last summer, sitting at a table in the sun beneath a big umbrella, sipping milk shakes; here was Chloe as a toddler in a pram, being pushed along some seafront somewhere, back in the days when Dad still had long hair and Mum had only one chin.

The photographs blurred, ran together, as the tears began to trickle from his eyes and run down his nose until they were forming dark coins on the thighs of his jeans. He felt a hand on his back and turned his head to see his mother, her features little more than dark smudges in his swimming vision.

'Why did it have to happen, Tim?' she said in a tiny voice. 'Chloe never hurt anyone.'

'I don't know, Mum,' Tim sobbed, twisting to hug her. 'I just don't know.'

They clung together until they heard the front door opening and closing, the sound of slow, trudging footsteps coming upstairs. Annette let go of Tim, sniffed and called out, 'Eric?' in a wavering voice. The footsteps paused and then resumed. Next moment Eric appeared in the doorway, looking haggard and stoop-shouldered. Blue and purple veins stood out at the sides of his temples.

He looked slowly round his daughter's room as if this was the last time he might see it and he wanted to commit it to memory.

'How was she?' Annette said with a kind of eager desperation. 'How did she look?'

Tim suddenly realised that his dad must have been to identify Chloe's body. His stomach turned over.

'Peaceful,' Eric said flatly.

He did not sound convincing.

20

Until the doctor had come and given her the pills, Felicity hadn't been able to stop crying. The memory of what she had seen when she had opened the stable door had been like a horrible picture in her head, a picture that had made her feel sick and frightened, and which wouldn't go away. Sometimes the picture had grown so big and vivid that it seemed to fill her so that she could hardly breathe. It was then that she had what the doctor had called her 'panic attacks'. She screamed and tore at her scalp and thrashed about because the urge to make the picture go away became overwhelming.

But then she had taken the pills, and quickly had begun to feel much better. The panic subsided and she felt calmer, even sleepy. The memory was still there, but it seemed more distant, like a fierce dog that had been locked in another room. You could still hear the dog barking, but you knew it couldn't bite you.

She had spent much of yesterday asleep – deep, dreamless naps, like sinking in feathers. And every time she had woken up, part of her had felt as though it was still asleep – the part that hurt, that brought the image of what she had seen in the stable into sharp focus. On a couple of occasions, the hard edges and the bad feelings had begun to creep back in again, and Mummy had had to give her more of the pills to make them go away. Felicity wished she could take the pills for ever. If she could, then nothing would seem bad ever again.

It was now Wednesday, and she had just surfaced slowly from what seemed like the longest, deepest sleep she had ever had. A weak sun was poking in through her curtains, laying a soft creamy light on her bookshelves full of Mallory Towers and Famous Five and the Black Stallion. The first thing Felicity saw when she sat up was the beautiful, hand-carved rocking horse Mummy had bought her last year. Daddy had kicked up a fuss about that because the rocking horse cost £890, and he said it wasn't as if she would even get any use out of it because the man at the County Show who had carved it had said it shouldn't be sat on by anyone older than eight. But Mummy had bought it for her anyway because Felicity had said she would love it even if she couldn't ride it. She had called the rocking horse Dancer, and when Mummy bought her a proper pony six months later, she had called that Dancer too.

Dancer. An image punched into her mind: blood, and purple insides coming out of Dancer's tummy, and his smashed-in head with his eyes sticking right out, glaring at her.

Her lungs seemed to tighten, and she jumped out of bed and ran out of the room. Barefoot, she ran along the upper landing, screaming, 'Mummy! Mummy! Mummy!' She ran into Mummy and Daddy's bedroom, which was empty. She ran back out on to the landing and then down to the wide staircase as if the horrible image of Dancer had escaped from her head and was coming after her.

She was nearly at the bottom of the stairs when Mummy came out of the breakfast room dressed in a cream jacket and skirt. Felicity ran up to her, threw her arms around her and buried her face between her breasts. 'Mummy,' she wailed, 'make the awful pictures go away.'

'Sh, darling, sh. Come with me and we'll get your pills.'

Just the thought of taking a pill made Felicity feel calmer. She clung to her mother as the two of them made their way to the kitchen. From here you could see Dancer's stable, but Felicity kept her eyes averted from it. Mummy got her a pill, and Felicity gulped it down with a glass of water.

'Now,' Mummy said, 'will you come and have some breakfast?'

'I'm not hungry,' Felicity said in a small voice.

'But you must eat, darling.'

'I'm not hungry,' Felicity repeated stubbornly.

Juliette sighed. 'Very well. But at least come and sit in the breakfast room with us. Then if you want to nibble something, you can.'

Felicity followed her mother out of the kitchen and through the house towards the breakfast room. They were crossing the hallway when the telephone rang.

Juliette sighed. 'You go on, darling. I'll join you in a moment.'

Felicity went into the breakfast room. The scene was just the same as yesterday: Daddy reading his *Times* and sipping coffee, Samuel buttering a piece of croissant.

Samuel eyed her warily. 'Are you all right, Lissy?' he said.

Just knowing that she had the pill inside her made Felicity feel calmer than she had when she'd woken up. 'Yes,' she said.

Daddy lowered his newspaper and looked at her. 'Joining us for breakfast are you, young lady?'

'Yes, Daddy.'

'Jolly good. You'll soon feel better after you've had something to eat.'

He went back to his newspaper and Samuel went back to eating croissants. Felicity sat stiffly on her chair, gripping the edge of the table with her fingertips, willing the pill to start working. This time yesterday she'd been finishing her breakfast too, and looking forward to saying good morning to Dancer before going to school. She closed her eyes - blood, purple innards, smashed skull. She opened them again at once, but still felt panic building up in her once more, her breath coming too quickly.

And then Mummy came back into the room, and whether it was her presence or the pill that was beginning to take effect, Felicity immediately felt a little calmer. She noticed that Mummy looked ... odd, her face mildly troubled, her movements somehow careful.

'Andrew, darling,' she said.

Daddy lowered his newspaper once again. 'Yes?'

'I've just had rather a peculiar phone call.'

'Peculiar? In what way?' Daddy said, frowning.

'Well, there was a man - at least I assume it was a man. He was hissing and whispering, and the line was poor, so it was something of a struggle to hear what he was saying. He told me to ask you about your dark secret.'

'My dark secret? Whatever are you talking about, darling?'

'He said to ask you what you did to him thirty years ago.'

'Thirty ye—'

Suddenly Daddy stopped talking, and a startled expression crossed his face. His cheeks, which were usually red and flushed, now turned a bright shade of purple. 'My God,' he spluttered.

Mummy frowned. 'What on earth's going on, Andrew?'

Daddy looked at her, his eyes bulging. 'Nothing,' he barked. 'Nothing at all.'

'Nonsense. I can tell by your reaction that you know exactly what the caller was referring to.'

'No, I don't. Or at least ... it was something that happened a long, long time ago, when I was a boy. It's not important.'

'Well, if it's not important, why don't you share it with us? I'm sure we're all terribly intrigued.'

Samuel was nodding, but Felicity looked scared. The expression on her father's face was frightening her. Daddy stood up. Scowling, he said, 'It's nothing, I tell you.' He looked as though he was about to storm from the room, but then something seemed to occur to him. 'This caller, did he give a name by any chance?'

'Well ... yes, that was another peculiar thing,' Mummy said. 'When I asked him who he was, he said – and I hope I heard this right – he said just to tell you that it was Mr Bad Face.'

21

Sitting in the tiny office at the back of the Portakabin, DI Farrington was munching the smoked turkey and salad in granary she had ordered from the deli across the road and hoping she would be left alone for the next ten minutes. From beyond the thin partition wall came the bustle of movement, the buzz of voices and the intermittent bleating of telephones.

The Portakabin, set up as a temporary incident room for Farrington's team, had been delivered around three in the morning, and positioned to receive optimum attention from shoppers, office workers, passers-by. It sat on an oval of grass studded with benches halfway up Bramwell's high street, sheltered beneath the century-old library, and flanked by a pub called The Crown on one side and a hairdressing salon called Snippets on the other. Annette Knight's flower shop, Bloomers, was across the road and three hundred yards along, though from here it was just out of sight due to the gentle curve of the high street.

Almost as soon as the town began to fill up, people were milling around the sandwich boards set up on the wet grass outside the

Portakabin door, their indignation at this ugly intrusion in their pretty town slowly turning to shock as they read the posters plastered to the boards. MURDER the posters announced in red block capitals, above a photocopied photograph of a smiling Chloe Knight. Beneath were rudimentary details about the killing and an appeal for information. Thus far the response had been heartening, though as yet enthusiasm to help had far outweighed solid evidence. Farrington's immediate team, consisting of three Detective Sergeants – including Lockwood – and a dozen Detective Constables, had logged names and addresses, collated information and followed up a number of leads, albeit without result.

Farrington swallowed the last of her sandwich and licked mustard from her fingers, wiping them on a grease-free corner of the sandwich bag before binning it. As she lifted a mug of cooling tea to her lips she thought about the murdered girl's parents. In the car on the way back to the station after seeing them last night, she had asked Lockwood for his opinions on the interview and on the parents themselves. He had shrugged, puffed out his cheeks.

'I don't think either of them did it. I don't even think the secateurs were used to implicate the mother. I think they were used as a kind of ... taunt, or planted by the killer to let us know that he was the one who broke into the flower shop. It would follow the pattern set by the phone calls and the rotten meat.'

'You realise all that could have been engineered by Eric Knight?' she had said.

He had given her a sidelong look. 'You don't really believe that, do you, boss?'

'No,' she had admitted.

She had had a further chat with Eric that morning, before accompanying him to the morgue to identify his daughter's body. Ostensibly this had been to gather more specific details about Chloe herself in the hope that something would lead them to her killer. From what Eric had told her, however, Chloe seemed a singularly unremarkable girl ... or perhaps not so much unremarkable as normal. She was happy at home and school, she had no major problems of which her parents were aware, and she had not fallen in with the wrong crowd or taken to staying out late or questioning her parents' authority. If Eric was to be believed, Chloe had been an ideal daughter, squeaky clean even. As requested, he had provided Farrington with a list of Chloe's friends and acquaintances, and of the people who knew both him and Jackie (though most of these, he had told her, neither of them had seen for years, and many of the names were without up to date addresses). Although Chloe's school year would be addressed en masse and her classmates questioned as a matter of course, the names on Eric's list would receive priority attention.

Farrington finished her tea in two gulps, suddenly realising she'd taken longer than the ten minutes for lunch she'd allotted herself. Although the well-oiled machinery of investigation was running smoothly all around her, and although she'd been without sleep for longer than she cared to remember, she couldn't help feeling a little guilty. The forty-eight hours following a murder were always the most crucial. Malingering was an unforgivable sin, which this would become if she sat here for much longer.

As she was rounding her desk there was a knock on her office door, and Lockwood entered. The sound of the newspaper that he tossed on to her desk was like a hand slapping a cheek.

'Local rag,' he said distastefully. 'Just came out. You won't like it, I'm afraid, boss.'

Farrington picked up the paper, flipping it open along its fold. A bold black headline assailed her: NEW AGE TRAVELLERS MURDER LINK. Accompanying the article was a copy of the same photograph that Eric had provided Farrington with last night: Chloe, her face shining with joyful life, wearing a black headband and the same grey school jumper that was now sealed in a bag in a pathology lab, shredded by the killer's knife and drenched with blood.

The sandwich she had eaten burned in her throat like bile as she read the story. Although not exactly inaccurate it was a highly subjective and covertly inflammatory piece, crammed with barely veiled insinuations, calculating sensationalism.

When she had finished she rolled the paper into a cudgel and slammed it down on the desk. 'This is all we need,' she said. Though her voice was not raised, the words were disgorged like pellets of venom. She tossed the paper on to the desk, where it unfurled, and rubbed a hand across her forehead.

'I can't believe the sheer crass stupidity of the press sometimes. Don't they realise what kind of trouble an article like this can lead to?'

'Course they realise,' Lockwood said. 'That's why they do it. Inflame public opinion, start a few fights, create more sensational news and sell more papers.'

'Get someone to go and talk to the editor of this rag,' said Farrington, 'read him the Riot Act. I'd do it myself if I wasn't snowed under.'

Lockwood grinned. 'Oh, for a totalitarian regime, eh, boss?'

'Don't baffle me with long words, Frank. I've got another headache coming on.'

22

It was a couple of days after the incident in the school playing fields before James Keeve felt able to cope with going back to work. Marjory had been alarmed at the state of him when he had crashed in through the front door on Monday night. She had coaxed him into the lounge and sat him on the settee, where, unable to stop shivering, he had jabbered out his story.

However, in the warm, light, sane surroundings of his home, James had been unable to convey the sheer terror of his experience. It had been like trying to describe a nightmare in which the sense of threat vastly outweighed the actual events. Despite the state he was in, he knew that his recounting of what had happened made his response to the figure sound like a wild over-reaction. Marjory, though, was as understanding and supportive as ever. 'If you really think this man was dangerous, you ought to inform the police,' she said.

'And tell them what?' James had responded, frustratedly, bitterly.

'That he chased you, that he tried to attack you.'

'But he didn't, that's the point. All he did was stand up and come towards me. He didn't even run. But it was the *way* he did it. There was something ... horrible about him, unnatural. But how can I tell the police that? They'd just think I was going off my trolley again.'

'You're not off your trolley and you never have been,' Marjory said firmly. She stroked his balding head and kissed him. 'Don't blame yourself for how you sometimes get, James. It's not your fault, it's not a weakness. It's like blaming yourself for having, I don't know - eczema or asthma.'

'It's an illness, you mean,' he replied. 'I'm mentally ill.'

'Oh, now you're starting to feel sorry for yourself,' she said, though not unkindly. 'If you carry on like that, I'm afraid I may have to bite your nose.'

She had been trying to make him smile, but James had been unable to oblige. He had been far too unsettled by the incident. And there had been something else too, something that nagged at him, something obvious but which his mind was hiding away, refusing to acknowledge. He had slept little that night, seeing that grey figure sliding upright against the chain-link fence and raising its hairless white head each time he closed his eyes.

Once, around dawn, he had drifted from a fitful doze to see the figure standing silently at the end of his bed, watching him and Marjory sleep. He had jerked fully awake, sat up and cried out, but when he looked properly the figure had gone.

It wasn't until Sally walked into the kitchen in her school uniform later that morning expecting Tizer to be there to greet her that James realised the dog had not come home last night. He felt a knot tighten in his gut and he pushed away the toast he had only managed to nibble. How could he have forgotten about Tizer? Was he losing it completely this time? He gripped the edge of the kitchen table as the walls seemed to close in around him. It had only been Sally's shrill, indignant voice that had hauled him back.

'Daddy, can you hear me?'

'What? Uh ... yes, of course I can, darling.'

'You looked all funny ... you looked *scared*.'

'Did I? Well, I ... I'm not. I mean, I'm fine. What is there to be scared of?'

He tried to smile, though his muscles felt stiff, unresponsive. Sally shrugged and said, 'Daddy, I can't find Tizer. He isn't *anywhere*.'

'Have you looked in the garden, darling?' Marjory said.

'Yes, he's not out there.'

'Well, maybe he's gone to visit his girlfriend.'

'He wouldn't do that without saying hello to me first.'

James glanced at Marjory. He felt as he always did during one of his bad times – sick, scared, shivery inside, constantly on the verge of panic without quite knowing why. He saw immediately that Marjory was fully aware of Tizer's non-appearance, and was grateful that she had been sensitive enough not to burden him with questions or accusations. He swallowed, licked his lips, and then, unable to keep the quaver out of his voice, he said, 'Tell her the truth, Marje. She's bound to find out sooner or later.'

Marjory sighed, and then said calmly, as if it was nothing to worry about, 'Tizer didn't come home last night, darling.'

Sally looked at her mother, puzzled, and then at James. 'But he always comes home,' she said.

'Well, he didn't last night, I'm afraid.'

'Where is he then?'

'We don't know.'

For the first time a look of alarm crossed Sally's face. Again James tried to smile, failed. 'You see, I ... I took Tizer for a walk ...' he began before his throat closed up and he couldn't say any more.

Quickly Marjory said, 'Daddy took Tizer for a walk, but Tizer ran off into the fog and Daddy couldn't find him. He looked everywhere – didn't you, James?' James nodded mutely. 'And he shouted and shouted until he was hoarse, but Tizer didn't come back. In the end Daddy had to come home without him.'

Sally was breathing heavily. She looked on the verge of tears. 'So where's Tizer now?' she asked again.

'We don't know, darling,' Marjory repeated patiently.

'But it's not foggy now! Tizer should be here! Why hasn't he come home?' Her voice was shrill, uncomprehending.

'He's probably just got a bit lost. Perhaps he'll turn up later,' Marjory said.

'Can I wait here for him until he comes back?'

'No, darling, you'd better go to school.'

'But I want to see Tizer. I want to see him *now*.' She burst into tears.

James felt like bursting into tears himself. He swallowed and said a little desperately, 'Don't cry, darling, Tizer'll come back. And if he doesn't I'll get you a new dog, a puppy.'

'I don't want a new dog. I only want Tizer,' Sally wailed.

'Hey, hey, come on,' Marjory said, crossing the kitchen to hug her daughter.

That had been twenty-four hours ago and Tizer still hadn't come back. Eventually Marjory had cajoled Sally into going to school, but James had been in no fit state to go to work. All day yesterday he had sat at home, trying to keep his mind empty, trying to keep the jitters at bay. Unable to face his daughter when she returned from school, he sneaked upstairs to bed, thinking that if she came in with the intention of talking about Tizer he would pretend to be asleep.

As he crossed the room to close the curtains, he glanced down into the front garden and saw the white-headed figure in the blue boiler suit standing on the lawn below the window. The figure was in the process of raising its head to reveal its un-right face. James jumped back into the room, almost wrenching the curtain from its runner, an inarticulate yelp of shock leaping from his lips.

He stood, his heart pounding coldly for several seconds, before venturing to the window again. He peeked down into the garden and saw that the figure had gone.

Later, when Sally had gone to bed, he ventured downstairs to see Marjory. He spent a couple of hours talking out his fears with her, purging himself. She had done her best to convince him that the figure he had seen – standing at the end of the bed, standing on the lawn looking up at the window – existed only in his imagination.

'What about what happened last night?' he said, his voice hoarse, weak, quivery. 'Was that just my imagination too?'

'I don't know, James,' she said gently. 'I wasn't there. Only you can answer that. But if you're sure it was real, if you're certain you saw what you say you saw, then I believe you.'

She had soothed him, calmed him, pulled things into perspective. He knew that sometimes he over-reacted to situations, allowed things to swell out of all proportion. He knew it and yet he couldn't do a thing about it, not by himself. He needed Marjory to be his voice of reason, to set him back on the straight and narrow.

He didn't run away from Sally's disappointment at breakfast that morning. Though his stomach began to flutter as he heard her feet thumping the stairs, he stayed where he was at the table, trying to make himself look as relaxed as he could, trying to smile.

Although he knew it wasn't in her nature, he nevertheless expected black, accusatory looks from her, expected her to blame him for Tizer's disappearance. He felt his fluttering stomach tighten as she entered the room and looked around, her face filled first with hope, and then despondency.

'I'm afraid he still hasn't come back, sweetheart,' he made himself say.

She sighed, her shoulders slumping, her satchel slipping to the floor. 'Will he ever come back, Daddy?' she asked him.

'I don't know. Maybe.'

'But where *is* he? What's he been doing? Has he been getting enough to eat, do you think?'

She came over to him and he opened his arms to her. He half-expected her suddenly to stop, scowl, say, 'You were the one who lost him. I'm never going to hug you ever again,' but she fell into his embrace, allowing him to squeeze her tightly.

'Maybe somebody found him and took him in. Maybe they've been feeding him and looking after him.'

'Who?' she said in a small voice.

'I don't know who. Somebody. Probably somebody nearby.'

She was silent. He knew she was thinking about this. Finally she said, 'But what if he likes the new people more than us? What if he wants to stay there?'

'He won't,' said James reassuringly.

'But what if he *does*?' Her voice cracked, threatening tears.

James kissed the top of her head. 'Tizer knows you love him. He knows you'd be missing him. And he loves you. Dogs aren't stupid, are they?'

A moment of reflection, then she shook her head, prepared to be convinced.

'I'm sure the people who are looking after him are trying to find out who Tizer belongs to. They've probably told the police and everything.'

'I hope so,' she said in a small voice.

'Try to look on the bright side,' he told her, and thought: Oh yes, great advice, James. Why don't you try taking it yourself once in a while?

There was another short silence, and then she said, 'It wasn't your fault that Tizer got lost, Daddy.'

'What?' he said, surprised.

'You couldn't help it that he ran away. He's a silly dog. He should have known better.'

James felt uncomfortable. I was the one who ran away, he thought. He wanted to confess this to her, but he knew she wouldn't understand. Instead he said, 'I'm sure Tizer didn't mean to run away. He probably just got lost in the fog.'

'But you didn't, did you?' she said. 'You found your way home.'

He remembered his headlong flight, remembered how he had crashed in through the front door and collapsed sobbing. Oh yes, he thought, I found my way home, all right.

Several minutes later, sitting at the breakfast table, concentratedly peeling the shell off the top of a boiled egg, Sally asked, 'If Tizer doesn't come back, Daddy, can we get a puppy just like him?'

'We can get one exactly like him,' James said.

'And can I call him Tizer, too?'

James wasn't sure whether she said 'Tizer too' or 'Tizer two'. However he smiled and nodded. 'Whatever you like,' he said.

He worked as a credit controller for a pharmaceutical firm which was situated on an industrial estate just outside Tewkesbury. Though the surroundings were a bit grim, the big open-plan office in which he worked was light and airy with a salmon-coloured carpet and lots of pot plants which were lovingly tended by Julie, one of the secretaries.

He got in half an hour early on Wednesday morning, still feeling a little jittery, but determined to be strong, determined to make Marjory proud of him. Dumping his briefcase beside his desk, he looked ruefully at the pile of stuff in his in-tray. He began to flip through it, prioritising, making a list of the calls he would have to make. He hoped there wouldn't be too many irate customers to deal with today. Most of the time he could handle it by making the customer believe he was on their side, but just occasionally, when he was feeling particularly brittle, the irritation of unpaid suppliers or customers who had been waiting too long for goods got to him.

He was trying to sort out an outstanding account with the medical centre that he, Marjory and Sally actually used when Jo Hines walked into the office. Jo had the desk next to his, mainly because their jobs sometimes overlapped. It was her task to, as she put it, 'seek out new accounts, a new customer base, to boldly go where no girl has gone before'. Jo was a bubbly brunette in her early thirties who travelled up and down the country at weekends attending *Star Trek* conventions. She wore a small gold Starfleet insignia pin on her lapel and had two photographs on her desk: one of herself and Patrick Stewart with their arms around each other, laughing into the camera (this had been taken, James knew, by her husband, Michael, at a convention in Chicago), and one of their three cats, Data, Geordie and Spock. Jo was currently pregnant, and had told James that if the baby was a boy he was going to be named James Tiberius and if it was a girl she was going to be Beverley Deanna.

'Hi, James,' she said, sounding as though she was genuinely delighted to see him, 'how are you?'

'Oh, so-so,' he replied vaguely, and indicated the cardboard box she was carrying. 'What have you got there?'

More than anything he had asked the question to change the subject, but she surprised him by placing the box on his desk.

'Parcel,' she said, 'for you. It was in the lobby downstairs, so I thought I'd bring it up.'

'For me,' he said, surprised. 'Who's it from?'

'Oh damn, I forgot to install my X-ray vision today. Hey, I've got a great idea. Why don't you open it and find out?'

He couldn't help but smile. Jo's good humour was infectious. He turned the box round, looking for a sender's address, and even lifted it up and looked underneath.

'It's quite heavy,' he said.

'Tell me about it.'

He began to pick at a corner of tape with a blunt fingernail. 'Whoever sealed this must have used a whole reel of packing tape. It'll take me an age to get into it.'

Jo opened a drawer in her desk and took out a pair of scissors. 'Try these,' she said, handing them over.

'Thank you.' James used one blade of the scissors like a knife, slicing the tape down the centre groove where the two flaps met. He then sliced along the outer edges of the box until he was able to raise the tape-encrusted flaps.

The instant he did so Jo recoiled, holding her nose. 'Phwarrr,' she exclaimed, 'what a stench!'

James shoved himself back from his desk, the castors of his chair squealing over the carpet. He thought he was going to throw up and clapped a hand over his mouth. The smell rising from the box was so awful it was beyond description. He had never smelt anything like it before. It filled the whole room, closed over his face like sweaty, stinking hands.

Though the box was open, he couldn't yet see what it was that smelled so bad. All he could see were strips of shredded paper used as packing.

Jo gagged and muttered something that James didn't catch. She staggered across to the big windows lining the back of the room and began to open them as wide as she could, one after another.

Other people in the office were taking notice now, pulling faces, placing hands or handkerchiefs over their noses, flapping at the air. Simon Hughes, the office clown, said loudly and nasally, 'If you're planning on offering around pieces of that brie, James, I think I'll pass, thanks all the same.'

Jo turned from the window where she had been gulping at fresh air. 'My God, James, what's *in* that box?' she said.

James had got up from his chair and was standing behind it now, staring at the box as if he thought whatever was in there would leap out at him. He turned to look at Jo, and then noticed that everyone else in the office was staring at him. He grimaced, managing to look both sickened and embarrassed, looking as though he wanted the floor to open and swallow him up. 'I ... I don't know,' he muttered.

'Then find out, man!' declared John Peacock, a tall, thin man with a domed forehead and a stern expression.

'How?' said James in a small, lost voice.

'Use my ruler,' said Jo. 'It's in the top left-hand drawer of my desk. Just ... just don't give it back to me afterwards.'

James grimaced his thanks and clumped across to Jo's desk. He felt clumsy, horribly aware of all the eyes upon him, as he opened the drawer and rummaged for the ruler. He found it, snatched it up, approached his own desk, extended the ruler towards the open box.

Cautiously he used the ruler to push aside the nest of shredded paper. The first thing he saw was a glazed but somehow glaring eye surrounded by black and white fur. His stomach turned cold and began to melt into the hollows of his legs as he revealed bared teeth, a blood-flecked muzzle. Then he saw a ragged edge of wound, blood, black things crawling ... He dropped the ruler with a clatter on the desk, felt the room spinning away from him.

Hands clamped on his shoulders, stopped him from falling. Jo's voice, sounding as though it was echoing down a hollow tube, said, 'What is it, James? What's in there?'

'It's Tizer,' he said, though the word emerged as less than a whisper.

'It's what, James? I didn't hear you.'

'It's Tizer,' he repeated, his voice audible this time, though strained. 'Or rather ...' A bubble of something – disbelief, disgust – lodged in his throat and he had to make a burping, sniggering, gulping sound to rid himself of it.

He heard the puzzlement in Jo's voice. 'Tizer? The soft drink, you mean? I don't under—'

'Tizer!' he all but shrieked at her. 'It's my dog, Tizer. He's cut off his head! He's sent me Tizer's head!'

23

Oonagh was torn from sleep, terrified and confused. Someone was pounding on the side of the trailer, the clanging din competing with her crashing heart. For a moment she was literally rigid with terror, fingers splayed, eyes wide open and glaring into the darkness. The din went on, the trailer rocking and lurching as though pummelled by giant hailstones.

Then it stopped. The trailer creaked once more and came to rest. Oonagh lay panting and shaking, trying to make sense of what was going on. She was so disorientated, and the silence now so absolute, that she could almost have believed the pounding had been part of some particularly vivid nightmare, a reaction to last night's events.

It had been Jewel Cantleigh who had picked her up from the mud and taken her back to the cosy little caravan she shared with Jake and her mother and their sandy-haired mongrel, Pooch. Oonagh had been glad to find Linda there, attempting to comfort a still-weeping Sara. Jake was slumped groggily over a table whilst Isobel Cantleigh, Jewel's mother, bathed a purple lump on his forehead that was like an extra bulging eyeball with a red slit of pupil. Jewel insisted Oonagh have a shower whilst she made herbal tea for everyone, but Oonagh could not seem to get warm, no matter how long she stood under the thin jets of hot water.

Later, swaddled in Jewel's voluminous dressing gown, she sat and listened to the adults angrily, incredulously, dissecting the night's events. Occasionally other neighbours called round to see if they were okay and to talk about what had happened.

Graeme and the rest of the men had started drifting back after a few hours, bedraggled and battle-scarred. The travellers would have moved on immediately then if the police hadn't ordered them to stick around. Neither Oonagh nor the rest of the half-dozen or so children in the group had been to school that day, and none of the adults had been to town; they'd stayed together, closed ranks and licked their wounds.

Around mid-day the police had been back, though only three of them this time, all plain-clothed, like the sergeant who had arrived at the tail-end of last night's trouble and tried to calm everyone down. Oonagh had not spoken to them, but Graeme had, and when Linda asked him what they were like he said they'd been polite, even apologetic.

It wasn't until then that the travellers had actually found out why the police had come in such numbers last night. At first they'd assumed it was to look for drugs, but now they knew it was because a girl had been murdered in the woods. The police didn't tell them who the girl was or anything else about the killing, however. Although they resented being regarded as automatic suspects, Graeme – ever reasonable – had said he could understand the police's attitude in a way, that the group's being there was simply a case of bad timing.

By nine that evening Oonagh was nodding to sleep on the sofa. Her father scooping her up and carrying her to bed felt like a portion of a dream. Oddly it was in that semi-conscious state that she thought of Tim for the first time that day. Because the travellers would stay together now until the police allowed them to go, whereupon they would up sticks and move as far away as possible, it seemed likely that she would never see him again, would never even have the chance to say goodbye. It was a shame. She had liked him. She had liked him a lot. She fell asleep thinking of his smile and wondering if there was any way she could get his address.

Now, a couple of hours later, she was lying perfectly still in the darkness, the echoes of the clanging blows that had woken her seeming to shiver through her body. Next door she heard her parents moving about, the sleepy murmur of Linda's voice. And underneath that she now realised she could hear another sound, like lots of people shouting all at once, though so distantly that their voices seemed wordless.

Still feeling delicate, she slid out of bed and switched on the lamp. Surely the police hadn't come back to cause more trouble, not after what had happened last night? She wrapped herself in Jewel's dressing gown, which she hadn't got around to giving back yet, deriving a little comfort from the soft perfume of apple-scented soap and patchouli oil that always emanated from Jewel's clothes and skin. Then, hitching up the trailing ends of the gown as though it was a wedding dress she was trying to keep free of mud, she padded through to her parents' bedroom.

Graeme was already up, standing barefoot and bare-chested in jeans in the middle of the floor, in the process of pulling a T-shirt over his head. Linda's head jerked up when she walked in, as if she had been fearfully half-expecting someone else. She was sitting up on the futon, pillows bunched behind her back, knees drawn up, red mane of curls an unruly tangle.

'A noise woke me up,' Oonagh said.

'Us too, sweetheart. Graeme's going to see what's going on.'

'Is it the police again?' Oonagh asked.

'I don't know why it should be.' Graeme dragged boots over his bare feet and hastily laced them up. 'Wait here, you two. I won't be long.'

'Be careful, Graeme.'

'Yeah, don't get arrested again,' said Oonagh.

Graeme looped his wire-framed spectacles over his ears, gave a vague smile, then left the room, pulling the door closed behind him. Oonagh and Linda both felt the trailer creak as he clomped up the corridor to the main room, and then give a slight lurch as he jumped off the step and down on to the grass outside.

For several long minutes Oonagh and Linda sat huddled together on the futon. Then suddenly there came a sound which made them both jump.

'That was a shotgun!' Linda cried.

Oonagh scrambled to her feet. 'I'm going to see what's going on.'

'You're not going out there,' Linda said.

'I'm going to look out of the window in the main room.'

Linda threw the duvet aside. 'All right, I'm coming with you. But don't turn any lights on. We don't want to draw attention to ourselves.'

Taking the lead, Linda opened the bedroom door. The two of them peeked out like children spooked by ghost stories, then crept along the narrow landing towards the main room. The creaking of the trailer all around them seemed far louder than it ever did in the daytime. They had reached the entrance to the main room, groping along in the dark, when the trailer gave a sudden lurch and the door that led outside eased open with a furtive click.

The two of them froze, Oonagh instinctively clutching her mother round the waist. They watched, wide-eyed, as a dark figure entered the trailer. Oonagh saw the black bulb of its head turning towards them. She was not sure whether the breathing she could hear was the intruder's or her own.

Then light flooded her eyes, blinding her. Before she could see she heard a voice. 'For God's sake, you two, you made me jump. What were you doing, creeping around in the dark?'

The glare slowly fading, Oonagh squinted at Graeme standing in the doorway. Beside her she felt Linda sag as though she'd been punctured.

'Graeme,' Linda said, half-relieved, half-angry, 'thank God.'

Graeme had opened the cupboard beneath the sink and was rooting about in there. 'Where's the hosepipe?' he asked.

Only now did Oonagh notice how grimy and sweaty he was, how his clothes reeked of smoke. 'What's happening, Graeme?'

Graeme had found the hosepipe now. Connecting one end to the tap, he started to uncoil it.

'A group of thugs from the town, about twenty of them. They came up here, tanked up, and started running riot, banging on the trailers, accusing us of killing that girl. Some of the guys went out to talk to them, but the gang just set about them with rocks and lumps of wood. Geoff's hurt really bad; Captain's taken him to hospital.'

'Oh God,' said Linda, raking a hand through her hair.

'Why do you stink of smoke?' asked Oonagh.

'The bastards set fire to Rob's VW. It's burning pretty fiercely. We're trying to put it out before it reaches the petrol tank.'

He was talking breathlessly, unravelling the hosepipe, trailing it out through the door. Now he sprang back up the steps and twisted the tap full on.

'We heard a shotgun being fired,' said Linda.

'That was Mike Jordan. He fired one over their heads and they all ran off. Probably saved Geoff's life.'

'Is Rob all right?' asked Oonagh anxiously. She liked Rob. He was an earnest blond-haired man in his early twenties who wanted to be a writer. He had bought the VW auto-sleeper second-hand for two hundred pounds and had been travelling with the group for about nine months.

'Physically he's fine, but he's really upset. Everything he owns is in that van.'

Graeme jumped down off the steps, grabbing the hosepipe before the water could reach the end and set it thrashing like a snake. Oonagh made to follow him, but Linda called her back and ordered her to get dressed and put some shoes on.

By the time she jumped down off the steps and ran round the side of the trailer the fire was almost out. Travellers surrounded the VW, directing jets of water from their own hosepipes at the last few stubborn gouts of flame. Though the VW had not been gutted, it was most certainly uninhabitable and very probably beyond repair. Black greasy smoke of such density that it resembled an expanding column of solid black rock poured from the shattered windows and rose into the night sky.

The stink of it caught in the back of Oonagh's throat and made her eyes water. Ash ascended into the air and sifted down over the camp. Even as the last flames guttered and died, the heat from the fire was still intense enough for Oonagh to feel her skin prickle with sweat. She spotted Rob sitting on the steps of Sara and Captain's brightly painted caravan, his head bowed as though he couldn't bear to watch the destruction of his home.

She plodded across, gritty ash still descending over the camp like dead petals, greying the air, mingling with the sweat on her skin. Sara had her arm round Rob's shoulders, but she was not saying anything, merely staring bleakly at the blackened, smoke-wreathed wreck. As Oonagh came closer, Sara shifted her gaze to look at her, pulling a face as if to say: Why does everyone hate us so much? What have *we* done to them? Oonagh, noticing Rob's feet were bare, knelt on the damp grass in front of him. Slowly he raised his head to look at her.

It was obvious he had been crying. His eyes were bloodshot and tear-tracks had been smeared through the grime on his cheeks. The expression on his face was one of such desolation that Oonagh felt like crying too. She reached out and took his hand. It lay in her palm like a dead fish. Before joining the group, Rob had had a lot of problems with drugs and bad relationships, and once he had tried to kill himself. She could feel the thick ridges of healed scar tissue on the underside of his wrist.

'All my work ...' he moaned. 'I've lost everything ...'

'No, you haven't,' Oonagh said as though willing him to believe it, 'you've still got us.'

Rob looked at the smoking ruin of his VW over which arcs of water were still being played. In a voice that sounded as though it was running down he said, 'I've got nowhere to live.'

'You've got a dozen homes to choose from,' Sara said. 'Anyone would be happy to put you up. You can crash with me and Captain if you like.'

Oonagh heard someone behind her and looked round. Linda was approaching, having dragged jeans and a sweater over her nightshirt.

'I'm going up to the farmhouse to call the police,' she said. 'Rob, will you talk to them when they arrive?'

Rob looked at her in disgust. 'What's the point? They won't do anything. They don't care what happens to us.'

Oonagh had never seen her mother look so angry, so determined. 'We've got just as much right to protection as everyone else.'
Sara reached up and pushed damp hair from her sweaty forehead. 'Try telling *them* that,' she said quietly.

Thursday 24 November

24

Although he couldn't remember falling asleep, Eric was certainly aware of waking up. His head felt like a magician's cabinet into which swords were being thrust, his throat felt scoured by steel wool, and whenever he moved, foamy waves of nausea surged and slapped against the walls of his stomach.

Yesterday, the first full day after Chloe's death, had been awful, each hour, each minute even, like a separate ordeal that had had to be endured. He and Annette and Tim had done nothing but cry and cling to each other, or sit silently, staring into space. Occasionally one of them had thrown out a question: Why had it happened? What had any of them ever done to deserve this? It was like sitting next to a black void that sucked up their tears and their anger and their questions but gave nothing in return: no comfort, no answers, nothing.

The police had been back once or twice, and a police counsellor, arranged by Farrington, had appeared too to try and give them some idea of what to expect in the next few days and weeks and months. Valerie Jones had come over with a chicken casserole which nobody felt like eating, and the press had set up camp outside, for a while ringing the doorbell almost non-stop until finally they had taken the hint and gone away.

When Annette and Tim had gone upstairs to bed sometime around eleven, Annette sedated and Tim exhausted, Eric had stayed up, unable to bear the prospect of closing his eyes and trapping himself with his thoughts. With nothing else to do he had smoked cigarette after cigarette, and had eventually wandered over to the drinks cabinet and found three-quarters of a bottle of Bell's whisky, which he had methodically worked his way through, tumbler after tumbler after tumbler, perhaps in the hope that he'd eventually find oblivion in the bottom of a glass.

He had never been a big drinker, and by the time Farrington and

Lockwood appeared on his doorstep – sometime after midnight, he guessed, though he couldn't be sure – he was staggeringly, speech-slurringly drunk. Lockwood had made him black coffee, and Farrington had told him that a group of villagers had attacked the travellers' camp because the local newspaper had inferred the travellers were involved in Chloe's death. She had therefore arranged a press conference for the following morning, which she wanted Eric to attend, if he felt up to it.

He told Farrington he'd be there, agreed to meet her at the police station at eight-thirty in the morning, and after that he couldn't remember any more.

Now, some hours later, he dragged himself from the settee where he'd been sprawled, and rushed upstairs, barely managing to reach the toilet bowl before vomiting. The sweet fermented stench of regurgitated whisky rose about him. When he had done, he slumped to the floor, feeling like a piece of wrung-out rag.

Eventually he rose to his feet, clutching at the sink for support, rinsed his mouth out with cold water that tasted sugary, and stumbled downstairs. The lounge and his clothes stank of stale smoke. He threw open the windows, recoiling like a vampire from the daylight. He put away the whisky bottle, dumped the contents of the ashtray into the bin in the kitchen and made himself some coffee.

It was only as he was drinking it that he glanced at the clock on the wall above the sink and saw that it was 8:22. He was halfway through a groan when the telephone began to ring. He dragged himself into the lounge to answer it, and was not surprised to find it was Farrington, calling to make sure he was up and about.

He told her he'd be there in twenty minutes, then bustled around as quickly as his fragile body would allow. He didn't much care how he looked, but changed his clothes anyway because the stink of smoke was rolling his stomach around like a dough ball in big grey hands. He swallowed two paracetamol and was tying his shoelaces when the letter box clacked and mail slithered over the doormat. He went into the hall and bent to pick up the fan of envelopes. When he straightened, his head swam as though he'd been getting too much or too little oxygen.

Certain he was either going to throw up or fall down, he groped his way to the stairs and sat. When the dizziness had passed, he glanced at his watch, and decided that he could afford to sit still for a few more minutes, recovering. He reached for the stack of mail and began to open it.

Most were sympathy cards, the majority of which were white with silver- or gold-embossed doves, flowers, crucifixes. Eric doggedly read the messages inside, even though part of his mind refused to take in the words of regret and condolence. People thought they were being kind by telling him what a wonderful girl Chloe had been, whereas in truth they were simply accentuating her loss. There were perhaps a dozen cards and Eric had opened eight or nine before he came to a bright orange envelope on which their name and address had been handwritten in neat block capitals.

The envelope seemed stiff enough to contain a card, but what kind? It couldn't be a sympathy card, not unless the company who'd issued it had an appalling grasp of etiquette. Eric tore open the envelope and pulled out what was inside. For long seconds, during which his breath seemed to become a solid block in the base of his throat, he stared at what he held in his hand, unable to believe his eyes.

It was a card, sure enough, but a child's birthday card, depicting a grinning pink cat balanced on a red ball, holding a bunch of balloons in its right hand. The three most prominent balloons were each emblazoned with a word. The first balloon read YOU, the second read ARE, and the third balloon should have read 6, but instead the word DEAD had been cut from a magazine or newspaper and Sellotaped crudely across the number, the top and bottom of which could still be seen.

YOU ARE DEAD. Eric swallowed, and it was like trying to force down a clod of earth. He was so stunned he didn't know what to feel. One thing was for sure: Annette mustn't see this. Dreading what else might be in store for him, Eric opened the card.

Beneath the usual trite rhyme, two words had been written in blue block capitals: I'M BACK. That was all. Eric turned the card over, but there was no other message.

I'M BACK. What did that mean? He looked at the front of the card again. YOU ARE DEAD. With sudden distaste, Eric thrust the card back into the orange envelope and tossed it on to the stairs as he pulled on the brown corduroy jacket that he usually wore to school. He remembered how Chloe had hated this jacket, how she used to say it embarrassed her to see him in it. He'd tell her he wore it because it was comfortable, and because he was damned if he was going to get chalk dust all over his decent clothes.

Suddenly, with a clarity that almost took his breath away, he pictured the expression she always gave him at such times – a combination of pity and contempt. Perhaps it was just him, but it seemed to sum up exactly that jumble of inconsistencies that constituted being a teenager. Self-confidence and uncertainty, arrogance and vulnerability, a naive but dawning awareness that the world and all its wonders were there for the taking, like gifts waiting to be unwrapped . . .

All at once Eric felt a surge of something that went beyond loathing, beyond rage. The intensity of the emotion frightened him; he was not a man used to such fury. He snatched up the orange envelope, took it in both hands, and was on the verge of tearing it into shreds when he recovered his senses enough to realise that it might turn out to be the breakthrough the police had been looking for. Stacking the rest of the cards in a neat pile at the bottom of the stairs, so that Annette and Tim wouldn't slip on them when they came down, he left the house.

It was quarter to nine when he arrived at the station. Farrington, wearing more make-up than usual, greeted him curtly, trying not to show her irritation at his lateness. She told him she'd brief him on the way to the community centre, where the press conference was to be held. Lockwood held the door open for him and Farrington ushered him out.

It wasn't until they were in the car that Eric showed them the card. Farrington took the orange envelope from him without a word, opened it, looked at the front of the card, read the message inside, then shook her head and muttered, 'Jesus.'

'What is it, boss?' Lockwood asked, glancing aside from the road for a moment.

Farrington showed the card to him.

'Sick bastard,' Lockwood muttered.

'We mustn't automatically assume it's from the killer, though,' said Farrington. 'There are a lot of sick people out there. Maybe one of them read about Chloe in the paper, or it could even be kids messing about.' She paused, looking thoughtful. 'It is an odd message, though, isn't it? "I'm back." Have you any idea what that might mean, Eric?'

It was the first time she had called him by his Christian name. Eric shook his head. 'No, sorry.'

'It suggests revenge, doesn't it?' Farrington said, twisting in her seat. 'Are you quite sure there isn't an ex-pupil who might bear a grudge against you? Someone you . . . caused to have expelled, say?'

Eric shook his head. 'No, I can't think of anyone. Besides, Jackie's been getting these messages too. It wouldn't make sense for an ex-pupil to persecute her as well, would it?'

Farrington was still looking thoughtful. 'No, I must admit it doesn't seem to make a great deal of sense. But all the same all possibilities, however unlikely, need to be explored. Do you think you could compile a list of pupils you've had problems with in the past?'

'I can't remember half of them,' Eric said.

'Just do your best. Use the school records to help jog your memory.'

She twisted back round in her seat and slipped the card carefully into its envelope. 'Local postmark,' she noted. 'Posted yesterday. Collected at one forty-five p.m.'

There was barely time now for Farrington to brief Eric before the press conference, but she did her best, and was getting him to repeat the essence of what she wanted him to say even as Lockwood was pulling into a parking space outside the community centre between a white van with a BBC North logo emblazoned along the side and a dusty red Clio with a Press sticker in the window. They were already late, but Farrington kept them sitting in the car just a few minutes longer until she was satisfied that Eric knew what was expected of him. 'Just remember,' she said, 'all you have to do is give a brief statement. If anyone in there asks you a question I'll answer it.'

They got out of the car and marched towards the olive-green double doors fronting the dismal, flat-roofed building. A smattering of bystanders, attracted by the TV vans, eyed them curiously, evidently in the hope of spotting a famous face. There was a uniformed constable just inside the door who respectfully pushed back his shoulders and raised his chin as they entered. A shabby entrance porch led to a short corridor inset with four doors. At the end of the corridor another door led into the main hall.

This was a large high-ceilinged room with long windows that let in plenty of light. Just inside the door, precarious-looking stacks of blue and red plastic chairs stood on either side. More of the chairs had been arranged in four semi-circular rows facing a long wooden table in front of the stage at the other end of the room. The last time Eric had been here was to see an amateur production of *The Mikado* in which one of Annette's friends who thought she was a good singer but wasn't had been starring.

Now the stage resembled a failed actor at the end of a bad show. It looked tired and grey and somehow lonely, blotchy red curtains sagging like dewlaps. The long wooden table in front of the stage, by contrast, behind which three more of the plastic chairs stood empty and expectant, was bathed in white light from the arc lamps that surrounded it, like a primitive sunbed.

This whole area was buzzing with activity. The four rows of chairs facing the table were occupied by journalists and TV people. Reporters sat drinking coffee out of paper cups, smoking cigarettes and gossiping with colleagues. There were sound men wearing headphones and wielding boom mikes like sickles, cameramen hefting their machines on their shoulders, vying for position. Cables trailed over the floor; photographers checked their cameras; a bald man with wiry black chest hair poking out of his shirt front was testing the microphones that had been taped to the table-top by bending to count into them, then straightening to raise his thumb to someone within the melee.

Because of the bare wooden floor, on which even the daintiest footsteps echoed like tap shoes, the entrance of the three new arrivals did not go unnoticed. There was a general shuffling as people turned to look at them, one or two sarcastic comments about their lack of punctuality. Farrington led the way, her face set, Eric close behind her, looking down at his feet. Flashbulbs began to go off all around them, their flares like hooks snagging at Eric's headache. He was peripherally aware of cameramen rushing towards them and then backing away as they advanced, their black, single-lensed cameras all but obscuring their faces, making them look like machines with human legs.

He was glad to get the barrier of the table between himself and the crowding attentions of the media, though in truth it offered little respite. There was no escape from the blazing arc lamps which made him feel as though he were being interrogated.

Farrington, at least, appeared self-confident. Hands laced in front of her, not squinting at all, she said, 'Thank you very much for coming, ladies and gentlemen. I must apologise for the unavoidable delay.' She introduced Eric and DS Lockwood, and then said, 'I assume you're all fully aware of the murder of Chloe Knight on Tuesday afternoon. What's going to happen is that I'm going to issue a statement which will provide you with as much detail on this case as is pertinent at the present time, and then I'll bring you up to date on the inquiry so far. After that, Mr Knight here will issue a brief statement, which I'd be grateful if you could all reproduce in your newspapers and show on your TV programmes. Only after that will I be prepared to answer questions, but I must stress that you direct all your enquiries to me. Mr Knight is not prepared to answer any questions at the present time.'

She looked around slowly as though to ensure that her authority was unquestioned, and then, calmly and concisely, began to run through the events of the past three days. Eric bowed his head and tried to close his mind to what Farrington was saying. When his turn came to speak he was almost caught unawares, and only looked up because his name seemed to jump out at him from the drone that he had made Farrington's voice become.

'There's ... a couple of things I want to say,' he began in a quiet, halting voice, after clearing his throat. 'First of all, if anyone knows anything about Chloe's murder ... or suspects anything about anyone that they know, they must ... must go to the police at once. He doesn't deserve to be protected. He's done ... an awful thing. The person who did this to my little girl is ... is a monster. He's torn our family apart ...'

His voice waned and he placed a hand over his mouth: a number of flashbulbs went off, capturing his anguish on celluloid. He took a number of deep breaths, and finally felt able to continue. 'And the other thing is that there's been a lot of nonsense about the ... the travellers being involved in Chloe's death. Well, I'd just like to appeal for calm on both sides. All this conflict is ... is only hampering the investigation.'

He paused to clear his throat again and looked up. Immediately he froze. For a long, long moment all sound, all movement in the hall seemed to cease. Despite the light that lay over his audience like a shimmering patina, Eric could quite clearly see Chloe standing at the back of the crowd of journalists, her face unscarred, her expression serene, her dark hair shining.

She was looking straight at him, and as Eric gazed at her she gave a nod and a little smile. That seemed to break the spell: a murmur rose from the crowd, a cameraman stepped to his left, obscuring Eric's view of his daughter.

'Chloe!' he blurted and jumped up, his chair tipping back and thumping into the edge of the stage. The murmur became a tumult of surprise and speculation. Perhaps it was simply the effect of the flashbulbs flaring all around him, but the faces of the journalists closest to Eric seemed to swell like over-ripe fruit, to bloat with eagerness. Despite himself, he had the presence of mind to realise that this was exactly what they had come for: a show of melodrama, of human emotion laid raw. This knowledge as much as the fact that he could see nothing beyond the white screen of flashbulbs, caused Eric to slump back in the seat Lockwood had righted for him, to lower his head into his hands.

'Eric! Eric! Eric!' The voice was Farrington's. She had her hand on his shoulder and was shaking him as though to rouse him from a nightmare. Instead of responding he brought his arms up over his head, hands locked behind his skull, elbows pressed together in front of his face. In his mind's eye he saw Chloe, beautiful and serene, smiling at him.

Farrington's voice cut in again. 'Eric! Are you all right?'

The vision of Chloe winked out. 'Leave me alone,' Eric muttered. 'Why can't you all just leave me alone.'

He looked up, in the vain hope of catching another glimpse of his daughter, of grasping another chance to consolidate that image of smiling serenity in his mind's eye. But all he saw were flashbulbs, like white eruptions of migraine piercing the dark spaces behind his eyes.

Friday 25 November

25

'I'm not really dead, you know,' Chloe said.

She and Tim were sitting on a park bench bathed in hazy sunshine, surrounded by trees and bright green, sweet-smelling grass.

'So why did you make everyone think you were?' Tim asked.

'It was just a joke. I didn't think everyone would take it so seriously.'

Somewhere in front of Tim the grass became a lake. Ducks quacked and flapped on the glittering blue water.

'When are you coming home?' he asked his sister.

'Tomorrow.'

'Oh, good. Shall I tell Mum?'

'No, I want it to be a surprise.'

Tim smiled. 'She'll be really pleased. And Dad too. Don't ever pretend to die again, will you, Clo? It's a horrible feeling.'

'Okay, sorry.'

Suddenly there was a noise like static, coming in waves. No, not like static. More like flurries of rain, pattering on canvas.

Chloe stood up and pointed. 'Those boys are throwing stones at the ducks. We'd better stop them.'

Tim ran after his sister, but all of a sudden he felt disturbed, restless, and then obscurely terrified that this beautiful, warm summer's day was about to be taken away from him. He tried to concentrate on the boys, hurling their handfuls of stones at the ducks, but they were indistinct, dark blurred figures; he wasn't even sure how many of them there were. All he could hear was the sound of their stones. Like rain on canvas. Like ... like ... like ...

Gravel on glass.

He woke up, and the summer's day was gone. Instantly he knew that Chloe was gone too, gone for ever. The darkness pressed in all around him. The dream had been sweet, but that only made the waking all the more bitter.

He swung out of bed, panting for air. His face felt cold, and when he touched it he found his cheeks were wet. He yearned for his sister to be alive again; he wanted it more than he'd ever wanted anything before. He raised his head and gazed into the darkness of his room.

A spindly black figure was standing at the end of his bed.

His breath stopped, and the figure melted back into what it really was – his easel, standing with splayed legs in the middle of the room. Tim stood up, feeling the coldness of the night pressing against his bare skin. He began to grope his way towards the light switch.

He had taken no more than three steps when the silence was shattered by a clattering sound that made him drop to one knee and throw up his hands as though attacked by a swarm of killer bees. The sound was so unexpected that it was a good five seconds before his nerves stopped jangling and he actually realised what it was. Heart racing, he looked up towards his curtained window.

The boys throwing stones at the ducks in his dream.

Gravel on glass.

He stood, lurched towards his window and pulled back the curtain.

His pounding heart gave another almighty lurch.

Chloe was standing in the back garden, waving up at him.

No, it wasn't Chloe. Chloe's hair was dark, not blonde. This was . . .

'Oonagh,' he whispered.

All at once, though he'd barely thought about her these past two days, he was really pleased, albeit puzzled, to see her. He waved to let her know he was coming, then dragged his dressing gown on over his pyjamas, and dashed silently through the house until he reached the kitchen. He switched on the light and unlocked the door. The kitchen clock informed him that it was 2:25 a.m.

Oonagh was virtually pressed up against the door, shoulders hunched, arms wrapped around herself. 'Can I come in?' she said. 'I'm freezing.'

Tim glanced behind him, as if afraid that one or both of his parents might be standing there. 'Yeah, course you can,' he said. 'Come on.'

As Oonagh entered, shivering, Tim crossed to the kitchen door and closed it quietly. When he turned back, Oonagh was sliding a chair from beneath the table and sitting down. She was wearing only a light jacket over a red sweater and jeans. Her lips were bloodless with cold.

The remnants of Tim's dream were still with him, and he felt so disorientated that for a long moment he couldn't think what to do or say.

Oonagh looked at him. 'Are you okay?' she asked. 'Your face is wet.'

Tim swiped at the tears on his cheeks, feeling vulnerable and embarrassed. 'I'm fine,' he growled unconvincingly.

Oonagh crossed her hands on the table and looked at them. A little colour was returning to her cheeks. 'I heard about Chloe,' she murmured. 'I couldn't believe it. I'm really sorry.'

'Yeah,' said Tim, and then couldn't say any more; he was afraid his voice would crack. He swallowed, cleared his throat, and eventually said, 'Do you want a drink or anything?'

'A hot one, yeah.'

'Coffee? Tea?'

'Cocoa would be nice, if you've got any.'

Tim found a tin of cocoa in the cupboard. It had been in there so long that the contents had hardened and he had to chip at it with a spoon. 'How did you know where I lived?' he said.

'I looked it up in the phone book.'

'Oh, right,' he said, then frowned again. 'But how did you know which room was mine?'

'I didn't, but I knew which one your mum's and dad's was because I saw them go up to bed. Or rather, I saw a light go on upstairs and then your dad appeared in the window and closed the curtains. So I avoided that one and threw gravel up at the others. Yours was the second one I tried.'

Tim nodded vaguely.

'You don't seem all that surprised to see me,' Oonagh said. 'Aren't you wondering why I'm here?'

Tim poured boiling water into two mugs, stirred them and carried them across to the table. 'I suppose so, yeah. I mean ... yeah, of course I am. I'm just a bit confused, that's all. You woke me up. I was dreaming about Chloe.' He gave a half-laugh that had no humour in it and rubbed his forehead, making his fringe stand up in spikes. 'Sorry, I'm not really thinking straight.'

'That's okay,' said Oonagh.

'So why *are* you here?' Tim asked. 'Not that I don't want you to be. It's really good to see you actually.'

'It's a long story. Did you hear that we'd been having some trouble at the camp?'

'Yeah, my dad told me. He did an appeal for calm which was on the news this lunchtime. Some yobs set a trailer on fire or something.'

'That's right ... well, more or less.' She told him about the initial trouble with the police, and the ensuing news story which had led to the attack from a group of drunken locals.

'Anyway, first thing this morning the police came back again, this time with a bunch of social workers. They said feelings in the village were running high – this was even before your dad's appeal had been on the news – so a decision had been taken to give the children ... how did they put it? ... temporary alternative accommodation until things blew over or until they decided to let us move on. It was awful, Tim. They just came and took all the children away. Some of the younger ones were screaming their eyes out. They didn't know what was happening.'

'But they can't do that, can they?' said Tim, 'That's like kidnap.'

Oonagh shrugged. 'All I know is that they did do it. Maybe they were given special powers or something.'

Tim shook his head. 'So where did they take you?'

'They put me in a police car and drove me straight round to this house where these foster parents lived. It was a place near York. The people knew I was coming. They must have organised it all the day before.' She fingered the bruise on her face and tried not to look upset.

Tim said quietly, 'It's all because of what happened to Chloe that they're doing this, you know. Everything's just ... just going wrong.'

There was a long pause. Then Oonagh said, 'Yeah, I know. I thought if we got together, we could help each other, maybe work out what to do.'

Tim looked at her. She had a little moustache of cocoa above her top lip. He said, 'There's nothing we *can* do, though, is there? Nothing's going to bring Chloe back.'

'No, I know,' she admitted softly. 'But the man who did it still needs to be caught, doesn't he?'

'Is that why you came? Because you thought that together we could catch him? There's millions of policemen after him, you know.'

Tim had seen Oonagh upset and angry before, but he had never seen her look unsure until now. 'I know that,' she said. 'I just ... well, I was at that house where they'd taken me, and I saw the headline in the newspaper, and I picked it up and read it, and I didn't know until then that it was Chloe who'd been killed, and I just thought ... well, that I had to see you, that's all.'

There was a silence as Tim digested all this. Then he said, 'Do the people you're staying with know you've come?'

'Of course they don't. I ran away, didn't I? I don't normally call on people at half-past two in the morning, you know.'

'How did you get here?'

'I hitched.'

'You didn't!' said Tim.

'Yeah, it's no problem. As long as you stand somewhere where there's lot of people about and only accept lifts from women, you're fine.'

Tim wasn't so sure about this, but was in no mood to argue. 'So what will you do now?' he asked.

Oonagh looked surprised. 'Well, I was hoping I could stay here with you.'

'*Here*!' Tim exclaimed, then realised how loud his voice had been. He shook his head and said quietly, 'Sorry, Oonagh, there's no way, especially not with Chloe and everything.'

'But I've got nowhere to go. If I go home, the police will come and take me away again.'

'Yeah, but there's no way my mum and dad would let you stay here. The first thing they'd do is tell the police themselves.'

'But if your mum and dad don't find out,' said Oonagh, 'it'd be okay, wouldn't it?'

'How are they not going to find out? You can't exactly hide under my bed.'

'I thought I could stay in the shed in the garden.'

'You what? You'd freeze to death. Besides, Dad'd find you. He's always going in there for stuff.'

'What, even now that it's coming up to winter? And with ... with everything else that's happened? I didn't think he'd feel like doing much gardening.'

Tim thought about it. Oonagh had a point. He couldn't actually remember the last time either of his parents had been out to the shed. 'You'd still be freezing cold,' he said.

'You could bring me blankets and coats and stuff. And some food and other bits and pieces. I wouldn't need much.'

'Yeah, but ...' Tim pulled a face.

'Oh, what's the problem, Tim? I thought you'd be pleased to see me. I thought we were friends.'

'I am. We are. It's just ... well, with everything else that's happened, it seems such a hassle. I mean, what will you use for ... like ... you know ... a toilet? And you'll need to wash and stuff. And what if we get found out?'

'Don't worry,' Oonagh said, 'I'll manage. If I want the toilet, I'll go in the bushes. And if you bring me some newspaper and plastic bags and toilet roll, I'll ... well, I don't really have to spell it out, do I? And you could bring me some soap and a bucket of water every now and again, and if your mum and dad go out, you could let me in for a shower. And if we get found out, well, so what? They're not going to throw us in prison, are they? The worst that can happen is that we'll get told off and I'll be sent back to those foster parents.'

She made it all sound so simple, so straightforward. 'Please, Tim,' she urged. 'We're both going through a bad time at the moment. We need each other.'

Tim sighed and looked at her. The cocoa was drying on her top lip. Her eyes were imploring.

'Okay,' he agreed reluctantly.

Oonagh's face broke into a dazzling smile and she clenched her fist in a gesture of triumph. She jumped up, circled the table and gave him a hug, which surprised them both, but which they felt they both needed. 'Thanks, Tim,' she said, her breath warm on his ear. 'I knew I could rely on you.'

26

Five hours later, Eric woke suddenly, breaking the surface of a sleep that had been like a cold, black sea. He sat up, and immediately felt the dark weight of his grief settle around his shoulders like an invisible cloak. Beside him Annette slept fitfully, murmuring, fidgeting, frowning and grimacing by turns as if trying on different expressions. Watching her, Eric felt an ache inside him, knowing that in an hour or two she would also wake up, and feel awful reality crash back into place around her. He had tried to comfort her as much as possible these past few days, but he might as well have attempted to hold back the sea. Besides, the way he was feeling himself, he hardly felt equipped to comfort anybody.

He staggered downstairs and made himself some black, sweet coffee. He thought about yesterday:

Chloe, standing at the back of the room, serene and beautiful, smiling at him ...

As he tipped his head back to pour the last of the coffee down his throat, he heard the letter box clack and the sound of post hitting the doormat. Instantly he remembered the orange envelope, the clown clutching its handful of balloons.

YOU ARE DEAD.

I'M BACK.

He stood up, full of a juddering apprehension, and hurried through the kitchen and the lounge, hitting his leg on the edge of the settee in his clumsy urgency, and stifling his blurt of pain as he dashed, limping, into the hallway.

This time the envelope, peeking out from its nest of brown-clad circulars and the sober white wrappings of sympathy cards, was the pink of healthy gums. Eric felt dread ripple through him. Had he known this would be here or had he just feared it? He was disturbed by the unshakeable thought that he'd willed it to be here by the strength of his foreboding.

He stooped and snatched up the envelope. His leg was throbbing as he tore the envelope open and dragged out the card inside, creasing it.

A teddy bear was clutching what appeared to be a heart-shaped cushion, a tear rolling down its right cheek. An arc of pink marsh-mallowy letters above the illustration spelled out MISSING YOU ... Beneath this someone had printed in black biro, pressing down so hard that the nib had almost gone through the card: HA! HA!

Eric felt sick. With trembling hands he opened the card and stared at the message inside:

I'M IN CHLOE'S ROOM.

He licked his lips and glanced involuntarily up the stairs, as if expecting to see a figure standing at the top, grinning down at him. I'M IN CHLOE'S ROOM. What the hell did that mean?

Trying to remain calm, Eric quickly ascended the stairs. The door to Chloe's room was closed. Nothing unusual there, but his heart beat a little faster as he placed his ear to the stripped pine and listened. As far as he could tell there was silence, though the blood in his own ears was roaring like a distant sea. He shoved the pink envelope into his back pocket, then pushed the door open.

The door brushed softly inwards over the wine-red carpet, hinges giving a squeak which made Eric's cheeks wrinkle in a grimace. He stepped quickly inside, blinking at shadows, head sweeping from one side of the room to the other. The air smelt faintly of talcum powder. He closed the door, strode quickly to the window and pulled back the curtains, admitting a pearly wash of daylight that highlighted the dust that was already collecting on the room's flat surfaces, like a crust growing over the past.

He turned back to face the room. There were only two places where an intruder could hide: under the bed and in the wardrobe. He crossed to the wardrobe first, grasped the handles of both doors and pulled them open. Coat hangers jangled softly like bones, the clothes that were draped over them swaying in a slow dance. On the left-hand side, narrow compartments held T-shirts, socks, underwear, leggings, jeans. Eric closed the wardrobe doors quickly before particular outfits could bring back memories of special occasions, happy times.

He dropped on to all fours and peered under the bed. Gathered among the dust were some old school exercise books, some box files, cassettes of out of favour bands, a grubby pair of espadrilles with frayed toes, a tennis racket and a biscuit tin.

Eric dragged out the tin, which kicked up enough dust to make him sneeze twice before he could stifle the third one. He listened for signs of movement in the house but it was as still as before. Reassured, he sat up, his back against the bed, and placing the tin on the floor between his knees he peeled off the lid.

The tin was full of plastic figures and animals from a variety of sources, some painted in life-like colours, others simply the single colour of the plastic they had been moulded from. There were cowboys and Indians, legionnaires and Arabs, fawn-coloured British soldiers and steel-grey German ones. There were cows and pigs and dogs; lions, tigers, elephants, penguins, sea lions and polar bears. There were Wombles, Clangers and Mister Men; Zebedee, Rupert Bear, Thunderbirds and Daleks. A Tyrannosaurus Rex, a Cheshire cat, a rubber skeleton. Footballers and Beefeaters and members of a marching band.

Eric pushed his hand into the jumble, the irregular plastic shapes pressing against his fingers before giving way, a child's treasure chest of memories, a seething, tumbling sea of colour. Tim and Chloe used to spend hours playing with these plastic figures. Eric recalled Chloe as a little girl, sitting cross-legged on the floor, inventing voices for pigs and elephants and crocodiles. While Tim re-enacted World War II with the soldiers, she would concoct complex games in which Lady Penelope and Rupert Bear would marry, do battle with the Daleks and then retire to their farm on which dinosaurs and polar bears roamed freely.

A splash of liquid fell into the tin, drenching a Red Indian wielding a tomahawk. Then another, this time landing on a green, horned monster with spiny body armour. The image of Chloe, so engrossed in her games that the house could have burned down around her without her noticing, was so vivid that it took Eric a few confused seconds to realise that the liquid was his own falling tears. He raised an arm to wipe the tears away.

'Don't cry, Dad.'

Eric turned, blinking. Chloe, sitting on the bed, chin resting on her upraised knees, arms entwining her legs, wore a look of concern.

'Don't cry,' she urged again.

Eric sniffed, dragged himself heavily to his feet, and sat beside her.

'I can't help it,' he said, his voice trembling a little. 'I miss you, Clo. We all do.'

'I know,' she said. 'I'm sorry.'

'Why did you have to go away? Why did you leave us?'

Chloe squirmed, looking uncomfortable. 'I didn't mean to, Dad. I didn't want to.' Her voice dropped to a murmur. 'I couldn't help it.'

Eric stood up and wandered over to the window. It was full light now. The sky was the white of a blank page. It hurt his eyes.

'We've been getting these cards through the post, Clo.'

'I know, Dad.'

'Do you know who sent them?'

Silence.

'Who did it, Clo? Tell me who killed you.'

There was no reply. Eric turned from the window to face the room.

The brightness outside gave the impression that a black smear of shadow was sliding across his vision, moving all the swifter when he tried to focus upon it. Chloe – the apparition, the memory, the perfect daughter – was gone, the section of duvet where she had sat unrumpled. Eric sighed, moved across the room, crouched to replace the lid on the biscuit tin, and shoved the tin back under the bed. He pulled the now bowed and creased pink envelope from his back pocket and glared at it.

I'M IN CHLOE'S ROOM.

But where, you bastard? Where?

He left the room, pulling the door softly closed behind him, and trudged downstairs to ring Farrington.

27

'Another one came this morning,' he told her in a hushed voice the instant he opened the door.

Farrington had had little sleep over the past three days and was feeling irritable. 'Another what?'

Eric raised a hand as if the volume of her voice was something he needed to catch and crush before it drew attention to itself. 'Please, not so loud. Annette and Tim are in the living room. If they found out about it, it'd only upset them.'

He drew the crumpled pink envelope out of his back pocket and silently held it out. Farrington put on a pair of latex gloves, then took the card from him, sliding it from its envelope. She read it, then handed it to Lockwood.

'I presume you've taken a look in Chloe's room?' she said.

'Yes, but I couldn't find anything.'

'And you've had no new thoughts on who the sender might be?'

'None.'

'Hmm.' Farrington looked dissatisfied. 'The card you gave us yesterday has yielded nothing so far – no marks of value, no clue as to where it might have been bought.' She took the card back from Lockwood and looked at the envelope. 'Local postmark again. Whoever's got it in for you, Eric, it seems that he, she or they are still in the area.'

'The murderer, you mean?'

'Who knows? Like I said yesterday, it could just be someone's idea of a joke.' She tapped the envelope on her fingers. 'Listen, Eric, if you receive another one of these, could you try to touch it as little as possible? Hold it by the corners or use gloves?'

'Yes, of course.'

'Good.' She took a polythene evidence bag from the pocket of her overcoat, dropped the envelope inside and put it back in her pocket. 'Presumably this is what you wanted to see me about?'

Eric nodded.

'Right. Well, while we're here, do you think I might have a word with Tim?'

'Tim?' Eric looked surprised. 'What about?'

'It would save time if I explained in front of all three of you.'

'Oh. Well ... yes, certainly.' He moved back to allow the two detectives to enter. They wiped their feet and followed him through to the lounge.

Tim glanced up when they entered. He was sitting on the settee, next to Annette, who looked washed out. She was wearing a dressing gown over a long nightdress, her hands crossed in her lap.

'The Inspector wants to talk to you, Tim,' Eric said, making it sound like a warning.

Tim immediately tried not to look alarmed. 'Me?' he said. 'What about?'

'Just a few questions, Tim,' said Farrington reassuringly. 'Nothing to worry about. I understand you're a friend of Oonagh Walsh's, one of the children from the travellers' camp?'

For an instant Farrington felt sure Tim was going to deny it. Then he said, 'Who told you?'

'Her parents,' Lockwood answered. 'I went to see them this morning.'

'Were you aware, Tim, that Oonagh and the rest of the children from the camp were taken into temporary care yesterday?' Farrington said.

Tim swallowed nervously. 'Er ... I think I saw something about it on the news.'

'And were you also aware that Oonagh Walsh has disappeared from the temporary accommodation she was placed in?'

'Disappeared?' said Eric before Tim could answer. 'What do you mean?'

'Perhaps disappeared is too dramatic a word. She's run away, either some time last night or this morning.' Turning to Tim again, her voice hardening just a touch, Farrington said, '*Did* you know about this, Tim?'

Tim looked hesitant, but he shook his head. 'No,' he said.

'Are you quite sure?'

'Yes,' said Tim, but looked to his father as if for guidance.

Taking his cue, Eric said, 'Look, what is all this, Inspector? You're surely not accusing Tim of having anything to do with this girl's disappearance?'

'I'm not accusing anyone of anything,' Farrington said curtly, and then, all but turning her back on Eric to make it obvious she wanted to talk to Tim without interruption, said more gently, 'You're not in any trouble, Tim, and neither is Oonagh. It's just that after running away, Oonagh didn't return home, and her parents have said that this is the only place they can think of where she might have come. Naturally, in light of what happened to Chloe, they – and we – are a little concerned, and are becoming more concerned the longer she remains missing. Now obviously I don't want to have to deflect people from the inquiry into Chloe's murder to look for this girl, but I'm going to have to if we don't find her soon, and I'm sure you wouldn't want that, would you?'

Tim looked uncomfortable, but he shook his head. 'No.'

'So if Oonagh *does* get in touch with you, you'll let us know straight away?'

Tim licked his lips and again looked to his father. This time, however, Eric simply frowned and said, 'You *don't* know anything about this girl running away, do you, Tim?'

'No,' said Tim with the disappointed indignation of one who feels let down by an ally. 'Why are you all blaming me? I wasn't the one who took her away from her family. None of this is my fault.'

Farrington leaned forward. In a measured voice she said, 'None of this is anybody's *fault* as such, Tim. Whatever you may have heard, Oonagh and the other children weren't taken away from their parents as a punishment. They were taken away to *protect* them from whoever might want revenge for being led to believe that the travellers had something to do with Chloe's death. They were all placed in very nice family homes with people who are used to having children staying with them – in fact, most of them seem to be treating the whole thing as a kind of holiday. So by running away, Oonagh has done nothing but caused herself, her parents and everyone else a lot of trouble and heartache.'

'Okay, okay,' Tim said, flapping at the air as if her words were buzzing around his face like mosquitoes. 'You don't have to go on.'

In stark contrast to Tim's agitation, Farrington looked icy cool. 'Do you have something to tell me then?' she asked.

Tim hesitated, then mumbled, 'No, I don't. Except that ... you don't have to patronise me. I'm not a kid.'

He tried to match the long, expressionless gaze that Farrington gave him, but failed. It wasn't until his eyes flickered from hers that she said, 'I'm sorry you think I'm patronising you, Tim. *I* think I'm just doing my job. Why do you think I'm being patronising?'

Up until now Annette had been silent, watching the exchange with a look almost of dispassion. Suddenly, however, she barked, 'What are you picking on Tim for? You should be trying to catch the bastard who killed my daughter, not treating us like we're the criminals.'

Farrington sighed and glanced at Lockwood, who raised his eyebrows. 'All right, Mrs Knight, we'll leave this for now,' she said, and then added pointedly, 'I'm sure that if Oonagh does try to get in touch with Tim, he'll be sensible enough to do the right thing.'

Tim stuffed his hands between his knees and gazed at the floor.

Lockwood said, 'Would either of you mind if we had another look in Chloe's room before we left?'

Eric looked prepared to give his assent, but before he could, Annette said, 'What for?'

Farrington glanced at Eric, whose eyes widened in obvious alarm that she would mention the card, but instead she said smoothly, 'Sometimes at the beginning of an investigation, Mrs Knight, details are overlooked whose importance only becomes apparent in light of further evidence. Now that we know a little more about Chloe, we'll be able to look at her room with fresh eyes, see if there's anything unusual or out-of-place or off-kilter that we didn't pick up the first time.'

'I don't want her things messed about,' Annette said.

'You don't have to worry about that, Mrs Knight,' replied Lockwood reassuringly. 'You won't even know we've been in there.'

Annette looked at Eric, who said, 'Well, if you really think it'll help, Inspector.'

'I do,' said Farrington. 'In fact, perhaps you'd like to accompany us, Eric. That way you can ensure we won't touch anything we shouldn't.'

'Um ... yes, okay,' Eric said, trying to sound casual, and led the way upstairs. In Chloe's room, he sat on the bed while Farrington and Lockwood began methodically to go through drawers and cupboards, to look under and behind furniture, to examine cassette cases and books and plants pots – anything that might contain a snippet of paper or a photograph that could lead them to make sense of the message inside the card.

When they had exhausted every obvious alternative, the two police officers moved across to the bed. Eric stood up while they carefully stripped off the bedding and examined it, looked under the mattress and then the bed itself. They dragged out the things from under the bed – the school exercise books, the tin of plastic figures – and went through those. In all, it took them twenty minutes to search Chloe's room as thoroughly as they were able. When they had finished they were grimy and frustrated.

'Nothing,' Farrington said in disgust. 'To do this properly, we'd have to get a team in, get the carpet up.' When Eric looked alarmed, she said, 'Don't worry, Mr Knight. I'm not advocating that *just* yet.'

Lockwood brushed carpet fluff from his trousers. 'It's my guess that that message doesn't mean anything anyway. Whoever wrote it was just trying to put the wind up you. Sick bastard.'

Farrington looked around, pursing her lips. 'Have you any idea whether Chloe kept a diary or had an address book, anything like that?'

Eric shook his head. 'Not that I ever noticed.'

'*I* know,' said a voice from the doorway.

Everyone turned to see Tim standing there. As though eager to make up for his earlier evasiveness, he said, 'I was walking past on my way to the loo, and I heard what you said. Chloe *did* keep a diary. She used to write in it every night before she went to bed. I know where she hid it.'

'Will you show us?' said Farrington.

Tim nodded and crossed to the dressing table, then went down on all fours and reached underneath. There was a tearing sound, and when Tim withdrew his hand there was a cloth-bound book in it, criss-crossed with flapping strips of brown packing tape.

'When she was being a pain, I used to threaten to tell you and Mum where it was,' he said.

'How come *you* knew she kept a diary and I didn't?' Eric said, feeling excluded in spite of himself.

'I came in one day when she was taping it under here. After that, she used to read me bits. It was all pretty boring stuff, really.'

'I know what you mean,' said Lockwood companionably. 'My sister used to keep a diary. I used to sneak in to read it when she was out.'

'I couldn't have done that without her knowing,' Tim said as if he was being accused of something. He peeled off the tape and turned the book over to reveal a metal clasp. 'I didn't know where the key was.'

'Ah, I think I can help you there,' said Lockwood unexpectedly. He dragged the chair from beneath Chloe's dressing table across the room, climbed up on to it and opened a suitcase that was sitting on top of the wardrobe. He reached inside and produced a small key. 'Try this. I noticed it earlier, but I just assumed it was for a padlock to lock the case, or perhaps the wardrobe door.'

Farrington took the key from Lockwood and the diary from Tim. She fitted the key into the lock and twisted it. The clasp sprang open.

She held the diary up like a waiter offering a platter of cold meats. 'Do you mind?'

Eric shook his head, and Farrington opened the diary somewhere in the middle, then flicked through to find the most recent entries. She began to read, provoking a silence which no one seemed willing to break. All eyes were on her face, but she remained impassive. After a couple of minutes, Eric could stand it no longer. 'Well?' he said.

Farrington gave a small frown and looked up. 'How much do you know about Chloe's relationship with this boy, Ben Wyatt?' she asked carefully.

Eric glanced at Tim. 'All I know is what Tim told me – that Chloe was keen on him. But I hardly think you'd call that a relationship. When I rang him up on the night ... the other night ... he claimed that he hardly knew her. Why do you ask?'

'Tim?' Farrington said.

'Like Dad says, Chloe fancied Ben and was trying to get him to go out with her, but I don't think she was having much luck.'

'And how about Ben Wyatt himself? You're a teacher at the school, Eric. Did you have any dealings with him?'

'I took him for English last year.'

'And what were your impressions of him?'

Eric shrugged. 'He was a nice enough lad. A bit cocky, full of himself, most of which comes from being big and strong and good-looking. A bit of a charmer with the girls. From a teaching point of view, though, he could do better. He's intelligent, but doesn't apply himself fully to his work.' He frowned, his curiosity getting the better of him. 'Why are you asking all these questions? As I've said, Chloe hardly knew the boy.'

'That's not the impression she gives here, I'm afraid,' Farrington said almost regretfully. 'Tim, what do you think of Ben Wyatt?'

Before Tim could reply, Eric said, 'What do you mean? What does the diary say?'

'Please, Eric, if you'll just bear with me for a few minutes. Tim?'

Tim shrugged. 'He's younger than me. I haven't really had anything to do with him. He's the cock of his year.'

'You mean he's a bully?'

'No, nothing like that. He's just ... hard. But he doesn't pick on people.' He shrugged. 'That's about all I know really.'

'*Now* are you going to tell us what all this is about, Inspector?'

'In a moment, Eric. I'm sorry to be evasive, but I do have to ask you a number of questions first.' Suddenly she seemed hesitant. 'In fact I'm afraid I'm going to have to ask you some rather intimate questions about your daughter. Perhaps you'd prefer to answer them in private.' She looked meaningfully at Tim.

Tim looked uncomfortable. Backing out of the room, nodding his head rapidly, he said, 'Er ... I was just on my way to the loo anyway.'

When Tim had left the room, Eric asked with a directness that seemed to suggest he was bracing himself, 'What *is* all this, Inspector?'

'Now, I want you to try and remain calm while I ask these questions, Eric,' said Farrington. 'I'm afraid this may be a little hard for you.'

Eric looked pale. He licked his lips. 'What is it you want to know?'

Farrington paused, sighed, and then said, 'Do you know whether Chloe was sexually active, Eric?'

Eric stared at her a moment, then shook his head. In a voice so controlled it sounded as if he was carefully weighing up every word, he replied, 'No, I don't think Chloe was sexually active.'

'Did she ever discuss it with you?'

'Well ... yes, Annette and I talked to her about sex. We always tried to be open about it. But Chloe never seemed inclined to try anything. She always had a pretty sensible attitude about things like that.' Though it was obviously a big strain for him, he tried to smile and said, 'God knows where she got that from. Her mother, I expect.'

'And how about when Chloe went out with her friends after school. Did you always know where she was?'

'She usually told us where she was going.'

'And you believed her?'

'Oh, yes. As I say, she was a sensible girl, very trustworthy. We've never given our kids cause to lie to us.'

'I see,' said Farrington. She sighed deeply, as if obliged to perform an unpleasant task. 'According to your daughter's diary, Eric, Chloe *was* seeing Ben Wyatt and had been for some time. Now either what's contained in here is fantasy, or Chloe and Ben were keeping their relationship secret for some reason.'

Eric hesitated, then asked, 'Can I see?' He stretched out a hand, but Farrington didn't immediately place the diary in to it.

'I ought to warn you,' she said, 'that the diary does actually detail quite explicitly various sexual encounters between Chloe and Ben Wyatt. A number of these encounters appear to have taken place in the woods where Chloe was killed.'

Eric took a deep breath and closed his eyes briefly. Then he said, more firmly this time, 'Please, I'd like to see.'

Farrington handed the diary over without another word. Eric turned it round and began to read it, his lips pressed together, his face grim. For a few minutes the only sound in the room was the ripple of paper as Eric turned the pages detailing his murdered daughter's apparently secret life. Then all at once, shockingly, the blue-bound book slipped from his fingers and he began to weep.

As he sank on to the re-made bed, Farrington moved forward, hesitated a moment, then placed a hand awkwardly on Eric's shoulder. Her voice sounded oddly hollow, as if the room they were standing in was empty and uncarpeted.

'I'm very sorry,' she said.

28

James came awake, his head fuggy with medication. For the past two nights the little sleep he'd managed had been beset with nightmares, dreams of being trapped or pursued. The most common had involved him stumbling through a squalid, stinking, unfurnished house, trying in vain to find a window or door that led outside. He had been full of panic because he knew that somewhere behind him was the headless body of Tizer, its legs moving in a kind of squeaky mechanical shuffle, like a wind-up toy, that in the context of his dream was utterly terrifying. Several times James had burst from this dream, shaking, sweating, even crying. The most recent occasion had been at dawn this morning, where he had sat up in bed with a shout of, 'No!' that had woken Marjory. She had done her best to comfort him, had made him change his sweat-sodden pyjamas and coaxed him to drink a cup of tea. Eventually, with the aid of two Tamazepam, he had fallen into a sleep too deep even for dreams.

Now, though, he was awake again, the effects of the drug clinging to him like tendrils of sticky matter. Something had woken him, but what? He had the impression that some sound, too intrusive to be ignored, had punctured his consciousness – a breaking of glass, perhaps, a crash of ... of *something*.

He shook his head in an attempt to clear it, but without success. 'Marjory,' he called, his voice rusty with sleep.

There was no reply, and her side of the bed was empty and cold. With an effort James focused on the bedside clock. Sluggishly his brain deciphered the position of the black hands on the white face. It was twenty past nine, pearly daylight washing through the thin curtains, filling the room. The pills should have enabled him to sleep until at least noon, if not later, which seemed proof enough to him that he couldn't have imagined or dreamed the sound that had woken him up.

He got out of bed, feeling heavy, cumbersome, as if gravity were increasing its grip, attempting to suck him into the floor. He crossed the room and opened the bedroom door. 'Marjory,' he called again, but again there was no reply. He padded out on to the landing in his bare feet, the house so silent that the thick carpet made his footsteps sound as though he was walking on densely-packed gravel. His surroundings still seemed hazy, his thoughts trapped half-way between reality and dreams. His breath struggled in his chest as though the air was thin. Dressed only in his blue and white pyjamas, he was vaguely aware of the cold. He reached the bottom of the stairs without even remembering the descent and moments later found himself in the lounge. Dazedly he looked around. As far as he could tell, everything was as it should be.

'Marjory,' he tried again. The air was so still that it made his voice sound sharp, almost brittle.

The sudden clamour of the telephone made him jump out of his skin.

Nerves jangling, he crossed the room to answer it. Its second ring was cut off as he fumbled the receiver from its cradle and placed it to his ear. Unable to remember either his name or the phone number, he simply said, 'Hello.'

There were ... sounds on the other end of the line. A series of furtive clicks, a scratching as though someone was scraping a key across glass. And faintly, behind a rush of emptiness, James thought he could detect a mewling noise, like and yet unlike a cat trapped down a well.

'Hello?' he said again, hesitantly this time.

The mewling paused, and another sound seemed to swell behind it, like a mass of whispering trying to form a single voice.

Suddenly, unaccountably afraid, James banged the receiver back into its cradle. He didn't want the intimacy of whatever that voice had to say, didn't want its words rising like creatures from the depths to caress his ear. He didn't want it getting into his head, didn't want it *knowing* him.

He backed away from the phone, as though cutting off the voice wasn't enough, as though he were afraid it might still ooze from the earpiece, given form by his simple acquiescence in picking up the phone and greeting it.

Behind him, out in the hallway, he heard a click: the sound of someone who didn't want to be detected closing the front door. Muzzily he wondered whether it might be Marjory, entering the house, trying to be quiet so as not to wake him. If it wasn't Marjory ... his heart began to thump uncomfortably. He loped clumsily towards the lounge door, pulled it open and stepped into the hallway.

He was just in time to glimpse a figure, dressed in blue, rounding the banister at the top of the stairs.

This time James didn't shout out. He blinked and rubbed his face, trying to sharpen his senses. But the drug in his system continued to muffle his thoughts, to blur the edges of his perception.

He began to climb the stairs after the figure, feeling as though he was ascending through a glass tube. The figure had reached the top of the stairs impossibly quickly, yet James had had the odd impression, even though he had only seen it momentarily, that it had been moving in slow motion.

He couldn't hear the creak of the landing as the figure (*please let it be Marjory*) moved along it, but that was because the blood racing through his heart was also racing through his clotted head, deafening him.

He reached the top of the stairs, wheezing. All except one door leading off from the landing was closed. The exception was his and Marjory's bedroom, the door of which was ajar. James tried to remember whether the other doors had been closed a few minutes ago, but couldn't.

Cautiously, feeling clumsy as a drunk, he approached the half-open door. He tried to speak Marjory's name, but his voice lodged in his throat like a wet rag. He stretched out a hand to the door, which seemed in his current state of mind to recede from his fingertips. When his fingers finally made contact with the door, they seemed small and distant, his arm ridiculously elongated.

He pushed at the door and it swung open.

He stepped into the room and saw the wardrobe door closing behind a figure in a blue boiler suit, its head shining like white plastic.

James's terror was an imploding star, an electric shock that tore through his body and contracted inwards to its core. He pictured again the hideous way the figure in the school playing field had somehow *slid* upwards into a standing position, the way its head had rotated on its neck in a slick yet mechanical way. He recalled the way it had moved, remorseless, machine-like, a nightmare given form.

And now here it was in his house, waiting for him, teasing him, hiding in his wardrobe like a childhood bogeyman.

James stumbled out of the room and along the landing, his legs refusing to respond quite how he wanted them to. Though his terror was stark, raw, his mind was still befuddled by the drug that gummed his thoughts. As he reached out for the banister at the top of the stairs, his feet somehow became tangled together and he fell. The stairs lurched sickeningly towards him, the steps reminding him briefly of teeth in a vast jaw closing on his body.

Then he was crashing down the stairs, rolling over and over, collecting pain as he went.

He came to rest at the bottom of the staircase on his back – stunned, winded, hurting all over. But alive.

He tried to rise; his body felt like one enormous bruise. Furthermore, the slightest movement caused his head to start spinning and made him feel sick. But he had to get away. He couldn't just lie here at the mercy of that ... that thing upstairs. Involuntarily he felt his eyes starting to close, and fought against it, but to no avail. He felt unconsciousness creeping up on him, seeping into the corners of his perception. Vaguely he became aware of movement somewhere close by, of someone or something coming towards him.

Then the someone or something was crouching down beside him. James imagined smooth white hands reaching out to peel back his eyelids, forcing him to gaze up into the awful face of the creature that had been stalking him. He was astonished, therefore, to hear a familiar female voice, full of concern, alarm.

'James, what's happened? Are you all right?'

Marjory's voice seemed to give him the strength to open his eyes. Looking up into his wife's worried face, he felt the threat of unconsciousness fading.

'I fell,' he said weakly.

'Are you hurt? Shall I call a doctor?'

He was about to shake his head, then thought better of it. 'No. I'm ... fine. Just a bit bruised. I'll be all right ... in a minute.'

'Where does it hurt?' she said. He felt her hands on him, her touch tender. 'Nothing seems to be broken.'

'We have ... to get out,' he said, reaching out to grasp her arm, feeling his strength returning. 'He's here.'

'Who's here?' she said.

'The man in the park. I saw him. He went into our wardrobe.'

He saw her frown. 'Are you sure, James?'

'Yes. Yes. He came in through this door. He went upstairs. I saw him.'

Marjory glanced at the door through which she had entered the house. 'But I locked this door on my way out to take Sally to school. It was still locked when I came back, and there was no sign of a forced entry.'

'But he's here. I saw him,' James protested feebly.

Marjory stroked his head. 'I'm sure you *think* you saw him, James, but you can't have done. You must have been dreaming. That's probably why you fell downstairs, because you weren't properly awake.'

'No,' James groaned. 'I saw him. I *did*!'

'Shh, James, take it easy. Those pills can make you think and see all sorts of funny things. I'll go upstairs and see if *I* can see him, shall I?'

'No,' James said, grabbing her again. 'Don't go up there.'

She disengaged his hand so easily it surprised him. 'Don't upset yourself, James. You're confused, that's all. Just lie there quietly. I'll be back before you know it.'

Then she was gone. He saw her walking upstairs; she seemed to float.

He forced himself to sit up, knowing that when she started to scream he'd have to go after her, despite his spinning head and battered body. He still felt sick, but not as much as before. He took a number of deep breaths, wincing as his ribs and back ached.

Then, to his astonishment, she was back, skipping down the stairs like a young girl.

He gaped at her, unable to think of anything to say.

'There was nobody there, sweetheart,' she said. She took James's hand and kissed him tenderly on the forehead. 'There was nobody there at all.'

Saturday 26 November

29

Tim fumbled for the grasshopper which was chirruping insistently in his ear. He found it and stifled it, except that it wasn't a grasshopper, it was a clock.

The luminous right angle of the hands told him that it was 3 a.m. and reminded him why he had set the alarm. He dragged himself from the warmth of his bed, shivering as the icy autumn air stripped away the insulation of sleep from his body. He was surprised he had been able to sleep at all after the way his conscience had been plaguing him since Farrington's visit the day before. As he pulled on his jeans, he felt exhausted rather than refreshed by the sleep that had finally stolen him, as though the anguish his dilemma presented had threaded its way through his unremembered dreams.

The house was so still as he crept downstairs that he could actually feel the air yielding before him, a chill less substantial than mist. He winced as he opened the door to the cupboard under the stairs, as though that might reduce the squeak the hinges made, and retrieved the sports bag he had concealed behind a row of Wellingtons. He winced again as he turned the key in the lock of the kitchen door, and didn't begin to relax even when the door was closed behind him and he was loping across the back lawn towards the dark block of the shed. At the shed door he turned and looked back at the house. There was so little moon that he couldn't even distinguish the windows.

Beyond the shed, the trees at the end of the garden rustled as though someone was seeking greater cover, or perhaps stepping forward to reveal themselves. Tim imagined policemen rising from the darkness all around him, and though the thought of being discovered alarmed him, there was a part of him that would have welcomed it. But then the breeze which had stirred the leafless branches whispered over him, ruffling his hair, and he sighed, resigned to the fact that his responsibilities could not be so easily sidestepped, after all.

He gave two raps on the door, and, after a pause, two more.

A couple of seconds passed before the key grated in the lock and the door was pulled open. 'At last,' Oonagh hissed at him. 'Where have you been all day?'

'I couldn't get away,' said Tim a little shamefacedly, for this was not entirely true; he had merely been putting off this confrontation. 'The police came this morning.'

'Don't they come every day?' said Oonagh, stepping back to let Tim enter, then closing the door behind him.

'Yeah, I suppose, but this time they came about you.'

She paused in the act of reaching for the bag Tim was holding out to her, and looked up at him. 'Me? What did they say?'

'Let's sit down,' Tim said, 'and I'll tell you.'

Oonagh led the way to the back of the shed, the interior of which was made narrow by a set of rusting metal shelves on which were stacked packets of seeds and garden implements, boxes of bone meal and lawn food, bundles of twine and towers of plastic pots. Larger garden tools hung from hooks on the walls, above a hosepipe coiled loosely on the floor like a sleeping python. Leaning against the opposite wall, beneath the window which looked out over the lawn, were Tim and Chloe's bikes, and beside them an electric lawn mower. Beyond all this, against the far wall, Oonagh had set up her camp.

The bundled up sleeping bag and blankets Tim had hastily provided for her last night reminded him of a nest, and if he had been a few years younger and this had been a game and Chloe had still been alive, he would have found it an evocative place - cosy and exciting and secret. Tucked away in one corner was the bucket Oonagh had been using as a toilet with a paint-spattered piece of plastic sheeting draped over it. Next to that was a toilet roll and the remains of her day's provisions. Tim had supplied her with apples, biscuits, Weetabix, milk, half a pot of coleslaw, some tomatoes and a thermos of orange squash. She could have had some cold ham and chicken too, but she had told him that even if she had been starving she wouldn't have been able to bring herself to eat animal flesh.

The two of them sat down on the rumpled sleeping bag, cross-legged and facing each other, like Red Indians about to hold a powwow.

'So what did they say?' Oonagh asked again impatiently.

'Aren't you going to look at what I've brought you?'

'In a minute. I want to know why the police should come to see you. Oh, I suppose Graeme and Linda must have told them that we knew each other.'

Tim told Oonagh about the visit from Farrington and Lockwood that morning, emphasising their threat to deflect people from the murder investigation if she wasn't found soon.

Oonagh shook her head in disgust. 'That's typical of them. I mean, how low can you get?'

'Maybe they've got no choice,' said Tim. 'Maybe they haven't got enough people to deal with everything.'

'Of course they have! They were just saying that to make you feel guilty, and to see if you really knew where I was. It's an obvious trick.'

'Well, I'm not so sure.'

'Oh come on, Tim! I can't believe you're being so gullible.'

'I'm not,' Tim said indignantly. 'You weren't there. You didn't hear them.'

'I don't need to,' said Oonagh. 'In fact, you should be able to realise how they were trying to con you just by listening to yourself now. I'm sure this Inspector Farrington made it all sound very reasonable.'

'Maybe it's you who doesn't want to believe you're causing so much trouble for everyone.'

There was a short, simmering silence, then Oonagh said, 'If that's how you feel, then I'll go. Is that what you want?'

The conversation was turning out how Tim had feared it might. 'Oh, I don't know,' he said. 'What did you have to go and run away for in the first place, anyway?'

'They took me away from my parents, Tim. They just came and took all the children away. What would you expect me to do – stand by and accept that?'

'They only did it for your own protection.'

'Is *that* what they told you?'

'Yes it is, as it happens.'

'Oh well, if they said it, then it must be true, mustn't it?'

Tim took a deep breath. He was getting so frustrated he could feel his throat closing up. Eventually he said, 'She also said that you were the only one to run away. She said most of the other kids are treating the whole thing like a holiday.'

'Then she's a lying bitch!' Oonagh shouted, suddenly more furious than Tim had ever seen her. 'When they came to take us away, some of the younger children were screaming – *really* screaming – and holding their arms out for their parents. It was horrible, Tim. People like that – policemen, social workers – they don't like us because they don't understand the way we live. We threaten them by not fitting into their little categories. That's why they're always trying to break us up.'

Her anger dissipated some of Tim's own irritation. He glanced at the window, and saw a black lattice of branches embedded with blue shifting splinters of sky. He had always liked the smell of the shed – soil and grass cuttings and fresh wood. 'What was the place like they took you to?' he asked, as though prepared to be conciliatory.

Oonagh shrugged moodily. 'It was okay. The people were nice enough, I suppose. I wasn't there long enough to find out.'

There was another short silence, then she said, 'So what are you going to do?'

'What do you mean?'

'Well, it's your decision, isn't it? Are you going to throw me out, or tell the police that I'm here?'

Tim sighed. He felt so mentally and physically exhausted that he couldn't think straight. He just wanted to sleep, or rather to blot out everything, erase the past few days. He could certainly do without all this extra hassle just now.

'I don't want them to stop looking for the person who killed Chloe and start looking for you instead,' he said.

'They won't,' Oonagh said softly, and then, after a pause, 'So, *are* you going to tell them?'

Tim sighed, then reluctantly shook his head. 'No, of course not. You know I wouldn't do that.'

Oonagh's hand in the dark was cool on his, but her lips were warm.

'Thank you,' she whispered.

30

When Farrington arrived back at her flat on the outskirts of Harrogate it was after 3 a.m. The first thing that struck her as she entered was the musty smell, like that of old houses that have been closed up for too long. Occasionally she had thought of this place as a sanctuary, though never really as a home. She'd been here over two years and still hadn't got around to stripping off the brown and white 1970s wallpaper and giving the place a fresh coat of paint – a task she'd put top of her list of priorities when she'd moved in. She switched on the hall light, dragged off her overcoat and hung it up, then wandered through to the living room whose bank of windows looked down on an area of tarmac and a block of residents' garages.

She pottered about for a bit – watering plants that she suspected were already beyond help, pouring away the milk in her fridge that had turned sour, flicking through the *Radio Times* to decide what she would set the video to record tomorrow even though she knew she would almost certainly never get around to watching it. When she had performed all her little rituals that made her believe she was actually in control here, she made herself a salad sandwich, poured herself a glass of wine from the bottle in the fridge she was slowly working her way through, kicked off her shoes and flopped on to her dusty settee.

There were times when she liked being alone, and times when she didn't. At the moment she hated it, which was unfortunately the way things tended to work. When she was in a relationship she all too quickly found herself craving independence, resenting the emotional complications and obligations that came with being part of a couple; when she had been alone for a while, however, she found herself wanting company, someone to talk to, to show her some affection and help her forget the daily grind of police work.

It was for this latter reason that she had never been out with a policeman and had no intention of ever doing so – which was probably why she had the reputation at work of being something of an iron lady. And yet the irony was, another policeman would probably have been able to understand her motivations better than most. Her relationships generally faltered because, however much she sometimes resented the demands of her job, she was fully committed to it, and was never really prepared, when push came to shove, to put the same energy into a relationship as she put into her career. Not that she ever openly admitted this to herself – instead she tried to convince herself that she simply hadn't yet found the right man. But in her heart of hearts she was coming to realise that she probably never would. Last time she had visited her mother, the old lady had used a word which Farrington had never given breathing space to before, but which, since then and despite herself, now nagged constantly at the edge of her mind. The word was: *spinster*. A horrible, archaic word loaded with all sorts of hateful implications. But just because Farrington was no longer young and yet still single, did that make her deserving of the title? Then again, if she wasn't a spinster, what was she?

She gulped at her wine, which combined with her lack of sleep, made her feel light-headed, a sensation she welcomed. Deliberately she turned her thoughts away from her own relationship problems and on to the relationship which she had spent most of the day investigating – that between Ben Wyatt and Chloe Knight. Even now she wasn't sure whether Ben and Chloe had actually had anything going between them, or whether the contents of Chloe's diary had simply been the fanciful imaginings of a love-struck teenager. She and Lockwood had spent most of the morning talking to Wyatt, first at his school and then later on down at the station. At first he'd been cocky, arrogant, demanding to know what they wanted to see him for, claiming – even before they'd accused him – that he hadn't done anything wrong. However, when he realised they meant business, his bravado had quickly evaporated, to be replaced by alarm, nervous indignation, and even – when he finally cottoned on to what they were interviewing him about – fear.

Lockwood had played the hard man, reading out selected snippets from Chloe's diary as though presenting Wyatt with irrefutable evidence. The boy's reaction had been one of astonishment; he'd steadfastly denied any involvement with Chloe Knight, had claimed he hardly even knew the girl.

'So what are you saying?' Lockwood growled. 'That we've got the wrong Ben Wyatt? That this is a case of mistaken identity?'

'I don't know. She ... she must have made it all up, I suppose.'

'And why would she do that?'

'I don't know.' He flushed red. 'I suppose ... well, she must have fancied me.'

'You *suppose?* Don't you know?'

'Well, I ... I suspected, I guess.'

'And what made you *suspect?*'

'Well, she kept making a point of saying hi to me at school. And then the other day her friend asked me if I'd sent her a present.'

'Her friend? And who might that be?'

'Just a girl in her class. Blonde, good-looking. I think her name might be Tanya something.'

'And *did* you send Chloe Knight a present?'
'No.'
'What made her friend think you had, then?'
'I don't know. I suppose Chloe must have got a present from someone and they thought it was me ... I don't know.'
The interview had gone on for a long time, with Lockwood firing questions at Wyatt, never allowing him to pause for even a second, and then every so often, just when the boy seemed to be reeling like a boxer who had taken too many punches, Farrington cutting in, her voice calm, reasonable, understanding, in the hope that Wyatt would lower his defences, open up to her.
'Look, Ben, we're not accusing you of anything. In fact, we'd like nothing better than to eliminate you from our enquiries. But to do that we need the truth. You do see that, don't you?'
'Well ... yeah. But I didn't do anything to Chloe Knight. Like I say, I hardly even knew her.'
'Knowing her doesn't make you guilty of killing her, Ben. Now, are you sure you didn't know her better than you're letting on?'
'No, I told you, I only ever said hello to her once or twice—'
'Because anyone who did know her well could be a big help in catching the real killer. You do see that, don't you?'
Halfway through the interview, Farrington passed Ben a sheet of paper and a pen and asked him to write the words, I'M BACK, in block capitals.
'Why?' he asked, looking, as far as Farrington was concerned, genuinely puzzled.
'Just do it,' Lockwood said.
Tim Knight had described Wyatt as 'cock of his year', but it was evident he was no delinquent: he had obviously never been in this kind of situation before. Thoroughly cowed by the treatment he had received, he swallowed and complied. Lockwood took the sheet of paper, scrutinised it silently and passed it to his superior. Farrington gazed at it for far longer than was necessary, her face deadpan, then sent the paper to forensic to be analysed. Eventually the assessment came back: Ben Wyatt's handwriting and the writing on the cards sent to the Knight household were not the same.
After they had let Ben go, with a warning that they might want to speak to him again, Farrington told Lockwood, 'I want Wyatt watched, Frank. Nothing heavy, I just want to be kept informed of what he gets up to. Also, get a couple of the boys to check up on his movements on the day Chloe was killed, paying particular attention to the hour or so either side of the murder.' When Frank had gone to do her bidding, she picked up Chloe Knight's diary and flicked through

it. 'Not such an innocent, after all, were you, Chloe?' she murmured. 'But then again, who is?'

Now, sixteen hours later, Farrington swung her legs to the floor and stood up. She was due to give a briefing on the progress of the inquiry at divisional HQ in just over five hours, which meant that she ought to get some sleep, but she was restless, unsettled, her mind buzzing like a trapped wasp. She went into the kitchen and grabbed the bottle of wine, then carried it back into the living room. There was nothing more exhausting than forcing yourself to sleep when your mind was resisting it. She might as well sit here, watch one of the numerous films she'd recorded and get quietly pissed. What did she fancy? Definitely nothing with cops in it. A love story? No way. Something funny? Yeah, something really knockabout. She rummaged through her tapes, selected *Uncle Buck*, and settled back with a glass of wine.

Five minutes later she was fast asleep.

31

It wasn't for himself that Eric had come to dread the post. It was the thought of Tim or Annette getting here before him, unwittingly tearing open one of the brightly coloured envelopes and being subjected to the kind of malicious shit he'd had to put up with these past two days. Tim, actually, he wasn't too worried about – he'd be upset, but he'd get over it quickly; he'd use his anger as a defence. Annette, though, seemed to be balancing on the rim of a precipice. He was afraid that the slightest nudge might send her on to the jagged rocks below.

He was sitting on the bottom stair, smoking a cigarette and casting anxious glances upwards. When he had crept out of bed, his wife had moaned and stirred for a moment, as if the cold air that had rushed into the warm gap left by his body was attempting to probe her awake. At Tim's door, Eric had listened but had heard nothing. Sitting on the stairs now, he wondered when the family ought to start making moves to get things back to a semblance of normality. He couldn't stay away from his job and Tim from school and Annette from the shop for ever. Brutal though it seemed, the outside world wouldn't wait for them; it would continue to grind on, leaving them further and further behind.

He glanced at his watch: 8:05. He'd been waiting here for almost forty minutes. He still had the sick feeling in his stomach that he'd had since reading Chloe's diary yesterday. Although as a teacher he was all too aware that teenagers were nowhere near as innocent as their parents often liked to believe, he couldn't escape the fact that his idealistic image of his daughter – his little girl, his unsullied angel – had been denigrated by what he'd read, just as his mental picture of her, laughing and happy and full of life, had been denigrated by seeing her dead, disfigured face in the morgue. It was no good telling himself to be sensible and mature about the thing either; his instinctive emotional reaction far outweighed any amount of reason. He wondered whether his response would have been the same if she had still been alive and he'd discovered her diary, and he decided that no, it probably wouldn't. If Chloe had been here he could have talked the thing over with her sensibly, put it into perspective. As it was, he somehow had to try and live with what he'd learned about her. Whether she had actually done all the things she'd detailed in her diary was beside the point; the fact was, she'd thought about them, she'd imagined them. He'd always tried to be open and cool about all things sexual – he was a product of the Sexual Revolution, after all – but in these circumstances he couldn't deny it was hard.

He heard the crunch of footsteps outside, then the door was opening its mouth and vomiting envelopes into the house. He stubbed out his cigarette in the ashtray on the stair by his side, then stooped to pick up the batch of envelopes, acutely aware of the sound of his own pumping heart and the postman's receding footsteps. There weren't as many cards this morning and he spotted the lemon-yellow one instantly. Remembering Farrington's instructions, he tweezered the very corner of the envelope between the tip of his thumb and forefinger and eased it from the pile.

He carried the envelope into the kitchen, holding it out before him as though it were a rotten fish. Once there he opened it using a kitchen knife with a long thin blade, and, again taking great care to touch it as little as possible, teased out the card inside.

It was a bright watercolour this time, a spray of flowers in a blue vase on a checked tablecloth. The vase stood in front of a window, through which could be seen a pastoral summer scene, two figures running through a distant golden cornfield. Eric spotted the most obvious amendment instantly. The message across the top, a scroll of golden writing reading HAPPY BIRTHDAY, had been crudely altered with a blue biro to read HAPPY DEATHDAY. He set his face, pressing his lips together, as though he was being observed by the sender and was determined not to give him the satisfaction of showing any distress. He was about to open the card when he realised that the two tiny figures in the background were recent additions to the artwork. They were only stick figures, crudely drawn with biro, but the leading figure was certainly a girl, long hair streaming out behind her, and the pursuing figure a man brandishing a triangle that was obviously supposed to be a knife.

Eric felt sick. Distastefully he opened the card. This time the message inside read: MBF – LOOK FOR ME IN STEFAN'S BIG PICTURE.

For a moment Eric was baffled. Who was Stefan? And what did MBF mean? Then it clicked. Stefan Edberg. Of course, Chloe's heart-throb. Immediately he realised how much Ben Wyatt looked like Edberg – similar athletic build, blond hair, chiselled features – which in turn brought a flash-memory of something he'd read in Chloe's diary: *Ben has got a very big cock. He likes me to ...*

He clenched his teeth and shook his head as if to dislodge the memory. Then, still carrying the card by one corner, he went upstairs. He was almost at the top when it suddenly struck him what MBF meant, and a shock of coldness washed through him. It was as though an internal eye which had been closed for a long time had suddenly opened.

MBF. It couldn't be. And yet his legs felt hollow as he crossed the landing to Chloe's room. His thoughts suddenly felt like clouds that were floating somewhere above his head, or dreams in which he was losing control. Bracing himself, he opened the door and went inside.

LOOK FOR ME IN STEFAN'S BIG PICTURE. Chloe's room seemed still as a photograph. Eric was almost afraid to look at the shaft of daylight slicing through the gap in the curtains for fear of seeing motes of dust not curling lazily as they should be, but hanging motionless in the air. He dropped the card on to Chloe's bed, and slowly looked around. There were many pictures of Stefan Edberg plastered around Chloe's walls, but the biggest seemed to be a poster stuck on the back of the wardrobe door. Eric approached it, aware that he was struggling to catch his breath. The poster seemed to zizz in front of his eyes, as if trying to come alive.

LOOK FOR ME IN STEFAN'S BIG PICTURE. Eric tried to calm himself enough to scrutinise the picture carefully, at first the tennis player himself and then the crowd behind him. Most of the crowd were wearing sun hats and dark glasses, their heads tilted slightly to the right. But there in the middle of the fourth row was a figure so out of place that Eric was astonished he had not spotted it immediately. He recoiled as though from a hot flame, stumbling into the bed with such force that he fell backwards on to it, crumpling the yellow envelope beneath him.

It couldn't be true. It was a nightmare he and Jackie had carried through their childhoods and beyond, a black and terrible secret they had never revealed to anyone.

When they had killed the neighbourhood bogeyman, they had all been twelve years old.

At the time none of them had known the bogeyman's real name.

They'd all just called him Mr Bad Face.

32

'Dad, what's wrong?'

Tim felt a weird sense of *déjà vu*. Except that the last time he had heard a sound in Chloe's room and walked in, it had been Mum sitting on his sister's bed. His Dad, though, didn't simply look beside himself with grief as Mum had done; he looked ... terrified, his face white, his hands trembling.

He looked up. 'Tim,' he managed to say.

Tim advanced a couple of steps into the room. 'Are you all right, Dad?'

'All right?' Eric murmured as if the concept was alien to him, and gave a small shake of the head. 'No, not really.'

'Is there anything I can do?'

Eric smiled, but it was a ghastly expression, as if invisible hooks were tugging at the sides of his mouth. 'Some coffee would be good,' he said.

Tim noticed a yellow envelope poking out between the duvet and the seat of his father's trousers, and reached for it.

'What's this?'

Eric twisted round so suddenly that Tim jumped back. 'Don't touch it!' Eric snapped.

'Why not? Who's it from?'

'It's nothing,' Eric said unconvincingly, then immediately amended himself: 'It's evidence.' Then his shoulders slumped. 'Oh, Jeez, I suppose I might as well tell you the whole story. Things have gone too far to keep secrets from one another.'

Wearily he nodded towards the wardrobe. 'Have a look at that picture there, Tim, and tell me what you see.'

Tim raised his eyebrows, but did as his father had asked. 'It's a picture of Stefan Edberg,' he said carefully.

'What else?'

'What do you mean, what else?'

'Do you notice anything ... odd about it?'

Tim looked again. Eventually he said, 'Not really. It's just Stefan Edberg at Wimbledon. He's about to serve. It's a sunny day.' He shrugged. 'What am I supposed to see?'

'What about the crowd?'

'The crowd,' Tim murmured, and gazed at the rows of faces in the background. 'Well, they're very blurred. Lots of them are wearing sunglasses and hats. Oh!'

'What is it?' Eric said, tension in his voice.

'I've just noticed this figure here.' Tim hunched his shoulders as he gave a small involuntary shiver. 'It's pretty creepy.'

The figure he was pointing at was sitting in the middle of the fourth row of spectators. Whereas most of the crowd were wearing pale summery clothes, this man was wearing what appeared to be a blue boiler suit. Also the man's head was not inclined to the right, following the play as the others were, but instead he appeared to be gazing straight into the camera lens and therefore out of the poster.

Neither of these factors would have seemed overly unusual, however, if it hadn't been for the man's face. Although all the background faces were blurred, most of them had pink or brown skin and features discernible enough to appear normal. This man, however, had a bald and somehow lumpy-looking head. Perhaps it was just a trick of the sun, but his flesh appeared unnaturally white and strangely shiny, like scar tissue or candle wax. Furthermore he seemed to have no ears and no nose, and the eyes and mouth were simply a triangle of black misshapen blurs in the face, the mouth in particular seeming to hang open as if the man was shouting or screaming.

'You *can* see it then?' Eric said. 'I thought it might just have been me.'

'Of course I can see it,' said Tim. 'What's going on, Dad? Do you know who this man is?'

Eric let out a long sigh. 'Come on,' he said, 'let's go to the study. I can't sit here with that looking out at me. And besides, I need a cigarette.'

In the study, he rolled and lit a cigarette, then drew on it as if sucking in life-giving oxygen. He kept the smoke in his lungs a long time before blowing it out. Finally he said, 'You know how I've always encouraged you not to keep secrets, Tim, to come and talk to me if you had a problem?'

Tim nodded.

'Yes, well, I've got a secret. A big one. I've never told anyone about it before. Not even Annette.'

Tim swallowed. 'What about Mum?' he said. 'Jackie, I mean. Does she know?'

Eric laughed harshly. 'Oh yes, Jackie knows. You see, this is her secret too. You might say it's what first brought us together.' He took another drag on his cigarette, leaned forward and fixed Tim with a penetrating gaze. 'When we were young,' he said, 'we did a bad thing. A really bad thing.' He paused, and then said in a hushed, oddly flat voice, 'We killed a man.'

Interlude: July 24 1965

'Why don't we go round the back of Mr Bad Face's house and see if we can see in through the windows?' said Andrew.

Eric lowered the binoculars he'd been using to observe number 39 and stared at his friend. Jackie and James, who were sitting on the floor of Andrew's bedroom, playing chess, looked up too.

Andrew Dullaston was a big, heavy-set boy who looked older than his thirteen years. He had a knuckly face and a pudding-basin haircut, which he thought made him look like one of the Beatles, but which Eric secretly thought made him look more like Bully Beef out of the *Dandy*. Dullaston regarded himself as leader of their four-strong gang, both because of his size and aggressive manner, and because his parents were a little richer than everyone else's, and ostentatious enough to ensure their son had a snazzier bike and better toys and games than his friends, including – the ultimate status symbol – a real leather football, which was far superior to the horrible balloon-light plastic things everyone else owned.

For a few seconds there was silence, then Jackie said tentatively, 'Are you serious?'

Dullaston sneered. 'Course I am. Why? You scared?'

'Course not,' Jackie snapped back. 'I was just wondering, that's all.'

'Won't it be a bit dangerous?' said James.

Eric cringed inwardly. James was always doing this, opening himself up to abuse. Eric didn't know why he did it; he wasn't stupid, so maybe he just couldn't help it. Maybe he had been placed on the planet for the simple sad purpose of waving red rags at bulls. Often it wasn't just *what* he said that riled Dullaston, but the way he said it. He was a small weedy boy with a soft voice and a timid manner – the exact opposite of Dullaston, in fact. However, it wasn't only his manner that rubbed Dullaston up the wrong way. There were other factors involved, over which James had no control. Dullaston was scornful of the fact that James was always a little down at heel and never had any money in his pocket, though Eric knew that this was because James' mother had found it hard to make ends meet after her husband's death when her son was just a baby. Also Dullaston hated the fact that James was a 'Mummy's boy', though again Eric felt nothing but sympathy when James shamefacedly excused himself at 7:30 each evening and trudged off home. If ever he was a few minutes late, his mother's piercing cry would ring down the street and across the playing fields behind the houses: 'Woo-oo, James, where are you? Time to come ho-ome.' On these occasions, Dullaston's teasing would become merciless. 'Ooh, it's time for beddy-weddy, Jamey-wamey. Is Mumsy-wumsy going to tuck you up with a nice hot cup of cocoa and read you a liddle story, den?'

Now Dullaston bared his teeth, his face bunching like a fist. 'Is it going to be a bit too scary for you, Jamey-wamey?' he said. 'Is it going to make you poo your little panty-wanties?'

'Leave him alone, Andrew,' said Jackie.

Dullaston's eyes widened. 'Or what will you do? Hit me with your handbag?'

Jackie scowled. Eric couldn't imagine her ever owning a handbag. Although she was a stunner, and all three of them secretly fancied her (even Dullaston, though he always showed it by trying to act big, perhaps in the hope that he would impress her enough to make her swoon into his arms), she was also a real tomboy. She was quite prepared to do anything that the boys did, and went on all their 'expeditions', which generally involved scrabbling about in some muddy river bed or other, getting covered with bruises and scrapes and nettle stings. She was also a better footballer and cricketer than most of them, and a better fighter too – she had once given Craig Stewart, their arch enemy from two streets away, a black eye and a bloody nose when he inferred that her mother was a prostitute.

'If I hit you, you wouldn't wake up till next week,' she said.

Dullaston held his belly and gave an exaggerated guffaw. 'Oh yeah? You and whose army?'

Jackie rose from her lotus position in one fluid motion and bunched her fists. 'I don't need an army to handle you,' she said. 'Want to try it?'

Dullaston pulled a pitying face. 'I don't fight with girls.' Then he poked the still-sitting James in the kidneys with his foot. 'Except for this one, maybe.'

James rubbed his back and pursed his lips but didn't say anything.

'Did you really mean it, Andy, about going round the back of the house?' said Eric in a deliberate attempt to change the subject.

Dullaston pushed out his jaw, as if he thought that Eric too might be challenging his idea. 'Yeah, course,' he said. 'Why? You gonna come?'

Eric glanced at Jackie, then shrugged. He didn't like the idea one bit, but he tried to sound casual. 'Yeah, I might do. If everyone else wants to.'

Perhaps to prevent Dullaston having another go at her, Jackie said quickly, 'Yeah, me too, actually. I'll do whatever.'

'And what about little Jamey-wamey?' said Dullaston. 'Are you going to come with us or are you going to run off home to Mummy?'

James looked trapped. When he cleared his throat it sounded as if he was squeaking. In an even softer voice than usual, he began, 'Are we just going to—'

'Speak up, I can't hear you,' Dullaston barked.

James cringed. He cleared his throat more vigorously and tried again. Fortunately his voice was a little stronger the second time. 'Are we just going to look in through the windows?'

'No, I thought we'd have a picnic in the back garden,' said Dullaston, then leaned forward and boomed, 'Joke,' as if James had taken him seriously, though in truth Dullaston hadn't even given him time to react.

James looked unhappy, but he didn't repeat his question. On his behalf, Jackie said, 'James is right. We need to decide exactly what we're going to do.'

'Why?' said Dullaston, rolling his eyes.

'Because this is like a special expedition, isn't it? If we were proper soldiers, we wouldn't just go rushing in without some sort of plan, would we?'

Sometimes Jackie had a way of manipulating Dullaston that Eric recognised and admired, especially when it came to deflecting attention away from James. Now Dullaston, who devoured war comics like there was no tomorrow, went all misty-eyed at the words 'special expedition'. 'Yeah,' he said, 'I suppose so. First, we need a name for it, though. We could call it Operation ...'

'Peeping Tom?' said James hesitantly.

Before Dullaston could pour scorn on the suggestion, which he would undoubtedly have done as a matter of course, Jackie said, 'That's a good idea, James. Operation Peeping Tom. Yeah, I like

that. What do you think, Eric?'
'Perfect,' Eric said.
'Okay, now that's sorted out we need a definite plan. What do you think we should do, Andy?'
They spent the next twenty minutes discussing their plan, which in the main took the form of trying to find solutions to various problems. The biggest of these was the fact that the high-walled back garden of number 39 Jasmine Road was only accessible via a narrow path that ran up the side of the house. If someone were to come up that path after them, they would be trapped.
'We'd just have to fight our way out,' said Dullaston, not without relish. 'We'd be all right, there's four of us ... well, three and a half,' he amended, looking at James. 'We could take weapons.'
'What sort of weapons?' said Eric.
Dullaston shrugged. 'Whatever you can get hold of. Sticks. Knives.'
'Knives?' said James, blanching.
'Our mums'd kill us if they caught us going out of the house with knives,' said Eric.
'Yours maybe,' said Dullaston with disgust. Everyone knew that his parents let him do more or less whatever he pleased.
'You could bring your spud gun, Andy,' said Jackie, 'and I'll bring my catapult. On a proper military expedition, they'd have weapons to *fire* at the enemy. They wouldn't attack them with knives.'
'They'd have bayonets,' said Dullaston.
'Not these days they wouldn't,' said Eric. 'They didn't have them in the war.'
'Yes, they did,' said Dullaston. 'I've seen pictures.'
The argument raged on, and by lunchtime was still unresolved. One thing the four of them did agree upon, however, was the timing of the expedition. Originally Dullaston wanted it to take place at midnight, all four of them sneaking out of their houses, leaving pillows bunched up beneath their bedclothes to fool their parents into thinking they were still asleep. However, once Eric had pointed out that they would be unlikely to see a thing through Mr Bad Face's windows in the pitch darkness, Dullaston reluctantly agreed to bring Operation Peeping Tom forward to two o'clock that afternoon.
Eric could hardly eat anything at lunchtime. As usual, Dullaston had pushed things a little further than the rest of them felt comfortable with, transforming the situation from a thrilling bit of fun into something nerve-wracking and potentially dangerous. This whole Mr Bad Face thing had started two months ago. It stemmed from the house at the bottom of the quiet, suburban cul-de-sac in Tewkesbury

where the four children lived with their families. For as long as Eric could remember the shabby house had crouched there in its overgrown front garden, each window reduced to a blind eye by drab greyish curtains which were always closed. It might have been empty apart from the fact that the milkman and the grocer made regular deliveries there, each of them taking their wares round the back, and every so often a rusty blue car would park on the pavement outside, and a dumpy, middle-aged woman would get out, jangling a set of keys like a warder in an old prison movie, and, like everyone else, would trudge up the narrow path that led round the back of the house.

All of this mysterious activity had naturally led to some speculation amongst the local kids over the years. The younger ones particularly would dare each other to run up the drive and rap on the front door before fleeing as fast as their legs could carry them. Eric had once asked his mother who lived at number 39, and she had said that it was a housebound old man who just wanted to be left in peace. For the last few years, therefore, he had barely given the house a second thought.

And then one Saturday morning in May, with the first whisper of summer in the air, Andrew Dullaston had dropped his bombshell. The occupant of number 39 was not a man at all, he told them, but a hideous monster.

Dullaston's bedroom window faced number 39, albeit at an oblique angle. The previous evening he had been looking through his binoculars when he had seen the curtains at one of the upstairs windows move just a little. Next moment he had caught a brief glimpse of the face of the thing that lived there.

'What did it look like?' Jackie asked warily.

'Get your bikes,' Dullaston replied, 'and I'll show you.'

The four of them cycled into town, James at the rear on the boneshaker that Dullaston always took the mickey out of, pedalling furiously to keep up. Eventually Dullaston skidded to a stop outside the cinema, and pointed at the poster for the film that was playing that week.

'See that?' he said.

Eric took off his glasses, cleaned them on his shirt and put them on again.

'Yeah,' said Jackie.

'Well, that's exactly what he looked like, I swear. Cross my heart and hope to die.'

The poster was for a Hammer horror film called *The Evil of Frankenstein*. It was all lurid reds and yellows, the foreground dominated by a picture of the monster with its lumpen, deformed face, and its square block of a head covered in scars.

For a few seconds, the four friends stood in silence, staring at the poster. Then James, still out of breath from pedalling, gasped wonderingly, 'You mean Frankenstein lives in that house?'

'Don't be stupid,' said Dullaston scathingly. 'I said it just *looked* like Frankenstein, I didn't say it was him.'

'Yeah, but someone could have got the idea from Frankenstein, couldn't they?' said Eric. 'They could have got a load of bits from dead bodies and sewn them together and brought it alive, couldn't they?'

Dullaston shrugged. 'Maybe.'

'Don't be stupid,' said Jackie. 'Frankenstein's not real.' Then she added as if to convince herself, 'Besides, where would they get all that electricity from to bring him alive?'

'Did this ... thing you saw at the window have a big square head and scars and everything?' Eric asked.

Dullaston nodded gravely. 'Yep. If Jamey-wamey had been there, he would've thrown an eppy.'

'No, I wouldn't,' James protested half-heartedly.

'Yes, you would. Don't argue with me or I'll punch your head in.'

James flushed, prompting Jackie to say hastily, 'Now that you've told us about this monster you saw, Andy, what are we going to do about it?'

They had come to the conclusion that it was their duty to observe it, to collect information and evidence, to build up what Dullaston called a 'dossier' (a word he had learned from reading about the exploits of Chip McGann, Superspy).

And for the past two months the four of them had been doing exactly that. It had been a deliciously thrilling time. They felt as if they were employed on a secret and dangerous mission, although there was a sense of security in the knowledge that if things got out of hand they could present their 'dossier' to their parents, or even the police, and let them take over.

Even the fact that there had been no further sightings of Mr Bad Face, as Jackie had christened him, since Dullaston had seen him at the window had not dampened the gang's enthusiasm. In fact, Eric secretly felt some measure of relief that he had not seen the creature himself. At school the four of them would pass each other notes full of speculative comments and wild theories. Eric would write something like, 'Maybe the woman with the blue car is the wife of a scientist and Mr BF is one of his experiments', and a little later he would receive a reply written in Jackie's careful script or James' crabbed handwriting or Andrew's thick scrawl: 'Maybe the keys she carries are for a dungeon under the house.'

All of these ideas and theories would be noted down in the 'dossier', a school exercise book with a yellow cardboard cover which Andrew kept in a suitcase on top of his wardrobe. Also in the suitcase was the body of 'evidence' that the four of them had collated over the past two months.

If pushed, Eric would have had to admit that some of the articles in here were a little dubious. There was an empty purse which someone might have dropped in horror when Mr Bad Face jumped out at them; a chewed stick which he might have used to sharpen his teeth on; a large bolt which might have fallen out of his neck. Indeed, if Eric had been asked whether he truly believed there was a monster living at number 39 Jasmine Road he wouldn't have known what to say. When he was with his friends, picking up on their enthusiasm, he *wanted* to believe, for the simple reason that it made life more mysterious and exciting. However there were occasions late at night, when everyone else was asleep and he was lying awake in the darkness, listening to the night sounds outside and the peculiar, often alarming creaks *inside* the house, when he would have given anything to know for sure that monsters didn't *really* exist.

He felt in need of such assurances now. It was creeping inexorably towards two. In ten minutes the four of them would be meeting at Andy's house, and five minutes after that they would probably be in Mr Bad Face's back garden.

What if Andy had been right and there *was* a monster living in that house? Or if not a monster, a madman, say, with crazed eyes and a slavering mouth? And what if that madman came bursting out of the back door with an axe in his hand? What if he knew they'd been spying on him and he was at that moment sitting there in the stinking darkness, waiting for them, surrounded by the rotting bodies of his victims?

Eric felt sick. Sweat was oozing out of his palms. He clenched his hands and looked out of the window. A week into the summer holidays, the sun blazing, the sky of such an incredible blue that it hurt his eyes to look at it. He should have been on top of the world, looking forward to long, blissful days of fun and relaxation, but thanks to bloody Dullaston he was sitting here with his stomach churning and his head swarming with dark and dismal thoughts.

I should have put my foot down, he thought. I should have stood up to him and said it was a dumb idea; the others would have backed me up. He sighed. Too late now. He forced down the last of the ham and tomato sandwich his mum had made so she wouldn't think he was sickening for something, then went into the garage to grab a cricket stump for a weapon. Hoping he wouldn't have to use it, he plodded down the street towards Andrew's house, the heat of the sun bearing down oppressively, like heavy hands on his shoulders and head. As he passed James' house, the front door opened and James came out and ran down the drive, waving. He looked even smaller and paler than usual. Eric noted that he wasn't carrying a weapon of any sort.

'Hi,' Eric said.

'Hi. I saw you walking past. Are you calling for Jackie?'

'No, I just said I'd see her at Andy's.'

'Oh, right.'

The two of them fell silent as they trudged down the road, both apprehensive for similar reasons but unwilling to expose their misgivings for fear of ridicule.

Jasmine Road resembled a gentle L shape. Eric and James lived close together at the top of the street, Jackie lived more or less on the crook of the L, and Andrew lived in number 34, down near the bottom, his house the only one from which number 39 was visible.

Eric and James passed Jackie's house, rounded the bend, and all at once both Andy's and Mr Bad Face's houses came into view. As if this had prompted him to speak, James suddenly blurted, 'Are you scared?'

Eric paused before replying, then he nodded. 'Yeah, a bit. You?'

'Yes,' said James, the word whooshing out of him as if he was mightily relieved to expel it.

'Hey, you two.' Jackie's voice came from behind them. They stopped and turned. She jogged to catch them up, her dark hair bouncing. She had a catapult sticking out of her back jeans pocket, and her front pockets were bulging with what Eric could only assume was ammo.

'Ready for Operation Peeping Tom?' she said.

'Yeah,' said Eric with as much enthusiasm as he could muster, avoiding James' eye.

'I'll be glad when it's over, to be honest,' Jackie admitted. 'I think this is one of Andy's stupider ideas. I don't think we'll see anything, though, do you?'

She sounded as if she was looking for reassurance. Eric, all too willing to give it, shook his head vigorously. 'Nah. I bet the curtains'll be closed round the back as well. We'll be all right. I mean, the milkman goes round there every day, doesn't he?'

'Do you think Andy really *did* see a monster?' James said tentatively.

Eric blinked in surprise. This was the first time in two months that anyone had actually questioned the validity of Andrew's story.

'I think he saw something,' Jackie said.

'I hope we don't find out what it was,' James murmured, almost too quietly for them to hear.

Dullaston answered the door on the first knock as if he'd been waiting impatiently for them to arrive. 'All ready?' he said in a voice full of eagerness. The three of them nodded. 'Good. Come on, then.'

As they trudged the fifty yards or so towards number 39, the sun beating down on them, Eric half-hoped some adult would emerge from a nearby front door to ask what they were doing, thus forcing them to abandon their expedition. However the street seemed deserted, as if everyone had gone out for the day, the baking heat and lack of a breeze creating a stillness that seemed somehow expectant.

On the pavement outside the rust-spotted gate of number 39 they stood for a few moments and looked up at the house. The path leading to the disused front door was choked with weeds which seemed by their very proliferation to have caused the cement to crack and crumble. The grass in the front garden, though parched and brittle-looking, had grown to waist height and was dotted with the acid-yellow heads of dandelions. The house itself looked grey and ill, slates missing from the roof, paint peeling like old skin from the woodwork around the windows. The big front window, long curtains so grey they seemed composed of dust concealing the interior of the house from prying eyes, reflected the summer sky, the ghost of an occasional fluffy white cloud sliding across the glass. The four of them would have to walk right past that window to get to the passage that ran down the side of the house. Eric again imagined some hunched, salivating creature crouching in the gloom, watching their shadows pass by with burning red eyes, then scuttling on spider-like limbs to the back door to greet them.

'Right then,' Dullaston said in a voice so full of bravado that Eric knew he was at least partly faking it. He shoved open the gate and led the way up the path, his spud gun slung over his shoulder. For the first time Eric noticed that he was limping, or at least walking stiff-leggedly – there appeared to be a foot-long pole or club stuffed down the back of his trousers. Eric wondered whether to ask him about it, then decided not to bother. He didn't particularly want to raise his voice this close to the house, and besides, it seemed as though Andrew had at least taken their advice not to bring along a knife, for which they ought to be grateful.

Passing the window was not one of Eric's favourite moments. He held his breath and kept his eyes firmly on Andrew's back. If he'd been aware of the curtains twitching even a little, he would not have been able to prevent himself bolting in panic, ploughing through the long grass of the front lawn and leaping over the low wall on to the pavement. It was almost a relief to reach the passageway that led between the side of the house and the tall fence that bordered the property next door, even though the passageway seemed dark and cool after the heat and brightness of the street.

All of them were creeping now. Even Andrew, with his curious, stiff-legged gait, was on his tiptoes. None of them spoke, or even established eye contact. Eric was trying to concentrate on keeping his breathing as quiet as possible.

He pushed his tongue out between his dry lips to separate them as they emerged from the passageway into the back garden, and tried to compose himself, to relax the taut muscles that had made him clench his teeth so hard they were aching. He turned to see Jackie trying not to look nervous, and beyond her James, who looked pale as marble, eyes wide in his head.

The back garden was a sun trap, hot as an oven after the coolness of the passageway. Eric felt beads of sweat hatch out under his hair, run together and form a trickle down the side of his face. He trapped it with a forefinger, flicking it away as he looked around. The back garden was as overgrown as the front. A dilapidated shed crouched in the far corner, its wood so rotted you could see right through it in places. It made Eric think of the decaying body of a large mammal – a whale, perhaps, washed up on a beach, flesh shrinking back, tearing apart to reveal the grey bones beneath.

The back of the house was as scabrous as the front. Eric was relieved to see that even here curtains were pulled across all the windows.

'Aw, look,' Jackie hissed, pointing this out and managing to sound genuinely disappointed, 'we're not going to be able to see anything through here either. We might as well go.'

'Not yet,' Dullaston said. He placed his spud gun on the ground, lifted up the back of his T-shirt and drew out the wooden club that had hampered his movements. Around the end of the club he had taped a thick wad of rag.

'What's that for?' James asked warily, as if he half-expected Dullaston to start beating him around the head with it.

'It's one of those things all the villagers carry in the Frankenstein films,' said Dullaston with obvious pride. 'I thought if we met Mr Bad Face we'd be able to hold him off with it. Look.'

He produced a box of matches and a small glass bottle full of clear liquid from his pocket. 'Petrol,' he said. 'We pour it over the rag and then we light it. Good, eh?'

Jackie raised her eyebrows. 'Yes, very nice,' she said, unimpressed.

'Pity you're not going to be able to use it, though, isn't it?'

'Who says I'm not going to be able to use it?' said Dullaston petulantly.

She shielded her eyes and made a big show of looking round the garden. 'Well, *I* can't see Mr Bad Face anywhere,' she said. 'What are you going to do? Knock on his door and wait for him to come out?'

'No. I'm going to go in and look for him,' Dullaston said.

That took the wind from her sails. She flinched back as if Dullaston had raised a hand to strike her, her eyes widening.

'You're not,' said Eric, his voice hoarse and shocked and louder than he intended.

'Why not?' said Dullaston.

'Well, because ... because you just *can't*,' Eric said, so appalled by his friend's plan he couldn't find the words to express himself. It wasn't just that there might be a monster waiting for them in there, it was also because Dullaston's suggestion went against everything that had been drummed into him as a child, his sense of right and wrong. You don't just walk into people's houses, uninvited. Only criminals did things like that.

'Well, I'm going to,' Dullaston said. 'You can come with me or you can wait here, I'm not bothered.'

'How will you get in?' said Jackie.

'I'll smash the window.'

'You *can't* do that!' spluttered Eric. It seemed to be all that he was capable of saying at the moment.

'Just watch me,' said Dullaston, stomping over to the window by the back door and raising his club. Eric clapped his hands to the sides of his head as if by blocking his ears he could somehow lessen the damage that Dullaston was about to do.

Then James said quietly, 'Why don't you try the back door first?'

Dullaston paused, looked at James as if he was beneath contempt, and seemed about to say something when Jackie nipped in front of Dullaston and did as James had suggested. With a click the door opened. Jackie left it ajar and stepped back smartly as if she expected something to lunge from the gloom and grab her wrist. For a few seconds the four friends stood and stared at the door as if it had opened of its own accord.

Then Dullaston said, 'Right, I'm going in. Are you softies coming with me or not?'

Eric and Jackie looked at each other, neither wishing to be the first to chicken out, whilst James just looked at the ground. Dullaston tutted disgustedly, scooped up his spud gun and without another word shoved open the back door and marched into the house.

The door swung to behind him. After a moment, through the gap, there was a burst of light as he lit his torch, which quickly faded to an orange flicker. Then the light moved away and was replaced by gloom and shadows once more.

For perhaps thirty seconds the three of them stood there, saying nothing, Eric bracing himself for the sound of running footsteps, or a scream, or even the reappearance of Dullaston himself, gibbering like a maniac, hair gone white with shock, face scarred with claw-marks. Then Jackie sighed and said impatiently, 'Oh bloody hell, I suppose we can't just leave him, can we?'

Without waiting for a reply, she shoved the back door open as if defying it to stop her, and followed Dullaston into the house.

The shadows inside had swallowed her up before Eric even had time to react. He looked at James, horrified and helpless. He could possibly have left Dullaston to his fate, but not Jackie. 'Oh God,' he said, and feeling like a little kid at the moment when the carriage bumps open the double doors into the Ghost Train, he lurched forward on hollow legs, bringing up his hand to shove the door open. It swung before him, and he stepped out of the sunshine into blackness.

At least that was what it seemed like at first after the intense brightness of the sun. It was a cool, smoky, musty blackness that moved against his face like cloth, and for several interminable seconds he could only stand rigid, hands clenched into fists, feeling helpless and horribly vulnerable. Then his eyes began to adjust; the shadows divided into grey blocky shapes, which quickly acquired enough detail to be recognised as the very ordinary objects they really were: a sink with taps, a cooker, a refrigerator, several work surfaces, a pantry, some wall cupboards. This was a kitchen, sparse and functional, with a vague smell of things being closed up for too long underlying the acrid stench of smoke from Andrew's torch, but clean enough.

At the other end of the room, her hand on the door handle that led deeper into the house, was Jackie.

'Eric,' she hissed, 'you followed me.'

He couldn't decide whether she sounded pleased or accusatory. He nodded, and then realising she might not be able to see the movement in the gloom was about to say something when there was a yawn of light behind him.

He turned to see James' small, thin frame silhouetted against the brightness outside before the door swung closed, like a chunk of darkness that appeared to absorb him.

'Hi,' Eric whispered. James jumped, and Eric realised that the smaller boy couldn't see him; his eyes would still be adjusting. 'Don't worry, it's just me,' Eric assured him. 'Jackie's over here. You'll be able to see us both in a minute.'

Almost immediately James was moving tentatively forward. Eric's eyes had fully adjusted now, to the extent that he knew the gloom was simply that of a room with thick dark curtains drawn across the windows, and not an unnatural darkness as he'd first thought. He could see James' eyes, which were round and dark as a lemur's.

'Come on, you two,' hissed Jackie urgently. 'Andy'll be miles away by now.'

Eric and James made their way across to where she was standing, by the door at the other side of the room. As she opened it, flickering orange shapes scampered forward to ambush them, blowing smoke into their lungs, making them cough. They clapped hands over their mouths, trying to stifle the sounds they were making; Eric's eyes bulged with the effort. In his free hand he kept a tight grip on the cricket stump, which felt like oiled metal in his sweaty palm.

At last the three of them were able to bring themselves under control. Eric's throat felt raw and itchy; he swallowed in an attempt to lubricate it. They moved forward into a hallway illuminated by the eerie light from Andrew's torch. Andrew himself was standing at the bottom of a flight of stairs which formed a sloping wood-panelled wall to their left, looking up, his face an orange mask.

The three of them made their way towards him. He looked as though he'd been there a little while because smoke from his torch had collected beneath the ceiling. The right-hand wall of the hallway was covered in heavy flock wallpaper which looked a deep red in the light from the flames. There was a door on the right at the end of the hallway, opposite the front door which was immediately to the left at the bottom of the stairs, the small window beside it curtained like every other window in the house. Eric was disturbed to see how heavily locked and bolted the front door was; there would be no escape that way if they needed it. The other door presumably led into the lounge with the big front window. Eric shuddered as he came near to it, noticing that it was open the tiniest crack, revealing nothing but a line of blackness inside.

Dullaston turned his head to scowl at them as they came alongside him. 'You made enough bloody noise, didn't you?' he whispered. 'Did you really have to cough like that?'

'It's the smoke from your stupid torch,' said Jackie.

'It doesn't bother me.'

'That's because it's drifting away from you.'

'Well, at least you can see, thanks to me,' said Dullaston.

'You can see anyway once your eyes have adjusted,' Jackie retorted.

'Yeah, but not well enough to tell if something's creeping up on you out of the shadows, not until it gets really close.' Suddenly Dullaston looked beyond Jackie to James, and his eyes widened. 'God, look at the size of that spider on Keevey's shoulder,' he hissed.

James jumped and swiped at first one shoulder, then the other. 'Where?' he squealed, loud enough to make Eric wince.

Dullaston cackled. 'Made you look, made you stare, made you soil your underwear,' he sang softly.

James looked as furious as Eric had ever seen him. 'You bastard,' he muttered.

Immediately the grin disappeared from Dullaston's face. 'Come here and say that, you little fart.'

'Pack it in,' Eric hissed, still eyeing the ominous black crack between the lounge door and its frame, 'he'll hear us.'

'Unless he's stone deaf, he'll already have heard you lot barking like seals,' said Dullaston.

'Look, let's stop arguing,' said Jackie. 'We're all in this together now. All for one and one for all, okay?'

Eric nodded. 'Definitely.'

'James?' Jackie said.

James was still brushing his hands nervously across his shoulders as if he wasn't entirely convinced the non-existent spider wouldn't suddenly materialise. He nodded too. 'All right,' he said.

'What about you, Andy?' said Jackie.

Dullaston looked at her contemptuously, then nodded at James. 'He's still a little fart.'

'It was James who said we should come in and back you up,' Eric hissed angrily, then tried not to show the surprise even he felt at the impromptu lie.

Caught off-guard, Dullaston looked at James with something like gratitude for a second, then the expression was snatched back out of sight like an errant toddler who had wandered out of a house into a busy street.

'I didn't ask you to, did I?' he said. 'I was all right on my own.'

'We'll go then, shall we?' said Jackie.

'I thought you said we were all in this together now,' Dullaston said quickly.

'We are,' said Eric.

'Well, you might as well stay then, I suppose, now that you're here.'

Eric felt a flush of warmth as Jackie turned and flashed him a secret smile, but this immediately turned to a vague disappointment as she bestowed the same expression on James.

Partly to hide what he felt was the obviousness of his emotions, and partly in an attempt to exorcise a personal fear, Eric indicated the lounge door as surreptitiously as he could and whispered so that nothing that might be lurking inside could hear him, 'Do you think we should have a look in here?'

'I've already looked,' Dullaston said.

'Was there anything in there?'

'Nothing much, only some half-eaten dead bodies that had gone all rotten and green.'

'Ha ha,' said Eric, trying not to betray the nervousness he felt.

'And some heads on poles with their eyes ripped out and brains dribbling out of their ears,' Dullaston continued, warming to his subject.

Angrily Jackie hissed, 'Be quiet, Andy, you're not funny.'

Dullaston grinned. 'The brains looked just like rice pudding.'

'I said be quiet!'

'All squishy and—'

'*Shh!* Listen.'

The urgency in Eric's voice was enough to make them all pause and stand motionless. Jackie and James looked fearful and expectant, Dullaston nonplussed that he had been interrupted in mid-flow. After a few seconds Dullaston said accusingly, 'What are we supposed to be listening for?'

'I thought I heard something,' said Eric. 'Voices.'

Dullaston rolled his eyes. 'It'll be someone walking past outside.'

'No, it sounded as if it was coming from upstairs.'

Dullaston raised his torch. The stairs seemed to pulse and bloat with amber light. 'You're cracking up,' he said.

'Why shouldn't Eric have heard voices?' said Jackie. 'There *might* be people upstairs.'

'Who?' challenged Dullaston.

'I don't know. Mr Bad Face and the woman with the blue car.'

'Her car wasn't outside when we came in.'

'Well, I don't know then.'

Still lingering at the back of the group, James said hesitantly, 'Maybe it's just Mr Bad Face, talking to himself. Mad people do that sometimes. They're called ... schizophrenics.' He stumbled slightly over the word.

Dullaston thrust his torch so high that the flames seemed almost to lick the ceiling. 'Let's go and see,' he said.

'I'm not sure we should,' said Jackie.

'Why not?'

'I don't know. It just doesn't seem right.'

'My mum says it's just an old man who lives here,' said Eric, uncertain whether he was trying to shame them into leaving or reassure himself.

'How would she know?' said Dullaston.

Eric hesitated, then said lamely, 'She just does.'

Dullaston sneered. 'You're just chickening out. I don't care what anyone says. I know what I saw through my binoculars. I'm still going up whether you lot come or not.'

He began to stomp up the stairs, making no attempt to keep quiet. It was so smoky in the house now that he was only about halfway up when his outline began to get hazy. It was here that he stopped, a strange expression coming over his illuminated face.

'What is it?' hissed Jackie.

Dullaston cocked his head, as if his ears were blocked with water. 'I can hear voices now, too,' he said.

Eric crept up the stairs to join him, both uncomfortable with the fact that he was still clutching the cricket stump, and grateful for the solid weight of it in his hand. He desperately wanted to be out of here, and not just because there might be a monster or a maniac waiting for them upstairs. Indeed, even if he had *known* there was simply a frail and bedridden old man up there he still wouldn't have felt any better. The thought of how an old man might react when he saw them, brandishing weapons and a burning torch, made Eric feel deeply ashamed. He'd probably be terrified; he might even be so shocked it would bring on a heart attack or something.

He stopped on the step behind Dullaston and listened hard for the voice that had been little more than a vague murmur when he'd heard it before. If it was an ordinary human voice, he might be able to use it as a means of persuading them all – Dullaston in particular – to leave. For a few seconds adrenaline caused blood to rush through his ears and he could hear nothing. He forced himself to stand absolutely still, to calm down, and suddenly he heard it. A faint but unmistakeable human voice, drifting down from upstairs.

The voice was male, with plummy tones, and had an odd, slightly distanced quality to it. It was Jackie who first realised why.

'That's not a real voice,' she said, 'it's a wireless. It's the cricket from Lord's. The Test Match. My dad sometimes listens to it.'

Eric realised she was right. Indeed, now that she had placed the voice, he fancied he could even hear the gentle click of leather on willow, the occasional ripple of applause from the crowd. It seemed so weird to be standing here on this dark staircase in this unknown house, feeling sick to the stomach with fear and shame, listening to something so quintessentially ordinary as a cricket commentary. Paradoxically, it made Eric feel more enclosed and stifled than ever, made him feel as if the hot, bright summer with its attendant sights and sounds and smells – lush green grass, droning bees, fresh strawberries – was a million miles away.

'I really think we should go now,' he said.

'Why?' said Dullaston aggressively.

Eric waved a hand in frustration. 'Because ... well, because monsters don't listen to cricket matches, do they? If there's someone up there, we'll scare them out of their wits. We'll get done for ... for trespassing, or breaking and entering, or something. They might think we're burglars.'

'Eric's right,' said James, who was standing behind Jackie at the bottom of the stairs, looking anxious.

Dullaston's face adopted his usual disgusted expression. 'You would say that, you little weed, wouldn't you?'

'Eric *is* right, though,' said Jackie. 'Come on, Andy, let's go.'

'No, why should I?' said Dullaston. 'I'm not coming all this way just to run off home again.'

'But this isn't *right*, Andy,' said Eric.

'Who says?'

'We all do,' said Jackie.

Dullaston tossed his head in dismissal, and was turning back to continue his ascent, when suddenly they all froze.

The cricket commentary had abruptly become louder as a door opened on the landing. Next moment they heard a voice, which made Eric turn cold inside.

'Who's there?' it said, but it didn't sound like a human voice, it sounded harsh and gurgling, somehow sludgy, like a swamp that was trying to speak.

The landing creaked above their heads as something moved along it towards the head of the stairs. The house was so full of smoke now it was like a grey mist. Eric gripped his cricket stump, which seemed suddenly pathetic, ineffectual. Smoke snagged in his throat as if composed of tiny, hook-like filaments, making him want to cough. None of them moved; they were all rooted to the spot by terror and fascination.

'Who's there?' the voice came again, grating and wet like a drowning Dalek.

It is a monster, after all, Eric thought. *Oh my God, oh my God, oh my—*

His racing mind seized up as the figure rounded the banister and was suddenly standing before them at the top of the stairs. It was bulky and hunched, and through the pall of smoke that surrounded it, Eric could see that there was something wrong with its head.

For what seemed like a long time, but could have been no more than a few seconds, Mr Bad Face and the four children confronted one another. Then Mr Bad Face drew in a breath that sounded like someone sucking spaghetti straight from the tin. 'What do you want?' he said, and his voice was harsher this time, more high-pitched, though whether with anger or fear Eric couldn't tell.

By way of reply, Andrew suddenly clomped up three more steps and thrust his burning torch towards the creature's face.

Mr Bad Face stumbled clumsily back with a squeal of terror, though not before the firelight parted the smoke and revealed his face. Eric thought his heart had stopped. Behind him, somebody screamed.

Mr Bad Face's head was lumpen and bald and misshapen. It was as if all the flesh had melted on the bone and then set again. In some places it was an angry red colour, puckered as though with burst blisters, and in others it was a waxy white, shiny like scar tissue. His eyes were sunk so deeply into his swollen flesh that they looked like empty black sockets, and his nose was nothing more than a bump in the centre of his face, with two ragged uneven holes torn in it. His mouth was bent and lipless, and inside it looked black; Eric could see no sign of teeth or tongue. Drool spilled from the side of his mouth and trickled down his chin, causing his white flesh to gleam like tripe.

Seeing his face broke the spell. The four of them turned and ran, Eric almost falling headlong down the stairs. It was a brief but nightmarish journey through the house. Eric felt sluggish, disjointed; his gasps for air only caused smoke to rush into his lungs. He was aware of bodies barging into him, or he into them; once he almost fell. When he finally burst out of the back door, the heat and brightness rushed at him like a comet, making pain explode in his head. He sank to his knees, certain he was going to throw up or pass out, or both.

Then someone grabbed him under the armpits and hauled him up. From their strength he felt certain it was Andrew until he heard Jackie's voice.

'Come on,' she said, her words distant and echoey, 'we have to get away from here.'

Somehow he managed to get to his feet, and with her help stumbled down the passageway at the side of the house. After the smoky atmosphere, the fresh air was making him light-headed and more nauseous than ever, as if the oxygen was too rich for him.

He didn't know how he did it, but he kept running, too sick and terrified and disorientated to appreciate that he was holding Jackie's hand. The four of them ran across the road, down Andrew's drive, and didn't stop until they were lying in the long grass of the field behind the house.

As Eric flung himself gratefully to the ground, grass seeds exploding around him, getting into his mouth and hair, he became aware that Andrew was lying in the grass with his face pressed into his hands, weeping. Eric felt shocked and distressed, but oddly touched by his friend's reaction. Then Dullaston rolled on to his back and removed his hands from his face, and Eric saw that he wasn't weeping at all, but laughing.

'God, that was brilliant,' he said, as if he had just come to the end of a roller coaster ride.

Eric was recovering now. He saw James slumped in the grass, arms wrapped around himself, almost catatonic with shock. Jackie was glaring at Dullaston as if she wanted to hit him.

'What do you mean, brilliant?' she said, sickened. 'How can you be so heartless?'

Dullaston gave her an almost pitiable look, as if she had no sense of humour. 'Did you *see* his face?' he crowed. 'Did you *see* it? I told you, didn't I? Bloody hell, he was *horrible*.'

'Shut up, Andy,' muttered Eric.

Dullaston rolled his eyes, still grinning. 'What's the matter with you lot? We saw what we went for, didn't we?'

'No, we didn't,' snapped Jackie. 'What are you, thick or something? He was a man, not a monster. Just a man who had something wrong with him. And we scared him out of his wits. We ought to be ashamed of ourselves.'

'I am,' said Eric. 'I feel awful.'

'Who are you calling thick?' Dullaston said, scowling.

'I want to go home,' said James, in a voice so small it was barely audible.

'Bugger off then,' said Dullaston. 'We don't want you around.'

'Why don't *you* bugger off?' said Jackie, her eyes blazing.

'Try and make me.'

'I will if I have to.'

'Come on then.'

'*Stop it!*' screamed James suddenly. His voice was no longer small, but shrill and hysterical enough to make them all jump.

For a few seconds there was silence, as everyone – Dullaston included – looked at James warily. He was breathing hard, staring ahead, and he seemed somehow coiled, as though he could spring into furious, frenzied action at any moment.

Finally Dullaston said, 'What's *your* problem?' though there was none of the usual venomous aggression in his voice. Indeed, he spoke almost quietly, as though James was a vibration-sensitive bomb he was afraid of setting off.

For a moment James didn't answer, then he shook his head as though Dullaston's question was so puerile it barely merited a response. However he said, 'If you don't know now, you never will.'

'What are you on about?' said Dullaston, genuinely perplexed.

Trying her best to sound reasonable, Jackie said, 'Don't you think it was wrong of us to have gone into that house, Andy?'

Dullaston looked at her, baffled. 'No, why?'

Jackie shook her head disgustedly. 'Forget it.' Then she stood up, brushing grass seeds off her clothes. 'Do you want to go for a walk, James?'

James hesitated a second, then nodded. He stood up, and the two of them wandered off.

Eric watched them go, feeling a little jealous. He wanted to run after them, to say, 'Hey, I'm not like Andy. Can't I come too?' But he stayed where he was, for fear of making a fool of himself.

When they were out of earshot, Dullaston said contemptuously, 'Look at them. A couple of girls.'

Eric's instinct was to snort non-committally to prevent himself being drawn into an argument, but he made himself say, 'We shouldn't have gone into that house, Andy.'

'Why not? It was only a bit of fun.'

'Not for that bloke it wasn't. We must have terrified him out of his wits.'

'Not as much as he terrified you,' said Dullaston. 'I've never seen anybody run so fast.'

'*You* ran too,' said Eric defensively.

'Only because you lot did. I'd have stayed if everyone else had.'

'To do what?'

'I don't know. We should've had a camera, shouldn't we? We could've taken a picture of him.'

Eric wrinkled his nose distastefully. 'That would've been awful. He can't help the way he looks.'

Dullaston sat up and began to pluck blades of grass out of the ground. He grinned suddenly. 'I was right, though, wasn't I? He did look like Frankenstein.'

Eric agreed but didn't want to voice it. It would be like condoning Andrew's callous disregard for the man's feelings. Instead he said, 'I wonder how he got like that.'

'Maybe he was born like it,' said Dullaston.

'No, he looked as if he'd been in an accident. A fire, maybe.'

'Did you see his nose?' said Dullaston gleefully. 'Just like a blob of plasticine with two massive holes in it. He looked like the Phantom of the Opera.'

'I thought you said he looked like Frankenstein,' Eric wanted to say, but didn't. The two of them lapsed into silence, and a couple of minutes later Jackie and James came back, having done a lap of the field.

'What happened to that torch thing you had?' was the first thing Jackie said to Andrew, as if she and James had been discussing it.

Dullaston looked at his right hand as if he half-expected the flaming torch still to be clutched in it. 'I don't know,' he said. 'I must have dropped it.'

'Where?' said Jackie.

'I don't know. Does it matter?'

'It might do. What if you dropped it in the house and started a fire?'

Dullaston looked momentarily scared, then he said, 'Mr Bad Face would've seen it. He'd have put it out.'

Eric suddenly realised he had no idea what had happened to *his* weapon. 'Oh no,' he said, 'I've lost my cricket stump. I've only got two now.'

Jackie gave him a withering look. 'So what? Who's bothered about a cricket stump?'

'I am. I only got them for my birthday.'

'If *you're* so bothered, why don't you go back to the house and check?' Dullaston said to Jackie scathingly.

'I think we should all go back,' she said.

'Go back into that house? You're joking.' Eric was unable to hide the horror he felt at the prospect.

'Not *into* the house,' said Jackie. 'We should be able to tell if everything's all right from the road outside.'

Eric hesitated. At that moment even the thought of looking at the house made him feel a blend of shame and dread. However, now that Jackie had raised the subject of the torch, he knew he wouldn't be able to rest until he was sure everything was okay. He nodded reluctantly. 'Yeah, all right.'

'Come on then. We'd better check now.'

Andrew tutted, but got to his feet, grabbing the spud gun he had thrown into the grass, and followed Jackie, James and Eric as they made their way towards the hole in the fence. They ducked through it, scaled the low wall into the Dullaston's back garden, then trooped across the lawn, up the path at the side of the house, and on to the drive. Jackie, eight feet in front of Eric, was the first to step out of the shelter of the house and into the sunshine. Eric saw her turn towards where number 39 was, and then he saw her stop and a look of absolute chilling horror cross her face.

'Oh no,' she whispered.

At once Eric felt his throat close up, his stomach lurch, then tighten. He ran the last few steps towards her, and again, stepping out of the shadows into the sun was like being hit with too much oxygen. James, standing at Jackie's shoulder, looked like someone in a film who had seen something he couldn't cope with. His face was slack with shock, his eyes glassy. Eric turned his head towards the end of the street.

Above Mr Bad Face's house, the brilliant summer sky had been ripped in half.

The darkness which seemed to be pouring through the breach in the daylight was actually a thick, almost solid-looking column of black smoke rising from number 39. People were milling about: neighbours. Eric recognised each and every one of them. His own mum was there, talking to Mrs Grainger. Eric wondered why the people he could see weren't *doing* something, instead of just standing around, watching, as if they were sick of the eyesore that was number 39 and glad to see it go. The top of his head felt as though it was swelling, about to burst, as if he was unable to comprehend the terrible magnitude of what they had done. He felt certain that the moment they were seen, they would be accused of causing this. Someone must have seen them going into the house or fleeing from it. He wondered what would happen to them. Would they be sent to Borstal? The idea terrified him. He was aware of Dullaston at his shoulder, and he half-turned to look at him. Dullaston looked back at him, as uncertain and as scared as Eric had ever seen him, and as if he saw some measure of accusation in Eric's eyes, he said, 'This isn't *my* fault.'

Jackie regarded him as if he was the most contemptible thing she had ever seen, and she said in a low voice, 'Don't you ever think about anyone but yourself?'

Then she marched up the drive and towards the crowd of people gathered around number 39. Eric hurried to catch up with her.

'What are you going to do?'

'I have to know if they got Mist— that man out.'

'You're not going to tell them what happened, are you?'

She glanced at him. 'What do you take me for?'

Eric saw a couple of people start to turn towards them, his mum included. He braced himself for the pointing fingers, the accusatory glares, the harsh voices. 'I'm sorry,' he wanted to shout, 'we didn't mean it.' His stomach was beginning to ache with tension. He could smell smoke, and hoped it was coming from the thick black column rising above the house and not from his own clothes.

He and Jackie were now too close to their neighbours to escape if the crowd decided to turn on them. Eric saw his mum scowl. 'Where have you been hiding?' she said.

Except she didn't say 'hiding'; Eric had just imagined her saying that. His mind went completely blank, and it was Jackie who said, 'In the park, playing football. What's happened, Mrs Knight?'

Eric's mother glanced at her. 'Mr Ryan looked out of his window and saw smoke coming from the house. He and Mr Jarvis went round the back and saw flames at one of the upstairs windows. They tried to get in, but they couldn't get through the smoke.'

Eric felt his stomach cramp with the panic he was trying to suppress. It took all his willpower to stop him doubling over. He couldn't believe how Jackie was managing to stay so calm, how she was able to speak, though admittedly her voice sounded strained when she said, 'Is anyone inside?'

Mrs Knight pursed her lips as if she was unsure how much to reveal. After a short pause, however, she said, 'We think Mr Straker must be. He never goes out. We won't know for certain until the fire brigade get here.'

Eric took a deep breath, making his stomach spasm with new pain, and croaked, 'Who's Mr Straker?'

'He's the man who lives there. Poor soul. You'd have thought he'd been through enough.' Mrs Knight frowned and said, 'Are you all right, Eric?'

'He's got stomach ache,' said Jackie quickly, taking her cue from the fact that Eric's hand was pressed to his belly like a compress. 'He ate too many sweets earlier. Has someone called the fire brigade?'

Mrs Knight frowned, as if Jackie had questioned her intelligence, and looked at her watch. Immediately her face turned anxious. 'Mr Ryan called them over five minutes ago. They should be here by now.'

As if on cue, all three of them suddenly heard the distant but approaching peal of a fire engine. No sooner had Eric's mother ushered them on to the pavement than the alarm increased in volume and pitch, and a vehicle so red and shiny it was like a slap to the senses sped round the corner and came to an angled stop half on the pavement in front of Mr Bad Face's house.

The doors opened and men in helmets and bulky protective clothes spilled out, and immediately began to unravel a hose the colour of clay. A couple of them ran round the back of the house with a retractable ladder. Mr Ryan hurried forward from the crowd of neighbours who had moved on to the pavement, to speak to the Fire Chief.

It terrified Eric to think that he and his friends were the cause of all this. He thought he'd rather die than face the shock and dismay his parents would feel if they found out. He couldn't stop thinking of Mr Straker either. Now that the man had a name, and by association a history, Eric's shame and regret at what they had done mushroomed inside him.

'Do the firemen know there's someone in the house?' Jackie asked anxiously.

'Yes, dear, don't worry. Mr Ryan will tell them.'

'Will they get him out all right?'

'I'm sure they'll do their best, dear.'

Jackie glanced at Eric, and he saw that she was going through exactly the same thing he was. Worry tautened her face to such an extent that it made her seem old, and almost ugly.

All they could do was watch the firemen go about their work, and hope against hope that Mr Straker would be all right. Eric imagined himself visiting Mr Straker in hospital, taking him flowers and chocolates to atone for what they had put him through; the thought comforted him a little.

He looked around for Andrew and James. There was no sign of Dullaston – he was probably watching proceedings from his bedroom window, lying low like an escaped convict – but James was sitting on the low wall outside Andrew's house, arms wrapped around himself as if he too had stomach ache, eyes wide and haunted. If everyone's attention hadn't been focused on number 39, he would have looked odd, even suspicious.

There was the sound of another siren, and suddenly an ambulance appeared, chased by a police car. The ambulance turned in the crescent at the bottom of the road, and backed up next to the fire engine, facing back up the street. The police car parked at the kerb outside Andrew's house and two uniformed officers got out. Eric held his breath, instinctively shrinking back so he wouldn't be seen. He half-expected the officers to pounce on James and drag him into the car, or at least walk down Andrew's drive and knock on his front door. However, despite the fact that James had become rigid, his face stark with alarm, they barely glanced at him before strolling the thirty or forty yards to where all the action was taking place.

'Why is the ambulance here?' Jackie asked, her voice high with anxiety.

'I expect it's to take Mr Straker to hospital, once they've got him out,' said Mrs Knight.

'And what about the police? Do they think someone started the fire on purpose?'

Eric cast Jackie an anguished glance, terrified that she might be giving too much away. However his mother said, 'No, I'm sure they don't think that. I think they just show up as a matter of course when something like this happens.'

All at once there was a bang and the window by the front door exploded. People jumped back, some letting out little screams, though they were well out of range of flying glass. Eric watched as flames sprang in twisting orange shapes from the window. He remembered what his mum had said, about flames first being seen at an upstairs window, and that suddenly struck him as odd. Surely Andrew had dropped his torch on the staircase, or even on the way out of the house? The only way the fire could have started upstairs was ...

The pain in his stomach turned cold, like a spear of ice, as a suspicion formed, then flourished. He sat down on a low garden wall to prevent himself creasing double. He tried to remember what had happened, but it was all a blur – he had seen Mr Straker's face and then he had run. Could it be possible that Andrew had not dropped his torch in panic at all, but had actually *hurled* it at the man?

Eric looked at Jackie to see if he could tell by her face whether the thought might have struck her too, but her eyes were fixed on the jet of water battering the front of the house. Then he saw her face change, her eyes and mouth widen once more with shock. Her sudden intake of breath was so sharp it seemed to tug her upright.

Two of the firemen had appeared from the back of the house, carrying a stretcher covered by a red blanket. Nothing of the person underneath was visible. The blanket stretched over the jutting feet at one end and the mound of the head at the other. A murmur started in the crowd, which – though wordless – seemed to convey a sense of speculation and dread. Eric was aware of Jackie starting to move, and suddenly she was pushing through the crowd, running towards the stretcher.

He climbed to his feet, wanting to shout at her to come back, but that would have drawn even more attention to themselves. She reached the stretcher just as the firemen got to the ambulance with it, and were handing over to the ambulance men, who were preparing to lift the stretcher into the back of their vehicle. Eric, watching in horror, thought for a second that Jackie was going to whip the red blanket away to see what sort of state Mr Straker was in. Then one of the uniformed policemen stepped forward to intercept her.

Eric couldn't hear what was being said over the rushing of water and the renewed mumblings of their neighbours, but he could guess from the gestures which Jackie and the policeman were making. She was demanding to know how the figure beneath the blanket was, whilst he was placating her, trying to move her away from the scene.

The stretcher installed, the ambulance men closed the back doors of the vehicle, one of them climbing inside to tend to the patient, and moments later the ambulance drove away. As it disappeared up the road, all the fight went out of Jackie; Eric saw her shoulders slump, her head droop forward.

'What's wrong with her?' Mrs Knight said, bewildered.

It still hurt Eric's stomach to talk, but he forced himself to say, 'She's just upset, Mum.'

His mother raised her eyebrows, but made no further comment. Eric watched nervously as the policeman led Jackie over to them, his hand on her shoulder. His face, however, was kindly and concerned.

'Are you the girl's mother?' he asked Mrs Knight.

'No, she's my son's pal. Her name's Jackie Foster. She lives at number 23.'

The policeman looked directly at Eric, who had to stop himself from flinching. 'Will you look after your friend, son? She's a bit overwrought.'

Eric made himself nod, and the policeman smiled, let go of Jackie's shoulder and moved away. Eric pulled Jackie across to the garden wall he had been sitting on, and said in a voice low enough so that his mum wouldn't hear, 'Are you all right?'

She sniffed and nodded, but she looked distressed.

'Is ... is Mr Straker all right?'

Jackie looked at him. She had a streak of dirt on her face and her eyes were wet-looking, though she wasn't crying.

'They wouldn't tell me.' Her voice dropped almost to a whisper. 'He's dead, Eric, I know he is.'

Eric felt scared, as if her words could make it true. His stomach throbbing, he said, 'No, he isn't. He'll be all right.'

'Why was that blanket over his face then?'

'Maybe they didn't want people to see what he looked like.'

She seemed to contemplate this for a moment, but then without warning she turned and flung her arms around him, burying her face in his neck. Shocked, Eric responded, putting his arms around her. He had fantasised about holding her, feeling her warm body against his, but he had never thought it would be like this.

'He'll be all right,' he repeated lamely. 'Don't worry.'

'No, he's dead, I know he is,' she said, and then she gave a sort of sob. 'And we killed him.'

Part Two:

The Good Mother

33

'And ... well, that's about it, really,' Eric said.

His voice was steady, but the hand which brought the cigarette up to his mouth was trembling. There were seven squashed butts in the dolphin-shaped ashtray on the desk, all of which had accumulated in the hour or so since he had begun his story. Despite the open window, the room was full of smoke. When his dad had told him about choking on the smoke from Andrew's torch in Mr Bad Face's house, Tim had felt as if he was there. He flapped a hand in front of his face now in a vain effort to disperse the acrid grey cloud, and said, 'He *was* dead, then?'

Eric nodded. 'We didn't know until much later when one of our neighbours, Mrs Richards, came round to give us the news, but yes, he died of smoke inhalation. Apparently his heart and lungs had been damaged in the war, and it didn't take much to kill him. I didn't sleep at all that night, and the next morning I was out before your gran and grandad and your Aunt Lesley had even woken up. We lived at the top of the street, but the minute you stepped out of the house you could smell the effects of the fire. In fact, for the rest of the holidays the air smelled charred, and even on hot, clear days there was a sort of graininess to it. It was as if there was a blight on summer, as if we were being haunted by what we had done.'

'And none of you ever told anyone about it?'

'No, we got together and we all swore that we'd never tell anyone. In fact, that was probably one of the last times all four of us *were* together. What happened brought me and your mum closer, but it somehow drove us apart from the other two. I suppose when we were all together it was too much of a reminder of that day. Even if no one talked about it, it was always there, bubbling beneath the surface.'

'Did you and Mum used to talk about it?'

'At first we didn't talk about anything else. For maybe ... I don't know ... three months, six months, we were consumed by guilt and shame and remorse. We relived that day again and again, went over it and over it, trying to ... make some sense out of what had happened, I suppose. We both knew Andrew was really to blame, but that didn't stop us feeling guilty. I mean, we were all in it together. If we hadn't agreed to go into that house with him in the first place, if we'd stood up to him, tried to stop him somehow ... that's what it always came down to in the end. If we'd done this or that or the other, then maybe the bad thing wouldn't have happened.'

He grimaced, perhaps thinking about Chloe, and then continued, 'We both had nightmares for weeks, and there were times when I thought if it hadn't been for Jackie I couldn't have coped – God knows how the other two did – but we were young and resilient, and in the end I suppose we got over it. Eventually we stopped crying on each other's shoulders and we started to enjoy one another's company. The guilt never really went completely away, but I suppose I came to terms with it by thinking that some good had come out of the tragedy – pretty selfish attitude, huh?'

Tim shrugged non-committally, then said, 'Did you ever find out why Mr Straker was ... well, the way he was?'

'Yes,' Eric said. 'Hang on a minute.' He twisted in his chair and opened the bottom left-hand drawer of the desk. Delving beneath piles of leaflets and newspapers, packets of photographs and old magazines, he dragged out an orange cardboard folder which looked as though it hadn't seen the light of day for a long time. He opened it and took out an old yellow newspaper clipping, which he passed carefully to Tim, as though he expected it to crumble into dust at any moment.

The headline across the top of the clipping read: WAR HERO DIES IN FIRE. To the left of the headline was a photograph of a young, handsome, moustached man in Air Force uniform, and beneath the photograph was a caption: John Straker in 1942.

Quickly Tim read the story, which told how the Lancaster Bomber in which John Straker had been rear gunner had crash-landed in 1943 due to the effects of enemy fire. Straker had been one of only two survivors of the crash, though he had suffered such horrific burn injuries that since the war he had lived the life of a recluse, refusing to see anyone except his beloved sister, Mabel, who had faithfully visited him at least twice a week for the past twenty-two years. Before the war, he had apparently had all that a man could wish for – a good job in a draughtsman's office, and a beautiful fiancée whom he intended to marry as soon as the war was over. The report concluded by pointing out the irony of surviving one conflagration only to die in another, and by stating that with the war now two decades past, it was often all too easy to forget that it was not only the dead who had lost their lives during that terrible conflict.

Tim handed the clipping back to his father, who muttered, 'Pretty big skeleton in the closet, wouldn't you say?' And then, almost reluctantly, as if being forced to ask a question he wasn't sure he wanted to know the answer to: 'Well, what do you think of me now?'

Tim shrugged. 'It wasn't your fault this man, Straker, died, Dad.

It was this Dullaston kid who took things too far. You didn't want anyone to get hurt, did you? You shouldn't be blaming yourself for what happened.'

'But I do blame myself to some extent, Tim, and I probably always will. And I'm not the only one.'

'What do you mean?'

'You've seen the poster.' Eric pulled the yellow envelope out of his pocket. 'Now look at this.'

Tim opened the envelope and took out the card. For perhaps two seconds his face remained deadpan, then it curled into an expression of revulsion.

'Sick bastard!' he blurted. 'Sorry, Dad, but ... what sort of person would do something like this?'

'Look inside,' Eric said.

Tim did so. Eric saw his son mouth the initials written there, like an inverted echo, before looking up and saying quietly, 'MBF. Mr Bad Face.'

'That's the third one I've had,' Eric said. 'The first one came on Thursday and had a message inside which said, "I'm back". The second one said, "I'm in Chloe's room".'

Tim stared at the card again, frowning as though the letters were coming alive in front of him, wriggling like insects.

'Who could have sent this?' he said.

Eric shrugged. 'You saw the poster, Tim. That was definitely him. Mr Bad Face. I'd put money on it.'

'But it can't be, can it, Dad?' Tim said. 'It must be some sort of trick.'

Eric's hands were still trembling slightly, but his voice was unnaturally calm. 'You mean ghosts don't come back from the dead and take revenge? They don't appear in posters of tennis stars and send malicious messages?'

'Well ... yeah,' said Tim. 'I mean, it's stupid, isn't it? It doesn't make sense.'

'No,' Eric agreed. 'It doesn't make sense. But then there's a great deal that hasn't made sense in the past few days.' He sighed and lowered his head into his hands, long white fingers encompassing his balding skull.

For a few seconds there was silence, and then Tim said, 'You're not just going to ... accept this, though, are you, Dad?'

Eric looked up. His eyes were bleary as if he hadn't slept for days. 'Accept what?' he said.

'Well, that some evil spirit has come back from the dead and is taking revenge on you.'

The words sounded ridiculous even as Tim said them, but that didn't prevent a little superstitious part of him from thinking, *What if . . .?*

Eric shook his head, made a brave attempt to smile. 'No, Tim, I don't accept it. That way lies madness. But, to be honest, I don't really know *what* to think.'

'Well ... who knew about what happened?'

'I told you, just the four of us.'

'So it must be one of you lot then. Well, not you or Mum, but Andrew Dullaston or this James Whatsisname.'

'Keeve,' supplied Eric automatically. He thought for a moment, and then said, 'Not necessarily. What if one of them told somebody else?'

'Who?'

'I don't know. Somebody vengeful enough to want to tear all our lives apart.' He shook his head. 'No, it still doesn't make sense. It all happened thirty years ago. Why wait until now?'

'Maybe whoever's doing it has only just found out,' said Tim.

Eric pulled a face. 'I don't see how. But even if that were true, I can't think of anyone who'd care enough to take things so far. Straker's sister, if she's still alive, would be about eighty now. And Straker himself never married, so he had no children.'

'When was the last time you spoke to either Andrew Dullaston or James Keeve, Dad?'

Eric waved a hand in the air. 'I don't know. Years ago.'

'Well, maybe you ought to try and track them down, find out if bad things have been happening to them too. If it's not one of them that's doing all this, maybe if you all got together you'd be able to work out who was.'

Eric looked at his son. There was a kind of desperation about him, as if this idea was a mission he needed to cling to, to busy himself with. It was this more than anything that made him nod and say, 'That's not a bad idea. But the addresses and phone numbers I've got for Andrew and James are over twenty years old. There's no guarantee I'll be able to track them down.'

'It's worth a try, though, Dad, isn't it?'

'Yes.' Eric nodded wearily. 'It's worth a try.'

'What about Mum? Jackie, I mean? She needs to be told too, doesn't she? Do you want to ring her or shall I?'

What Eric really wanted was to lock himself away for a while, to throw up his hands and shout, 'Stop!' Twice in his career he had attended the funerals of pupils who had died of cancer, and on each occasion he had looked at the grieving parents and had thought: This is the ultimate nightmare. How can you cope? How can you even function?

Now he knew. You coped because your natural human resilience *made* you cope, and you functioned because however bad you felt, your motor kept chugging away and the days kept turning and life moved on. Even when things seemed too much to bear, like today's discovery that Chloe had been murdered because of him, because of something he had done in the past, you carried on. After all, what else could you do, except perhaps be driven insane by grief and guilt? But insanity wasn't a matter of choice, it wasn't an indulgence, like a long, deep sleep or a soak in a hot bath or an expensive meal. Either you went insane or you didn't. And if you didn't, and you had a responsibility to protect yourself and your family from whoever or whatever was out there, then you just had to get on with it.

And yet, however great his sense of responsibility, Eric knew there were some things that at the moment he simply could not do. One of them was to ring Jackie and tell her that the childhood trauma they thought they'd buried long ago had resurfaced. He felt too brittle to cope with the shock and bewilderment that he knew would be her response. And so he said, 'Would you mind doing it, Tim? I'm not sure I can face it just now.'

'Yeah, sure,' Tim said. He got up to leave the room, but at the door he hesitated. 'None of this is your fault, you know, Dad.'

Eric pressed his lips together in what he hoped resembled a smile, and gave a nod to show that he appreciated his son's support. Tim left the room. The instant he did so, Eric groaned and stretched and closed his eyes. Tim had spoken to Jackie every day since Chloe's death, but Eric hadn't spoken to her since she had rung him up on the night of the murder, after receiving the strange phone call. He felt bad about that, as he felt bad about many things. It wasn't that he was not concerned about his ex-wife; he questioned Tim after each phone call, and knew from talking to him that she was okay, that her boyfriend, Gareth, had been staying with her, and that she had received no more threats or strange messages over the past few days.

Yesterday, after the latest interrogation, Tim had said testily, 'If you're so worried about her, Dad, why don't you ring her yourself?' However, up to now, Eric had been unable to bring himself to do that. Speaking to her at present would be, for him, too much of a reminder of the intimate emotions - both good and bad - they had once shared. He knew, of course, that now this Mr Bad Face business had come to light, he would have to overcome all that. Sooner or later they would have to talk.

Tim seemed to be gone a long time, but eventually Eric heard his son's footsteps on the stairs, and he opened his eyes at the same instant that Tim reappeared in the doorway.

'How was she?' Eric asked.

Tim shrugged. 'Shocked. Upset. She wants to talk to you.'

'Is she still on the phone?' Eric said, trying not to show his reluctance.

'No, she wants to talk to you face to face. She's going to drive over tomorrow. I said we'd meet her in Bertolucci's at twelve o'clock.'

'You did what?'

'Well, I thought if you got in touch with the others today, you could all meet there.'

'Oh, Tim, you could have discussed this with me first.'

'How could I? Mum was really upset. I couldn't say, "No, you can't come over", could I? If you didn't want her to come, you should have spoken to her yourself.'

Tim was red-cheeked with indignation. Eric raised a hand in a conciliatory gesture. 'No, you're right. I suppose the sooner we meet the better. It's just ... hard for me, you know.'

'I know,' said Tim. 'It's hard for me too.'

Eric wondered how much his son understood about how he felt. Sighing, he said, 'What else did she say?'

'Well, there were a couple of things. One was that she wondered whether you were going to go to the police.'

Eric blinked. Until this moment he hadn't thought about that, but now that he did he realised he would have to tell Farrington about the fire. He wondered whether after all these years, the four of them would be charged, and if so, with what? Arson? Manslaughter? The thought that the information that might lead the police closer to his daughter's killer could also result in prison sentences for himself and his friends would have been blackly comic if the situation hadn't been so tragic.

'I ... don't know,' he said slowly. 'What does Jackie think?'

'I think she wants to talk to you about it. You can't not go, though, can you, Dad? Not if one of the other two killed Chloe.'

'Let's just see whether I can get in touch with the other two first,' said Eric. 'Find out what they have to say. We'll decide then, shall we?'

Tim pursed his lips, but eventually nodded.

'You said there were a couple of things,' said Eric. 'What was the other one?'

'Mum's boyfriend's got to go to Germany on business tomorrow morning, and she's going to be on her own. I wondered if she could stay here.'

The idea appalled Eric for a number of reasons. 'I don't think so, Tim,' he said.

'Why not? It'd be better if we were all together.'

'Better for who? You know Annette's a bit funny about Jackie. She hasn't seen her for years as it is. She'd hate it if Jackie came to stay, especially at a time like this.'

'You'd hate it, you mean,' said Tim.

Eric was taken aback, which caused him to sound defensive. 'Jackie and I get on perfectly well.'

'Well, what if I go and stay with her then?' Tim said.

'No, Tim, that's not a good idea either. I don't want the family spread about just at the moment, I want us all to stick together. And besides, think how Annette would feel. She's just lost her daughter. She'd think she was losing her son as well.'

'No, she wouldn't. It'd only be for a little while.'

'Believe me, that's not how she would see it.'

'But Mum's on her own! Don't you care what happens to her?'

Eric thought of the tomboy who had hauled him to his feet when he had fallen in Mr Bad Face's garden, and who had stuck up for James when Andrew Dullaston had been getting at him, of the young woman he had accompanied on protest marches against the bomb, whom he had once made love to under the stars within sight of Stonehenge, and who had gone through absolute hell giving birth to their son – the son who was now standing indignantly before him.

'Of course I care about her,' he said. 'I care about her very much.'

'Then how can you leave her to fend for herself when there's a psycho on the loose? What if he got her? How would you feel then?'

Eric lowered his head into his hands. This was so unfair. He had enough to contend with without this extra dilemma. He knew that whatever decision he made, he would end up hurting someone. 'Isn't there anyone else she can stay with?' he said. 'What about Beryl?'

Tim looked scornful. 'You know Jackie and her mum don't get on very well. Besides, Beryl's nearly eighty. She wouldn't be much help.'

'Friends, then.'

'Dad, she should be here with us. Whoever this Mr Bad Face is, he can't get us if we're all together.'

Eric knew Tim was right. On her own, Jackie was appallingly vulnerable. If she ended up like Chloe just because he was unwilling to put up with the awkwardness her presence would cause for a little while he'd never forgive himself.

He sighed deeply and said. 'All right, Tim. Talk to Annette about it. But if she says no, we'll have to think of something else.'

'She won't say no, Dad,' said Tim. 'I know she won't.'

Eric raised his eyebrows. He dreaded to think what Annette's reaction might be. 'Don't bank on it,' he murmured.

34

Andrew Dullaston was not in a good mood. He should have been playing golf now with Neale and Marcus, after which he had arranged to meet Juliette at the Yachting Club for lunch. But instead here he was, stuck in the office on a Saturday morning, trying to resurrect a deal that he'd thought cut and dried when he'd left for the weekend at 3 p.m. yesterday.

It was Mortimore's fault, of course. Incompetent arsehole. Dullaston should never have left him to tie up the loose ends of the Erickson contract. He had only done so because Carlton had virtually ordered him to, just to give the useless sod something to do, and because Dullaston hadn't seen how even Mortimore could make a pig's ear of this one.

He should have known better. The recollection of Mortimore's voice on the phone that morning still made him flush with rage.

'Andrew, hi, Peter here,' he had said in that smug, brisk way of his. 'Listen, the Erickson deal has hit a snag. Be grateful if you could just pop in and sort out one or two things. It is your baby, after all.'

The 'snag', as it turned out, had been caused by Mortimore's ill-advised attempt to improve on the terms that Dullaston had spent weeks thrashing out by inserting an additional software option just as Erickson were preparing to sign. Although this additional option would have added just a negligible few thousand to a contract that was already worth millions, the effect was devastating, akin to dropping a big, greasy spanner into the delicate workings of a vast and expensive machine.

Now Erickson were threatening to pull out of the deal altogether, saying that they were not happy doing business with a company that resorted to underhand tactics. Dullaston had spent all morning trying to placate them, not least by tilting the contract further in their favour as a gesture of goodwill, or, as he had phrased it in the fax to which he was currently awaiting a response, 'in an effort to illustrate Carlton-Strong's heartfelt regret at this unfortunate misunderstanding at such an advanced stage of negotiations'.

As it was, Carlton-Strong looked likely to lose at least quarter of a million on the deal. Dullaston had already promised himself that if they lost the deal altogether, he would personally wring Mortimore's neck – and sod the fact that he was Carlton's sister-in-law's husband. Indeed, if they did lose this contract, then perhaps Carlton might finally realise that blood was only thicker than water when the brain it serviced was capable of competent thought. Although Dullaston was not yet a partner in the company, he knew Bob Strong was eager to have him aboard. When that day came, the first thing he aimed to do was to rid himself of liabilities like Mortimore – if the man hadn't single-handedly managed to bring the company to its knees by then, of course. Perhaps, with Bob Strong's help, Carlton himself might even fall if pushed hard enough.

But for now all Dullaston could do was wait. He was alone in the office, Mortimore having sloped off home soon after he had arrived. Although Dullaston was grateful that the man had not hung around to stick his nose in where he might very likely get it bitten off, he had to admit that the silence only added to his tension. The last time he had been for a medical check-up, his blood pressure had been way too high, and Dr Swanyck had told him to lose weight and reduce his stress. Dullaston snorted. He'd defy anyone to lower their stress levels when they had Mortimore to deal with on a day-to-day basis.

The phone rang. Though Dullaston had been waiting for it, he still jumped like a startled gazelle. His heart was pumping so fast that he felt breathless when he snatched it up. Composing himself, he brought the receiver to his ear and said, 'Carlton-Strong. Andrew Dullaston speaking.'

'Andrew?' The voice on the other end of the line sounded ... odd. Full of wonderment, as if the caller couldn't quite believe he'd got through. Dullaston was thrown completely. He had been expecting Van Beuran's Dutch-accented English, which previously had been full of warmth and humour, but this morning had sounded cold and sharp as ice splinters. For a moment all he could think was that Mortimore was ringing to find out how things were going. It would be just like him to tie up the line when Dullaston was waiting for the all-important call.

'Is that you, Peter?' he said coldly.

'Peter? Uh .. no. It's ... er ... well, hopefully you'll remember me. Eric. Eric Knight.'

'Eric Knight?' said Dullaston like the unappreciative victim of a practical joke.

'Yes. You remember. We used to—'

'I remember,' said Dullaston briskly. 'You lived up the road from me when we were children.' He glanced at the clock: 11:47. Van

Beuran had promised to get back to him that morning. 'What is it that you want?'

'Well, I ... er .. I just wondered how you were.'

Dullaston felt a sense of unreality, coupled with a building irritation. 'How am I? I'm fine.'

There was a pause as though Eric was expecting him to say more, then the voice on the other end of the line said, 'Oh good, good. So ... nothing ... *untoward* has been happening this past week or so? To you, I mean?'

For a moment, Dullaston wondered whether Knight could somehow be referring to Mortimore's tampering. And then he remembered Felicity's pony, and the phone call which had dredged up a part of his past he'd convinced himself he'd all but forgotten, and which had preyed on his mind more than he'd ever let on to Juliette.

'Untoward?' he snapped. 'What the hell are you talking about?'

'Sorry. I'm not making myself very clear, am I? I just wondered whether you'd had any ... threatening phone calls or letters, anything like that?'

For a moment something cold tingled through Dullaston's chest and arms, almost making him shudder. Then he shook it off and said angrily, 'Why do you ask? Have you sent me some?'

'No,' said Eric as though shocked by the idea. 'It's just ... well, I've received some myself, that's all.'

'Have you?' said Dullaston, so startled that he forgot to sound angry.

'Yes. And it's not just that.' Eric paused and then said quickly, 'On Tuesday night, my daughter, Chloe, was killed. Murdered.'

Dullaston felt a weight drop into his belly. 'Murdered?' he said.

'Yes.' Another pause. 'I think it might have something to do with what happened.'

A few days ago, Dullaston might not have immediately realised what Eric was referring to, but now he did. On Thursday night he had even had his first fire dream in many, many years. He knew that some people thought he was stupid and insensitive, but he had his fears just like everybody else. He simply didn't like to show them, that was all. Fear and uncertainty were weaknesses, and if someone threatened to expose your weaknesses then you had to fight them by throwing up a shield composed of something strong, like ruthlessness or anger. Brusquely he said, 'Look, I'm sorry to hear about your daughter, Eric, but I really have to go. I'm waiting for an important phone call.'

'I doubt the call you're waiting for will be as important as this one,' said Eric.

'Indeed?' said Dullaston, and then, as a thought struck him, 'Do you mind telling me how you got this number?'

'I rang your old house. The man there had your forwarding address, so I got the number from Directory Enquiries. I spoke to your wife. She seemed very nice. She said I'd be able to find you here.'

The trouble to which Knight had gone to track him down disturbed Dullaston. He was not a man used to being disturbed; he was a man used to being in charge of situations. 'Look,' he said, 'I haven't got time for this. What is it that you want?'

'I think we should meet,' said Eric. 'My daughter has been murdered, and both Jackie Foster and I have been getting ... threatening messages from someone claiming to be Mr Bad Face. It seems that someone's out to get us all.'

'Preposterous,' said Dullaston. 'All that was over a long time ago.'

'Tell that to the person who killed Chloe,' said Eric.

Dullaston was silent for a moment, and then he said, 'How do I know you're telling the truth?'

'What?' said Eric.

'How do I know *you're* not responsible for what's happened?'

'So something *has* happened to you?' said Eric.

'I didn't say that.'

'As good as. What's been happening, Andrew? Believe me, I only want to help.'

'The police are handling things, thank you very much. They're all the help I need.'

If he thought mention of the police was going to scare Eric off, Dullaston was disappointed. 'Have you told the police about Mr Bad Face?' Eric said.

'Of course not,' Dullaston snapped.

'Why not?'

'Because ... because it's not relevant.'

'Because you don't know what'll happen to you if you do, you mean?'

Dullaston scowled into the phone. 'I don't believe I'm having this conversation.'

'So why don't you put the phone down on me?'

'I might just do that.'

'Listen, Andrew, Jackie and I are meeting in a cafe called Bertolucci's on Bramwell High Street at noon tomorrow. Bramwell's a small town between Harrogate and York, just off the A1. We're meeting to talk about what's happening, to try to find some answers, to decide whether we should go to the police, that sort of thing.'

'So?' said Dullaston.

'So it would be good if you could be there.'

'Impossible.'

'Just think about it, Andrew, please. Oh, and by the way, I don't suppose you know how to contact James, do you?'

'Who?'

'James Keeve. He used to—'

'Why should I have kept in touch with him?' Dullaston said as if he found the very idea an insult.

'Why indeed?' said Eric, and suddenly seemed to have run out of things to say. Awkwardly he said, 'Well, I'd better go. Perhaps I'll see you tomorrow.'

'I doubt it,' said Dullaston.

After Eric had put the phone down, Dullaston sat for a few minutes, listening to his crashing heart, trying to swallow. His hands were trembling and he clenched them angrily. Whatever was happening here, he wouldn't let it get to him. He wouldn't.

When the phone rang again, he almost jumped out of his skin. He tried to compose himself, allowing it to ring four times before picking it up. His throat was dry as he croaked a greeting, but this time it was Van Beuran calling to say that Erickson were accepting the deal. 'Oh, that's marvellous, Mr Van Beuran,' Dullaston said, not feeling marvellous at all. 'I promise you, you won't regret it.'

Within ten minutes the contracts had been as good as signed. Dullaston put the phone down, angry that the celebratory mood he should have been in had been spoiled. Almost unwillingly he reached for a desk jotter and snatched a fountain pen from the inside pocket of his jacket. He unscrewed the lid, and then paused with his hand hovering over the page for a moment, as if he was being asked to sign the contracts to a deal he had little faith in. Finally he scowled, and almost reluctantly, pressing on the paper so hard he was in danger of tearing it, he wrote: BERTOLUCCI'S. BRAMWELL. 12:00. He screwed the lid back on his pen and put it in his jacket, then tore the sheet from the jotter, folded it into his pocket and stomped out of the office.

35

Eric put the phone down, his expression woeful. 'I'm not sure I handled that very well.'

Tim pulled a sympathetic face. 'Yes you did, Dad. It's not your fault he was stroppy. From what you've told me about him, it doesn't sound as if he's changed much.'

Eric crossed the room and slumped into his armchair. 'I take it you could hear what Andrew was saying?'

Tim nodded.

'It certainly sounds as though something's been happening to him too, doesn't it? Something serious enough to involve the police.'

'Unless he was lying to make you think he was a victim too,' said Tim.

Eric thought for a moment, then shook his head. 'No, Andrew's always been the sort of person who goes at things like a bull in a china shop. He's many things, but he's not devious.'

'Do you think he'll turn up tomorrow?'

'Who knows? At least he heard me out. I think he's worried, but whether or not he'll be able to overcome his pig-headedness is another matter.'

'I suppose this makes James Keeve our number one suspect now, doesn't it?' said Tim, and then when Eric smiled thinly in response, he asked, 'What's so funny?'

'If you knew James you'd understand why I was smiling. He was always so timid and quiet.'

'Don't they say the quiet ones are the worst?' said Tim. 'Besides, people change. Maybe he got into body-building or something.'

'Or just went mad,' said Eric. Suddenly his face was deadly serious. 'The person who's doing this would have to be mad, wouldn't he?'

Tim nodded. 'An A1 mental case.'

A short, odd silence fell between them as if each were momentarily preoccupied with their own thoughts. Then Tim said, 'Are you going to ring James Keeve then, or what?'

'I'll get my book,' Eric said. He did so, and a minute later was listening to a telephone ringing and ringing, his hand gripping the receiver so tightly it was turning his palm numb. Finally he put the phone down. 'No answer. I'll try again later.'

'Maybe he's not there because he's here, stalking his victims,' Tim almost said, but didn't. Both of them looked at the ceiling as they heard the creak of movement from upstairs.

'Annette,' Eric said as if identifying bird song. 'When are you going to speak to her?'

'Later,' said Tim. 'I'm going to make some coffee. Do you want one?'

'Does Dolly Parton sleep on her back?' Eric murmured automatically, but neither of them felt much like smiling.

As Tim was spooning coffee into a couple of mugs, Eric appeared in the kitchen doorway and said, 'I've just had a thought. Have you any idea where Chloe got that poster from?'

Tim paused and frowned. 'I'm ... not sure. I think it was a present.'

'A present?' Eric said. 'From whom?'

'I'm not sure.' And then Tim's face cleared. 'Actually, I think it might have been from Ben Wyatt. I vaguely remember Clo saying something about that.'

A strange expression crossed Eric's face. He looked both startled and grim at the same time. High spots of colour appeared on his cheekbones and his lips compressed into a terse line. 'Right,' he muttered, 'forget the coffee. I'm going out.'

'Where?' Tim said, surprised at his dad's sudden change of mood.

'I'm going to see Ben Wyatt and make him tell me the truth,' Eric said.

36

Nose to tail traffic crawled down Bramwell High Street. Eric sat hunched over his steering wheel, eyes searching restlessly for a parking space. A woman carrying a baby came out of the chemist's and awkwardly unlocked the Fiat parked at the kerb. Eric touched the brake and his car dwindled to a halt. He indicated, then waited as the woman strapped the baby into its seat, rounded the car, got in, removed the crook-lock and started the engine. When she finally indicated right to pull out, he revved the car and twisted the wheel, all but nudging the Fiat out into the road. The 'Baby On Board' sticker in the Fiat's back window seemed to waggle at him reprovingly.

Ever since Tim had told him he thought Ben Wyatt might have given Chloe the poster, Eric had been gripped by a steely determination to get to the bottom of the boy's association with his daughter. Normally he weighed up the pros and cons of a situation before plunging in, but this was no ordinary situation, and no ordinary day. Although he knew he was very probably acting so spontaneously simply in order to assuage his own sense of accountability for Chloe's death, and although he knew Farrington had spoken to Wyatt and released him, and would undoubtedly frown on Eric's decision to confront the boy directly, it didn't deter him from his mission.

After driving away from the house, he had gone straight round to where Ben Wyatt lived, having managed to recall the address from when he had rung the boy on Tuesday night. Mr Wyatt, who answered the door, was a tall, imperious man with grey hair swept back over his ears, flared nostrils and a jutting chin. When Eric told him that he was one of Ben's teachers and that he needed to speak to him urgently, Mr Wyatt replied that he thought Ben had gone to meet his friends at the coffee bar on the High Street. Eric thanked him and got back into his car. Although Mr Wyatt didn't know the name of the place, Eric knew that he was referring to Bertolucci's. It was the only coffee bar on the High Street and on Saturdays was *the* place to be seen among fourteen- to seventeen-year-olds.

From where he was parked, Eric could see Bertolucci's on the other side of the road. It was a glass-fronted place which generally had teenagers not only filling the shop with their gossip and laughter, but also hanging around outside, as though the place was so packed they had been squeezed out on to the pavement. Today, though,

Bertolucci's looked half-empty, a fact which Eric realised with a shock must be due to Chloe's murder. Teenagers were staying indoors because they or their parents were worried that they might become the next victim of the knife-wielding maniac they perceived to be stalking the town. It was odd how Eric kept forgetting that Chloe's death was far more than simply a family matter. It was also a massive police investigation, a media sweetmeat and the source of the fear that was evidently gripping Bramwell. Thinking about this, Eric's hands tightened on the steering wheel he was still holding, and for a brief moment he thought that everyone on the street was staring at him. However, when he looked up he couldn't see anyone who was.

He glanced again at Bertolucci's, the name painted on the plate-glass window in looping chocolate-brown script, edged with silver. As he did so, four boys emerged from the coffee bar, each carrying a can of Coke as though it was a membership requirement for their group. Eric felt something jump in his throat, his chest tighten. This was one of these quirks of fate that were never meant to happen in real life. One of the boys was Ben Wyatt.

He was about to shove open his door when he heard a sigh from the seat beside him. He turned to see Chloe gazing out through the front windscreen, a dreamy expression on her perfect, unblemished face.

It was obvious who she was looking at. Eric followed her gaze. Ben and his friends were playing the fool now, two of the boys taking swigs from their cans and spitting great brown arcs of Coke at each other. They were laughing and dodging out of the way as Coke spattered the pavement like vomit. One of the boys jumped back and collided with an old lady pushing a shopping cart. Although he apologised immediately, and even helped her to pick up her spilled groceries, Eric could see the other boys – Wyatt included – were finding it hard to stifle their laughter.

He was surprised by the intensity of the anger that suddenly surged through him, and turning back to Chloe, said bitterly, 'What do you see in him?'

For the first time Chloe tore her gaze away from Ben Wyatt and looked at her father. She was radiant, her hazel eyes sparkling.

'He's strong, he's confident, he's good-looking. He's just ... perfect,' she murmured.

'He's an ill-mannered yob,' Eric said, knowing even as the words left his mouth that this wasn't like him at all, he who was normally so tolerant, a defender not a condemner of youth.

'He's fifteen, Dad. He's full of life, that's all.'

Full of life. The words cut deep. Feeling intrusive, but nevertheless compelled to ask the next question, he said, 'Chloe, about your diary ...'

She frowned. 'What about it?'

'All the things you wrote in there ... about you and Ben. Were they true?'

She looked away again. For a moment he thought she wasn't going to answer. Then she said, 'What do you think?'

Eric shook his head. 'I don't know what to think, Chloe. I don't know what to think about anything any more. My whole world has turned upside down.'

'But what do you want to *believe*, Dad?' she said earnestly.

'I want to believe ... I want to believe it's not true, that none of this is true.'

'Then believe it,' she said simply. 'Believe what you need to, just to get by.'

Eric nodded, unconvinced, and glanced out of the window again. The old lady's groceries had been returned to her shopping cart now and the boys were sauntering off down the road, laughing and shoving each other.

When he turned back, Chloe was gone. He thought he detected a hint of perfume in the air, though when he sniffed again, hoping to capture it, he smelt only leather and exhaust fumes.

He got out of the car and dodged through the traffic to the opposite pavement. Wyatt and his cronies were about fifty yards ahead of him, moving slowly. They looked as if they hadn't a care in the world; as if they had nothing to do and all day to do it. Eric saw Ben throw back his blond head and laugh like a donkey. *He's full of life*, Chloe had said.

Full of life.

The anger that had surprised Eric seized him again. He had never been a violent or short-tempered man, but this anger was ferocious, like a vice that would crush his head if it didn't find an outlet. It made him furious that Wyatt, of all people, could appear so carefree when Chloe was dead. Hardly aware of what he was doing, he suddenly started running towards the boys, shouting, 'Hey! Hey, you!'

One of the boys turned and saw him, said something to the others. And then they were all turning, watching him approach, trying to conceal expressions of nervousness, bewilderment, surprise.

Eric thudded to a stop a few feet away from them, red and panting, his heart racing not just from exertion but from the rage that seemed to have replaced the blood in his veins.

'I want a word with you, Wyatt,' he said, and then raising his voice as if he wanted everyone to hear, 'It's about my daughter.'

Wyatt looked wary. There was a red flush to his cheeks. He glanced around at his friends, who were staring back at him.

'Your daughter?' he said nervously. 'Look, Mr Knight, if it's about that diary of hers—'

'I want to know where you got that poster from and why you gave it to her.'

Ben couldn't have looked more startled had Eric suddenly started speaking to him in Japanese. He cleared his throat, and evidently working hard to retain his cool, said, 'What poster? I'm sorry, Mr Knight, but I don't know what you mean.'

Eric lurched a step closer. 'Oh, yes you do. You know perfectly well what I'm talking about.'

Ben licked his lips. People were stopping in the street to stare at the two of them now. 'No,' he said, trying to keep his voice from wavering, 'I don't.'

'*Don't lie to me!*' Eric suddenly bellowed, his face turning crimson. '*Don't you DARE lie to me!*'

Fear surfaced on Ben's face and he took a step back. Those kids whose parents had let them out were streaming from Bertolucci's now to see what was going on. It was obvious that Ben felt trapped between beating a hasty retreat and saving face by trying to maintain the fearless devil-may-care persona that the boys respected and the girls fancied him for. Speaking quickly and quietly, almost pleadingly, he said, 'Look, Mr Knight, I'm really sorry about what happened to Chloe, but I had nothing to do with it, honest. All that stuff in her diary, she just ... made it up. So why don't you .. I dunno ... go home and have a lie down or something.'

To Eric, Wyatt's words sounded patronising and dismissive rather than conciliatory. It was the last straw. His rage engulfed him, took him over completely, and he flew at Ben. He hit him side on, and the two of them fell sprawling on the pavement. People came running from all sides, some to try and break up the fight, others simply to watch, even a small proportion to goad the combatants on.

Eric, of course, was unaware of his audience. The rage inside him was all-consuming now; he had even lost sight of the fact that he was supposed to be avenging his daughter. He simply wanted to tear and kick and gouge and punch, to inflict as much pain on his opponent as he could. He fought frenziedly, uncontrollably, his vision a blur, his throat raw from screeching out his fury. If Ben was fighting back, then Eric didn't feel the blows. He was beyond physical pain now, beyond everything but the basic animal urge to destroy as he himself had been destroyed.

And then, vaguely, he was aware of being yanked backwards, lifted up, of his blows no longer connecting but slashing at empty air. He saw a smear of faces around him, recognised - even in that briefest of instants - expressions of shock and horror, excitement and delight.

And then, let go, he stumbled backwards, felt his right leg hit something hard; a dull, crunching collision that was not quite pain, but which soon would be. He wondered what he had collided with - a postbox? A litter bin? A parked car? The thought flashed through his mind in a fraction of a second, as did the realisation that his momentum was still carrying him backwards, that he was stumbling now off the edge of the pavement and into the road. Instinctively he pinwheeled his arms for balance, though he already knew that there was nothing he could possibly do to stop himself falling.

When his head hit the tarmacked concrete, white pain burst up through the back of his skull. His teeth clicked together so violently he thought they'd splintered. But the pain was not as bad as the sounds he heard: the sudden chorus of horrified screams, the screech of brakes and squeal of tyres. He squeezed his eyes tight shut, wondered - almost casually - what it would be like to have the wheel of a ten-ton truck run over your head.

The sounds seemed to go on for ever, and then they stopped. Eric opened his eyes.

The tyre, stinking of hot rubber, its treads pitted with stone chips, was less than an inch from his face.

37

'Right then, Eric, perhaps you'd like to tell me what the hell you thought you were playing at?'

Detective Inspector Farrington had not had a good morning. After spending an uncomfortable half-hour in Detective Chief Superintendent Cruikshank's office, trying to explain to her superior officer why their investigations into Chloe Knight's death had been getting them precisely nowhere despite the accumulation of evidence, she had then driven with Frank back to Bramwell, in order to co-ordinate the 10 a.m. search involving both police and volunteers for the missing girl, Oonagh Walsh. Although a heartening number of townspeople and travellers had turned up to aid in the search, a disruptive local element – mainly young men hostile to the travellers – had also put in an appearance. Their leader, barrel-chested and slab-faced, had tried to shame the scattering of townspeople into abandoning the search, describing them as traitors, scum-lovers. He went on to say that if Oonagh Walsh was gone, then bloody good riddance to her, and that the town's task should not be to try and find the girl, but to drive out the rest of the murdering slime she had rolled in with.

The travellers, thanks largely to the efforts of Oonagh Walsh's father, had shown admirable restraint in the face of the insults and accusations hurled at them, leaving it to Farrington and her men to deal with the problem. Inevitably a number of scuffles had broken out between the troublemakers and police, and it had taken half a dozen arrests to restore order, which meant a further stretching of resources already at snapping point.

And even after as thorough a search as they could manage, Oonagh Walsh had still not been found, although this, of course, was both a curse and a blessing. The last thing Farrington wanted was for the girl's body to turn up as Chloe Knight's had. And yet she was all too aware of time marching on, of another morning slipping by with nothing being achieved.

And now this: Eric Knight and Ben Wyatt brawling in the town's high street. Farrington had already listened to Wyatt's side of the story. Now she wanted to hear Eric's.

He was a pitiable sight. Rumpled and grimy, with a cut on the back of his head that had leaked blood into his thinning hair, he slumped forward over the interview table, arms stretched out, hands meshed together. By his side was a plastic cup of what Farrington knew to be disgusting coffee from the vending machine in the hall, and an ashtray containing the crumpled butts of four cigarettes.

His linked thumbs moved agitatedly, but he didn't look up. Shamefaced, he mumbled, 'I know it was stupid. I'm sorry.'

Farrington sighed, and a little more gently she said, 'Why did you do it, Eric? What were you thinking of?'

Eric shrugged. 'I don't know. It was just . . . a brainstorm. Everything got on top of me and I lost control for a while. I needed someone to hit out at.'

'So you chose Ben Wyatt?'

'Yes.'

'Why?'

Eric spread his hands palm upwards on the table as if to show he had nothing to hide. 'Well, because of the diary, I suppose. Because of what that boy did . . .' He grimaced, and amended himself, 'Because of what Chloe wrote in her diary.'

'You think that what Chloe wrote was true, do you?'

'My daughter isn't a liar.'

'No, but what was written in that diary wasn't lying exactly, was it? I mean, who was she lying to, except herself? We're all of us surely entitled to our fantasies, aren't we, Eric?' When he didn't reply, she went on, 'Even if what Chloe wrote in her diary *was* true, does that give you any right to do what you did?'

Eric grimaced. 'Of course not. But like I say, I lost control. I really don't know what came over me.'

Farrington looked at Eric for a long moment. Then she said, 'Wyatt told us that you accused him of giving your daughter a poster, that you demanded to know where he had got it from. What was all that about?'

Eric looked suddenly uncomfortable. 'Oh . . . that was nothing.'

'Come on, Eric. It must have been something to make you fly off the handle like that.'

Avoiding her gaze he muttered, 'Oh, it's just that Chloe was given a poster that I was led to believe was from Ben Wyatt. I just wanted to know why, if he claimed he hardly knew her, he'd given her a present.'

'Hmm.' Farrington sat back and then asked bluntly, 'Do you think Ben Wyatt killed Chloe, Eric?'

Eric looked up, surprise on his face, almost as if the thought had never occurred to him. 'Well, I . . . I don't know,' he stammered.

'But you must have some pretty strong opinions about him – strong enough to drive you to attack him in a crowded street, at least.'

'I've already told you, that was because of what Chloe wrote about him in her diary. It was eating away at me, I couldn't come to terms with it. If Chloe hadn't been killed, things might have been different; I might have been able to talk to her. But it was as though Wyatt had spoiled my memories of her, dirtied them somehow. I know that sounds irrational, but it's how I felt. I just had this ... anger inside me that I needed to get out.'

Farrington nodded. 'I can accept that. But I have to admit, this business over this poster still puzzles me. According to Wyatt and a number of witnesses we spoke to, you were demanding to know *where* Wyatt had got the poster from. They all said you seemed to regard that as very important.'

'So?' said Eric, once again looking uncomfortable.

'Well, surely *where* he got it from is irrelevant? Isn't the important thing from your point of view the need to establish whether or not Wyatt actually *did* give Chloe this gift?'

Eric scowled. 'I suppose so, I don't know. As I've said I don't know how many times, I was confused. I didn't know what I was saying.'

'Describe this poster to me,' said Farrington.

A strange look crossed Eric's face. 'Why?' he said.

'I'm just curious, that's all.'

Eric looked at her a moment longer as if he thought she might be trying to catch him out, and then warily he said, 'Well, it's ... it's quite big. It shows Stefan Edberg just about to serve at Wimbledon. You've probably seen it yourself already. It was on the wardrobe door when you searched Chloe's room.'

'Ah,' said Farrington ambiguously, and then abruptly she asked, 'What is it you're not telling me, Eric?'

Eric tried, and failed, not to look guilty. Flushing, he said, 'Nothing. That is ... I mean .. I've told you everything I know. I've got nothing else to say.'

Farrington stared at him for a good fifteen seconds. She had learned over the years that a disbelieving silence was often more effective than a barrage of questions for eliciting a confession. But although Eric squirmed, his face continuing to burn red, he remained silent.

Finally Farrington leaned forward and said quietly, 'I hope you're telling me the truth, Eric. Because if you *are* hiding something, I promise you that sooner or later I'll find out what it is.'

38

Smoothly Andrew Dullaston turned the wheel of his BMW, and swept up the driveway of the Georgian country house that he and Juliette had bought with her parents' money. Gravel crunched under his tyres as he swung the car round in front of the building's elegant, sunlight-dappled facade and cut the engine. He got out, breathing in the country air, trying to calm himself with its crisp freshness.

All the way home his mind had been filled not with his triumph at finally securing the Erickson deal, but with the conversation he'd had with Eric Knight. The man's phone call had disturbed him far more than he'd ever let on to anybody. Just what the hell was going on? He thought he'd put all this Mr Bad Face business behind him years ago. Could it all be some sort of scheme that Knight had engineered himself, but if so, for what purpose? Perhaps the man was some kind of gold-digger, hoping to use that unfortunate business in their childhood as a lever with which to blackmail him? If that was the case, then he was going to get a great deal more than he'd bargained for. Actually, in some ways this was the most comforting option because at least Dullaston would know what he was dealing with, though he had to admit he couldn't quite bring himself to believe it. Perhaps the best thing would be to attend this meeting tomorrow and see what – if anything – transpired.

He locked the car and marched into the house. Although the front door was unlocked, no one answered when he called out hello. He tried again, but the only response was the echoes of his voice, rebounding from the high ceiling and wide staircase.

Strange. The children might have gone to see their friends, but Juliette should be here; she wouldn't have gone out and left the house unlocked. Besides which he had seen her white Golf parked in its usual spot on the drive, and despite the beautiful countryside hereabouts she had never been one for walking. She was not overfond of nettles and mud and flies; she liked an environment she had control over.

He moved towards the staircase and then stopped. Had he heard a sound coming from the lounge to his right? All at once he was wary. He thought of Eric Knight's phone call again; the man had rung his home number before ringing Dullaston at the office, hadn't he? If he or whoever was carrying out this campaign of intimidation had dared to come here . . .

Dullaston snatched a stout walking stick capped with the bronze head of a foxhound from the rack beside the front door, and hefted it in his hand. Never one for creeping about, as whoever was in the lounge had seemed to be doing, he stomped forward, twisted the handle of the closed door and shoved it open. This room was a sun trap, the patio doors flanked by large windows making the opposite wall seem to be composed almost entirely of glass. Beyond the windows and the patio, a lawn like green velvet fell away to flower beds and a line of trees, which were shedding curls of gold each time the wind blew. Dullaston's immediate gaze, however, was not drawn to the view beyond the glass but to the glass itself.

With the stark autumn light pouring through, the streaks and splashes of blood looked to be glowing, their colour so vivid that that alone would have been enough to make anyone flinch. It seemed like a long time to Dullaston before he could tear his eyes away from the streaks of red that were like screams given colour and shape, though in truth it was no more than a couple of seconds.

And then he was registering all the other terrible details in the room. More blood, this darker, though no less shocking, on the walls and the floor and the furniture. Pools and gouts of it, jagged streaks like dark lightning bolts up the pale wallpaper. So much blood. An impossible amount. Far more, surely, than could be contained in a human body.

And then, still less than ten seconds since he had entered the room, Dullaston saw his family. The sofa had been turned to face the window, so that it had its back to him. What he saw was three clumps of hair, like nests, peeking over the back of the settee. His daughter's hair, ash-blonde, was stained with blood.

The walking stick, his only defence, fell from his numb fingers.

He stumbled forward like a man who'd forgotten how to walk. His stomach felt as if it was peeling away from the inside, as if he was on the verge of sliding into a great chasm that was opening in his mind. He circled the sofa. More blood. So much more. The sofa was dripping with it, gleaming with it; his family were clothed in it, head to toe. They were propped together like drunks or dolls, heads thrown back, eyes and mouths wide open, idiot expressions on their faces. Felicity's eyes were facing in opposite directions; Juliette's tongue lolled from her mouth, coated with blood like a flap of liver. Each of them had been stabbed and slashed and hacked. Samuel's left cheek hung in shreds, exposing his back teeth in a crazy, terrible grin.

Dullaston fell to his knees. He felt his mind tearing apart like something soft, felt himself receding, into a faint or madness. A sheen of darkness, thick and fuzzy, seemed to drape itself over the room, like dust sheets over furniture. Under cover of this darkness, a figure detached itself from the sideboard across the room that it had been crouching behind and came towards him. Dullaston saw it approaching, and he tried to scramble to his feet, but he felt heavy, lethargic, and the figure was upon him before he knew it. He looked up at the figure's face, and he recognised it. His mouth dropped open, and a murmured denial, repeated over and over, squeezed its way out of his throat.

So incredulous was he that he never even saw the thin-bladed knife that killed him. Never even felt it when it pierced his heart.

Sunday 27 November

39

Eric couldn't sleep. For over an hour, he tossed and turned next to Annette – who seemed to be in a state deeper than sleep, lying on her back, motionless as a carved saint on a tombstone – before finally throwing back the covers and going downstairs. He went into the kitchen and poured himself a large whisky, then sat at the kitchen table as he sipped it, staring out of the window beside the back door, which was like staring into nothingness. He wished his mind could be as empty as the darkness outside seemed to be, but it was crammed with dilemmas and ambiguities, emotions as sharp and painful as broken glass. Should he have told Farrington the truth about the poster? He felt bad that he hadn't, but when it had come down to it, he hadn't been able to; the time hadn't seemed right. But didn't that mean that as well as being responsible for Chloe's death, he was also now responsible for protecting her killer by withholding information? He gulped at his whisky and then rubbed at his forehead. He needed a cigarette. He got up out of his chair to fetch one.

When he returned, Chloe was sitting at the kitchen table. 'Hello, Dad,' she said.

Eric sat across from her, put the slim roll-up between his lips and lit it. 'Hello.'

She flapped at the smoke that drifted into her face. 'I thought you'd given that up.'

'I have.' He took another drag, and said, a little shamefacedly, 'I had a bit of an argument with your boyfriend.'

'A fight, you mean? You made his nose bleed.'

'I know. I'm ashamed of myself. I wanted to know if he'd given you the poster, and if he had, to find out where he got it from.'

'Did he tell you?'

'No.'

'Why not?'

'He said he didn't know what I was talking about.'

'And did you believe him?'

Eric was silent for a long moment. 'Not at the time.'

'And now?'

'I don't know.'

'You don't know much, do you, Dad?'

Eric wasn't sure how to answer that. Before he could decide, Chloe said, 'Do you really think Ben killed me, Dad?'

Eric looked at her. She was so beautiful, so pure, just as he remembered her. 'I don't know,' he said, and then shook his head vigorously. 'No,' he admitted. 'No, not really.'

'So who do you think *did* kill me, then?'

An image rose in Eric's mind – a white, waxen face, staring out from the poster on the wardrobe door. Now, in the dead of night, with the house silent around him, he could almost believe that Straker's vengeful spirit *had* come back to haunt them.

Chloe leaned forward, her voice dropping to a Halloween whisper. 'Mr Bad Face. Is that who you think it was?'

His stomach kicked, as if the mere mention of the name would bring the creature here, ploughing through the darkness, through the dead hours, towards him.

He glanced at the kitchen window, half-expecting the nothingness to part, to see that terrible lumpen face peering in.

'Of course not,' he said, trying to make it sound as if he was treating her comment as a joke. 'He doesn't exist.'

'Doesn't he?'

'No. You know as well as I do that people don't—' And then he realised what he was about to say and his voice dropped to a murmur '—come back from the dead.' Abruptly despair overwhelmed him and he began to weep. 'I'm sorry, Chloe,' he sobbed. 'I'm so sorry. Please forgive me.'

But Chloe was gone, without even saying goodbye.

Trying to sniff back his tears, Eric reached out both hands, one for the whisky bottle, one for the tumbler. However his fingertips hadn't even connected with glass when he heard a sound. He froze, his gaze jumping instinctively to the window by the back door. He wasn't entirely sure, but it had sounded very much like the scuff of a boot heel on the concrete path that surrounded the house.

As before, the darkness outside the window seemed impenetrable, as if a black sheet had been stretched across the glass. Sitting in the brightly lit kitchen, Eric suddenly felt horribly exposed, felt as though the window was a two-way mirror that only whoever was on the other side could see through. He stood up so abruptly that his chair skidded backwards, and then he scuttled across the room to the light switch. He switched off the light and hurried through into the lounge, pulling the door shut behind him. Although he felt a little foolish, it didn't lessen the uncomfortable thudding of his heart, the tingling across his arms and shoulders as he shuddered. Had he really heard something? Ought he to ring Farrington just to be on the safe side? In the circumstances she'd be sure to send someone to check it out. But what if she came along personally, using the visit as an excuse to start grilling him about the poster again? In the end he decided to leave it for now, promising himself that if he heard one more sound he'd ring her; if not, he'd assume it had been a cat or a wind-blown leaf or any one of a hundred more likely things.

He walked across the sitting room and sat in his armchair, feeling tense but trying not to show it, as though he had an audience. He crossed and uncrossed his arms, and then did the same with his legs. He picked up the *Radio Times*, opened it at the letters page, and stared at what was written there without taking any of it in; his mind was too focused on the anticipation of a sound breaking the silence to concentrate on anything else. Seconds stretched into minutes, and little by little he began to relax, to convince himself that the sound he had heard had been nothing, after all. He decided to brave going back into the kitchen to fetch his whisky, and was just pushing himself up out of the chair when he heard a tapping on the window behind him.

He jumped so violently that a muscle in his shoulder seemed to wrench, sending a hot knife of pain into the back of his neck. He spun round, feeling dizzy, half-expecting to see someone already standing there, the window wide open, curtains billowing in the wind. There was no one, of course: just the dining table and chairs in the alcove before the curtained window that faced the back garden. The window was locked, but the glass behind the curtains suddenly seemed to him such a flimsy barrier, so easily breakable. Loath as he was to approach it, he knew he couldn't simply ignore the tapping, which thankfully had now stopped. He blundered forward on jelly-legs, around the dining table, his hip catching one of the chairs and making it clatter.

His hands were shaking so much that he almost tore the curtains from their hooks as he grabbed them. He was horribly aware that if whoever had knocked on the window was still there, he and they were now no more than a couple of feet away from each other. He yanked the curtains back in three jerky movements and peered out, his fear coalescing into a hard lump that was rising up through his stomach towards the back of his throat. Immediately his shock caused the lump to lodge in his chest, a hot, tight ball of pain.

Mr Bad Face was there on the other side of the glass, staring in at him.

Eric didn't think he had ever experienced real terror until that moment. The way he had felt as a kid when he had seen Straker for the first time was nothing compared to this. It was an instinctive, primeval, all-encompassing emotion. He couldn't scream, couldn't move, could do nothing to prevent his bladder releasing a spurt of urine that felt warm as blood, then cold as ice, on his skin. For several seconds he was held rigid, gazing into the face from a hundred childhood nightmares. And then all at once his legs seemed to give way, to turn as watery as the piss that was running down them. He stumbled backwards, tripped over something and fell, hitting his head on the table leg on the same spot he'd hit it that morning on the road after his scuffle with Ben Wyatt.

The pain was immense. It felt as though the back of his skull had been split with an axe. Blackness swarmed in like an invading army, threatening to overwhelm his senses. Eric fought desperately to remain conscious, but even so, for long seconds he could do nothing but lie helpless on the floor, hovering in a limbo between consciousness and unconsciousness. And then, gradually, the darkness began to recede and he felt a little of his strength returning. He managed to raise himself groggily on to one elbow and gaped up at the window, trying to bring his vision into focus.

Mr Bad Face was gone.

Eric's relief was superseded almost instantly by anxiety. *Where* had he gone? Was he creeping around the outside of the house, looking for a way in? Eric sat up, which made his head swim. He put his hand to the back of his skull and it came away bloody. Feeling dizzy and unco-ordinated he crawled on hands and knees to the phone, picked it up and punched the memory button that should put him straight through to Farrington. The phone rang four times and then was picked up, but it was a male voice which said, 'West Yorkshire CID incident room. Detective Inspector Farrington's office.'

Eric, still half-lying on the floor, the phone clutched to his throbbing head, heard the lounge door open behind him and soft footsteps cross the carpet.

'Please help me,' he whispered.

40

'Mum!' Tim cried, hurrying across to the table by the window where Jackie was nursing a cappuccino, 'how are you?'

She stood up and embraced him tightly. 'All the better for seeing you,' she said. 'Where's your dad?'

'Parking the car,' said Tim. 'He'll be here in a minute.'

They sat down. Jackie was wearing a long blue dress with a split up the front, silver trainers with platform heels and more make-up than usual. Even so, she looked tired and edgy. She glanced at Tim, flicking dark hair back from her face.

'Now that you're actually in front of me, I don't know what to say,' she said.

'You don't have to say anything,' said Tim.

'Of course I do.'

'You've said it all on the phone.'

'The phone's different. It's a machine. People don't say what they really think on the phone when they can't see the other person's face. Also they make things out to be better than they really are, so it doesn't make the other person feel so helpless. There's not a lot you can do when you're seventy miles away, is there?'

'There's not a lot anyone could have done,' Tim mumbled, and then lifted his gaze from the table where it had fallen. 'How are you anyway?'

She shrugged. 'Scared. Shocked. But coping. Like I say, I feel a whole lot better for seeing you. I just hope that the three of us can come up with some answers.'

'There might be four of us,' said Tim. 'Dad spoke to Andrew Dullaston yesterday. Something's definitely been happening to him too, but it's a bit touch and go as to whether he'll turn up.'

'My God,' said Jackie. 'That'd be quite a reunion. How about James? Did you get to speak to him too?'

'No, we tried quite a few times, but there wasn't any answer.' He leaned forward and confided, 'I think it's him that's doing all this.'

Jackie was unable to prevent a burst of laughter escaping her. 'James?' she said. 'No way. If you met him, you'd know what I was talking about.'

'That's what Dad says,' said Tim, 'but it stands to reason, doesn't it? If you four were the only ones who knew about Mr Bad Face, and three of you are getting ... what's the word?'

'Persecuted?'

'Yeah, persecuted. Then it must be the other one, mustn't it?'

'Unless someone else has found out,' said Jackie.

'But who? Me and Dad couldn't think of anyone who'd be mad enough to do all this.'

At that moment the door to Bertolucci's opened and Eric walked in. Tim noticed the look of shock on Jackie's face when she saw her ex-husband. He had to admit, his dad looked particularly bad that morning: haggard, deathly pale, sunken eyes. He leaned forward and murmured, 'I should have said – Dad reckons he saw Mr Bad Face last night. In the flesh.'

Jackie barely had time to disguise her look of startlement before Eric spotted them and came over.

'Jackie,' he said, his voice sounding drained of all energy, all emotion, 'how are you?'

Jackie stood up as she had done when Tim had approached the table, but this time the object of her affections was not so compliant. She had to actually reach out and all but grab Eric and pull him towards her.

'I'm fine,' she said. 'My poor Eric. I'm so sorry about everything that's happened.'

'It's not your fault,' Eric said awkwardly. Although Jackie was hugging him, his own arms were down by his sides. He looked relieved when she let him go and sat down. 'Can I get anyone a drink?' he said.

Jackie said she was fine with her cappuccino; Tim ordered a Coke. As soon as Eric was out of earshot, Jackie leaned forward and said, 'He looks absolutely terrible. Has he been like this since ... since it happened?'

Tim shrugged. 'I suppose so, off and on. He's pretty bad this morning, though, because of what he says he saw last night.'

'You say he actually *saw* Mr Bad Face?'

'That's what he reckons. All I know is that I heard this thump about two o'clock in the morning. I came downstairs to find him lying on the floor, phoning the police. He was terrified and his head was bleeding.'

'His head? Had he been attacked?'

'No, he fell and banged it, nearly knocked himself out. Anyway, the police came and had a good look round, but they didn't find anything.'

'My God,' said Jackie. She pursed her lips and then said cautiously, 'You don't think he's going a bit ...'

'What? said Tim defensively.

She decided to rephrase the question. 'You don't think he's started seeing things, do you? I mean, with everything that's happened, I wouldn't be surprised.'

Tim looked troubled. 'Why don't you ask him yourself?'

Eric came back with a Coke and a coffee. 'I was just telling Mum about last night, Dad,' Tim said, as if to pre-empt and thus avoid accusations of collusion.

'Ah,' said Eric, sitting down.

'Do you really think you saw him, Eric?' said Jackie.

'I don't think, I *know*,' said Eric.

'But ... well, you can't have done, can you?'

'Can't I?'

'No,' she said, distress making her impatient. 'You know as well as I do that Straker died in the fire.'

Eric sighed and stirred his coffee. 'Yes,' he said softly.

'So you can't really have seen him, can you?'

Eric didn't reply.

'*Can* you?' she snapped.

'Why don't you tell Mum what happened, Dad?' Tim suggested.

Eric did so, in a quiet, measured voice, taking frequent sips of his coffee. Afterwards Jackie, looking scared and bewildered, asked, 'What did you tell the police?'

'I said I thought I'd seen someone prowling around outside the house, but it had been too dark to see their face.'

'And you're sure it was ... Straker's face? You're sure it was exactly the same?'

Eric frowned as if he was having difficulty recalling the exact moment when he had opened the curtain. Finally he replied, 'It was how I'd always remembered it.'

'And what about the rest of the body?' said Jackie. 'Was that like Straker too? All sort of ... twisted and hunched?'

Eric thought about it for so long that Tim and Jackie thought he was never going to reply, but at last he said, 'I really only noticed the face, but I got the impression he was ... a big man. Powerful.'

'Then it can't have been Straker, can it? It must have been somebody made up to look like him, somebody wearing a mask.'

'It didn't look like a mask,' said Eric.

'Come on, Eric. Even Straker's *real* face looked like a mask.'

Eric looked too weary to argue. 'The question now, of course, is whether we should tell the police all that we know.'

Jackie shrugged. 'I don't think we've really got a choice, have we?'

Eric ran his finger round the rim of his coffee cup, then looked up. 'But you realise that'll mean telling them about the fire, don't you? About what we did?'

She nodded. 'Of course I do. But I don't think that really matters any more, does it? It all happened such a long time ago now.'

Eric looked suddenly agitated. 'Just because it happened a long time ago doesn't mean it doesn't matter. A man died because of us, Jacks. Thirty years, fifty years, even a hundred years doesn't make that go away.'

'I know that. But we were children, Eric. And besides, you and I weren't even the ones who started the fire. What do you think they're going to do? Arrest us?'

'I don't know. They might.'

'Then it's a risk we'll just have to take, isn't it? We can't afford not to.'

He looked at her a moment, then nodded. 'Yes,' he said, 'I suppose you're right.'

'When are you going to tell the police, Dad?' said Tim. 'Shall we go and see Inspector Farrington now?'

'Shouldn't we wait for Andrew?' said Jackie.

'It's nearly half past,' said Tim. 'I don't think he's going to come.'

'I think I'd rather be at home when we tell her,' said Eric. 'Besides, if she comes to us we can show her the poster.'

'I'll leave you to it then,' said Jackie.

'What do you mean?'

'Well, I can hardly come back with you, can I? I don't think Annette would appreciate it if I turned up.'

Tim looked at his father and then said. 'Actually, Mum, we were hoping that you'd come and stay with us for a bit.'

Jackie looked astonished. 'What?'

'Well, we thought with you being on your own, it'd be a lot safer if we all stuck together until this Mr Bad Face person is caught.'

Jackie smiled at her son. 'It's a lovely thought, Tim, but I don't think Annette would be too happy.'

'No, she's fine about it,' said Tim. 'I spoke to her yesterday, told her everything about Mr Bad Face. She said that if you wanted to stay, you could.'

Flabbergasted, Jackie looked at Eric. 'Is this for real?'

Eric grimaced. 'I'm not sure it was quite as simple as that.'

'Ah,' said Jackie. 'What really happened, Tim?'

Tim frowned at his father as if he'd let him down, then said reluctantly, 'Okay, Mum said no way at first, but I said that if she didn't let you stay then I'd come and stay with you so you didn't have to be on your own. In the end she said you could stay, but you had to keep out of her way.'

'Sounds like an offer I can't refuse,' murmured Jackie.

'You have to see it from her point of view, Jacks,' said Eric. 'She's just lost a daughter. She doesn't want anyone in the house right now.'

'Least of all me?'

Eric shrugged and pulled an apologetic face.

'*We* want you, though,' said Tim. '*Don't* we, Dad?'

'I'd hate to think of you on your own just at the moment,' Eric said.

Jackie looked out of the window. It had started to drizzle. A man hunched by an orange Volvo was feeding green skittles to the giant domed helmet of a bottle bank. She thought of how awkward it would be with Annette if she stayed at Eric's, but then she thought of her silent apartment, of being woken in the dead of night by weird phone calls or worse. Finally she turned back and placed her hands on the table as if to push herself to her feet.

'All right,' she said, 'I'll give it a go if you will.'

41

Annette sat on the settee in the lounge, silent and still. To a casual observer it might have seemed as though she was meditating, at peace with herself, but in fact the opposite was true. Chloe's death had reduced her to a mass of inconsistencies, paradoxes. How, for instance, could you feel numb and yet in so much pain? How could you hardly bear to imagine what your daughter must have been through in her last moments of life, and yet feel you were being eaten up inside because you didn't know exactly how she had died? How could you view the world through a haze of grief, refusing to acknowledge it, and yet at the same time possess senses that were so finely tuned they seemed like stripped nerves, endowing sounds with a clarity, smells with a sharpness, colours with a vibrancy they had never had before?

And why, after being faced with the ultimate nightmare, with the worst thing that could ever possibly happen to you, did the most inconsequential argument make you feel as though your world was falling apart all over again?

Last night Tim had come to her and had told her a long, incredible story about how Eric and his friends had inadvertently caused the death of a man they'd thought was a monster when they were children, and how Chloe had been murdered by someone who now appeared to be taking revenge for this man's death. Annette had listened to the story, mostly in silence, with a growing sense of unreality, a sense that the world was slipping away from her, that she couldn't quite grasp how it worked any more. Not that she would be sad to see it go; she wanted no part in a world where a young, beautiful, innocent girl could be tortured and butchered, could have the years ahead simply taken away as if her life didn't matter.

It was only when Tim proposed that Jackie should stay with them for a while that she snapped back into herself. She had refused, perhaps more vehemently than she should have done, but Tim had not been prepared to take no for an answer. He had threatened to go and stay with his real mother to prevent her being on her own.

At the time this, to Annette, had seemed like the last straw, the ultimate betrayal. Her already fragile emotions had crumbled and she had become hysterical. She had accused Tim of emotional blackmail, of kicking her when she was down, deserting her in her hour of need. It had been an ugly, awful scene. Tim, she knew, had been terribly upset by her accusations, but had remained adamant. 'I don't *want* to desert you, Mum,' he had said as if pleading with her to understand, 'but if she's on her own, this man might get her and then just think how you'll feel.'

In the end, unable to bear any more, Annette had screeched, 'Oh, just do what you want! I don't care! I don't care about anything any more!'

'Does that mean she *can* stay?' Tim had said.

'I've told you, do what you like. I don't care.'

He had stumbled to the door as if blinded by distress. As he had groped for the handle, she had said, 'I don't want anything to do with her, though. I want you to keep her out of my way.'

Afterwards, her tears had been bitter and prolonged; she had felt as if she was losing everything she had ever held dear. Now, though, sixteen hours later, she had had time to reflect on the awful exchange with her son (*my only child now*, she thought) and to rue her knee-jerk reaction.

It was only natural, in light of what Tim had told her, that he should feel concern for Jackie. And so as a way of apologising to him, and of avoiding more conflict, which she didn't think she could handle just now, Annette had decided to make the best of the situation. That didn't mean she wasn't still dreading the woman's arrival, but she had vowed to be, if not welcoming, at least civil to her. She had had a bath and got dressed, and had even brushed her hair and put on a little make-up for the first time in days.

Now she was waiting, staring straight ahead as though in a trance, her senses almost preternaturally sharp. Each sound that reached her ears seemed separate and distinct, and it was not just the internal sounds of the house, like the ticking of the clock on the mantelpiece and the whisper of the central heating, but the external ones too: the rattling of wind through trees made brittle by Autumn, the joyful shriek of a child (*oh, Chloe*), the constant but distant rumble of traffic.

How long she had sat there she wasn't sure; time still seemed as meaningless to her as it had on the night she'd been told of Chloe's death. Some time earlier, Eric, who had looked dreadful and seemed edgy (had seemed, too, as if he was keeping something from her), had all but begged her to come along to Bertolucci's with him and Tim, saying he didn't want her to be here on her own. However, she had refused, had said she wasn't going to be scared out of her own home, and that if the man who had killed Chloe came looking for her she would do to him what he had done to her daughter. In the end, reluctantly, Eric had left with Tim, exhorting her to keep the doors locked, to stay by the phone, and to call the Joneses across the road and then Inspector Farrington if she got so much as an inkling that anything was wrong.

That must have been several hours ago, she supposed. Two at least, perhaps three. Now she raised her head very slightly, her shoulders tensing, as she heard the sound of an engine detach itself from the distant rumble outside and turn into the street, coming closer.

It was odd. Before Chloe's death, she would have said that all car engines were much of a muchness, virtually indistinguishable, but she knew before it even stopped that this was Eric's Escort approaching; the engine seemed as distinctive as a voice now.

Behind Eric's car was another, this one – she would guess from the sound of it – newer and more compact; a Golf perhaps. Both cars pulled up in front of the house and cut their engines. There was the sound of doors opening and closing, and then she heard a woman's voice say, 'It's a long time since I was last here. It feels weird to be back.'

'Things haven't changed much,' Eric said then, which caused a band of anger and contempt to tighten across Annette's forehead.

Oh no, she thought bitterly, our little girl's dead, that's all. Just a minor thing. But apart from that, everything's exactly the same as it's always been.

She tried to calm herself as she heard footsteps approaching up the path, the sound of a key in the lock, the door opening, a murmured invitation to enter. Despite her intentions, she couldn't make herself look up when Eric and Tim and their guest entered the room. It would have felt too much like deferring to the woman, putting herself at a disadvantage, and so she remained where she was, staring straight ahead, until someone moved into her line of sight.

It was Tim. He knelt down in front of her and said, 'Mum, we're back. We've, er ... brought Jackie with us.'

Now she turned her head to appraise the woman. She couldn't suppress her satisfaction at realising that Jackie Foster was nervous, full of trepidation. And neither could she prevent herself thinking: Too much make-up. Ridiculous shoes that are far too young for her.

'So I see,' she said, trying – for Tim's sake – not to sound too cold.

'Hello, Annette,' Jackie said hesitantly. 'How are you?'

'Oh, I'm on top of the world. What do you expect?' Annette responded instinctively.

Even before the sentence was fully out of her mouth she was seeing Jackie recoil and Tim clench his teeth in anguish, and thought to herself: This is going to be harder than I ever imagined. Raising a hand, she said, 'Sorry,' but couldn't bring herself to offer an explanation.

'No, no, I should be the one who's apologising,' said Jackie. 'It was a stupid question.'

She paused, and then, as though encouraged by Annette's silence, said, 'I was so sorry to hear about Chloe. It's an awful ... *awful* thing.'

Annette felt something flutter in her throat. She swallowed it with an effort. 'Yes. Thank you,' she murmured.

42

Later, when the adults went upstairs to look at the poster in Chloe's room (Annette tagging along, Tim suspected, to make sure Jackie didn't touch anything), Tim sneaked out of the house to see Oonagh. He hadn't been to see her for over twenty-four hours, and his guilt at that was combined with a measure of eagerness and anxiety. Eagerness because it had occurred to him that Oonagh might have seen something last night to add weight to his dad's story, or even to shed new light on what his dad had seen; and anxiety because it had also occurred to him that whoever had been prowling around the house might also have seen Oonagh.

After filling a plastic Sainsbury's bag with enough provisions to keep her going for the next day or two, he squelched across a lawn plastered with yellow leaves to the shed. As he knocked, shoulders hunched against the drizzle, he cast anxious glances back at the house. What would he do if Oonagh didn't answer? Convince himself she was asleep and come back later? Try to break the door down by himself? Go to fetch his father? He waited. Five seconds. Ten. He began to get a jittery feeling in his belly. He knocked again, louder, certain that his father's curious face was going to peer out of the sitting room window at him at any moment.

Another ten seconds passed, and the jittery feeling was slowly building towards panic, when there was the grind-thunk of the key in the lock from inside, and the shed door was pulled open a couple of inches. A face peeped out, the eyes wary and resigned, a smudge of dirt on one cheek. 'Oh,' Oonagh said as if surprised, 'it's you.'

'Who did you expect it to be?' Tim said, pushing the door open just wide enough to slip inside, then closing it behind him.

'You didn't give the knock,' she said accusingly, 'so I thought somebody else must have found out about me.'

'Oh no, sorry,' said Tim, 'I forgot.'

'Where have you been anyway? I've been bored stiff. You said you were going to bring me some books to read this morning.'

'Yes, I know, I'm sorry, but I couldn't get away. There was too much going on.'

They sat down on the jumble of bedding against the far wall and he told her about his dad seeing the figure outside the window last night. He asked her if she'd seen anything, but she hadn't; she'd been asleep. He went on to tell her about the meeting with Jackie in Bertolucci's, and about her coming to stay with them for a few days.

Oonagh raised her eyebrows. Tim had told her all about Mr Bad Face yesterday when he'd come out to see her after speaking to Jackie on the phone. 'What does your mum think about that?' she asked.

Tim pulled a face. 'Not much. Things are pretty tense in there. I sort of guessed that the two of them didn't get on, but I never really realised how much Annette hates Jackie.'

'It's the competition,' said Oonagh.

'What do you mean?'

'Well, your mum must feel threatened by Jackie coming to stay. I mean, Jackie is your real mum and your dad's ex-wife. Perhaps Annette thinks that you'll decide you like Jackie better than her, or that she and your dad will become close again if they're forced together for a few days.'

'There's no chance of that,' said Tim uncomfortably. 'Jackie and Dad are just friends now. She's only here because of this Mr Bad Face stuff.'

'Stranger things have happened,' said Oonagh, but Tim shook his head vehemently.

'There's no way Dad would leave Annette,' he said, 'and neither would I.'

'Well, maybe you should tell Annette that, not me,' said Oonagh.

Tim thought about that, his scowl fading. Finally he nodded. 'Maybe I will.'

He looked around, thinking that if he was in Oonagh's situation he wouldn't be able to stick living in here for more than a day or two. The shed was cold, with a hard, dirty floor, she was having to use a bucket for a toilet which she covered with a plastic sheet between times, and she was eating only snacky foods – bread, cheese, fruit, biscuits, chocolate. Nothing hot, nothing cooked.

Tim had provided her with a bottle of water, soap, toothpaste and a towel, but she still looked grubby and her clothes were beginning to smell pretty stale. He had told her that if ever the house was empty and he knew the family were going to be out for long enough, he would leave a key under the flower pot outside the back door so she could let herself in for a shower.

'I can't stay long,' he said now. 'They'll start to wonder where I am.'

'I wish you could stay all night,' she said, and then blushed when he looked at her. 'What I mean is, it's so boring stuck in here all the time with nothing to do. Did you bring me those books?'

'No, I couldn't. If I'd gone upstairs and come down with an

armload of books someone would have been bound to have asked what I was doing. But I'll try and get them to you later. I'll put them in a plastic bag and stick them behind the bin. You can get them when everyone's gone to bed. How are the batteries in your torch?'

They talked for ten minutes or so as drizzle continued to weep down the shed's solitary window and the sky deepened towards a premature dusk. Their faces were mostly in shadow when Tim said, 'I'd better go.'

Oonagh sighed, but nodded. As Tim stood up she said, 'Actually, I was going to ask if you'd do me a favour.'

He shrugged. 'If I can. What is it?'

'Well, it's just that Graeme and Linda will be worried sick about me, so I wondered whether you could go and see them, tell them I'm all right? I know it means going off on your own, and being near the woods, so please say no if you're not happy with the idea.'

'Are you sure you want your mum and dad to know where you are?'

'Of course. They'll be going frantic, wondering what's happened to me. I hate the thought of putting them through that.'

'But won't they want to come and get you?'

'I expect they'll *want* to, but they're not stupid. They'll realise it's best if I stay here for the time being.'

The time being. Such a casual phrase, but Tim wondered briefly just how much longer Oonagh could go on living in his dad's garden shed.

'God, if that was my mum and dad, they'd come and get me straight away. They'd probably feel as though they had to tell the police where I was as well, just to avoid anyone getting into trouble.'

'Maybe you underestimate them,' said Oonagh. 'I mean, your dad and Jackie have kept their secret about the fire all these years, haven't they?'

'Well ... yeah, I suppose so. But they're going to tell the police everything now.'

Oonagh shrugged. 'So anyway,' she said, 'what do you think about going to see Graeme and Linda?'

Tim considered for a moment and then said, 'Yeah, I'll go.'

'Are you sure?'

'Yeah. I was thinking of asking Mum and Dad if I could go back to school tomorrow anyway. I could go and see them in my dinner hour.'

'But won't it worry you, walking down those country lanes on your own, being near to the woods?'

'You sound as though you're trying to put me off now.'

'No, I just want to make sure you know what you'll be letting yourself in for.'

Well, I suppose I will be a bit nervous, but it's all quite open round there, isn't it? If anyone comes for me I'll see them from miles off.'

Oonagh, however, now looked doubtful. 'I don't know. Maybe it's not such a good idea, after all.'

'Yes it is,' said Tim. 'I'll be fine. I'm not going to stay in the house for the rest of my life. If anyone tries to attack me, I'll kick them in the balls and run off.'

He spoke with a bravado he didn't altogether feel, but Oonagh said, 'Well, all right then, if you're sure.'

'I am,' said Tim firmly. At the door he added, 'And I'll get those books to you later, I promise.'

'Be careful,' Oonagh said.

'Don't worry,' said Tim, and forced himself to grin. 'Books don't frighten me.'

43

The man who had killed Chloe Knight had arranged to meet Farrington in a pub or a club whose name she couldn't remember. He had said to be there at 7:30, but it was five minutes to that now and she was still rushing around her flat, trying to find the socks she wanted to wear. She had turned the place upside-down looking for them, but they hadn't turned up. She didn't know why, but it was vitally important that she wear them.

Eventually, however, she knew she had to give up looking. She'd washed her hair, but hadn't had time to dry it, and it was hanging lankly over her face, dripping on her shoulders. She hadn't had time to apply any make-up either. She ran into the bathroom, feeling sick with urgency, looking for her make-up bag and a towel. She was wondering what Cruikshank would say when he found out she'd missed her appointment with the killer because she couldn't find the right socks to wear. He'd say it was because she was a *woman*, he'd say a *man* wouldn't care about his socks or his hair or his make-up. A *man* would have seen it as more important to have been there on time, a *man* would have caught the killer and brought him to justice. It was because she was a *woman* that she hadn't caught the killer. Everything she did wrong was because she was a *woman*.

It wasn't until she was on an extremely slow-moving bus that she remembered she had a car, and wondered why she hadn't used that. It would have been a hell of a lot quicker than this bloody bus, which seemed to be stopping every fifty yards or so to pick people up. And now that she thought about it, she didn't even know where this bus was going; it was probably not going anywhere near where she wanted it to go, wherever that was. What was worse, it was now stuck in a traffic jam, surrounded by cars, four or five lanes of them, an immovable gridlock of bumpers, stretching out on both sides.

She stood up, deciding to get off and run. If she ran fast enough, maybe the killer would still be there, waiting for her in the pub. But as she rose from her seat, she became aware that everyone in the bus, which was now so full that there was a seemingly impenetrable wall of bodies crammed in the aisle between her and the door, was looking at her and sniggering. She looked down and with a cringing shock of embarrassment realised that in her haste she had forgotten to put her clothes on.

The trill of her alarm clock mercifully jolted Farrington from the nightmare. She broke the surface with clammy threads of it still clinging to her like seaweed. Her hand groped blindly towards where she knew the alarm clock should be, but encountered only empty air. Abandoning the search, she pushed herself into a sitting position and used her fingers to prise her eyes open. The blurry room which was slowly coming into focus was not the one she expected to see.

She'd thought she was in bed, but in fact she had fallen asleep, fully clothed, on the settee. It was only then that she realised the trilling hadn't stopped, and that it wasn't her alarm clock at all but the telephone. She would have liked a few moments to orientate herself, but there wasn't time. She dragged herself off the settee, blundered across the room and placed the receiver to her ear.

'Hello. Farrington,' she said, trying to sound more alert than she felt.

'Boss, it's Frank. Did I wake you up?'

'Er ... yes you did, but that's all right. What time is it?'

'About four.'

The room was gloomy, steeped in shadow. The sky beyond the window was a boiling blue stew. 'Four when?' Farrington said, willing her mind to click into gear.

'Sunday afternoon. Remember I sent you home to get some rest about nine this morning?'

She wasn't too disorientated to bridle at his words. '*You* sent *me* home?'

Lockwood chuckled. 'I can see you're waking up, boss. All right,

I *suggested* you go home. You'd been working round the clock again, doing yourself in. There wasn't much happening here, so ...' He let the rest of the sentence dangle.

It was all coming back to her now. What Lockwood had meant was that the investigation had been at a standstill and she'd been getting into a state about it, trying to make things happen but only succeeding in winding herself and everybody else up. She hadn't really wanted to break off, but Lockwood had managed to persuade her that in the long run a few hours' sleep would be the most beneficial thing for her. The trouble was, when she'd got home she hadn't felt like sleeping at first, because whenever she closed her eyes she saw Cruikshank sitting behind his desk, telling her in that smugly sympathetic way of his that she'd given it her best shot, and that he appreciated that, oh yes he did, but it was plain to everyone that the inquiry was getting nowhere and that he thought that now was the time for a fresh approach. Or, to put it another way: Bye, bye, little girlie, pat on the head. You've had your fun, but now it's time for the big boys to move in and sort things out.

She supposed that eventually she must have dozed off and taken her anxieties down into her dreams. Trying to shrug them off now, she said, 'So, Frank, what's happening?'

'Quite a lot actually. We've got four more bodies.'

'*Four*!' she all but screamed. Sleep fell away from her in an instant. 'Jesus Christ! What's going on down there?'

'It's a family – mother, father, son and daughter. Butchered like Chloe Knight. And you'll never guess where they were found: in Annette Knight's flower shop.'

Farrington's mind was racing. 'Do we have an ID?'

'Yes, boss. How much do you want to know over the phone?'

Farrington wanted to know it all, but she made herself say, 'Tell me when I get there, Frank.'

'Okay. See you in ... what? Half an hour?'

She felt the urgency of her nightmare pressing in on her again. 'Twenty minutes,' she said, and put the phone down.

44

There were two police cars and a fire engine parked at the kerb outside Bloomers when Farrington arrived. She parked her own car on double yellows in front of the hardware shop across the road, and got out.

The first thing that struck her was the smell – smoky, like Bonfire Night – and then she saw threads of smoke drifting from the back of the shop like wispy grey hair blowing in the wind. Around the front of the shop a police barrier had been erected, yellow tape snapping between metal supports. Grey screens had been placed over the front windows inside the shop to prevent the public peering in, giving the building a blind, abandoned look.

Already, despite the fact that this was a cold, drizzly Sunday afternoon, a small crowd had gathered, for the most part silent and huddled, like mourners waiting for a funeral to begin. Farrington crossed the road, skirting the crowd, heading towards a uniformed constable standing stolidly at the entrance to an alleyway which led, presumably, to the back of the shop. As she slipped into the dark mouth of the alleyway, the constable stood aside for her, acknowledging her with a respectful nod.

There were a lot of people in the back yard of Bloomers, some looking purposeful, others just standing around talking. A number of uniformed constables were scanning the ground, looking for evidence. A couple of her own men, who obviously preferred to be out in the rain than inside the smoky shop, nodded at her, murmuring greetings. Back here the smell of smoke was stronger, more acrid; the air was hazy with it. It was rising from the open back door of the shop, from a burnt-out litter bin, in fact, that Farrington could see sitting in the short corridor that led to what looked like an office. The bin was sitting on a patch of flooring which looked as though someone had dropped a bag of soot on to it from a great height. Smoke was still rising from the bin, and forming a greasy black cloud just below the ceiling, despite the fact that the whole corridor was awash with grimy-looking water. Farrington was no more than two steps into the corridor when smoke caught in her throat and made her cough. She found a handkerchief and placed it over her nose and mouth.

In the office the smoke was not so concentrated, though it still seemed to hang in the air and begrime the walls and furniture, giving her the impression she was viewing the world through a dirty lens. It was here she found Lockwood, talking to a bearded man in bulky yellow fireproofs who had a helmet tucked under his arm. Lockwood had his arms folded and was perched on the edge of a desk, but pushed himself upright when he saw Farrington as if he thought she might reprimand him for slouching.

'Boss,' he said, by way of greeting, 'this is Dave Morgan, the fire chief. He and his men were first on the scene.'

Farrington shook Morgan's hand. 'You didn't say anything about a fire, Frank. What the hell's been going on here?'

Lockwood frowned as if he thought her annoyance was directed at him. He nodded at Morgan, who said, 'We got the call about an hour ago. Bloke who owns the post office across the road saw smoke rising from the back of the shop. When we got here, we found the back door forced open, and that bin that you passed on your way in sitting there with flames pouring out of it. The bin had been stuffed with rags and then it looks as though petrol was poured over the top and set alight. Plenty of smoke, but not very serious. Our first thought was that kids had done it.

'Then we went in to the front of the shop, just to check over the premises, and that was when we found the bodies.' He shook his head. 'Jesus, I've seen some things in my time ... Anyway, that's when I called you lot.'

'So when you arrived, how long would you estimate the fire had been going?' Farrington asked.

'Not long. Ten minutes at the most. A fire like that would create a lot of smoke almost straight away, plus it was still contained within the litter bin, more or less.' He scratched his beard with stubby fingers. 'You know, when I first saw those bodies I thought whoever had started the fire had done it to burn the place down, try to get rid of the evidence. Then I realised it wasn't that at all.'

'No,' Farrington agreed. She had already worked it out. 'He started the fire to draw attention to the place. He wanted those bodies found.'

'But why?' the fire chief said. 'He's taking a bit of a risk, isn't he? I mean, he can't have been gone more than ten minutes before we showed up.'

'He's an exhibitionist,' said Farrington. 'He's proud of his work.'

'Sick bastard,' said Morgan. 'People like that, they want bloody stringing up.'

They left Morgan to clear up and went into the front of the shop. The SOCO was photographing the bodies from all angles, his flash highlighting the vivid contrast between white flesh and red blood. The four bodies were in a heap on the floor as if they'd been huddling together for protection when they were killed. The man was on the bottom, face down, limbs at crooked angles, his golfing jumper and grey slacks stained maroon with blood. The woman was lying face up, head resting against the man's shoulder, eyes half-closed, sticking her bloody tongue out for the camera. The boy was lying cross-ways across the man's back and the woman's legs, slashed face turned to the side (if he'd been alive he'd have had a good view up the woman's skirt which had rucked up over her knees and thighs). The girl, who could have been no older than eleven or twelve, was draped across the top of the group, glaring at the ceiling, cross-eyed and accusatory, her mouth open in a frozen snarl or scream. Her right arm was bent back and the hand curled into a rigid claw.

Farrington forced herself to look for a good thirty seconds, blinking every time the flash went off beside her, trying to channel everything she felt into a cold and purposeful fury. Finally she breathed deeply, filling her lungs with the smell of death, and turned to Lockwood who had been standing silently by her shoulder.

'Who are they?' she asked.

Lockwood reached into his jacket pocket. He was wearing a pair of latex gloves; everyone in the building was wearing gloves of one sort or another. He withdrew a transparent plastic evidence bag containing a black leather wallet and held it out. Farrington fumbled in her pockets, found her own gloves and pulled them on. She took the bag from Lockwood, unzipped it and withdrew the wallet. Inside were forty-five pounds in cash, credit cards, a photograph of the family taken on a sunny beach somewhere, smiling into the camera, and a membership card for a Yachting Club printed with the name A. Dullaston and an address in Kent.

'Nice and convenient,' Farrington said. 'Not only did the killer want the bodies found, he also wanted them to be easily identified.' She put the wallet back into the bag and zipped it up. 'All right, what else have we got?'

'Well, Boam's not here yet to confirm it, but we're virtually certain that these people weren't killed here,' said Lockwood. 'Considering the injuries, there's nowhere near enough blood. Also, there are spots and streaks all the way through the shop, which would seem to indicate that they were dragged in here and dumped.' He pointed at the floor, where the said spots and streaks of blood had been enclosed within a series of yellow chalk rings, like ancient markings.

Farrington looked at him incredulously. 'But that would mean the killer must have parked outside the shop and dragged the bodies across the pavement and up the alleyway one by one.'

Lockwood gave a wry grimace. 'Looks like it.'

'Jesus, the guy's got some gall. And I suppose nobody saw a thing?'

'Well no, the bloke who reported the fire *thinks* he remembers seeing a dark-coloured transit van parked outside the shop for a while earlier this afternoon. Unfortunately, most of the shops around here are purely business premises, all of which, apart from the newsagent's and the cafe, are closed on Sundays. There are one or two flats upstairs, but mostly it's offices. We might get more once we put out a general appeal for information. A lot of people drive through the High Street en route to the A1, so if we could jog the memories of any of those we might be on to something.'

'Hmm,' said Farrington. She was not optimistic. From Annette Knight's flower shop you could see cars coming from a good two hundred yards away in each direction. She wondered how long it would take to drag a body, presumably wrapped in sheeting, from the back of a van, across the pavement and into the alleyway. Five seconds? Ten at the most? Although it seemed an outrageously risky thing to do, she wouldn't be at all surprised if nobody had seen a thing. It was incredible, actually, how little attention people paid to what went on around them. There had been a case she had worked on where a man had pushed a wheelbarrow containing a corpse draped with a tarpaulin through the centre of York on a busy Saturday afternoon, and not one person had found it even slightly suspicious.

'Any prints?' Farrington asked.

The SOCO looked up from his camera. 'Sorry, boss, nothing at all. The guy must have been wearing smooth-fingered gloves.'

Farrington pulled a face, though she wasn't surprised. 'I presume the Kent boys are checking out the Dullastons' address?'

Lockwood nodded. 'We're just waiting to hear back from them.'

'Can you liaise with them personally, Frank? I want to know if their forensic comes up with anything. Also, they'll be doing house-to-house. Tell them to ask whether anyone remembers seeing a dark-coloured transit van in the area.'

Lockwood nodded again. 'I suppose we're not wrong in assuming that this is the same guy who killed Chloe Knight, boss?'

'Is that a serious question, Frank?'

'Well ... no, I suppose not. It's just that with them being killed such a long way away. And then the m.o. isn't exactly the same either, is it? I mean, the Knight girl had her eyes put out and her fingers chopped off. There's none of that here.'

Farrington looked down at the bodies again, pursing her lips. After a moment she said, 'He cut Chloe Knight's fingers off with her mother's secateurs because he wanted it known that he was the same person who had broken into the shop that morning. He didn't need to do that with the Dullastons. Just dumping the bodies here and then drawing attention to them with the fire was his way of telling us that we're dealing with the same man.'

'But why kill these particular people?' said Lockwood.

'I'm hoping Eric Knight can tell me that.'

'You think the Knights and the Dullastons knew each other?'

'It seems likely, doesn't it? If the Dullastons were chosen at random, why did the killer go all the way to Kent? Why not just choose a family from the village?' She peeled off her latex gloves and shoved them into her pocket. 'I'm going to go and see Eric Knight now, see what he's got to say for himself. In the meantime, you get on to Boam and tell him to shift his arse, and then get on to Kent and tell them to shift theirs.'

'Will do, boss,' Lockwood said, and then called after her, 'Be careful,' as she strode out.

Farrington raised a hand, carefully stepping over the chalk-ringed spatters of blood. 'Don't worry, Frank, I always am.'

45

'Inspector,' said Eric when he answered the door. 'I was just about to call you.'

'Really?' said Farrington as if she didn't believe a word of it, and stepped smartly over the threshold. 'May I come in?'

Eric stepped back as she entered, and then preceded her through to the lounge. 'The Inspector's here,' he said when everyone looked up. He introduced Jackie, who shook Farrington's hand and said, 'Did Eric say we were just about to ring you?'

'Yes,' said Farrington. She sat down and crossed her legs, but didn't lean back. She looked officious and alert. 'What about?'

Eric glanced at Jackie and puffed out his cheeks. 'It's rather a long story. It's about something that happened to us ... me and Jackie, that is ... when we were kids.'

Somewhat haltingly he began to tell her the story of Mr Bad Face. However, he had only got as far as naming the other members of the gang when Farrington sat bolt upright in her seat and snapped, '*Dullaston?*'

Taken aback, no one said anything for a moment, and then Jackie asked, 'Do you know him, Inspector?'

Farrington was as flustered as Eric had ever seen her, but trying hard to regain her composure.

'Er ... yes. Yes I do,' she said. 'Or at least I know the name. It's ... um ... come up in our investigations.'

'How?' asked Jackie.

'Is he a suspect?' said Tim. 'Have you questioned him?'

Farrington paused a moment, then shook her head. 'No, he's not a suspect, and no, we haven't questioned him. Though *you've* already managed to answer the question that was my main reason for coming here.' She raised a hand as though to deflect the quizzical looks she was receiving. 'Why don't you go on with your story, Eric? I'll explain how I know Andrew Dullaston later.'

Aided by Jackie, and occasionally Tim, Eric told her the rest. Farrington listened, stony-faced, and when he had finished, said, 'Why didn't you come to me with all of this as soon as you realised?'

Eric looked a little shamefaced. 'I wanted to talk to the others first. And besides, I didn't know what would happen to us. About the fire, and the fact that Straker died in it, I mean.'

'Do you think we'll be charged, Inspector?' Jackie asked.

Farrington pursed her lips. 'That's not for me to say. Though off the record I'd guess that little will come of it.' She leaned forward in her seat and looked hard at Eric. 'But you realise you should have come to me straight away, don't you, Eric? By withholding this information, you could have seriously hampered the investigation into Chloe's death.'

He nodded miserably. 'Yes, I'm sorry.'

'Next time you ring me *immediately*, do you understand? Day or night, no matter how trivial or sensitive you think the information is, I want to know.'

Eric had turned crimson now. 'Okay,' he mumbled, and then tried to smile. 'Now I know how my pupils feel.'

Farrington leaned back a little, though not enough to look comfortable.

'You were going to tell us about Andrew, Inspector,' said Jackie.

'Yes, I was, wasn't I?' said Farrington, sounding reluctant. She looked for a moment as though she was debating how best to approach the subject, and then she said, 'You say you spoke to Andrew Dullaston yesterday morning, Eric?'

'Yes.'

'And it was the first time you'd spoken to him in ... what? Ten years?'

'More like twenty.'

'Ironic,' murmured Farrington. 'Can you remember what the exact time was when you spoke to him?'

Eric looked at Tim. 'Half eleven?' he ventured.

Tim nodded. 'Maybe even a bit later. Quarter to twelveish.'

Farrington nodded and sighed. 'I think you'd better prepare yourselves for a shock,' she said.

Jackie looked at her, her eyes widening. 'He's dead, isn't he?'

'I'm afraid so,' said Farrington.

'Oh God,' Jackie whispered, sounding more scared than upset, and put a hand over her mouth.

Eric looked numb but he asked, 'What happened?'

As plainly as she could, holding nothing back, Farrington told them the details. When she revealed where the bodies had been found, an already sickened-looking Eric opened his mouth in disbelief and said as though being strangled, 'Oh my God, you're joking!'

Jackie looked sick too, and unable to say anything, but Annette, who had been largely silent up to now, merely looked angry.

'It makes no difference to me,' she said. 'The business can rot anyway, as far as I'm concerned.'

Jackie began shaking her head slowly from side to side as though to deny what Farrington had been telling her. Finding her voice, albeit barely, she said, 'Whoever this is, he's destroying our lives piece by piece, taking us apart.' She began to snivel. 'How can someone do something like this? How can anyone kill a child? Someone like that can't be human, can they?'

No one replied, and ten minutes later Farrington left with the poster and the card, saying that her main priority now was to find James Keeve and talk to him, though whether as suspect or potential victim she didn't know. As she drove away she felt enraged and helpless, her hands white-knuckled on the steering wheel. She was acutely aware that even if she were to catch this madman today, it would neither bring back the lives he had already snuffed out nor rebuild those he had shattered.

46

Tim had been as good as his word. He had left a load of books wrapped in a plastic bag behind the dustbins for her. It had been a risk getting them – Oonagh had half-expected a face to appear at the lounge window in response to the squelching of her footsteps on the sodden lawn, or light to blaze suddenly through the kitchen window and the glass-panelled door which the bins were parked beside. However she had made it back to the shed without incident, clutching her prize as if it was the most valuable thing she had ever owned. Earlier she had vowed that once this was over and she was back with Graeme and Linda, she would never complain of being bored ever again. Indeed, more frequently as time had gone on, she had even found herself wondering whether it might have been better staying with the nice foster couple in their big, warm house, after all, though of course one advantage of being here was that she got to see Tim. She had come to rely on his visits, which, infrequent though they were, were like brief blazing moments punctuating endless hours of greyness.

She didn't much like her dependence on him – it made her feel weak, insecure – but she couldn't deny that her feelings for him were growing stronger and stronger. Whenever that special knock sounded on the door, her stomach gave a little twizzle of excitement. She had never been in love before, and the thought of it scared her, and also saddened her a little. If her life went on as it always had, then any romantic relationships she might form were bound to be doomed to failure. At least having all this time had given her the chance to really think about her life, though she wasn't sure that that was such a good thing, because the more she thought about it the more confused she became. She wanted to stay with Tim, but she also wanted to be away from here, back on the road with her parents. She realised that sooner or later, four or five years down the line perhaps, she was going to have to make a decision.

Before she could lose herself in a book until she started to feel sleepy, there was one more task to perform. This was to empty the bucket that Tim had provided for her to use as a toilet. Not only was it smelly, but it would probably become a health risk if she didn't empty it soon. She picked up the bucket, unlocked the shed door, pushed it open a crack and peered out. All seemed quiet, an orange glow behind the lounge curtains being the only thing that prevented Tim's house being silhouetted against the darkness.

It was bitterly cold. A strong wind was causing the trees at the bottom of the garden to rustle as if something was moving in them. The trees were where Oonagh was heading. They were only twenty or thirty feet behind the shed, but from here they looked like a solid wall of blackness. Tim had said there used to be an orchard behind the house, but most of it had been ploughed up to make room for further housing. Nevertheless the trees remaining were still plentiful enough to stand six or eight deep, almost like a miniature forest.

There was less chance of Oonagh being detected here, even if someone did switch on the kitchen light in the house, and so she took the journey slowly, the bucket swaying in her right hand. It wasn't very full, but she didn't want to slip and spill the contents over herself. The grass was swampy beneath her feet, far worse here as she approached the trees than it had been nearer to the house, and before she had covered half the distance her feet were damp with water that had seeped through the old, scuffed leather of her boots. Oonagh always wore boots, as did most of the travellers and their children, but these, which she'd had for well over two years now, were getting past their best.

She reached the trees and slipped between them, water dripping from above, sodden leaves brushing against her face. The ground underfoot was even softer here, slippery with wet leaves, but Oonagh pressed on until she came to a knee-high wooden fence that marked the boundary between the Knights' house and the one that backed on to it. Holding the bucket away from her to avoid backsplash, she upended it, holding her breath. She shook it to get out the last few drops, then turned to head back to the shed.

And then she froze, like a deer detecting a predator.

Had she heard the sound of someone moving close by, or had it been merely the rush of wind in the trees? She glanced around, but saw nothing except a dark jumble of trees and bushes, any one of which might be a motionless watching figure. She stepped calmly behind the nearest tree, where she squatted down on her haunches to listen. She put the bucket on the ground and placed her palms on the tree's gnarly wet bark to stop herself losing her balance. The wind was crashing through the trees, causing branches to sway and creak above her head. The moment it dropped, however, she heard what she thought she had heard before, and this time there was no mistake: it was the squelch of footsteps, coming towards her.

Scared, but trying not to make any sudden moves that might draw attention to herself, Oonagh peered around the tree, craning her neck in both directions. She could see nothing, and for a second couldn't help imagining a set of huge footprints simply appearing in the wet ground, as some invisible entity made a beeline for her hiding place. Her belly was jumping now, as if encouraging her to leap up and make a run for it, but she remained where she was. Unless Footsteps had actually seen her stepping behind the tree she was safer here for the time being. Another flurry of wind dashed by, drowning out the footsteps for a few agonising moments - moments in which Oonagh kept expecting a vast misshapen figure to loom from nowhere, hands like bear's paws reaching out for her.

And then, before she heard the figure again, she saw it, off to her right, a tall, dark shape, flickering between the trees as it came towards her. It was moving purposefully, accompanied by the squelch of footsteps which she heard when the wind dropped again, and by a deep, slightly rasping breath. It was too dark to see the figure's features, to see anything in fact but a tar-black silhouette that seemed almost to merge into the substance of the trees and then squeeze out again on the other side, but she saw enough to know that the figure was tall, broad-shouldered, powerful-looking.

She rose slowly, hands climbing the bark of the tree, feeling suddenly very vulnerable squatting down on her haunches. Her legs tingled with pins and needles, and she wondered, if she had to make a run for it, whether they would be reliable enough to support her.

Mr Bad Face, she thought, and shuddered. Suddenly she was grateful that it was a murky night, that clouds were obscuring the half-moon. Oonagh knew that having a scarred face didn't automatically make a person a monster, just as she knew that murderers didn't always look like the monsters that many of them really were. However put the two together and you were faced with something more than human, something with the power to terrify on an instinctive, primal level. It was this fear that was beginning to build in Oonagh now. One glimpse of that face in the moonlight, and she knew she would be up and running like a rabbit.

The figure came closer, arms swinging by its sides, face still thankfully obscured. Oonagh readied herself to run the moment it lunged towards her; until then she would cling to the desperate hope that she hadn't been spotted, just as she was clinging to the trunk of the tree, its rain-soaked bark, dark and soft as moss, embedding itself beneath her nails.

Closer, and closer still. Oonagh moved from one foot to the other, legs itching to run. The figure was five feet from her hiding place, and then three, and then no more than a foot away, just the other side of the trunk, in fact. If the tree had not been there Oonagh would have been able to reach out and touch it on the shoulder: *Tag, you're it.*

And then, miracle of miracles, the figure was walking straight past the tree, its rasping breath and squelching footsteps fading as it did so. Mr Bad Face hadn't seen her, hadn't smelt her, hadn't sensed her. Or perhaps he had and he simply didn't care about her. Perhaps she wasn't part of the equation.

All at once her legs felt watery, and she slumped down, knees splatting in the sodden mound of leaves at the base of the tree. She felt light-headed and silly, as if she wanted to laugh and cry at the same time. But she forced herself to remain silent, and even when the figure had gone, when it had blended into the darkness and disappeared, she made herself count slowly to six hundred before moving. Then she stood up, picked up her bucket and cautiously made her way back through the trees and across the lawn to the shed.

She was unsteady on her feet, and it seemed as though her thoughts were drifting above her head like balloons, anchored to her mind by invisible strings. Oonagh had never been drunk, but she had always imagined that this was what it would be like. She made it back to the shed without incident, slipped inside and locked the door behind her. Only then did she begin to shiver violently, as though with fever, and to giggle at the same time. Crossing the wooden floor, she slumped on to her mound of bedding and dragged her sleeping bag tightly around her. The giggles, which were hard and painful as pebbles in her throat, subsided relatively quickly, but the shivers remained with her for a considerably longer time.

47

Tim was up in his room, drawing to take his mind off things, when he remembered that he had told Oonagh he was planning to go back to school tomorrow and would use his lunch hour to see her parents. If that was still going to happen, he ought to broach the subject now with his mum and dad. He put aside his pad, on which he'd been sketching caricatures of film stars – Johnny Depp, Kim Basinger, Jim Carrey – working from photos in *Empire* magazine, and went downstairs.

No one seemed to have moved since he had left the room an hour ago. The TV was on, the sound turned down low; Jackie and Annette were staring at it, though both seemed preoccupied with their own thoughts. His dad was flicking through yesterday's paper as though in the hope of finding something absorbing enough to occupy his mind for ten minutes. Despite the TV and the wind howling outside, it seemed unnaturally quiet in the room. Tim wondered whether anyone had said even a word since he had left.

'Hi,' he said when Jackie glanced up and offered him a tired smile.

'Hi, Tim. How's it going?'

'Okay,' he said, and squeezed into the gap between his dad and Annette on the settee.

'I thought you were going back to your flat to pick up some of your stuff,' Tim said to Jackie. He had to be careful not to call her 'Mum' when Annette was around.

'We've decided to leave it until tomorrow,' Jackie said, evidently referring to herself and Eric. 'I think I can cope until then.'

Tim nodded, and then tentatively said, 'Actually, I was thinking of going back to school tomorrow.'

Annette, who hadn't even acknowledged his arrival, suddenly jerked beside him, like some dormant thing coming to life. 'No, you're not,' she said.

'Why not? I've got to go back sometime.'

'Not until this maniac's caught.'

'But he might not be caught for ages yet. I can't miss all that school.'

'It's more important that we all stay together. I don't want to lose you as well.'

Tim remembered Oonagh's words earlier, her assessment of Annette's hostility towards Jackie. 'You're not going to lose me,

Mum,' he said, and glanced frustratedly at his father, who unexpectedly spoke up for him.

'I'll take Tim to school, Net. I'll drop him off right at the door, and pick him up at the end of the day. As long as he doesn't go wandering off by himself, he can't come to any harm.'

Tim felt guilty at his father's words, but said, 'You see, I'll be all right. I just need something to do, something to take my mind off things.'

Annette glared at Tim as if he'd said something unforgivable. 'All right,' she muttered, 'you go to school if that'll "take your mind off things". I only wish I could forget about Chloe just as easily.'

Tim looked dismayed. 'That's not what I meant,' he said.

'Net, that's not fair,' said Eric. 'Tim feels just as bad about Chloe as you do.'

'*Bad*?' Annette exclaimed, and made a throaty sound of scornful disgust. 'That doesn't even *begin* to describe how I feel.'

'All right then,' said Eric, frowning. 'Awful. Devastated. Is that more appropriate? We're all feeling it, you know, however you want to describe it.'

'*Well, why don't you show it then?*' she screeched at him suddenly, making Tim jump.

Eric, normally the most mild-mannered of men, found himself losing his temper for the second time that weekend. 'We have been showing it, not that you'd bloody notice, you've been so wrapped up in yourself. Just because Tim and I don't spend all day walking around like zombies ...' He took a deep breath, struggling to bring himself under control. 'We've all got our different ways of dealing with it, that's all,' he said more calmly.

'But I'm not *dealing* with it,' Annette said bitterly. 'I'm not even beginning to *deal* with it. Do you want to know how I really feel? Do you? I feel as if my heart's been torn out, I feel as if there's nothing worth living for any more. I wish I'd been the one who'd been killed, not Chloe, so that I didn't have to go through all this.'

'Don't say that,' Tim said miserably.

'Why not? It's true.'

'Look, I think we all need to calm down,' Jackie said. 'Have a cup of tea or something.'

Annette swung round, her eyes blazing. 'What the hell has this got to do with you? How dare you tell me how to behave in my own house!'

'I wasn't—' Jackie began, but Annette had only paused to draw breath to yell, 'You can't even begin to know how I feel! You don't know what it's like to be a real mother!'

'That's enough!' Eric shouted, his voice booming off the walls. 'You've got no right to speak to Jackie like that.'

'Oh, you would stick up for *her*, wouldn't you?' Annette snarled. 'You're finally showing where your fucking priorities lie. Well, you're welcome to each other as far as I'm concerned.'

She jumped up and stormed out of the room, slamming the door with such force that a picture fell off the wall. Tim wasn't sure whether he heard Annette start crying before the sound was superseded by her footsteps pounding upstairs.

For a few seconds nobody moved or spoke. Then Eric let out a groan which seemed to deflate him, and Jackie said shakily, 'How did that happen?'

'It was all my fault,' Tim said. 'I shouldn't have said anything about going back to school.'

'No, it wasn't your fault,' said Eric. 'It's just that Annette's like a pressure cooker at the moment, she needs to let off steam every now and again. She didn't really mean what she said; she just can't help herself. I'd better go and see how she is.'

As he stood up, Jackie did too. 'Look, perhaps I'd better go home,' she said. 'I don't think this is working out.'

'Oh no,' Eric said, 'you're staying here. There's no way we'd let you go back now, after what's happened to Andrew and his family.'

'I'm a tough cookie, you know,' said Jackie.

'Not tough enough,' said Eric.

'I could always beat you at arm wrestling.'

'Somehow I don't think you'd get the chance to challenge the guy to an arm wrestling contest.'

She sighed. 'No, you're probably right. It's a horrible feeling to think there's someone out there who hates you enough to want to kill you. Look, you go and see how Annette is, and I'll put the kettle on.'

After Eric had gone upstairs, Jackie went through to the kitchen, followed by Tim. 'Are you okay, Mum?' he asked her.

She smiled at him. 'Don't you worry about me. I'm a tough old bird.'

Tim hesitated, then said, 'Annette's not usually like this, you know. She's usually really nice.'

'I know, Tim,' said Jackie. 'I don't blame her after what's happened. I'd probably be the same if I was her.'

She carried the kettle to the sink to fill it, but just as she was reaching for the tap, a pounding from the front of the house made the two of them jump.

'What now?' Jackie said. She put down the kettle and looked

around, then grabbed the serrated bread knife from its wooden block. 'Come on.'

She and Tim went through the lounge and into the hallway, Jackie holding the knife out in front of her. In the narrow hallway the pounding was abominably loud.

Jackie reached the door and shouted, 'Who's there?' just as Eric appeared at the top of the stairs.

'Let me in.' It was a man's voice that answered her, and it sounded terrified. 'Please, let me in.'

Jackie glanced at Eric, who was coming down the stairs now. 'Open the door,' he said, 'but be careful. No, on second thoughts, let me do it.'

He reached the bottom of the stairs, took the knife from her and stepped forward. Taking a deep breath, he pulled the door open.

Immediately he jumped back as a figure lunged towards him. Tim saw a small, plump man wearing a rumpled suit. The man must have been leaning on the door, because he fell forwards into the hallway, palms thumping the carpet to prevent his face doing the same. He scrambled into the house, legs kicking behind him. 'Close the door, close the door,' he implored.

Eric did so, shutting out the howling wind. He was still holding the knife out before him, and Tim thought the man was lucky his dad hadn't thrust it instinctively forwards when he'd fallen into the house. The man scrambled into a sitting position and looked up at them, wide fearful eyes blinking behind steel-rimmed spectacles, thinning hair sticking up every which way, tousled by the wind. He looked like a city gent, an accountant maybe, or an insurance broker, who had been through a rough time.

For a few seconds nobody spoke, and then Jackie broke the silence. In an astonished voice, she exclaimed, 'My God, it's James.'

48

Ten minutes later, James Keeve was sitting in the lounge, a blanket around his shoulders, a mug of tea in his hands. Every so often a bout of shivering would grip his body, causing the surface of the tea to ripple. He made Tim think of walkers he'd seen on the news who'd got lost on the moors in bad weather and had had to be rescued by helicopter. Back in the hallway, when Jackie had said, 'My God, it's James,' James had looked up and had said, almost in a kind of wonder, 'Jackie, you're here. I didn't expect—' Then his face had changed, had seemed to fall; the fear that had momentarily faded with the joy of seeing Jackie had reasserted itself. 'He's been after you too, hasn't he?' he said.

There was a beat of silence, and then Eric had lowered the knife. 'Yes, James,' he said, 'he has.'

Now they were all gathered in the lounge, waiting to hear James' story. Even Annette was there; while Jackie had made tea for everyone, Eric had gone upstairs to tell her who had arrived. After a few minutes she had followed him down, looking sullen, and had seated herself on a corner of the settee, drawing up her knees.

'I can't believe you're here, James,' Eric said. 'I've been trying to call you since yesterday.'

'Yesterday,' James repeated, as if it was a concept he couldn't quite grasp. 'I was ... that is, *we* were ... out most of yesterday. Shopping. Doing normal things. Having a normal day.' His face suddenly creased as though in pain, and in a choked voice, he said, 'Maybe if I *had* spoken to you yesterday, none of this would have happened.'

None of what, James?' Jackie asked gently.

'He took them,' James said. 'He took my wife and my little girl. He took them away from me.' He released a thick, rubbery sob, and his head drooped, chin resting on his chest.

Eric glanced at Jackie, who moved forward and knelt in front of Keeve, placing her hands on his shoulders. 'Hey, James,' she said, 'we're all here. We're here to help you.'

James glanced up. His eyes were red, his bottom lip trembling. 'Has anyone told Andrew about this?' he said shakily.

This time it was Jackie's turn to look to Eric. He grimaced and said as if apologising, 'I'm afraid Andrew's dead, James. Someone killed him.'

'Oh God,' James whispered, and his head slumped again. 'It was him. You know that, don't you? He's going to kill all of us, and there's nothing we can do to stop him. Nothing.'

Tim had noticed that no one had yet said the words 'Mr Bad Face'. He wasn't sure whether this was simply because they were refusing to accept that the ogre from their childhood had come back, or whether, despite any amount of rationality, the name still held a kind of superstitious dread for all of them.

'Yes there is,' said Jackie firmly. 'There's no way he's going to get us, not now we're all together. Whoever this is, he's only a human being. And there's only one of him, but there's five of us. Plus we've got the police on our side. We'll be okay.'

'A human being?' said James, bewildered.

'Of course,' said Jackie. 'What did you think, James? That Mr Bad Face—' (now that she said it, Tim noticed she said it with defiance, almost like a challenge) '— had really come back from the dead to take revenge on us?'

'Well, I . . . I don't know,' said James. 'I mean . . . I've seen him! I've seen his face.'

'So have I,' said Eric.

'But we agreed that was make-up, didn't we, Eric?' said Jackie. 'A mask. They can be very sophisticated nowadays.'

'But why?' James said. 'Who would do such a thing? And who knows except the four—' He grimaced and amended himself, '—the three of us?'

'Did you ever tell anyone about what happened?' Jackie asked.

'No, no one.'

'Are you sure?'

He looked at her and Tim saw the timid, frightened boy his father had described yesterday peering out from behind the podgy, middle-aged face. 'Yes.'

Jackie sighed. 'Then I don't know who's doing it. But I do know it's not who we're supposed to think it is.'

'But I've seen him,' James said again, like a little boy trying to convince his elders that he's telling them the truth.

'Perhaps you'd better tell us your story, James,' Eric said, 'and then we'll tell you ours.'

James nodded and gulped at his tea. 'I suppose it started on . . . on Monday night.' He told them about taking Tizer for a walk in the playing fields and seeing the white-headed figure in the blue boiler suit, told them about his reaction to it (adding that he'd suffered with his nerves for years as if it was something to be ashamed of), told them about going back to work on Wednesday morning and the parcel he had received.

Jackie put a hand over her mouth. 'God, that's horrible,' she said. 'I was sent some rotten meat, which was bad enough, but this ...' She shook her head, sickened.

'Presumably you told the police?' Eric said.

'Yes, I told them. They took it all very seriously, asked me if I knew of anyone who'd do something like this, and why.' He looked down at his hands, and in a quieter voice added, 'They weren't much use in the end, though, were they? They didn't stop ... stop *him* taking my family away from me.'

'So ... so what happened after you got the parcel?' Jackie asked.

'I went home. I was in a right state. I *am* in a right state. I'm not sure I can take much more of this.' He sighed, continued, 'Nothing else happened on Wednesday, but then on Thursday I got a card through the post in a red envelope.'

Tim noticed his father draw up his shoulders. He himself felt the prickle of gooseflesh down his arms and back.

'I wish I'd been able to bring it with me,' Keeve said, 'to show it to you, but the police have got it. I have got something else with me, though, that I'll come to in a minute. It's in the car, in my bag. Actually, I know this is terribly rude of me ... I mean, I haven't seen you for ... I don't know ... twenty years, but I was sort of hoping you'd ... put me up for a little while – you know, once you heard what I'd got to tell you. I ... I mean you don't have to, if you can't, or if you don't want to. It did cross my mind that maybe you'd think I was crazy if nothing had been happening to you, and I wouldn't have blamed you for that. But when you opened the door and you had that knife in your hand, and Jackie was here, well ... I sort of put two and two together. I guessed that you must have seen him too.'

He faltered, looked around at them all like a man who has woken to find himself surrounded by strangers.

'Tell us about the card in the envelope, James,' Jackie said gently.

'Oh. Yes. It was ... a child's birthday card. Some Disney thing with ... with Pluto and Mickey Mouse on it. Except that where it said "Happy Birthday" along the top, someone had scraped it off and had written "I'M BACK" in capital letters.

'I took the card to the police and they asked me more questions, but I could tell they didn't really know what to do next. I'd told them about the figure in the field, though at the time ... I don't know ... something inside me refused to acknowledge who the figure might be. Not that I could have told the police anyway. They'd have thought I was crazy.'

His teeth clenched in a ghastly, humourless, desperate grin. 'The next thing that happened was on Friday, two days ago. Sally came home from school with a cardboard tube with her name on it. Normally, I wouldn't be home when she got back, but because of all that had happened I was off work. I was in a pretty bad way, seeing things that weren't really there. At least . . .' His voice tailed off for a moment and he shivered. Then he said, 'I was on medication, you see. Anyway, when Sally arrived home with this tube, I said to her, "What have you got there?"'

'It was a poster, wasn't it?' Eric said.

James blinked in surprise. 'Yes,' he said, 'it was. How did you . . .' And then his face cleared. 'You've had one too, haven't you?'

Wind flailed suddenly at the house like something trying to get in. James flinched and glanced behind him. Even Tim hunched his shoulders instinctively.

When the wind died down, James said, 'It was a poster of Boyzone. You know, the pop group? It was a big poster. It showed them in concert, sort of from the side of the stage. Most of the left of the picture was taken up with a sea of faces, mostly young girls screaming. You could only see the first couple of rows, and even they were quite blurred, and then the rest of the crowd just sort of blended into a dark mass of heads.

'Because I wasn't feeling very well, I only glanced at the poster, and said something like, "Oh, that's nice. Where did you get that from?" I was trying to appear as normal as I could. Of course, Sally knew that Tizer was missing, but she didn't know about the parcel or the card. She said something about some friend at school giving it to her – I must admit, I wasn't really listening properly – and then she went upstairs to put it on her wall and I didn't give it a second thought.

'This brings us up to yesterday. Marjory suggested that the best thing was for us to try to take our minds off what was happening by going out for the day. So in the morning we went shopping, and then we had lunch in a pub, and then we drove out to the country. Perhaps if I'd stayed in and spoken to you, Eric, things would have been all right. I would have realised what was happening, and I could have taken precautions.'

'It wasn't your fault, James,' Jackie said. 'You weren't to know.'

'Besides,' said Eric, 'if you're married now, I was probably calling the wrong number. I was calling the old number on Jasmine Road.'

'Ah,' said James, 'in that case it wouldn't have made any difference. I haven't lived there for years.'

'Do you want to tell us the rest of it, James?' Jackie said.

He nodded. 'Going out on Saturday helped me to put things to the back of my mind a little bit. I even half-managed to convince myself that the police would find whoever had it in for us and sort it out, and I slept a bit better last night than I had been doing.

'This morning we were short of milk. Marjory said she'd go and get some from the shop, but I said, "It's okay, I'll go". I drove down there. I was only away fifteen, twenty minutes. When I arrived home the first thing that struck me was how quiet it was. I'd left Marjory eating toast in the kitchen, and Sally watching a video in the lounge. She's crazy about Wallace and Gromitt ... you know, "The Wrong Trousers"?' He smiled wistfully, then swallowed and shook his head. 'I called out their names, but there was no reply. I started to feel worried again, and I went all round the house, looking for them, getting more and more agitated. I looked in rooms two, three times, as if believing that somehow I'd missed them the first time round. I looked in cupboards and under beds. I even dragged out the steps and looked in the attic space. By this time I was starting to walk around in circles like a headless chicken. I didn't know what to do. Then the telephone rang.'

James paused and took a deep breath, as if the next part of his story was going to require enormous resolve to tell. He was still gripping his mug in both hands, though the tea in it must have been cold now.

'I went downstairs and answered it,' he said. 'At first I heard nothing, just the usual clicks and hisses on the line ... and then I heard this voice. It whispered at me, but – this is hard to describe – it wasn't like a normal voice; it was somehow ... unearthly. It made all the hairs stand up on the back of my neck.'

He shuddered so suddenly that Tim jumped. 'The voice seemed to come not just from the phone, but from all around me. It was ... horrible. I felt as if the voice's owner was right there in the room with me. And not only that, but as if he was right inside my head as well, as if he could see my thoughts.

'The voice said, "Don't you know who I am, James?" I was so terrified I couldn't even answer. Then it said, "Look for me in the poster, and you'll know me". Then the phone went dead. I dropped it and then I scrabbled about on the floor for it, thinking that if I didn't put it back in its cradle, the voice would come again, would crawl out of the phone, like ... I don't know ... like a snake or something.

'I realised straight away what it meant, and I ran upstairs to Sally's room. She'd put that poster right above her bed. I looked at it, stared at it, and that's when I saw him.' He shuddered again, closing his eyes for a moment as if to blot out the memory.

'Mr Bad Face,' Tim said, as though to defy the taboo that the name had become.

James nodded. 'He was standing there in the crowd, staring out of the poster. Staring right at me. The picture was blurred, but this time there was no doubt in my mind who it was. It was as if a dam had burst. I recognised him immediately. He was just as I remembered him – that white, scarred face ...'

He screwed up his eyes and pressed his lips together, clasping the mug tightly. He looked as though he was praying.

'Were there any signs of ... well, a struggle?' asked Jackie. 'Any signs that your wife and daughter had been taken forcibly?'

James opened his eyes and looked at her. 'No. That was it, you see. He made it look as though Marjory had ... well, as if she'd left me, and taken Sally with her. There was a suitcase missing, some of Marjory's and Sally's clothes and possessions, bank books, credit cards, things like that. I told the police, but despite everything else that had happened it was obvious that they thought she'd left me too. In fact, the sergeant I spoke to suggested that she might have gone *because* of what had been happening, because she couldn't take any more.'

Jackie glanced at Eric and then said carefully, 'Look, James, I don't mean anything by this, but ... well ... are you quite sure that Marjory *didn't* just leave of her own accord? I mean, if there were no signs of a struggle ...'

She broke off as James stared at her in dismay.

'If you knew Marjory, if you'd seen us together, you wouldn't have asked that,' he said. 'We love each other. She would never have left me in the lurch like that. Never.'

'Okay, I'm sorry, James. Really. I should never have asked.'

He looked hurt, bewildered, betrayed.

'So what happened once you'd been to the police?' Eric asked.

'I ... I thought of you. All three of you. I wondered whether you'd been seeing him too, whether anything had happened to you or your families. I couldn't stay in the house, because it made me feel frantic with worry for Marjory and Sally, and helpless, not knowing what to do. Also, it made me feel like ... like a sitting duck, just waiting for him to come back. So I decided to pack a bag and drive over here. I had a Christmas card which you'd sent me about fifteen years ago, Eric, and I prayed all the way over that you were still at the same address.'

'You could have phoned,' said Jackie.

'I didn't want to use the phone, not after last time. I felt if I picked up *any* phone, I'd hear that horrible voice whispering to me. I didn't even turn on the radio on the way over in case the voice came out of there as well. Besides, I felt I had more chance of making you listen to me if I saw you face to face. And so ... here I am.'

He shrugged dejectedly. Jackie crossed to him and gave him a hug.

'And it's good to see you, James. Despite the circumstances, it really *is* good to see you. And don't worry, we'll help you get your wife and daughter back.'

He looked at her, a spark of hope in his eyes. 'You really think there's a chance?'

Again Jackie glanced at Eric, and then she nodded vigorously. 'Of course there is.'

'Actually,' said Eric, 'although it might sound strange, I think that what happened to your wife and daughter might actually be an encouraging sign.'

James blinked at him incredulously.

'What do you mean, Dad?' asked Tim.

'Well, think about it. Before now, our Mr Bad Face, whoever he is, has simply ... well ... killed people, and he hasn't exactly been concerned about covering his tracks. Remember what the Inspector said about him? She said he was arrogant, that he thought he was too clever to be caught, and that in the end that would prove his undoing. And yet on this occasion he's taken precautions, he's made it look as though James' wife and daughter have just walked out on him. Don't you think that sounds as though he wants to keep them alive for some reason?'

'But why?' Tim said. 'As hostages?'

Eric shrugged. 'Perhaps. Maybe he's going to try and blackmail you, James.'

'But I haven't got any money,' James protested.

'I think Mr Keeve should tell Inspector Farrington what he's just told us,' said Tim.

James groaned. 'Not more police. I don't think I can face being treated the way they treated me this morning.'

'But the Inspector's different,' said Tim. 'She knows what's going on. She'll believe you.'

Eric nodded. 'Tim's right, James,' he said. 'You can tell the Inspector your story, just as you've told it to us. She knows all about Mr Bad Face, the fire, everything.' He was already reaching for the phone. 'Do you feel up to talking to her now, or would you prefer me to?'

'I suppose I'd better,' said James. 'Do you have the number?'

Eric showed him the button to press that would put him straight through to Farrington. He looked nervous as he waited for someone to answer, passing the receiver from one hand to the other, wiping his sweaty palms on his trousers. The others tried to make it look as though they weren't listening to his conversation, so as not to make him even more nervous than he already was. He repeated the story he had just told, answered some questions, gave his address, and at last, rubbing his forehead wearily, said, 'No, I haven't got any photographs on me, but I can give you their descriptions.'

Jackie was pretending to flip through an old copy of *Hello*! magazine, but Eric could tell she was listening intently to what James was saying. Despite the circumstances, he had to profess a certain amount of curiosity himself in finding out what kind of woman James had married.

'Marjory's forty,' James said. 'She's quite slim with ... with dark shoulder-length hair. Last time I saw her she was wearing a white dressing gown and a ... a nightshirt.

'Sally is seven. She's got blonde hair, and is quite small for her age, very slim. She was wearing ... uh ... pink pyjamas, I think.'

A few minutes later he put the phone down. 'Well, that's that,' he said. 'At least the police are actually looking for them now. Inspector Farrington wants me to call in tomorrow morning.'

'I think perhaps it's time we told you our story now,' said Eric, though he didn't look as though he was relishing the prospect of telling it.

Indeed, over the next half hour he became choked up on a couple of occasions and had to pause. Tim and Jackie helped him along where they could, but Annette merely sat silently, wearing her stony face like emotional armour that deflected the arrows of her husband's grief. James listened with an expression of horror on his face, occasionally letting out a little moan of fear or distress. When Eric had done, James slumped forward and said, 'This is awful. Awful. Who's doing it to us?'

No one replied, and for a few seconds there was silence in the room. Then Jackie said, 'You mentioned about showing us this poster, James?'

'Yes, it's ... it's in the car. I'll go and fetch it.' He put down the mug he had been holding and stood up, the blanket slipping from his shoulders. 'Actually,' he said a little shamefacedly, 'would you ... would you stand by the front door and watch me to my car and back? I know it sounds silly, but ... I can't stand being outside on my own in the dark.'

Jackie agreed, and the two of them went into the hallway.

As soon as they were out of earshot, Tim asked, 'Are you going to let Mr Keeve stay with us, Dad?'

'Well ... yes. I think so. Of course,' said Eric.

'Where?' said Annette. 'We haven't the room. Not if *she's* staying as well.'

'But we can't just turn him away. You've seen what sort of state he's in.'

'Jackie could sleep in my bed and Mr Keeve could sleep down here on the couch,' Tim said. He glanced warily at Annette, and then added as if it was an afterthought, 'I could sleep in Chloe's room.'

Annette's eyes were suddenly blazing. 'No. I don't want anyone sleeping in Chloe's room.'

'But, Mum—'

'No buts. No one sleeps in Chloe's room.'

'I didn't mean in her bed,' Tim said. 'I meant on the Z-bed.'

'No.'

'But I won't touch anything.'

'No, Tim!'

Tim scowled. Gently Eric said, 'Come on, Net, don't you think you're over-reacting? Chloe wouldn't have minded Tim sleeping in there.'

'But *I* mind,' said Annette.

'Why?'

'Because it's Chloe's room.'

'But Chloe doesn't need it any more, Net,' Eric said as gently as he could.

Abruptly, shockingly, Annette burst into tears. She reached out for her husband, and at first Tim thought she wanted to flail at him for what he had said, but then he realised she simply wanted to be held. Eric looked surprised, but moved forward and took her in his arms, rocked with her as she cried. 'Shh, my love, shh, shh,' he whispered into her hair.

Jackie and James came back into the room, James with a holdall in one hand and a large cardboard tube in the other. 'Oh,' Jackie said, coming to an abrupt halt, 'I'm sorry. James and I will ... um ... we'll make some more coffee.'

Annette looked up, her face blotchy with tears, strands of hair sticking to her face. 'If you're going to stay here, this is something you'll have to get used to,' she said.

Jackie looked as though she thought she'd been unfairly rebuked, but she said, 'Is there anything I can do?'

'Actually,' Eric said, 'some more coffee *would* be nice.'

Five minutes later everyone was back in the lounge, cradling mugs of fresh coffee. Annette, looking washed out, had stopped crying, but was still sniffing. Eric nodded at the cardboard tube that James had propped up by his chair, and said, 'I assume that's the poster?'

James glanced at the tube as if it was full of poisonous snakes, and nodded.

'Can we see it?' asked Jackie.

James picked up the tube, gingerly slid his hand inside and pulled out the poster. He dropped it on the floor, where it unrolled a little, but not enough to reveal the picture. Jackie went down on her hands and knees and rolled the poster out. She asked Tim to put his foot on one edge to stop it rolling back up, whilst she held the other side down.

'Oh my God,' she said after a moment, 'I see him. There he is.'

Everyone craned forward with the exception of James, who did the opposite, pushing himself back into his chair, clutching his steaming mug to his chest like a talisman.

Mr Bad Face was not as prominent in this poster as he had been in Chloe's, but he was nevertheless instantly recognisable. He was near the front of the stage, surrounded by screaming girls, his bald head like a shiny white balloon amid a forest of upraised arms. His face was partly in shadow, his features rudimentary as in Chloe's poster. Considering what was happening around him, his presence seemed grotesque in the extreme.

Jackie sat up straight, letting go of the poster, a violent shudder running through her. Without the pressure of her hand, the edge of the poster flipped up and rolled towards Tim's foot like a trap. 'So creepy,' she said. 'How does he do it? How does he manage to blend in so perfectly?'

'You can do that with computers nowadays,' Tim said. 'Get yourself put into a picture, get the picture printed up. It's easy.'

Jackie looked distastefully at the rolled-up poster. 'I still think it's creepy. And what's creepiest of all is the fact that someone would go to so much trouble just to scare us.'

'I'm not scared,' Annette said, suddenly and fiercely, the skin around her eyes still puffy from crying. 'Whoever he is, he's done the worst that he can do to me. This is what I think of him.'

She lunged from the settee, a sudden blur of activity, grabbed the poster from the floor and frenziedly began to attack it. They all watched silently as she tore the poster to shreds, crumpled it in her fists, scattered it around like confetti. She was breathing hard through her mouth as she did it, her hair hanging over her face. She looked like a wild woman, a savage from the hills. When the poster had sustained as much damage as she could inflict upon it, she dropped gracelessly on to her knees and scooped the torn and crumpled pieces into a pile.

'Tim,' she said, standing up, clutching two great handfuls of mangled paper, 'come with me.'

Tim followed Annette into the kitchen. Eric, Jackie and James all looked at each other, and then they jumped up too and hurried after Tim. They arrived in the kitchen in time to hear Annette say, 'Open the door.'

Tim did so, and Annette went out into the back garden, her hair flying around her face in the wind, her clothes flapping. She raised her head and screeched, 'Are you watching, you bastard? This is what I think of you!'

She opened her hands and released the torn shreds of the poster. They whirled and spun around her for a few seconds and then the wind carried them away into the night. 'If you come near me,' she screamed, 'I'll do the same to you! Can you hear me, you bastard? *Can you hear me?*'

Tim watched the bits of poster swirling and fluttering across the lawn like a flurry of white petals. He wondered what Oonagh, if she was still awake, was making of all this. Despite himself, he half-expected Mr Bad Face to appear in response to Annette's challenge, a powerful, unstoppable figure striding from the darkness, his scarred and melted face gleaming like the moon.

But although Annette stood for several long seconds, head raised defiantly, fists clenched at her sides, the only reply she received was the voice of the wind, baying like a distant but approaching pack of wolves.

Monday 28 November

49

'Playing footy, Knighty?' Steve Collins said, finding Tim in the locker room two minutes after the lunchtime bell had gone.

Tim shook his head. 'I can't. I've got to see someone about something.'

'Want me to come?'

'Nah, it's ... well, it's sort of private, you know.'

Steve looked at him for a few seconds and then said, 'Yeah, okay. Well, I'll see you in double French this aft.'

Tim nodded and Steve sloped away.

School had been okay, except that all Tim's classmates, even his best friends like Steve and Andy, were treating him like a delicate piece of bone china. Not one person had mentioned Chloe, or even asked how he was feeling. It was as though they thought he would break down if they so much as dared to scratch the surface of his emotions. Even some of his teachers had been as bad, treating him warily, avoiding eye contact. All morning Tim had been aware of sidelong glances cast in his direction, but whenever he had turned the culprit had glanced guiltily away – all except for Sarah Longman, whom Tim and quite a few other boys in his class had secretly fancied for ages, who had graced him with a dazzlingly sweet and sympathetic smile.

He dragged his jacket out of his locker and put it on, then stuffed his bag in there. He took the quietest route out of school – down through the music rooms and out by the main entrance, bypassing the playground. Although he was apprehensive about walking to the travellers' camp, he nevertheless breathed a sigh of relief when he was outside the school gates and heading down the hill towards the posh houses beyond which lay the farmland and the woods. Why did people have to treat him as some sort of freak just because his sister had died? Didn't they realise that by avoiding the subject completely they were making it obvious it was the one uppermost in their minds? He wanted people to tell him jokes, flick paper pellets at him, would even have welcomed Steve grabbing his arm and giving him one of his world-famous Chinese burns. A week ago, if Sarah Longman had smiled at him like that, Tim would have basked in the glory of it all day, but now he just felt like a charity case.

The sky was white but somehow lightless, as if the town was enclosed within a vast paper dome. Chimneys paled into mist as if houses were slowly disappearing from the rooftops down. The wind had dropped but it was cold, very possibly the coldest day of the year so far. Tim kept glancing behind him as he walked to make sure he wasn't being followed, but he didn't really feel nervous until the big houses petered out and suddenly he was on the dust track that curled its way down between farmers' fields to the dark bulk of the woods.

Seeing the woods, the place where his sister had died, all at once made Tim feel afraid and alone. It was so quiet. All he could hear was the faint chirrup of birdsong and the faraway chug of a tractor motor, sounds that were so much part of the landscape that they seemed almost negligible. He trudged down the dirt track, eyes moving constantly from the dry-stone wall on his right to the one on his left. If anyone reared up from behind one of those walls with murder on their mind, it would all boil down to a simple question of who could run the fastest. Fifty yards ahead was the farm where the farmer lived who had let the travellers set up camp on his land, but he would probably be out on his fields somewhere by now. Tim thought that if he was pursued, his best bet would be to run to the travellers' camp, see if he could find help there.

Rubble trickled ahead of him as he trudged downhill. Once past the farm, the camp came into sight, away to his left, and Tim began to jog towards the gate in the wall through which numerous vehicles had passed in the last few days, wearing deep ruts in the soft ground. Last week, when he had visited the camp with Oonagh, it had seemed an exciting place, but now it seemed sad, forlorn, cowering beneath the pearly vastness of the sky. The fact that he couldn't see a soul also made it look as though it had been abandoned, as if the adults had decided that it wasn't worth staying on here now that their children were gone.

He trudged towards the camp up the slight incline. Beneath the frozen crust of its top layer, the ground was gooey as toffee. By the time he reached the Walshes' trailer, noting the burnt-out remains of a camper van standing like a memorial to the violence which had taken place here, his shoes and the cuffs of his trousers were caked with mud. He glanced around him uneasily as he knocked on the Walshes' door, certain that numerous eyes belonging to faces he couldn't see were scrutinising his every move.

A crow cawed, making him jump, a split-second before the trailer door was pulled open. The thin, bearded face that peeked out looked vulnerable with trepidation. Blue eyes blinked at Tim from behind round-lensed spectacles, and then recognition dawned and the expression on the face softened.

'Tim, hi,' Graeme Walsh said, sounding tired and relieved. 'Every time someone knocks on the door, I think it's going to be the police. Would you like to come in?'

Tim did so, first of all unlacing his shoes and leaving them on the metal steps outside the door. Because the sky seemed so reluctant to share its light, a lamp with a stained-glass shade had been turned on, suffusing the main room with an orange glow. Floating down the short corridor that led to the bedrooms and the kitchen, was the sound of flute music, lilting and melodious.

'I'll just tell Linda you're here,' Graeme said, gesturing towards the source of the sound, and then added hesitantly, as if feeling he ought to offer an explanation, 'Playing her flute is the only thing she can settle to at the moment.'

Tim nodded, perching himself on the edge of the settee. Moments later he heard the flute music stop, and then Linda say in surprise, 'Tim? What for?'

Tim licked his lips. He couldn't help being nervous at the prospect of passing Oonagh's message on to her parents. He wondered whether they would be angry at having had to endure days of needless worry.

Graeme came back into the room. 'She's just coming. Can I get you anything, Tim? Herbal tea? Apple juice?'

'No thanks, I'm fine.'

Graeme sat on the rocking chair, which creaked beneath his weight. Quietly he said, 'The police told us what happened to your sister, Tim. I'm so very sorry. It's a terrible thing.'

'Yes,' said Tim, 'thanks.' Although grateful that Graeme hadn't avoided the subject like everyone at school, he still wasn't sure how to react. There was a short awkward silence, and then he said, 'I'm sorry about all this stuff that's happened to you because of it.'

Graeme wafted a hand as if it was of no consequence. 'It's not your fault. It's the authorities who have been a little ... heavy-handed, shall we say?'

Linda entered the room, looking as tired as her husband. 'How are you, Tim?' she asked.

'All right, thanks, Mrs ... er, Linda,' said Tim.

She crossed the room and without hesitation hugged him tightly, much to his surprise and embarrassment. 'We were so shocked to hear about your sister. It must be an awful time for you and your family.'

'Yes,' said Tim, relieved when she let him go. 'I was just saying to ... erm ... Graeme how bad it is, the way the police have been treating you since it happened.'

Linda sat back on her heels, pushing hair out of her eyes. 'You know they took Oonagh away, don't you? All the children, in fact.'

'Yes,' said Tim. He licked his lips again, crossed his arms.

'Actually, that's why I'm here. I've come to tell you that ... that Oonagh's okay.'

Graeme jerked upright in his seat as if on strings. Linda's eyes opened wide, and she said breathlessly, 'You mean, they've found her?'

'Well ... not exactly. I've spoken to her. She asked me to come and see you, to let you know she's okay. She didn't want you to worry.'

Linda looked at Graeme, her mouth widening in a grin of joy and relief. Seeing her expression, Tim thought: Why couldn't he and Mum and Dad have received good news about Chloe? Why couldn't he have seen a smile like that on his mum's face?

Graeme still looked bemused. 'Did she tell you where she was?'

'Er ... well ... I actually spoke to her face to face. She's ... um ... been living in our shed.'

'You mean she's there now?' said Linda.

'Yes.'

'So ... when did she arrive?' said Graeme.

Tim felt uncomfortable. 'Um ... Thursday night. She came straight to me when she ran away from the foster home.'

'You mean she's spent four nights in your shed?' said Graeme.

'Yes. I know I should have come and told you earlier, but I couldn't get away. My mum doesn't like me being out on my own at the moment. I'm only here now because I sneaked out of school at lunchtime.'

To Tim's surprise, Graeme threw back his head and laughed. 'I don't believe it. Oh, this is great. I presume your parents don't know that Oonagh's in the shed?'

'No. I keep sneaking her out food when I can. I've taken her some blankets and stuff, and things to wash with and all that. I've been looking after her.'

'I bet you have,' said Graeme. 'You're an absolute gem, Tim. How can we ever thank you?'

'You mean you don't mind?' said Tim. 'You're not angry?'

'Why should we be angry? Oonagh's all right. It's the best news we could ever wish for. I'm so happy I could ... I could dance naked round this field.'

'That'll give the cows something to talk about,' said Linda, grinning.

Graeme laughed again. 'I knew she'd be all right. Didn't I say she'd be all right?' All at once his enthusiasm turned to consternation, and he gave Tim a look of apology. 'Oh hell, I'm forgetting myself, aren't I? I'm forgetting what happened to Chloe, what you must be going through.'

‘That’s all right,’ said Tim awkwardly. ‘I’m glad you’re happy.’

Linda leaned forward and squeezed his hand. ‘What you’ve done is an incredible thing, Tim,’ she said, ‘especially considering what you must have been going through this past week. You’re a really amazing person.’

Tim felt his cheeks blazing. ‘I’m not really,’ he said. ‘Oonagh turned up and asked for my help, that’s all. I couldn’t just tell her to get lost, could I? I mean ... she’s my friend.’

‘Well, I think she should be extremely grateful to have such a wonderful friend,’ said Linda.

Tim gave an uncomfortable smile and shrugged, and was happy, five minutes later, to say goodbye and leave. After forcing Tim to accept two crumpled ten pound notes for Oonagh’s upkeep, Graeme apologised for not being able to offer him a lift back to school.

‘I know for a fact that the police are keeping tabs on our vehicles,’ he said. ‘Captain picked them up on his CB when he drove into town yesterday.’

‘They still don’t trust us,’ said Linda. ‘They still think we’ve got Oonagh hidden away somewhere.’

‘I wouldn’t be surprised if they still suspect us of having something to do with your sister’s death too,’ said Graeme quietly.

‘You don’t think they’ll have seen me come here, do you?’ Tim asked, alarmed.

Graeme shrugged. ‘It’s possible. Depends on exactly *how* closely they’re watching us. I suppose we’ll find out soon enough.’

This time, as he trudged back up the hill, Tim kept imagining he could see uniformed policemen ducking behind bushes and crawling through long grass, but whenever he turned to focus, the dark shapes at the edge of his vision would always resolve themselves into tree branches or fence posts or patches of shadow. He came parallel with the farm, and veered instinctively away from the metal gate, knowing that the stone sheds with their corrugated iron roofs that flanked it would make perfect hiding places. He was within three feet of the dry-stone wall on the right-hand side of the track, still eyeing the sheds warily, when the figure that had been crouching behind it suddenly loomed up beside him.

A second later, too quickly for Tim to react, the figure had vaulted the wall and grabbed him. The hand that encircled his upper arm was large and had a tight, painful grip. Tim’s head jerked round to stare up into the figure’s face, expecting to see scarred, shiny white flesh, rudimentary features.

What he did see, however, was a bony, scowling face framed by dark straggly hair and a dark beard. Tim recognised the man immediately. It was Mike Jordan, who had warned him off when he had come to the camp to call on Oonagh last week.

'Get off me,' Tim said, struggling. His initial surge of terror had already given way to relief, and now anger.

Mike Jordan, however, simply tightened his grip. 'Or what?'

'Or I'll shout for help.'

'Try it, and I'll rip your fucking tongue out.'

'I'll have you arrested for assault.'

'I don't think so.'

'Just ... let ... me ... *go*!' On the final word, Tim swung round and aimed a kick at Jordan's shins. However his lack of mobility hampered him and Jordan evaded the attack easily. He brought up a big-booted foot and swung it behind Tim's kicking legs, scooping him from the ground. Only at that point did he let go of Tim's arm, shoving him backwards, so that Tim landed on his back on the stony ground, banging his head hard.

For thirty seconds Tim could only lie there, unable to draw breath, certain his spine had snapped. When the black stars in his head began to disperse, he propped himself groggily on to his elbows, to see what Jordan was doing. The man was leaning over the wall, retrieving items he'd evidently left there when he'd vaulted it: his shotgun and a rough sack whose underside was stained maroon with fresh blood. Tim's first thought was that the sack contained a severed head; it looked about the right size and shape.

Then Jordan swung the sack over his shoulder and Tim saw there was a softness to its contents. Not a head, then; rabbits, maybe, or some kind of birds, pheasants perhaps.

Gingerly he sat up, rubbing his throbbing head, picking bits of grit from his hair. His spine felt as though it was on fire. With the same casual gesture that Tim remembered from the previous week, Jordan hefted his shotgun in his hand, then flicked it up, pointing it at Tim's face.

Tim felt his stomach go cold, but he wasn't as scared as he had been last week. Maybe it was because so many terrible things had happened since then that he was becoming inured to them.

'Are you going to shoot me?' he said, amazed at the calmness of his voice.

'I might do,' said Jordan.

'Why?'

'Why not?'

'Well, you'd go to prison, for one thing. They'd put you away for years and years.'

'Not if they didn't catch me.'

'Yes, but they would catch you, wouldn't they? They always do.'
Jordan looked at Tim as if he was a piece of shit he'd just scraped off his shoe. 'I told you not to come poking round our camp. We're sick of people like you, causing trouble, blaming us for everything. I told you what would happen if you came back, didn't I?'
'I'm not here to cause trouble. I came to pass on a message to Graeme and Linda Walsh.'
'We don't want your fucking message.'
'They did. They were really pleased. Why don't you ask them?'
Without warning, Jordan took four strides forward and kicked the bottom of Tim's right foot hard. It bent Tim's foot right up, his toes almost touching his shin. Tim howled in agony, then began to breathe hard and fast to keep back the tears that wanted to burst out of him.
'Don't get smart,' Jordan said.
Tim glared at Jordan, so furious that this man should dare to treat him like this after all he had been through that he couldn't prevent his mouth running away with him.
'I'm not scared of you,' he hissed. 'Oonagh was right. You're a thug and a creep.'
Jordan kicked him again, this time in the right thigh. What was most frightening was that his face as he did it was deadpan, the violence channelled, almost machine-like.
Tim cried out and rolled in the dirt, instinctively drawing his head into his hunched shoulders and cupping his balls, expecting a fusillade of blows and kicks. Instead he heard Jordan say, 'You stay away from here in the future, you understand? And if you tell anyone about this, I'll finish the job.'
Then he was walking away, his feet thumping the earth. Tim listened until the footsteps had faded entirely, then he rolled slowly on to his back and pushed himself into a sitting position.
He hurt all over, and his clothes were covered in dirt. He began to cry then, partly from the pain, but mostly because of the *unfairness* of it all. Hadn't he been through enough? Wasn't it time the scales tipped back in his favour? He wiped his tears away, angry with himself for crying. Then he took a few deep breaths and climbed painfully to his feet. It took him over forty minutes to limp back to school, by which time it was ten minutes into the start of afternoon lessons. He felt exhausted by the effort it had taken, his body damp with sweat despite the coldness of the day. Hoping his absence hadn't set any alarm bells ringing, he limped into the nearest toilet. He washed his face, cleaned the dirt off his clothes as best he could, retrieved his bag from his locker, stuffed his jacket in there in its place, and then went to his lesson. His foot, thigh and back still hurt

enough to make him limp, but the pain wasn't as bad as it had been. Everyone turned to look at him as he entered Mrs Tate's Maths lesson twenty minutes late. He started to mumble an apology, but Mrs Tate, who would normally have torn him to shreds with that piercing, Scottish-accented voice of hers, merely glanced at him in the askance, slightly embarrassed way he had become used to, and muttered, 'That's all right, Timothy. Sit down.'

The rest of the afternoon drifted by. Tim sat through Mrs Whelan's double French lesson and didn't take anything in. It didn't really matter because throughout the entire ninety minutes, she treated him as though he wasn't there. Tim suspected his teachers had been given a directive to go easy on him for a few days, allow him to get used to the idea of being back at school.

Normally he would have walked home with Steve and Andy, but when they asked him after the last bell if he was coming, and he told them it was okay, his dad would be picking him up, they could barely hide their relief. Tim didn't really blame them. He knew how awkward they felt around him just now. He retrieved his jacket from his locker and walked round to the car park. There was the familiar blue Escort, his dad hunched in the driver's seat, hands clutching the steering wheel as though eager to be off.

'Look at them all, staring and whispering. I feel like an exhibit in a freak show,' Eric said when Tim opened the passenger door and got in.

'Tell me about it,' said Tim wearily, dumping his bag between his feet.

Eric's expression softened. 'Not such a good idea, coming back, eh?'

'Oh, it was all right. People didn't know how to treat me, that's all, even some of the teachers. It was like I had a disease or something.'

'It won't last long. Things'll be back to normal before you know it.'

'Yeah.'

'I'm really proud of you, Tim, the way you've handled all this, coming back so soon. You've shown a lot of courage.'

Tim looked at his father and gave him a friendly punch on the arm. 'Give over, Dad.'

'I mean it. You've been a tower of strength to your mum and me.'

On the drive home, Eric told Tim what he and the rest of them had been doing that day. After a visit from the counsellor, which had been arranged by Farrington, he and Annette had accompanied Jackie back to Nottingham to pick some things up from her flat, while James had kept his appointment with the Inspector.

'And tonight James and Jackie have decided to take us out for a meal,' he concluded.

Tim wrinkled his nose. 'That's a bit weird, isn't it? We usually only go out for meals when we're celebrating somebody's birthday or something.'

Eric slowed the car as the lights turned to red at a pedestrian crossing on the high street. People made shapeless by thick coats hurried across the road, heads hunched as though weighed down by the deepening dusk.

'It's to give us all a bit of a breather, a change of scene,' he said. 'Besides, nobody feels much like cooking at the moment. I think it's an okay idea.'

The amber light flashed and Eric eased the car forward again. Tim hunched down in his seat, trying to find a comfortable position for his aching back and leg. As they passed Bloomers, its interior still hidden from curious eyes by grey screens, he shuddered and thrust his hands into the pockets of his jacket, feeling a chill that had nothing to do with the cold.

At once his right hand came into contact with something that puzzled him, or rather a number of somethings, for there were objects in his jacket pocket that he couldn't remember putting there, and that he couldn't identify by touch alone. He thought of pencils encased in rubber, and then of thin sausages gone hard and dry in the sun.

Taking one of the objects between his thumb and forefinger, he lifted it from his pocket, held it in front of his face and looked at it. There was an instant of utter disbelief, and then he was screaming and flinging the thing away from him, his body jerking back so suddenly in his seat that his spine felt as though it had come apart.

Instinctively Eric ducked, his hand yanking down on the steering wheel, causing the car to bump up on the kerb in front of the Nat West bank. Fortunately there were no pedestrians on that stretch of pavement; if there had been, he would have mown them down.

It took him just a few seconds to regain control, but it seemed like for ever. Horns blaring angrily behind him, he twisted the steering wheel to the right, bringing the car back on to the road.

Tim, meanwhile, was still screaming, struggling frantically against his seatbelt and trying to rip his jacket from his body as if it had turned into a coat of nettles and was stinging him mercilessly.

Somehow managing to keep his head, Eric pulled the car into the kerb and stopped. He twisted in his seat and grabbed his son's shoulders as he struggled and squirmed.

'Tim!' he shouted. 'What's wrong? What's the matter?'

'Get this off me!' Tim screamed. '*Get it off me*!' He was still struggling with his jacket, though he was in such a confined space that he wasn't having much success.

'Calm down, Tim! Calm down!' Fear was making Eric angry. He shook his son. 'For God's sake, calm down!'

His words seemed to have some effect. Tim's struggles became less violent, but his eyes were still wild and he was still breathing so fast that Eric felt sure he'd hyperventilate.

'That's it, now just tell me what's the matter,' Eric said, forcing himself to lower his voice.

Tim stared at his father. 'They're in my pocket, Dad,' he sobbed between gasps for breath. 'They're in my pocket.'

Only then did Eric remember his son throwing something away from him. Vaguely he recalled it hitting the windscreen and bouncing back to land on the dashboard. He turned his head to look at the object, and then for a long, long moment he just stared, unable to believe what he was seeing.

Sitting on the dashboard, the nail black, the other end a knob of gristle and bone and dried blood, was a shrivelled human finger.

50

'So what happened then?' Oonagh said, shocked and sickened.

'We went to that cabin-thing that the police have set up near the library to see Inspector Farrington. I gave her my jacket with the fingers still in the pocket, all except the one I took out. My dad picked that one up with a tissue and put it in an empty crisp bag.'

It was three hours after the incident, and Tim still looked shell-shocked. When Oonagh had opened the shed door to his knock, she'd been alarmed by how ashen he looked, by the haunted expression on his face.

'What did the police say?' she asked. 'Did they know who the fingers belonged to?'

Tim raised his head as if it required great effort. 'They were Chloe's,' he said.

Oonagh's hand flew to her mouth. 'Oh God, no. Did they tell you that?'

'They didn't have to. My dad guessed. When he asked the Inspector straight out, we could tell we were right just by the look on her face.'

Oonagh hesitated a moment, then reached out and hugged Tim. She began to stroke the back of his head. There was a lump just under his hair. When she touched it, he flinched.

'Sorry,' she said. 'Does that hurt?'

'A bit. Not as much as my back and leg.'

'Did you get knocked about a bit when your dad nearly crashed the car?'

'No. Mike Jordan did this to me. I've not had a good day.'

Oonagh sat bolt upright. 'Mike Jordan? What do you mean?'

Tim told her about his encounter at the camp earlier that day.

'Oh God, that's my fault. I should never have asked you to go.'

'It's not your fault,' said Tim. 'Mike Jordan's just a psycho. You can't blame yourself.'

'No, but I should have realised he might be around, and how he might react to you after the last time.'

'I'd still have gone. It was worth it just to see the expressions on your mum and dad's faces.'

Oonagh smiled. 'Were they really pleased?'

'Ecstatic. A bit over the top actually. Your mum kept telling me what an amazing person I was for looking after you.'

'Well, you are,' said Oonagh, 'you're really amazing.' When he looked up, giving her a watery smile, she kissed him on the mouth.

It was a tender kiss, but not a long one, an expression of affection and comfort, rather than a prelude to passion. Tim responded, but when they broke away, Oonagh saw that his face was troubled.

In a soft voice he said, 'It was horrible, Oonagh. I can't get it out of my mind. Every time I think about how I put my hand in my pocket and touched those things, I just feel sick. And the way it looked ... all shrivelled and ...' He shook his head suddenly, and covered his face with his hands.

Oonagh held him silently for a minute or more, until finally Tim pulled his hands away from his face and gasped as if he'd been holding his breath. 'I'd better go,' he said.

'So soon?'

'Yeah, Mum and Mr Keeve are taking us out for a meal – not that I feel much like eating. Actually, that's what I wanted to say: I'll leave the spare keys under the mat outside the back door so you can let yourself in for a shower. We'll probably be gone a couple of hours, so you'll have plenty of time.'

'Okay, thanks,' said Oonagh. They stood up together. 'Oh, I almost forgot. Something really weird happened to me last night. It wasn't as bad as what happened to you today, but it was pretty creepy.'

Quickly she told him about the figure in the trees at the bottom of the garden.

'You sure it wasn't Mr Freeman?'

'Who?'

'The man who owns the house behind ours.'

Oonagh shrugged. 'I don't know. I suppose it might have been. But what was he doing, poking around in the trees in the middle of the night?'

Tim hugged himself as if he was cold. 'I hate all this. This feeling of being watched all the time, of being ... I don't know ... hunted. I mean, whoever put those things in my pockets must have come into school today. It's like he's playing with us, like he's just showing us that he can come and get us any time he wants.' He scowled, suddenly angry. 'I wish I had a shotgun. If I ever saw him I'd blow his head off.' Then he smiled weakly. 'Do you think Mike Jordan'll lend me his?'

'He might do if you ask him nicely,' 'Oonagh said.

At the shed door, they kissed again, then Tim slipped out, back to the house. He'd told Oonagh that they were due to leave for the restaurant in fifteen minutes, but she waited for half an hour just to be sure, then ran in a crouch from the shed to the dustbins outside the back door. The Knights had left a lamp on in the lounge, which she could see glowing behind the closed curtains, but the rest of the house was in darkness. Nevertheless Oonagh paused for a moment, listening, before breaking cover and scuttling to the back door. She lifted the black rubber mat, soggy with rain, that was sitting there. There were no keys, but there was a note, damp and dirt-smeared. She carried it to the lighted lounge window to read it. It said: OONAGH. COULDN'T FIND THE KEYS, SO HAVE LEFT THE LAUNDRY WINDOW OPEN FOR YOU – THE LITTLE ONE ABOVE THE DUSTBINS. HAVE A GOOD SHOWER. SEE YOU LATER. LOVE, TIM.

She smiled, folded the note and put it in her pocket.

51

The restaurant was called the Herb Garden, and had evidently been an apothecary's shop in its dim and distant past. A feature had been made of one wall, which resembled a vast wooden filing cabinet full of tiny drawers, each inscribed with the Latin name of the drug it had once contained. In truth, however, the place seemed more junk shop than anything: shelves and surfaces were cluttered with paraphernalia, as if diners through the years had left small tokens of appreciation for the meals they had eaten. There were frosted bottles and brightly coloured feathers, old teddy bears and unusual stones, spiny shells and battered tins that had once contained tea or butterscotch tablets or gravy powder. The whole effect could so easily have made the place seem cheap and tacky, but in fact it came across as delightful, unpretentious, homely. Unfortunately, on this particular evening at least five of the Herb Garden's thirty or so customers were in no mood to appreciate its charms.

The meal, which Eric had told Tim he thought was an okay idea just a minute or two before Tim discovered pieces of his dead sister in his jacket pocket, had turned out to be a mistake, after all. The change of scene, intended to give them all some respite from their awful situation, was in fact having the opposite effect. The laughing, relaxed groups of people on the tables around them were serving only to emphasise their plight, to make them feel more isolated than ever. As a result, conversation between them was stilted, intermittent, sometimes downright excruciating.

Tim, who wasn't even listening to the little that *was* being said, was spending most of his time pushing his chicken chasseur around his plate and rearranging his vegetables. He couldn't get his awful experience from that afternoon out of his mind, the sensation of thrusting his hand into his jacket pocket and touching all those ... *things*. He must have washed his hands at least a dozen times since, but it did not feel like nearly enough. It seemed to him that his skin was indelibly tainted, that no account of scrubbing would ever erase the horror of touching his sister's dead and shrivelled flesh. Every so often he glanced up from his plate to see his dad and James eating stolidly, Jackie picking at her food like a bird, Annette staring at the salad she'd reluctantly ordered as if willing it to disappear. Tim admired his dad for managing to eat at all, for maintaining the pretence of what passed for normality for someone in his situation.

The two of them had decided not to tell Annette about the fingers. 'It would only upset her more than she already is,' Dad had said. 'She doesn't need to know.'

Nobody ordered dessert, though Eric, Jackie and James ordered coffee and petits fours. Afterwards, Eric produced his cheque book, but James held up a hand.

'No, Eric, this is my treat.'

'*Our* treat,' said Jackie. 'We'll split the bill down the middle.'

They paid the bill and went outside. It had turned very cold in the hour or so since they had entered the restaurant. Their breath formed a cloud of vapour above their heads.

'Let's get in the car and get the heating on,' Jackie said, hugging herself and hurrying across the car park.

She had driven them here in her white Golf. As she reached it, a little ahead of the others, she stopped suddenly and they all saw a hand fly to her mouth.

'What is it, Jacks?' Eric said, hurrying up to her.

'Look,' Jackie breathed, pointing at the car.

They had all seen it now. 'Oh no,' James whimpered.

On the car's white bonnet, in dribbling letters that looked as though they had been written in blood, had been daubed the words: YOU WILL ALL DIE.

52

James fell to his knees as though about to bring up the meal he had eaten. 'I can't take much more of this,' he groaned.

Jackie was still staring at the splash of letters on her car, one clenched fist pressed to her mouth. 'How did he know we were here?' she demanded, her voice flinty with suppressed hysteria. 'It's like he's watching us all the time.'

Everyone looked around as if expecting to see a figure with a white, scarred face standing some distance away, observing them. Seeing no one, they turned their attention back to the car, yet although the letters on the bonnet seemed to mesmerise them, none of them seemed willing to get too close, as if the car was some ferocious animal which they had cornered, and which was now snarling and taking swipes at them with big taloned paws.

Abruptly Annette said, 'I'll call the police,' then she turned and walked back to the restaurant.

As if his wife's words had roused him from a deep sleep, Eric rubbed a hand across his forehead. 'I think we should leave the car here and walk back to the house,' he said. 'The police'll want to examine it. He might have left fingerprints.'

Jackie nodded, and looked at Tim. He still seemed entranced by the drooling red letters. She glanced at Eric, then the two of them went over to Tim, their feet crackling on the grit on the tarmac. Jackie hesitated a moment, glanced behind her to make sure that Annette was out of sight, then put an arm around her son's shoulders.

'Come on, Tim,' she said, 'let's go.'

Tim didn't resist. As Jackie led him away, Eric hoped that the thought that had crept into his own mind hadn't also occurred to Tim.

Was that Chloe's blood on the car? Had the killer, as well as removing pieces of her body, drained some of it for the express purpose of tormenting them with messages and threats? Eric wanted to banish the notion, but his mind wouldn't leave it alone. Where was the best place to drain blood from the human body? The jugular vein? Had Chloe's killer slashed her throat and then calmly held some container beneath the gushing blood as she twitched and tried to scream?

He was still trying to shake off the thought when Annette came back. She seemed disturbingly calm, though Eric noticed that she averted her eyes from the car, almost as if she was studiedly attempting not to acknowledge it.

'The police are coming,' she said. 'They said not to touch anything.'
'Do they want us to wait?' Eric asked.
'I'll wait. I'll wait in the restaurant and then get one of the policemen to run me back later.' She glanced at her son, who was now standing independently, a little apart from Jackie. 'You get Tim home.'
'Would you like me to wait with you?' said Eric.
'No. I don't want Tim going home with strangers.'
'Jackie's not a stranger, she's his mother,' Eric stopped himself saying. Instead he said, 'All right. Are you sure you'll be okay?'
Annette's face and voice were icily calm. Not for the first time she said, 'Whoever killed my little girl can't hurt me any more than they have already.'
Eric kissed his wife, watched as she walked back across the car park to the restaurant to wait for the police, then went across to his son and said, 'Tim, would you help me with James?'
Tim looked at his dad for a moment, then he swallowed and nodded. The two of them helped James to his feet. He swayed between them as if drunk.
'Are you all right to walk?' Eric asked.
'Yes ... yes. I'll be all right in a minute. Thank you.'
They began the fifteen-minute trudge back to Stonecroft Avenue. By the time they got there, Jackie's teeth were chattering like maracas.
'I'll make some coffee, shall I?' James said as they entered the house, stepping into a delicious wave of warmth.
Eric nodded, then sat Jackie by the fire, turned it right up, and went to fetch her a blanket. Tim slumped in the armchair, hugging himself, and closed his eyes. Eric was draping the blanket around Jackie's shoulders when there was a clatter and a cry from the kitchen. The three of them jumped. 'Oh my God, what now?' Eric said. He scrambled up from his crouched position and rushed out of the room. The others followed, Jackie gripping the blanket like a cape which flowed behind her.
There was a mug on the kitchen floor, and the door into the back garden was standing open. James was nowhere in sight, though even as they were registering all this there came another cry from the darkness outside, this one more a squeal of terror than anything.
Eric ran to the back door, Jackie just behind him. The garden was dark, the moonlight minimal, but as he reached the threshold of the open door, he saw the silhouette of a hulking figure in the middle of the lawn, standing over a crumpled bundle that could only be James.

Eric came to such an abrupt halt that Jackie ran into the back of him, popping him out of the doorway and causing him to sprawl on the paving slabs between the house and the lawn. As if alerted by their presence, the figure turned its head towards them, and in the meagre light that was spilling into the garden from the kitchen they could all see that the figure was bald and that there was something wrong with its face.

Jackie dropped the blanket as her legs turned to water and she staggered forward, only stopping herself from falling by grabbing hold of the door frame. 'My God,' she hissed through her clenched fists. 'It's him! It's really him!'

Eric scrambled to his feet, swaying a little. The figure turned and calmly, almost arrogantly, strode towards the trees at the bottom of the garden.

'He's getting away, Dad!' Tim shouted, squeezing past Jackie out of the back door. He grabbed his dad's arm and tugged it. 'Come on, we can get him. There's two of us.'

Eric pulled Tim back. 'No,' he said. 'It's too dangerous.'

'But he killed Chloe, Dad! He killed her!'

'I know,' Eric said, anguish on his face, but still he made no move to pursue the figure, and held tight to his son's arm to prevent him from doing so.

The hulking figure stepped into the trees at the bottom of the garden and was swallowed by blackness. Tim, who had been tense in his father's grip, now slumped. 'We could have caught him, Dad,' he said. 'He killed Chloe.'

'I know, Tim. But he's a madman. It's best to let the police deal with it. He could have had a knife or an axe or anything.'

Tim pulled himself from his father's grip and looked at him accusingly. 'We could have caught him,' he said again, and his lips curled with scorn. 'You were scared!'

Eric said nothing. Jackie, meanwhile, had recovered enough to realise what they should be most concerned about. 'James,' she said, pushing past them and heading in a shambling run towards the black bundle lying motionless on the lawn.

She fell to her knees beside the bundle, muddying her skirt and tights, Eric and Tim bringing up the rear.

James was lying on his front, cheek pressed into the muddy grass. His spectacles, unbroken, were lying a couple of feet away. His eyes were closed and he had blood which looked black in the moonlight matted with the thin hair on his crown.

'Is he dead?' Tim asked.

As if in answer, James gave a small groan and tried to push himself up with his arms, his face creasing with pain and effort.

'Just lie still, James,' Jackie said. 'You're okay. We're here now. The person who attacked you has gone.'

She stroked his shoulder gently to reassure him. James groaned again, and his face and body relaxed.

'I'll phone for an ambulance,' Eric said, rising to his feet.

'Hurry. It's freezing cold out here.'

Eric ran back to the house. Tim watched him go.

'We could have caught him,' he muttered darkly, 'if *he* hadn't been so scared.'

'Don't be too hard on Eric, Tim,' Jackie said. 'He didn't want you to get hurt, that's all, and neither did I.'

'He didn't want to get himself hurt, you mean.'

'That too, I suppose. You can hardly blame him for that, though, can you? Weren't you scared as well?'

'I didn't think about it. I was thinking of Chloe.'

'Well ... *I'm* glad Eric did what he did,' Jackie said. 'I wouldn't want to lose either of you.'

Tim was silent for a moment, then he said sourly, 'I wish I'd had a gun. I'd have killed him, then.'

Jackie smiled briefly and stroked Tim's hair. Then her gaze flickered past him to the open back door of the house. 'Come on, Eric,' she said. 'What are you doing in there?'

As if in response, Eric reappeared, picking up the blanket that she had dropped in the kitchen. 'The ambulance'll be here in about five minutes,' he said. 'They said to keep James warm until they got here.'

In fact, the ambulance arrived in three and a half minutes, though it seemed more like ten. Jackie travelled with James in the back of the ambulance whilst Eric and Tim followed in the car.

'What about Mum?' Tim said.

'I rang the restaurant and spoke to her after I'd rung for the ambulance, told her to meet us at the hospital.'

They couldn't keep up with the ambulance, which was racing ahead of them, skipping red lights. The hospital was fifteen minutes' drive away, a white, modern building on the outskirts of York, with landscaped gardens flanking a large, well-lit car park. They were almost there when Eric said, 'Are you disappointed with me, Tim?'

'What for?'

'For not going after ... well, you know.'

Tim turned and stared out of the window. Finally he said, 'No.'

'You sure?'

'Yeah.'

'You don't sound it.'

Tim sighed and looked at his father. 'It's just ... he was right there, Dad. But I know you're right. It would have been stupid to have gone for him. He could have stabbed you first, then me, then he could have gone after Mum.'

Eric nodded slowly. 'That's right.' There was a pause, and then he said, 'But I just wanted you to know, Tim ... I still feel rotten. About not going for him, I mean. Considering what he's put us through.'

'Yeah,' Tim said, and looked out of the window again. 'I know, Dad.'

They parked as close to the hospital as they could and went through a pair of double doors into the Casualty department. Eric was talking to the girl on the reception desk when Jackie appeared at the end of the corridor that led to the treatment rooms.

'How is he?' Eric asked her the moment she was within earshot.

'They don't know yet. They're looking at him now, but the ambulance man said it didn't look too serious.'

'Are *you* all right?' Eric said. He reached out his hands as if to catch Jackie or hug her, but when she didn't respond they drifted back down to his sides.

'Fine,' she said, trying to smile. 'Well, a bit shaky. I could do with a cup of tea.'

The tea from the dispenser was weak and smelt like perfume, but they all sipped at it as though parched, wreathing their faces in steam.

'He came to in the ambulance a bit. I spoke to him,' Jackie said.

'What did he say?'

'Nothing much. He managed to tell me what happened, though he was a bit woozy. From what I could gather, the ... um ... the attacker just walked into the kitchen, hit James on the back of the head and dragged him into the garden. James seems positive that it was you know who. He kept grabbing my sleeve and saying, "It was him, it was him", as if he really wanted me to believe it.'

'It was just someone dressed up like him, that's all. James would hardly have had a chance to get a good look at him before he was knocked out.'

'But he seemed so sure,' Jackie said.

'So what are you saying now? That it really *is* him?'

'No, of course not,' Jackie said, frowning. Her hands curled around the white plastic cup. 'It's just ... oh, I don't know. I'm too shaken up by all this to even think straight any more.'

They lapsed into silence, vacantly watching the bustle going on around them. Eric glanced at his watch, and was surprised to see it was only 10:25. With all that had happened, it felt like the early hours of the morning. A few minutes later, a male nurse with the build of a rugby player appeared at the end of the corridor leading to the treatment rooms and ambled towards them.

'Excuse me,' he said to Jackie, who had her back to him, 'are you the lady who came in with Mr Keeve?'

Jackie twisted in her seat, face hardening with alarm. 'That's right. Why?'

The nurse glanced at Eric and Tim. 'Are you relatives of Mr Keeve's?'

'No, we're friends,' Eric said.

'What's happened to him?' Jackie demanded.

The nurse held up both hands as if trying to placate a dangerous patient and said quietly, 'No, no, he's fine. His wounds were mostly superficial. I've come to tell you that he's got a slight concussion, and that we're going to keep him in overnight for observation, so you might as well go home.'

'Can't we see him?' asked Jackie.

'Well, there's nothing much to see. He's sleeping now. It'd be best if you came back in the morning.'

Jackie looked around, and said, half to herself, half to Eric, 'He'll be all right in here on his own, won't he?'

Eric understood her meaning but the nurse obviously didn't. In the tone of one who was used to soothing over-anxious relatives, he said, 'Don't worry, he'll be fine.'

Tuesday 29 November

53

Despite, or perhaps because of, all that had happened, Tim was asleep the instant his head touched the pillow. It seemed no time at all, however, before he was jerking awake again, filled with the certainty that there was someone in the room with him.

The first thing he saw when his eyes popped open was a pale, misshapen face looming in the darkness. His feet kicked him into a sitting position, causing the Z-bed to lurch, threatening to flip up and tip him out. He dragged his duvet up to his chin, but as he opened his mouth to call out, the face changed back to what it really was – his white T-shirt draped over the back of the chair in front of Chloe's dressing table. His lips twitched into a grimace of relief. He could see now that the T-shirt looked nothing like a face.

Something had woken him, though, he was certain of that. Slowly he scanned the room, squinting as though in the belief it would sharpen his vision enough to slice through shadow. The only place an intruder could hide was under Chloe's bed, which was behind him; the wardrobe was inaccessible because the Z-bed would prevent the doors from opening more than an inch. Tim peered at the dark gap between Chloe's bed and the floor, but he might as well have had his eyes closed. Moving slowly, he eased the duvet from his body and stood up, wincing at the way the Z-bed creaked as he shifted his weight on it, then padded over to the light switch.

He was still a few feet away from it when he heard a sharp click from across the room, somewhere near the dressing table. Instantly he dropped into a crouch. He must have made a mistake, thinking the bed was the only hiding place; there must have been room to hide between the dressing table and the wall. And whoever had done so had now risen up, and the click had been the sound of a gun being cocked, a gun which was now pointing at him.

For the split-second it took for these thoughts to rush through his head like a hurricane, the supposition seemed perfectly logical and acceptable. Then Tim realised that if somebody *had* risen up from behind Chloe's dressing table, he would have been able to see their silhouetted form, framed by the brownish light seeping through the closed curtains of the window.

He rose slowly to his feet again, breathing heavily, gazing so hard at the place where the click had come from that his eyes became sore. He blinked as he felt them beginning to water, and just at that moment the click came again.

This time Tim knew what had made the sound instantly; it was a pebble hitting the window. Oonagh, he thought, remembering how she had attracted his attention a few nights ago, and hurried across the room. However, as he reached out to pull the curtain aside he became suddenly wary. Chloe's window looked out over the front garden, not the back as Tim's did; would Oonagh risk coming all the way round here? Besides which, how did she know he was in his sister's room and not his own?

Cautiously now, he eased aside the curtain until there was a large enough gap for him to look through. He could see only the right-hand side of the garden from here, and not very clearly. The street lights didn't make much of an impression on the shadows cast by bushes and the hedge; indeed, they only deepened them. Reluctantly Tim craned forward until his forehead was almost touching the glass – which was when a slim shadow detached itself from the mass beneath the hedge and beckoned to him.

Tim saw orange light flash on golden hair. So it *was* Oonagh. What was so important that it couldn't wait until tomorrow? He waved, then slipped back into the room and dressed quickly, wincing at the ache in his leg as he pulled on his jeans.

He was halfway down the stairs when he heard the murmur of the TV coming from behind the closed lounge door. Someone obviously couldn't sleep, which was hardly surprising after that evening's events. He tiptoed to the bottom of the stairs, crept across to the front door and painstakingly began to unlock it. When he finally got it open, freezing air rushed at him, making him gasp. Tim slipped outside, closing the door behind him. It was so cold it seemed to cut right through his clothes and skin. He stood on the doorstep and peered for a moment at the alien, shadowed landscape of the front garden, trying in vain to distinguish what the stripes and blocks of feeble orange light from the foliage-enshrouded street lamps were illuminating. At last he could stand the cold no longer and stepped down on to the path. Assuming that Oonagh had gone before him and expected him to follow, he readied himself to run nimbly round to the back of the house, and only just managed to stifle a cry of fear when a shadow tore itself from the main mass beneath the hedge and moved soundlessly to intercept him.

'Bloody hell, Oonagh,' he hissed as she reached him, 'you nearly gave me a heart attack.'

'Sorry,' she whispered. 'I waited for you. I thought we'd be safer together. Come on.'

She clutched the sleeve of his sweater and dragged him round to the back of the house. They didn't speak until they were inside the shed and Oonagh had closed the door. It was only marginally warmer in here than it was outside. Oonagh crossed to her mound of bedding, picked up a blanket which she tossed to Tim, then sat cross-legged on the floor, dragging a sleeping bag around her until only her head poked out. For the first time Tim noticed that she was cleaner than she'd been the last time he had seen her. Her face looked pink and fresh and her hair was frizzy and caught what little light there was in golden flashes.

'I see you got your shower then,' he said, sitting down to face her.

'Yes. That's how I knew where you were.' She looked a little embarrassed. 'I had a look around the house. I wanted to see what your room was like. When I saw your clothes and the Z-bed in your sister's room I realised you must be sleeping in there.'

Under normal circumstances, Tim might have teased her for being nosey, whilst secretly feeling pleased that she was showing enough interest in him to want to see his room, but now he simply nodded and said, 'So what did you want to see me about?'

A strange look crossed her face. 'I saw something really weird tonight. *Really* weird.'

'What was it?' he asked, not sure that he could bear to face any more weirdness today.

'Well, you know when you came back from going out, and your dad's friend was hit on the head, and you all rushed out and Mr Bad Face was there, and then Mr Bad Face walked off into the trees, and an ambulance came, and you all went off again?'

Tim nodded.

'Well, I saw what *really* happened.'

'What do you mean?'

'About ten minutes before you all came out, I heard someone moving around outside the shed. At first I thought it was you, but then when you didn't knock, I realised it must be somebody else and so I pushed myself into the corner and pulled the blankets up over my head, hoping that if somebody *did* come into the shed, they wouldn't notice me in the dark. Anyway, the sounds didn't go away, and I was getting more and more nervous, and more and more curious; I couldn't understand why someone was moving around outside the shed and not trying to get in. In the end I couldn't stand it any longer and so I crawled out from under my blankets and crept over to the window and had a look out. And who do you think was crouching there, just outside the window, literally three feet from my face?'

'Who?'

'Mr Bad Face.'

'You're kidding!'

'I'm not. I saw him up close. He had a bald head with wispy bits of hair sticking to it, and his skin was white and scarred, just like you'd told me.'

'Bloody hell. Did he see you?'

'No, he can't have done. But at first when I ducked down I didn't know whether he had or not. My heart was beating like mad. I was absolutely terrified. Luckily when I saw him he was facing away from me, watching the house. I only saw him in profile, and only for about half a second up close.'

'God,' said Tim. 'So what happened then?'

'Well, I waited a bit longer, and then I heard him move again. He must have been standing up, because the next thing I heard was the sound of him moving away from the shed. I decided to risk another look out, and guess what I saw.'

'I can't guess,' Tim said impatiently. 'Tell me.'

'You know that friend of your dad's? The one who was hit?'

'Mr Keeve,' said Tim.

'Yes, him. I saw him walking across the back lawn towards Mr Bad Face, who had moved into the middle of the lawn to meet him. The two of them met up and started just ... well ... chatting.'

'Are you sure?'

'Positive. They talked for a couple of minutes, and that Keeve man kept looking over his shoulder as if he was nervous of being seen from the house. Then eventually he went back into the kitchen and I heard him cry out and drop something, as if he'd been attacked. Anyway, next second he came running back out of the house and up to Mr Bad Face. He turned his back on him and hunched his shoulders as if he was bracing himself for something. Then he gave this sort of squeal as if he was terrified, and just as he did that Mr Bad Face whacked him on the back of the head with a club or an iron bar or something. Keeve fell down, and Mr Bad Face put his club away, then stood there over him, waiting for you lot to show up. When you did, he strolled off into the trees.'

A heavy silence followed Oonagh's story. Tim was shaking his head, as if trying to deny what she had told him. Eventually he said, 'I don't get it.'

'What don't you get?'

'Well ... any of it really.'

Oonagh shrugged. 'I don't see that there's anything not to get. Presumably Keeve and this Mr Bad Face character are in it together.'

'But they can't be!'

'Why not?'

'Well ... because Mr Keeve's been staying in our house.'

'So?'

'But he's my dad's friend! He seems so ... so normal.'

'A lot of psychopaths seem normal.'

'But if it's been him all along, why didn't he just kill us all last night when he had the chance, when we were all asleep?'

'I don't know,' said Oonagh, and then frowned as a look of horror crossed Tim's face. 'What is it?'

'I've just thought – the fingers in my pocket. You don't think ... you don't think Mr Keeve actually killed Chloe, do you?'

Oonagh looked almost apologetic. 'He might have done. Him or this Mr Bad Face character, or maybe both of them together.'

'Oh God,' Tim breathed, 'I can't believe it.' He shook his head and said again, this time even more incredulously, 'He seemed so ... *normal*.'

'He must have been acting,' said Oonagh. 'Playing a role, to make you all trust him.'

'But he told us his wife and daughter had disappeared,' Tim said almost indignantly. 'He seemed to think Mr Bad Face had taken them.'

'He probably killed them himself. Or maybe he never even had a wife and daughter.'

'But he spoke to the police. I heard him.'

Oonagh shrugged. 'It would take the police a while to check out his story though, wouldn't it? Or maybe he just dialled the number and then put his finger on the disconnect button while no one was looking. Were you watching him closely all the time?'

'No, I ... I suppose not. But why would he get Mr Bad Face to whack him on the head, enough to put him in hospital? He could have been badly hurt.'

'I suppose that was just another part of his plan, a way of throwing you off the scent maybe. That doesn't really matter now, though, does it? What's important is that he doesn't know we know about him.'

Tim rubbed his head. 'I can't take all this in. We'd better tell my dad.'

'What do you mean, "we"?' said Oonagh. '*I'm* not telling him. I don't want anyone to know I'm here. You can tell him yourself.'

'But how can I tell him and leave you out of it?'

'Tell him that you saw what I saw from an upstairs window.'

'Don't be daft. He'll want to know why I didn't tell him earlier, like in the car on the way to the hospital. No, you'll have to come with me, Oonagh.'

Oonagh scowled. 'There must be some way we can work this to leave me out of it.'

'No there isn't. And remember, the only reason you're here is because of all the trouble at the camp because of what happened to Chloe. Once Keeve's been arrested, you'll be able to go back to your mum and dad, won't you?'

'I'm not so sure. Knowing the authorities, they'll probably think of some other reason to split us up.'

'But it's got to end some time,' said Tim. 'You can't stay here for ever, can you?'

Oonagh was silent for a moment, then reluctantly she said, 'No, I suppose not ... All right, then. I'll do it. But only because I like you.'

Tim stood up. 'Thanks,' he said. 'Come on, then.'

'Hang on, there is one other thing.' Oonagh took something that clinked out of her jeans pocket. 'After you'd gone off to the hospital, I saw something shining on the lawn. I went out and found this. One of you must have dropped it.'

She held up the object. It was a single key on a keyring, attached to a metal tag.

Tim took the key and held it up to the window. He was just able to make out the words SINCLAIR & McPHEARSON on the tag, underneath which was a telephone number.

'Is it yours?' asked Oonagh.

'No, and I don't think my dad's got a key like this either.'

'That means it's either Jackie's or Keeve's.'

'Or Mr Bad Face's,' said Tim. He pocketed the key. 'I'll show it to my dad. Come on.'

The two of them trooped round to the front of the house and in through the door that Tim had left unlocked. This time he didn't bother keeping quiet. He opened the door and called out, 'Hello! Can anyone hear me? It's Tim!'

Seconds later the lounge door was snatched open and Eric appeared, a look of alarm on his face. 'Tim,' he said, 'what's the matter? Are you okay?' and then, noticing Oonagh, he did an almost comic double-take. 'Who's this?'

'This is my friend, Oonagh, Dad.'

Eric looked bemused. 'Well, what's she doing here? And why are you dressed? Where have you been?' Then his son's words registered and he said incredulously, 'Oonagh? You mean the girl from the camp? The one the police have been looking for?'

Tim nodded, abashed.

Eric looked from Tim to Oonagh, then back to Tim again. 'Perhaps you'd better tell me what's been going on here,' he said.

54

Farrington was going through the paperwork for the umpteenth time in the vain hope of spotting something she'd missed. At the moment she was looking at the forensic report she'd received from Kent CID, detailing their findings at the Dullastons' house. It did not make for pleasant reading, nor did it provide any significant leads about the identity of the killer. She knew it was a pointless exercise. The reports had been checked and cross-checked by human and computer so many times that one dog-tired detective giving them another once-over in the early hours wasn't going to make a blind bit of difference. Sudden flashes of inspiration were the domain of cheap crime novels and TV cop shows; they didn't happen in real life. And yet she still stuck doggedly to her task, if only to make her feel as though she was doing *something* constructive.

She pushed aside a photocopied thirty-year-old newspaper report on the tragic, lonely death of John Straker, and was wondering whether going off home to bed would be worth the guilt she'd feel for doing so, when someone tapped on the door to her office. The door opened before her mouth could and Lockwood leaned in. Farrington's immediate assumption was that he was going to ask for permission to go home, but then she noticed that there was a certain energy about him, and she sat up straighter in her chair, feeling something leap inside her.

'What is it, Frank?' she asked quickly.

'I've got the Knights and Jackie Foster outside, boss, and you'll never guess who's with them?'

'Frank Sinatra? I don't know, I give up.'

Lockwood looked like a magician about to pull a rabbit from a hat. 'Only Oonagh Walsh,' he told her, 'the missing girl.'

Farrington tried hard not to look as surprised as she felt. 'Oonagh Walsh!' she repeated. 'Where did she spring from?'

'She hasn't said yet. All they've told me is that they want to see you.'

Farrington used the arms of her chair to push herself into an even more upright position, and began to gather the reports together on her desk. Hurriedly she covered Boam's report on Chloe Knight, paper-clipped to which were candid close-ups of the girl's horrific injuries. She took a quick look round the tiny, makeshift office, just to ensure there was nothing on the walls that would disturb them, then gave a curt nod. 'Show them in. I want you here too, Frank, to hear what they've got to say.'

Lockwood nodded, opened the door wider and stood aside like a butler, wafting a hand towards the open door. The three adults and two children trooped into Farrington's office. The Inspector's attention was caught immediately by the girl with the honey-coloured hair. It was only now that she could admit to herself that she had never truly expected to ever see this girl alive. The girl's clothes were grubby, but she looked clean and well fed. The girl stared back at Farrington with a mixture of defiance and resignation.

'So you're Oonagh Walsh,' Farrington said evenly, 'the girl who's been giving us so much trouble.'

Oonagh's face hardened. 'I didn't ask you to look for me.'

Farrington smiled as if the girl's retort had amused her, and waited for Lockwood and Eric to distribute the chairs Lockwood had dragged in from the outer office. 'Perhaps you'd like to tell the Sergeant and me where you've been?'

'Not really,' said Oonagh, as if the conversation was boring her.

Farrington looked at Eric, who was perched on the edge of his chair, hands dangling between his knees.

'Eric?'

Eric nodded at Tim, standing beside Oonagh to his right. 'I think Tim'd better tell you, Inspector.'

Tim looked uncomfortable when Farrington turned her attention to him, but before he could say anything, Annette leaned forward. 'None of this is relevant,' she said bluntly.

'Isn't it?' said Farrington.

'No. We haven't come here for all this. We've come here to tell you who killed Chloe.'

Farrington felt a jolt of excitement so strong it was like electricity. Outwardly, however, she appeared calm. 'I think you'd better explain,' she said.

Annette glanced at the girl. 'Oonagh, would you tell the Inspector what you saw?'

For a moment, Farrington thought Oonagh was going to toss her head and refuse to co-operate, but then she nodded and said, 'For the past few days, I've been living in the shed in Tim's back garden ...'

She began to tell her story, but as soon as she mentioned Keeve walking out of the house to speak to Mr Bad Face, Farrington held up a hand.

'Wait a minute,' she said. 'What's all this about James Keeve? Where the hell did he spring from?'

Eric looked as surprised as the Inspector. 'He showed up last night,' he said. 'He rang you to tell you about his wife and child. He said he was coming to see you this morning.'

Farrington shook her head. 'Believe me, this is the first I've heard of any of this. As far as I'm concerned, we're still looking for Keeve.'

'Well, we know where he is,' said Eric.

'Then perhaps you'd better tell me. And then you can fill me in on what I've been missing.'

Two minutes later, Lockwood was arranging for a couple of men to rush to the hospital where Keeve had been admitted. While he was doing that, Eric hurriedly related the events of the past twenty-four hours (omitting the part about Tim finding Chloe's fingers in his jacket pocket, which Farrington already knew but Annette still didn't). After he was done, Oonagh took up the story again, concluding with the finding of the key.

Eric took a handkerchief-wrapped package from his pocket. He placed it on the desk in front of Farrington and carefully unfolded it. The key, with its tag attached, lay inside.

'It doesn't belong to any of us,' he said. 'It must belong to either James or the man he's working with.'

'It'll have my fingerprints all over it,' Oonagh said. 'I never thought.'

Farrington read out the name on the tag. 'Sinclair and McPhearson. What's that?'

When nobody replied, she looked up. Eric shrugged.

'Frank,' Farrington said to Lockwood, who had re-entered the room a few minutes earlier, 'would you check this out for me? When you've found out what the key's for, try to get a spare, then get forensic on to this one.'

'Right, boss,' Lockwood said, leaning over Eric's shoulder to take the handkerchief which she had gathered up and was holding out.

As he exited the office, Jackie sighed and said, 'I still find it hard to believe that James is responsible for all this. He was always so gentle, so ... so vulnerable.'

'I know,' Eric said. 'I can't believe it either.'

Annette glared at Jackie fiercely. 'Will you both stop calling him *James* all the time,' she snarled.

Eric looked surprised. 'But it's his name.'

'He's a monster. He doesn't deserve a name. He killed our little girl!'

'We don't know that for certain yet, Mrs Knight,' Farrington said.

'*I* know!' Annette retorted. 'He killed her. He's a monster, he doesn't deserve to live. And to think that he's been in our house –

sitting on our chairs, sleeping on our sofa, drinking from our mugs.' She drew her hands into fists and shuddered. 'I want everything he touched destroyed,' she hissed. 'I want it taken out into the garden and burned. The carpet too. I want all trace of him ... eradicated.'

Eric put his arm around his wife's shoulders and tried to draw her towards him, but she was like a rock. 'Hey, hey,' he said, 'come on, Net. We've nearly got him now.'

'I mean it,' she said fiercely. 'I'm not setting foot back inside that house until you've got rid of everything he touched. I'd be able to smell him. It makes me sick just thinking about it.'

Farrington held up her hands to quell Annette's outburst. She could understand the woman's feelings, but it was getting them off the point somewhat. 'Why didn't you mention James Keeve when I saw you this afternoon, Eric?' she asked.

Eric shrugged. 'It never occurred to me, I suppose. I assumed you'd already spoken to him.'

'This afternoon?' said Annette. 'Why did you see the Inspector this afternoon?'

Eric looked uncomfortable. 'Oh, Tim and I called in on the way home,' he said, trying to make it sound casual.

'What for?'

'Oh ... nothing really. Just to see if there were any developments.'

Annette glared at her husband so ferociously that he had to look away. 'You're lying.'

'No I'm not.'

'Yes you are, I can tell. What's going on?'

There was silence for a moment, and then Tim said miserably, 'You really don't want to know.'

Annette's gaze was jumping between her son and her husband. 'Don't keep things from me, I'm not a child.' When still no one said anything, she shouted, 'Tell me!'

'It's something about Chloe,' said Tim, 'something not very nice.'

'Tell me,' she repeated.

'I found some ... things of Chloe's in my pocket,' Tim said. 'Things that only the killer could have put there.'

Annette stared at him, lips pursed, and then asked, 'What kinds of things?'

'Oh God,' groaned Tim, half-turning away.

'Believe me, Net, it's best if you don't know,' Eric said quickly.

She rounded on her husband. 'I know what's best for myself, thank you very much!' She swung back to glare fiercely at Farrington. 'I want to know. You tell me.'

Farrington looked at Eric, who shrugged. Evidently taking this as a go-ahead, she said, 'There's no easy way of telling you this, Mrs Knight. The items that Tim found in his pocket were your daughter's fingers. They were missing from her body when we found her on Tuesday night. Now we know that her killer took them away with him.'

Annette's eyes opened wide in horror. Her hands flew to her face, fingers digging into her cheeks as if she wanted to claw away her own flesh. '*No!*' she gasped, and then screeched out the denial: '*No! No! No!*'

'What did you tell her for?' Tim shouted at Farrington, but before she could reply, Annette had jumped up from her chair, knocking it over, and was running for the door.

For a few seconds there was pandemonium in the office. Eric jumped up too and lunged at his wife, wrapping his arms around her waist, stumbling and wincing as she aimed vicious kicks at his shins. Jackie went to help him, and seconds later the door opened and two burly policemen burst in to investigate the cause of the commotion, only adding to the crush and confusion.

Farrington was standing now, her desk distancing her from the melee by the door, yelling, 'Sit down, Mrs Knight! Please, sit down!'

Annette, though, seemed beyond all reason. 'Let me go!' she was screaming. 'Let me go! I want to kill him!'

Eric, Jackie and the two policemen clung to her thrashing body like a human straitjacket until her furious energy began to dwindle. All of a sudden she slumped, her head dropping forward, and began to sob. Cautiously Jackie and then the two policemen relinquished their hold on her, leaving Eric to steer her back to her chair and sit her down. She slumped against him and he put his arms around her.

For a few seconds nobody moved or spoke, and then one of the policemen said tentatively, 'Er ... do you want us to stay, boss?'

'No,' Farrington said, 'you can go. We'll be all right.'

'Well, if you're sure,' the constable said, eyeing Annette doubtfully, then he and his colleague lumbered from the room.

Gently Farrington said, 'Are you all right, Mrs Knight?'

At first there was no response, then Annette gave the tiniest of nods.

'Would you like a cup of tea or coffee?'

This time there was no response at all. Farrington let it pass.

'I'm sorry to have distressed you,' she said, 'but if it's any consolation, the ... er ... the fingers were removed after death. Chloe wouldn't have felt any pain.'

Annette gave no indication that she had heard. Eric looked up and said, 'She'll be all right, Inspector. It was just the shock, that's all.'

Farrington nodded. Tentatively, Jackie asked, 'Why do you think Ja ... er, Keeve is doing this, Inspector? I mean, I still find it so hard to believe. As a kid he was always so timid. He hated violence.'

'Against himself, you mean?' said Farrington.

'Well ... yes, but he never showed any violent tendencies towards anyone else either.'

'Things happen, people change,' said Farrington. 'Or maybe as children you simply never saw the signs, never saw what he was capable of. Children can hide things well, just as adults can. Tell me about him.'

Eric and Jackie looked at each other, and then, somewhat haltingly, told Farrington what they knew about their erstwhile friend. It wasn't much.

'What I don't understand,' said Tim, 'is why he came to see us in the first place. I mean, he came to us, we didn't go to him.'

'My guess would be that he felt distanced from the effects of his actions,' Farrington said. 'Most of the time killers don't think about the terrible distress they're going to cause to their victims' families, or they don't care. But sometimes they actually relish the emotional repercussions of their actions – it makes them feel powerful, important. I think Keeve wanted to experience your grief and fear first-hand. He wanted to drink in your suffering like ...'

'A vampire?' Oonagh suggested.

'A vampire, yes.'

'But that's horrible,' Jackie said.

Farrington nodded.

'So you think that's why he didn't kill us when he had the chance?' said Eric. 'Because he was enjoying watching us suffer?'

'Well, it's only a guess,' said Farrington.

Jackie shook her head in disgust and disbelief. 'But that's ... so evil. I just can't believe it.'

'To us, it is evil,' Farrington agreed, 'but if Keeve is our man he probably wouldn't think like a normal person. Going by experience, I'd say he's almost certainly dysfunctional, by which I mean he'll have a warped world view. What he's doing probably doesn't seem evil to him; it may seem like ... like a mission, something he has to do. To you and me it's horrific and pointless, but to him it will make perfect sense; in fact, it may very well be the whole point of his existence.'

'But he's always seemed so ... so normal,' said Jackie. 'When he arrived at Eric's he seemed as scared and nervous as we all were. Same old James. He certainly didn't seem mad, or even weird. I never at any time thought there was anything strange about him.'

'Just because he's dysfunctional doesn't necessarily mean he can't read situations, or adapt to them.'

'You make him sound like some sort of ... I don't know ... chameleon,' said Eric. 'Something not quite human.'

'Not at all. It's a different way of thinking, that's all. The obsessive killer filters out all other distractions, focuses totally on the matter in hand. But he's still a human being, just like the rest of us. As we've proved, he can still make mistakes and he can be caught.'

'And what about this other person he's been working with?' said Eric. 'Will he be the same?'

'Possibly. Who knows? Often, when partnerships are involved, you'll find that one partner is dominant over the other. The submissive one is likely to hero-worship the dominant one, and will go to any lengths to please them.'

A perfunctory tap on the door interrupted her, and Lockwood entered, his face grim. 'What is it, Frank?' she said.

'I've got some good news and some bad news,' Lockwood said. 'The good news is that we've traced the key. Sinclair and McPhearson is a firm that rents out storage space, based at the Lowfields industrial estate just outside Leeds. It seems that our key is for one of four lock-up garages in Bramwell, adjoining number twenty-two Singer Lane. Roger's gone to meet the manager down at the unit to pick up a spare key, and I've sent Steve and Mark over to Singer Lane to keep tabs on the place until we get there. There's actually a serial number on the key itself, so the manager, a Mr Coombs, was able to tell me pretty quickly who'd rented the place once he got over to the unit. The name he's got logged is a Mr John Straker, who gave his address as thirty-nine Jasmine Road, Tewkesbury, Gloucestershire. He says the guy rented the place about three weeks ago.'

'Thirty-nine Jasmine Road. That was Straker's address, the house we burned down,' said Jackie.

Farrington glanced at her, then turned back to Lockwood. 'And the bad news?'

Lockwood grimaced apologetically, as if being the messenger of bad tidings made him responsible for them. 'I'm afraid we were too late to get Keeve. He discharged himself from the hospital an hour ago.'

55

Singer Lane was in the south-east corner of Bramwell, over a mile beyond the school and the main street. It was an amorphous, largely forgotten area in which imposing though dilapidated houses stood with uneasy defiance among chunks of untamed countryside. The lane itself was little more than a rutted, muddy track, running behind a short terrace of turn-of-the-century red-brick cottages. Adjoining the terrace were fields studded with trees that looked gnarled and twisted now in the approach to winter, and the occasional clump of woodland that stood out black against the deep blue of the night sky.

As Farrington's car, driven by Lockwood, jolted slowly down the lane towards the cluster of lock-up garages they had been assured were down here, the trees that overhung the road like giant sculptures of spiny black hands seemed to jerk and twitch, given life by the lurching headlights. They had only travelled forty yards, and already the lane was becoming narrower, the trees denser, the potholes more treacherous. Farrington was beginning to wonder whether there was some second turn-off that they had somehow missed, when all of a sudden the lane widened out and they were in a muddy clearing.

The first thing she saw was the back of Steve Wesker's car, or rather the twin red gleams of his reflector lights as their own headlights swept across them. The four garages were harder to pick out. They were overgrown with so much foliage that it looked as though the land was attempting to reclaim them.

Lockwood pulled in behind the other car, though at an angle so that their headlights were facing the garages. He turned the engine off, but left the lights on. As he and Farrington pulled on latex gloves, Steve Wesker and Mark Monroe, the two DCs that had been sent down here to keep an eye on the place, got out of their car and came towards them. Wesker, young and a little too cocksure for his own good, was adjusting his tie as if he was expecting a TV camera crew to turn up. Monroe was older and bulkier, with a sandy moustache and thinning hair. He had his hands thrust into his pockets, and Farrington saw him shiver with the cold and blow a plume of air from his mouth. She patted the pocket of the canvas police jacket she'd pulled on to ensure her torch was there, then got out of the car.

'All quiet?' she said.

'As the grave,' said Wesker with a grin.

'Which one is it?' Farrington asked, looking at the garages.

'Coombs said number two,' said Lockwood, 'which I assume is that one.'

'Right then, let's get to work. I assume you've both got your gloves on?'

Monroe gave a brusque nod; Wesker held up his gloved hands like a man doing a puppet show. The four of them trudged across the mud towards the garages. Lockwood bent to insert the key into the door's low central handle and gave it an experimental twist.

The whole row creaked and shifted a little as if about to collapse at any moment; the foliage that curled around the peeling garage walls and over the corrugated iron roofs rustled as if something that lived in it had been stirred from sleep.

'Wrong door?' suggested Farrington.

'No, just a bit stiff. That's it!' Lockwood took the rust-speckled handle in his left hand and twisted it. 'Welcome to Wonderland,' he said.

The door groaned and rattled as it rose up and over on powerful springs. The harsh light from the car headlamps fell into the garage, squeezing between the long black shadows of the four police officers. Four torches clicked on almost simultaneously, chasing down the rest of the shadows, eradicating them.

The garage was wider and deeper than it seemed from outside. It contained a shabby, dark brown transit van, two battered old chests of drawers which stood side by side along the back wall, and some old shelving which looked as though only cobwebs held it together.

'Dark van,' Lockwood said.

Farrington nodded. 'Let's get it open, shall we?'

Monroe stepped forward, pulling a crowbar from the inside pocket of his jacket. Less than a minute later he stepped back, red and sweating. The van door hung open. Farrington pulled the doors back and all four of them shone their torches into its interior. The van was empty save for several lengths of bundled-up plastic sheeting. The sheeting was heavily stained with what looked like dark, crusted splashes of blood.

'Must be what he used to wrap the Dullastons up in,' said Lockwood.

'Travel in style and comfort,' murmured Wesker.

'All right,' said Farrington. 'Mark, you have a poke about in the front of the van, see what you can come up with. The rest of us'll have a look through these drawers.'

Monroe nodded, and the four of them skirted the side of the van, Wesker scowling at cobwebs as if defying them to come anywhere near his nice suit. As Monroe went to work on the lock of the front passenger door, the three other officers fanned out. Farrington moved to the right-hand chest of drawers, the larger of the two, which consisted of three large drawers with small cupboard-like compartments on either side. She crouched down and pulled the right-hand compartment open, and was ambushed by dust, which made her jerk her head back, choking. The compartment was empty, save for a fat black spider which quivered in the centre of a thick funnel of web.

Lockwood was standing to her left, pulling open drawers which protested loudly as if they hadn't been subjected to this kind of treatment for years. Standing to *his* left was Wesker, who was tackling the smaller of the two items of furniture, this consisting of four drawers, no cupboards.

'Nothing in here,' Lockwood said, the bottom drawer jerking open an inch at a time.

The words had barely left his lips when Wesker leapt back as though something had jumped out of one of the drawers at him, a half-formed expletive, '*shiiiii*—', bursting from his mouth.

Farrington and Lockwood swung round. Even Monroe, who had got the van door open and was shining his torch under the seats, his fat backside sticking up in the air, jerked up, eyes wide as if expecting trouble.

'What is it, Steve?' Farrington said, rising to her feet.

Wesker had recovered enough to look sheepish. Nevertheless his finger was trembling as he pointed at the chest of drawers.

'In the drawer there ... there's a face.' He cleared his throat, as if that might cover up the warble in his voice.

Lockwood glanced at Farrington, then the two of them moved to the drawer Wesker had indicated. It was the second drawer down, and Wesker had pulled it perhaps a third of the way open before jumping back. Lockwood shone his torch on it now as Farrington grabbed the handle and, hardly aware she was drawing a deep breath, yanked it open.

In her time on the force, Farrington had seen so many dreadful sights that she now believed she could face the worst of what the world had to offer without flinching. Nevertheless, when she opened the drawer, a brief and unusual spark ignited her imagination, and for a split-second she saw what Wesker had seen. She saw a face which had been peeled from the gleaming musculature it had once masked, saw the gaping mouth which had once framed teeth and a tongue, the blank, eyeless sockets. The force with which she had yanked the drawer open caused the face to roll sickeningly forward, folding in on itself as it did so. Farrington didn't jump back, though she did have to fight down the fleeting, ludicrous notion that the face was somehow alive, that it had been waiting for someone to release it and was now flopping towards her in a ghastly and pathetic bid for freedom.

Then the world clunked back on to the right track, and she realised that what she was looking at wasn't a face at all, but a mask. There were other things in the drawer too – a rubber skull cup with wispy hair attached, some thick, greasy sticks of white, blue and red stage make-up, cartons containing powders of various hues, creams, make-up brushes, cotton buds.

Farrington reached into the drawer and took out the mask, draping it over her hand, holding it up. 'Boys,' she said, 'meet Mr Bad Face.'

Wesker gave an unsteady grin and shook his head.

'And I would've gotten away with it too if it hadn't been for you meddling kids,' muttered Lockwood.

Farrington took a polythene evidence bag from her pocket, unfolded it and put the mask inside. 'I'll take this back, show it to the Knights and Jackie Foster. Have you looked in the rest of these drawers, Steve?'

'No, boss, I was just about to.'

Wesker moved forward and opened the third drawer down. This contained what at first appeared to be rags, but on closer inspection turned out to be a crumpled sweatshirt and a pair of canvas trousers, both covered in dried blood. Wrapped in the centre of the sweatshirt was a long-bladed gutting knife, so coated with blood that the sweatshirt had to be peeled away from it. The fourth drawer down was empty. The van, too, yielded nothing more than a map of the area and some chewing gum wrappers.

'Okay,' Farrington said when they were done, 'let's get forensic down here, give the place a thorough going over. Mark and Steve, I want you to wait until they show up.' She looked around once more as she peeled off her gloves, a distasteful expression on her face. 'Come on, Frank, let's get out of here. I could do with some fresh air.'

56

When Farrington arrived back at the Portakabin, it was to find that her office had become a dormitory-cum-tea bar. Tim was lying on the floor, dozing, body curled into a question mark. Oonagh was actually sitting on Farrington's chair, slumped over her desk like a murder victim in an Agatha Christie novel. The three adults were silently drinking tea, Eric taking puffs on one of his thin little roll-ups between sips from his cup. They looked as though they had done nothing else *but* drink tea since she had left, judging by the mound of crumpled white plastic in the waste bin.

'Did you find anything?' Eric asked, looking up as she came in.

His voice roused Tim, who groaned and unfurled. Oonagh raised her head slowly, her face squeezed into a squint.

Farrington nodded, reached into her pocket, extracted the polythene evidence bag and held it up.

'My God,' said Jackie.

'Handsome fellow, isn't he?' said Farrington. 'I take it this is your Mr Bad Face?'

Eric was looking at the mask, his lips pressed together. 'I suppose it must be,' he said. 'Can I have a closer look?'

'Please don't take it out of the bag,' said Farrington as she handed it over.

The bag crackled in Eric's hands as he tried to smooth out the mask through the polythene. It was made of thick, textured material that looked like rubber, curled at the edges to fit more easily over the face, with slightly ragged holes for the eyes and mouth.

'Is it him, Dad?' Tim asked, craning over his father's shoulder to see.

'Yes, I think so.'

'You don't sound too sure,' said Farrington.

'No, well, it's just that it looks so crude, doesn't it? I feel a bit silly now to think that it scared the wits out of me. When I saw that face in the poster it really knocked me sideways, and then on Saturday night, when I saw him standing outside the window ... well, I didn't know *what* to think. But now ... to be honest, I don't know if it even really looks that much like John Straker. I mean, there's a resemblance, of course, but ...' He turned to Jackie, who was sitting beside him. 'I don't know, what do you think?'

Jackie nodded. 'I know what you mean. When I saw him in the

garden tonight it was a real shock, but now ... yes, it doesn't look that much like him, does it? Not really.'

'We did find some other materials,' Farrington said. 'A piece to cover the hair, make-up paints and brushes, that sort of thing. I should imagine that the overall effect was quite convincing. And remember, you only saw the figure on a couple of occasions, and then only briefly, when it was dark.'

'And I suppose you sort of expected to see him too, didn't you?' said Tim. 'I mean, after the poster and the cards ...'

'Exactly,' said Farrington. 'Keeve manipulated you in such a way that even a reasonably convincing likeness was likely to produce the desired effect.'

'Even so,' said Eric, 'I feel a bit foolish. I mean, we all know that it had to be somebody dressed up, but it still gives you a hell of a shock when you're on your own in the middle of the night and you're confronted with this ... apparition. All your reasoning goes right out the window, and you start to believe all sorts of things.'

'I know what you mean,' said Jackie. 'When I saw him this evening standing over Jame ... er, Keeve's body, my first thought was, "My God, it's really him!"'

'Have you found Keeve yet, Inspector?' asked Eric.

Farrington shook her head. 'Not yet. But we've got virtually the whole of the West Yorkshire police force out looking for him. It's only a matter of time.'

'So what should we do in the meantime? Go home and wait for news?'

'You might as well. I'll get a couple of men to accompany you. With your permission, I'd like to issue you with live-in, round-the-clock protection until Keeve is caught.'

'You don't think he'll come back for us now, do you?' said Jackie.

'I don't know. He has gone to enormous lengths to victimise you so far, and now that he's burned all his bridges he might just try something reckless.'

'What about me?' Oonagh said suddenly. She was still sitting in Farrington's chair, hands tapping lightly on the desk.

Farrington allowed herself a smile. 'Oh, I expect we can find someone to run you home.'

'Back to Graeme and Linda, you mean?'

'Graeme and Linda?'

'Her mum and dad,' explained Tim.

'Oh, I see. Well, in that case, yes, back to Graeme and Linda.'

Oonagh grinned. 'Brilliant! So I won't have to go back to that foster home? I mean, ever?'

'I don't think there'd be much point in sending you back there, do you?' said Farrington.

'No,' said Oonagh. She turned to Tim. 'Well, see you, Tim. Thanks for everything.' She blushed, suddenly shy. 'Thanks for looking after me.'

'No problem,' said Tim; he was blushing too. 'Thanks for telling us about Keeve.'

There was a moment's pause, then abruptly Oonagh stepped forward, gave Tim a brief hug, then stepped back.

'Can I go now?' she said to Farrington.

'Yes, if you like. I'll find someone to take you. But we'll probably need to speak to you again, and we may need you to give evidence in court. Are you prepared to do that?'

'Of course,' said Oonagh. 'Bye everyone.'

The three adults murmured their goodbyes.

When she was at the door, Tim called, 'Oonagh?'

She turned back. 'Yes?'

'Will I see you again?'

She seemed to consider, then shrugged and smiled. 'Maybe,' she said.

57

The ground on which the travellers' camp stood had been reduced to a lake of mud with all the comings and goings of the past week. An insipid sun was hauling itself over the horizon as a car containing Farrington, Lockwood, Mark Monroe and Steve Wesker jolted up the slight incline towards the huddle of trailers, camper vans and Land Rovers. The blackened remains of the VW still stood in the spot where it had burned six days ago, like a testament to the victimisation these people had suffered since Chloe Knight's death.

'Park here, Frank,' Farrington said when they were still some twenty yards from the first of the mud-spattered trailers. 'It'll only seem intimidating if we drive right in amongst them.'

Lockwood complied, easing the car to a stop and cutting the engine. Through the windscreen, Farrington could see a fat woman in sloppy black Wellingtons, hanging out washing on a line stretched between two trailers, and two men standing chatting beside a caravan decorated with large, brightly coloured flowers like some remnant from the Sixties. As the car pulled up, all three stopped what they were doing and turned to regard the new arrivals, their expressions hovering somewhere between hostility and curiosity.

'That bloke there with the dreadlocks,' murmured Lockwood, 'his name's Spencer Forbes, known as Captain. It was his arrest that led to the incident the other night.'

'Are he and his friend likely to cause trouble, do you think?' asked Farrington.

'Hard to say. They might, when they realise what we're doing, protecting their own and all that.'

'Okay,' said Farrington, 'well, let's just do what we've got to do and get out. We're heading for the blue caravan over there. Hopefully we'll be gone before most of them here have even finished their Weetabix.'

The four police officers got out of the car and trudged towards the camp. Farrington, at their head, tried to look casual, unhurried, unthreatening. When she came within earshot of the two men by the flower-decked caravan, she smiled and called out, 'Morning, gents.'

Captain, who had been leaning against the caravan, pushed himself upright. 'Changed your mind, have you?' he said.

'About what?'

'About Oonagh. Come to take her away again?'

'No, no, nothing like that,' said Farrington.

'So what are you here for then?' said the other man, who was somewhere in his twenties, rangy and blond-haired.

'Just following up a few developments in our inquiry, Mr ...?'

'Takes four of you, does it?' said Captain before blondie had a chance to supply his name.

Farrington smiled as though Captain had made a witticism, and strolled on. The fat woman had gone back into her trailer now, in order, Farrington hoped, to keep out of their way rather than rouse a few supporters.

The blue caravan they were heading for was two along from the Walshes. Farrington wished they could have done what they were about to do three or four hours ago when they'd brought Oonagh back and everyone was asleep. But of course, they hadn't had the information then: forensic had only just begun their work at the lock-up. Farrington sauntered up and knocked politely on the door. She caught a waft of frying bacon, which made her stomach twinge. It was a long time since she had either slept or eaten, but although she could have eaten something she certainly wasn't sleepy; she was running on adrenaline.

She allowed herself a glance behind her as she waited for the door to be opened. Her three accompanying officers looked tense rather than casual, Wesker moving from foot to foot as if the ground was too hot to stand on. Captain and blondie were still watching her every move, though at a distance; there was no sign of anyone else. So far, so good, Farrington thought, and turned back as the door opened with a click.

Through a gap of no more than six inches, a bony, straggly-bearded face peered at her. 'What?' the face said.

'Mr Jordan?' Farrington asked.

The eyes in the face swivelled to regard her companions and then turned back to her. 'Yeah,' it confirmed, more cautiously.

'Mr Jordan, may we come in, please?'

'Why?'

'If you'll just allow us to come in for a moment, we'll tell you.'

'I'm busy,' the face said, and then reared back as Farrington leaned forward to scrutinise it.

'What's that in your beard, Mr Jordan?'

'What do you mean?'

'Looks like ... traces of glue to me. What do you think, Frank?'

'Stage make-up, I'd say,' Lockwood said.

Realisation swept across Jordan's face and he slammed the door shut.

Instantly Farrington leaped forward and shoved at the door; either it was locked or Jordan was hanging on to the handle from the inside. She stepped back to allow Monroe and Wesker room to manoeuvre. They ran at the door, floundering a little in the mud, and slammed their shoulders into it. The caravan shuddered with the impact, and the door flew open so violently that Wesker tripped over the raised threshold and fell sprawlingly inside. Someone inside the caravan swore; there was the sound of things falling and breaking. Within two seconds of the door opening, Monroe and Lockwood were inside, jumping over Wesker's prone form. Farrington brought up the rear.

The caravan was dingy, poky. There was a pan of bacon frying on a grease-encrusted stove, though in the enclosed space it didn't smell so appetising. The first thing Farrington saw when she stepped inside was Jordan at the far end frantically trying to load a shotgun. Then Monroe slammed into him with such force that Farrington could have sworn she saw the traveller lifted clean off his feet. Both men crashed into Jordan's bunk, which collapsed beneath them, and then into the far wall. The impact caused the caravan to judder so violently that the frying pan fell off the cooker, shedding its cargo of sizzling bacon and hot fat.

Farrington and Wesker, who had now risen to his feet, jumped back to avoid getting splashed. At the other end of the caravan, Monroe was pinning Jordan down whilst Lockwood put handcuffs on him. Jordan was not putting up much of a struggle; the full weight of Monroe's considerable bulk had knocked all the fight out of him. The shotgun was lying broken-backed on the floor, one cartridge in the chamber, the other coated in hot fat, having rolled against the cooker.

Farrington walked forwards, stepping over the mess on the floor. Monroe and Lockwood, both panting, were crouched either side of Jordan, who was lying in the debris of his wrecked bed. 'I can't breathe, you've broken my fucking ribs, I can't breathe,' he groaned.

'Mr Jordan?' Farrington said. 'Mr Jordan, can you hear me?'

Jordan squinted at her, his face creased in pain. 'My ribs,' he gasped, 'I can't breathe. I need a doctor.'

'Oh dear, how sad, never mind,' Farrington said briskly. 'Michael Alexander Jordan, I'm charging you as an accessory to the murders of Chloe Knight, Andrew Dullaston, Juliette Dullaston, Samuel Dullaston and Felicity Dullaston. I must caution you that you do not have to say anything, but that anything you do say will be taken down and may be used in evidence against you. Is that clear?'

Jordan groaned. Farrington looked at Lockwood and Monroe and gave a brief nod.

'I think that means yes,' she said. 'Let's go.'

58

'We found Mike Jordan's fingerprints at the lock-up. They matched the ones we took when we brought him in after the trouble at the camp last week,' Farrington said.

She was sitting in the Knights' lounge, drinking tea. It was four o'clock in the afternoon, getting dark outside. When she had first entered the room, clutching a plastic bag which was wrapped around something she wanted to show to the Knights and to Jackie Foster, she had been curious to see blankets draped over the settee and one of the armchairs. Then she had remembered Annette's insistence that everything that Keeve had touched be taken outside and burned. A compromise had been reached, it seemed, though an uneasy one. Annette was sitting on the only untainted armchair, her knees drawn up as if she didn't want her feet to go anywhere near the carpet that her daughter's killer had walked on.

'Do you think it was Mike Jordan who did the actual killing, Inspector?' asked Jackie. She was sitting on the shrouded settee with Eric and Tim. PC Beatty, one of the two policemen whom Farrington had assigned as live-in protection until Keeve was caught, was in the kitchen, drinking tea, eating biscuits and reading the *Daily Star*.

'We don't know yet. He claims he had nothing to do with the murders. He says that Keeve was paying him a hundred pounds a day to run errands and to dress up in the Mr Bad Face gear. There's no escaping the fact that he must have known what Keeve was up to, though, and was simply turning a blind eye. In my book, that's as bad as being directly involved.'

'A hundred pounds a day is a lot of money to pay someone just to frighten us,' said Eric. 'I didn't realise Keeve was so rich. What did he do, rob a bank?'

Farrington gave a tired smile. She'd had very little sleep over the past forty-eight hours, and her reserves of adrenaline were now running low. 'Nothing so dramatic,' she said. 'As we suspected, Keeve never had a wife and daughter. He'd been living with his invalid mother until her death four months ago. They made a lot of money in 1980 by selling the house in Jasmine Road and buying a smaller place, a bungalow on the other side of Tewkesbury. Plus he had a reasonably good job as a credit controller with a pharmaceutical firm – that much of it at least was true – and nothing to spend his money on. He wasn't extravagant and he didn't have any vices.'

'Except killing people,' muttered Tim.

'You don't think he'd been saving up his money for this, do you?' said Jackie. 'Planning it for years?'

'I don't know. Perhaps his mother's death sparked it off. We'll find out when we catch him.'

'You've still got no idea where he might be?' said Eric.

'Not yet. If Mike Jordan knows, he's not telling us. But we'll keep working on him.'

'Were Jame— sorry, *Keeve's* fingerprints found at the lock-up too, Inspector?' asked Jackie.

'No. It seems Mr Keeve was more careful than Mike Jordan. He was just unlucky that there was a witness to his meeting with Jordan in your garden, and that the key fell out of his pocket when he fell down.' She took a sip of her tea. 'We did find more than enough evidence at his bungalow to convict him, though. Extensive files on all of you and the Dullastons, negatives and photographs of the mask, a bill from the printer who printed up the posters. We spoke to the printer, incidentally, who said he remembers Keeve telling him the posters were meant as a joke for a friend.' She reached down and picked up the plastic bag-wrapped package that was propped against the chair. She opened the bag out, reached inside it and produced a hardbound black book with a red cloth spine, which she held out. 'We also found this. I thought you might want to take a look.'

Eric took the book from her, a quizzical expression on his face. He opened it at the first page and was confronted by lines of neat, cramped, handwritten prose.

'What is it?' he asked. 'A journal of some kind?'

'Read it,' said Farrington. 'Tell me what you think.'

Eric frowned and began to read. '"Tizer," James Keeve shouted. "Tizer, here boy ..."'

He read on, his face growing ever more bewildered. At last he shook his head slowly and said, 'I don't understand. This is the story James told us about himself, about how he took the dog for a walk and saw the figure in the playing fields.'

Farrington nodded. 'That's right.'

'But who wrote this?' His face suddenly cleared. 'It was James, wasn't it? This was his way of ... of creating a persona for himself.'

Jackie took the book from Eric and began to leaf through it. 'But why write it like this, in third person?'

'Perhaps Keeve found this the best way to relate to the character he wanted you to believe he was,' Farrington said. 'Maybe doing it this way, creating dialogue, atmosphere, exploring the character's thought processes, made this alternative James Keeve more real for him, more immediate.'

'But why *third* person?' Jackie insisted. 'Why not first person?'

Farrington shrugged. 'He may have been confused in his own mind as to who exactly he was. Perhaps he didn't want to risk aspects of his own personality creeping in to the character of this other James Keeve and spoiling the illusion. Or it could be that he actually does think of himself in the third person – killers sometimes do. It's a way of distancing themselves from their actions.'

'Like schizophrenics giving names to the different aspects of their personality as though they're separate people, you mean?' said Jackie.

'Well ... yes, I suppose so,' said Farrington doubtfully. 'But schizophrenics aren't necessarily killers. Most of them aren't even violent.'

Jackie shuddered and handed the book back to Farrington. 'It's horrible to think of ... of Keeve planning all this, working everything out in such obsessive detail.'

Farrington nodded. 'But it's only a matter of time now before we pick him up. It's nearly over.'

'For you, maybe,' Annette said. It was the first time she had spoken since Farrington had come in.

Farrington looked at her with some surprise. 'I'm sorry?'

'I said, it's nearly over for you,' Annette muttered coldly. She drew herself into an even tighter huddle, as if she wanted to disappear completely. When she next spoke, her voice was more despairing than angry. 'It'll never be over for us.'

Wednesday 30 November

59

James Keeve sat motionless, legs drawn up, podgy hands resting on his knees. His gaze was fixed; he barely blinked. He was the eye of the storm, the centre around which all things revolved. He watched the patterns of the dust and the patterns of the darkness, and he sensed that soon it would be time.

60

As he reached for the sweet pickle, PC Chris Cutler was thinking about his son, Nathan's, fourth birthday, the day after tomorrow. He was hoping that by then this maniac would be behind bars. He didn't want to miss Nathan's party for the second year running.

It would be chaos, of course, utter, unadulterated chaos. Kids running around, shrieking and laughing, falling over and hurting themselves and bawling their eyes out until something distracted them and they were off, shrieking and laughing again. For the adults present, it would be like being caught up in a human whirlwind, but Cutler was looking forward to it far more than he'd ever let on to his mates at the nick.

He loved kids, loved their simplistic, innocent, wide-eyed view of the world. After a hard and depressing day shovelling the shit of humanity, Nathan was a tonic, a joy to come home to. Last year Cutler had missed his son's birthday because he'd been working on that body in the river case, the one they'd never got anyone for. Angie had told him later that all the kids had started throwing paper plates around like frisbees before Nathan's little friend, precocious, uncontrollable Archie from the playgroup, had decided that throwing plates was boring, that it was much more fun to throw food. When Cutler had arrived home that evening, the house had looked like a bomb site. Angie and Nathan had been asleep on the settee, both of them exhausted. Cutler had cleaned up around them, scooping trampled sausage rolls out of the carpet, putting mashed paper cups and torn wrapping paper into black bin liners. Once the bin bags had been tied up in the back porch and the carpet more or less reclaimed, he had picked Nathan up, a warm, floppy, red-cheeked bundle, and had carried him upstairs, undressed him, put him in his pyjamas and put him to bed without the boy even stirring. It was weird, but despite being bone-tired, he had actually enjoyed cleaning up. It had made him feel that he had made at least a small contribution to Nathan's special day.

Cutler began to spread sweet pickle on his cheese sandwich, and wondered whether the DI would allow him and young Beatty to vary their shifts so that he could make it to Nathan's party. He'd raised the issue once, tentatively, but Farrington had just looked at him in a don't-bother-me-with-trifles-I've-got-far-more-important-things-to-think-about sort of way, and he'd thought it prudent on that occasion not to press the issue. He knew Farrington could be a hard-nosed bitch at times, and he knew she had no family of her own, but Cutler didn't honestly think it was too much to ask. At the moment he and Beatty were rotating in twelve-hour shifts. Beatty was doing the day shift – six in the morning until six at night – and he was doing the graveyard shift. What Cutler wanted was to vary the shifts so that they went from eight till eight instead of six till six. Nathan's party started at four in the afternoon, so the way it was looking at the moment, Cutler would only be there for the first hour or so before he had to head off to work.

He'd spoken to Beatty about it, and the lad was agreeable, and Cutler was more than happy to work the fourteen-hour shift necessary to implement the changeover. All he had to do now was catch the DI in a good mood, but it had to be sometime today, because tomorrow night would be his last chance to do the fourteen hours before Nathan's party.

He cut his sandwich in half, then picked up the kettle and crossed the kitchen to fill it at the sink. It was two-thirty in the morning, and all was quiet. The Knights and their house guest were in bed, and Cutler was about to settle down with a sandwich, a cup of tea and a video. At least he'd be there to see Nathan opening his presents in the morning this year, he thought, as he turned on the tap; last year he had even missed that. The boy was crazy about Winnie the Pooh at the moment; he had a cuddly Winnie the Pooh that he carried around with him everywhere, Winnie the Pooh pyjamas, Winnie the Pooh videos, Winnie the Pooh books, you name it. For Nathan's birthday, he and Angie had gone to the Disney shop in York and had bought him a Winnie the Pooh lunchbox and a Winnie the Pooh colouring book with a set of paints. Cutler suspected that Nathan's initial interest had been sparked by the sheer joy of being able to yell, 'Pooh! Pooh! Pooh!' when asked what bedtime story he would like.

It was while water was still spattering into the kettle that Cutler felt the curious cold sensation in his back. It was as though someone had pressed ice cubes against his spine, but even as this thought crossed his mind the sensation changed, became a hot gushing as though a cup of liquid had been emptied down his back, wetting him through his clothes. He had barely registered this new sensation when the pain kicked in, a terrible, biting, twisting pain, a red-hot corkscrew of agony that seemed as if it would cut him in half. Suddenly he felt dizzy and sick and horribly weak. The room spun around him. He dropped the kettle, which crashed into the sink.

Holding on to the sink as if his life depended on it, he managed to turn himself around. The room was receding now, disappearing down a swirling black corridor. He could hear the blood roaring in his ears, the pump-pump of his heart which seemed in sync with the terrible pain that was engulfing him.

And then, swimming into view, he saw a face, small and distant, as though viewed through the wrong end of a telescope. It was a plump face, and somehow dusty. And beside the face was a stick of oily red light.

No, not light: a knife. The knife Cutler had cut his sandwich with. Except that now the knife was red. It was covered with blood. With *his* blood.

'Please,' he whispered, wanting to explain to this man about Nathan, about his birthday the day after tomorrow, about how he would be four, about his party, his Winnie the Pooh lunchbox.

But the words wouldn't come. His voice, like his life, was draining out through the hole that the knife had made in his back.

He tried again: *please*. But this time the word was nothing more than a sigh, an exhalation.

Darkness closed in around the plump, dusty face, filling in the white and the red.

Pooh, Daddy, Pooh, Nathan screamed, as though trying desperately to make him laugh.

The words echoed down the long black tunnel with him.

Pooh, Daddy, Pooh.

61

The silly cow actually looked shocked. So she wasn't a fucking robot, after all. How long had he been here? Eighteen hours? And for the first time he had said something that had caught her off-guard, that had made her look vulnerable, like a proper woman was supposed to.

His triumph, though, was all too short-lived. A split-second and then the visor came down again, the voice, hard as ever, battering at him. Her questions had been relentless, like blows from an iron bar banging repeatedly down on his skull.

'What did you just say?' she demanded, her voice bouncing back off the scabby cream walls. 'What did you just say?'

Despite her clamped expression, there was a gleam of sweat on her upper lip. She brought up a hand – one flick and the sweat was gone.

But it was a victory, however small, something to be relished. Jordan smiled through the pain in his ribs and took a long drag on his cigarette.

62

'Wake up, Tim. Come on.'

The voice was soft, implacable, but it curled around Tim's dreams with the slow strength of a snake and strangled them. Tim groaned resentfully. He was dog-tired, but his mind was so busy with tension that when he slept he felt as if he was only dipping beneath the surface of sleep, not reaching the real deeps where he wanted to go.

'Go away,' he murmured, clinging to the warmth and the darkness, his body aching where Mike Jordan had kicked him. Whoever the voice belonged to, whatever it wanted, it could wait.

'No,' the voice said. 'Wake up.'

And suddenly Tim felt a shock of cold as his duvet was pulled away.

'Hey,' he complained, groping down towards his ankles in the hope of catching hold of the flapping end of the duvet and yanking it back over him. But his hand encountered only empty air, at least until another hand closed over his wrist and held it tight. Tim was more than half-awake now, but what brought him all the way was the sudden stinging pain in his forearm, like that of a nettle which had somehow got into his skin. The hand holding his wrist let go as Tim jerked his arm back, his eyes snapping open, an involuntary yelp leaping out of him.

There was someone in his room, standing by his bed. Leaning over him, features a blur of shadow. Tim was awake, but disorientated. He struggled to sit up. His arm was aching now, throbbing. He put a hand over the source of the pain, and was startled to feel the slippery wetness there.

Blood!

With the feel of his own blood came realisation. It hit him like a convulsion, turning his stomach inside out, terror surging in his heart, making it race. Tim knew without question that the man standing beside his bed was James Keeve. He leaped up as though his mattress had burst into flames, tried to scramble off the other side of the bed, but Keeve lunged and grabbed hold of Tim's good arm and, using Tim's own momentum, twisted it behind him.

'Let go of me!' Tim screamed. 'Let go of me! Help! Help! Dad, help!'

'Your father can't help you,' Keeve said softly. 'No one can. Now, stop struggling and stop shouting or I'll cut you again.'

It was hard to deny his instincts, but Tim made his body become as still as his terror would allow. He was shaking uncontrollably, his limbs twitching, teeth chattering. Like his heart, his mind was racing, racing so fast he could hardly think.

'That's better,' said Keeve. His voice was still soft, but oddly detached, as though he was in a trance. 'I want you to get off the bed now, Tim. We're going downstairs.'

Tim obeyed as Keeve let go of his arm, his body feeling jerky and strange as he pushed himself to his feet.

'All right,' Keeve said when Tim was standing, shivering, at the side of the bed. 'Let's go.'

Tim flinched as Keeve moved towards the door in the darkness, silently, smoothly, despite his bulk. 'You're n-not going to h-hurt me, are you?' he whimpered. 'P-please don't hurt me. We haven't d-done anything to you.'

Keeve didn't react; it was as though Tim hadn't even spoken. He opened the door of Tim's room, and as light from downstairs crept in, Tim saw him properly for the first time. Small, plump, dishevelled, dusty, bespectacled and balding. He should have been pathetic, but he wasn't. Somehow, it was his sheer ordinariness that made him terrifying. He was the sort of man you'd pass in the street or sit next to on the train without ever guessing what he was capable of.

Then light fell on the knife that Keeve was holding loosely in his right hand, point downwards, and Tim felt a black, vertiginous wave sweep through him. The knife was smeared with blood, dripping dark spots on the carpet. Tim groped for the edge of the bed, needing something solid to hold on to. He couldn't pass out now, and leave himself at the mercy of this psycho, he just couldn't.

He didn't, though it was a close thing. When Keeve next spoke, his voice sounded mushy and distorted in Tim's ears. So much so that Tim had to say, 'S-sorry, what? I-I d-didn't hear you. I-I'm not f-feeling very well.'

Keeve paused for a long moment, as if Tim had been deliberately obtuse. However the bland, almost placid expression on his face didn't change, and at last he said, 'You walk in front of me. But don't try to escape because I'll catch you. I want you to walk slowly down the stairs and into the lounge. Do you understand?'

Tim nodded quickly, jerkily, and taking a deep breath moved away from the bed. To follow Keeve's instructions he had to walk towards him, towards the knife, which his every instinct was screaming at him not to do. He kept thinking of the blood on the knife. Whose was it? Was it his own? Had Keeve cut him that badly? So far he hadn't dared look at his arm in the semi-light for fear of what he might see.

A few feet away from Keeve he stopped, his legs refusing to take him any further. His whole body was shaking, as though from extreme cold. He knew that one step more would bring him within striking distance of Keeve's knife. He stood for perhaps three seconds before Keeve asked him mildly, 'Why have you stopped, Tim?'

Tim couldn't answer, couldn't bring himself to draw attention to the blood-smeared knife. He knew it was ridiculous, but he felt if he mentioned the knife it might prompt Keeve to use it, whereas if he didn't Keeve might forget he had it in his hand. He knew he had to give Keeve some sort of answer, though; he couldn't just stand there mutely.

In the end, rather lamely, he whimpered, 'I-I don't know. I can't m-move, that's all. I ... I ...' He floundered to a halt.

Keeve nodded, the light flashing on his spectacles. 'Yes you can. I'm not going to cut you when you walk past me. Didn't I say I wanted you to go downstairs, into the lounge?'

Tim made a small sound in this throat, and with a huge effort of will forced himself to move again. He was four feet from Keeve now, then two, then he was passing right by him. He felt the man's breath on his hair; his nostrils filled up with the man's smell.

It wasn't actually an unpleasant smell – it was dusty, indefinable, faintly aromatic – but to Tim there was something rotten and awful about it. It was as though the reek of the evil he had done oozed from Keeve's pores like sweat.

Feeling his gorge rise, Tim plunged past Keeve, so eager to put a little distance between the two of them that he stumbled and almost fell on the landing. He recovered, shaking with reaction, hoping Keeve wouldn't interpret his clumsiness as an escape attempt.

An agonising pause – five seconds, ten. Then Keeve said, 'Walk forward. I'll be just behind you.'

Tim walked on hollow legs to the head of the stairs. As he did so, he noticed the black square in the ceiling above his head – the attic entrance minus its panel of white wood. Instantly he realised how Keeve had got into the house. He must have had the spare key, which was why Tim had been unable to find it yesterday, and had come back after discharging himself from the hospital last night and let himself in whilst they were all at the police station. Knowing that Keeve had spent the whole day in the house with them while the police had been looking for him made Tim feel sick. Instinctively he looked for, and then reached out to, the banister rail, and saw his arm for the first time.

Immediately another wave of dizziness swept over him. He closed his eyes, took a few deep breaths, thought: *It's not so bad, it's not so bad.*

It wasn't, in fact, but in his present state of mind any intimation of violence only seemed like a promise of more to come.

There was quite a bit of blood, most of it drying now, from a wound perhaps three inches long but quite deep. In the past few minutes, he'd been so focused on holding himself together that he'd forgotten the pain, but now that he could see the wound it began to throb and sting again.

He opened his eyes and continued slowly down the stairs, clutching the banister rail as though it was a lifeline. Behind him he could hear Keeve, the creaking of the stairs as he put his weight on them, his soft, slow breathing.

He reached the bottom of the stairs, and turned along the hallway, stopping outside the closed lounge door. There was no sound from within. He put his hand on the handle, but lingered there a moment, suddenly afraid.

'Open it,' Keeve said.

Without turning, still staring at the door, Tim said, 'W-what's in here?'

'Open it.'

I don't want to. I'm scared. What if . . . what if . . .

Tim turned the handle and opened the door.

The room was full of bodies.

That was his first impression. Bodies. Three of them. Two on the floor, one covered in blood, the other on the blanketed settee. His whole body seemed to clench in shock, the sensation so violent that he thought it might stop his heart. Then he saw that the bodies were moving, the one on the settee wriggling like a fish. The one on the floor that he'd thought was covered in blood raised its head and looked at him.

It was his dad, and he wasn't covered in blood at all, he was wearing maroon pyjamas. Beside him, in a long nightshirt, legs and feet bare, was Jackie. She looked scared but defiant, strands of her dark hair sticking to her face. Annette was on the settee, wriggling and thrashing, looking more furious than scared.

All three were tied up with washing line, and Mum's mouth was stretched open as though something had been stuffed in there and then taped up, presumably because she had been shouting at Keeve. Tim wondered how Keeve had managed to tie them all up. Maybe he'd done it when they were asleep, or maybe he'd held the knife to one of their throats and made them tie up each other.

'Tim,' Jackie said, her voice a gulp of relief, 'are you all right?' Then, noticing her son's arm, 'What has he done to you?'

'It's all right,' Tim said, 'it's just a scratch, that's all.'

'Kneel down and put your arms behind you,' Keeve said.

'W-why? What are you going to do?'

'Leave him alone, James,' said Jackie fiercely. 'He's got nothing to do with this.'

'Kneel down and put your arms behind you, or I'll cut your mother. She bit me, look.'

A hand appeared over Tim's shoulder, right beside his face. A podgy hand, bristly with small black hairs. There was a crescent of teeth marks on the ball of the thumb.

Tim knelt down and put his hands behind his back. He felt like a prisoner awaiting execution. He hunched his shoulders, half-expecting to feel cold steel across the back of his neck. He heard Keeve fumbling about, then felt something being wrapped around his wrists. More washing line. It felt quite loose until Keeve yanked on it, drawing it tight enough to make Tim cry out.

'Stand up, walk to that armchair there and sit down,' Keeve said when he had done. This time it wasn't just his hand that appeared over Tim's shoulder, but the knife as well, some of the blood congealing on it now. The knife pointed at the armchair across the room – the one Annette had been sitting on for most of the day, knees hunched up as if the rest of the place was contaminated.

Tim shied away from the knife, another small sound escaping him, then stood up on shaky legs and did as Keeve asked, stepping between the bound bodies of Jackie and his dad.

The kitchen door was ajar, and from here Tim could see into the kitchen. What he saw made him look away quickly, his stomach flipping over. The body of the policeman who was supposed to be here to protect them, was lying very still in a pool of what was most definitely blood.

He sat on the armchair, awkwardly because his hands were behind him. Quickly Keeve knelt in front of him and tied his legs together. Just for a second, Tim considered lashing out with his feet, kicking Keeve as hard as he could in the face. But the consequences of what might happen if he didn't knock Keeve out or make him drop the knife made him hesitate, and seconds later the chance was gone.

Keeve walked back across the room and sat in the other armchair. For a few moments he just looked at his captives, his grey eyes seeming to contain a blankness that went on for ever. Then a faint smile appeared on his face, and he put the knife carefully on the shrouded arm of the chair as if it were a cup of tea. 'Well,' he said, 'here we all are.'

For a few moments nobody replied. Then Eric raised his head and, struggling to keep his voice steady, said, 'Look, James, what is all this? What are you doing it for?'

Keeve turned his bland gaze on Eric. He continued to give the eerie impression of being controlled, calm and alert, and yet at the same time not quite all there. 'Don't pretend you don't know, Eric. You were there when we burned the house down. You and Jackie and Andrew and me.'

Eric frowned. 'But that was years ago, James, and nothing ever came of it. What has it got to do with what's happening now?'

Keeve picked up the knife and began toying with it, idly testing the stickiness of the blood on the blade with his thumb. Then he put it back down and said mildly, 'I know what you're doing. You're humouring me, playing for time. You think you're being very clever.'

'No, not at all. I just—'

'You always thought you were better than me. Just because I was small and not very strong, just because you could stay out later than I could, just because I didn't always want to do the things that you wanted to do.'

'No, James, you've got it wrong,' said Jackie. 'You were our friend. We liked you.'

As if she hadn't even spoken, Keeve said, 'But I'm strong now, aren't I? You're not laughing at me now.'

'We never laughed at you, James,' said Eric.

'Behind my back, when I wasn't there. I wasn't stupid, you know, I knew exactly what you were doing. Laughing at me, just because my mother cared about me.'

He picked up the knife again and squeezed it. He'd begun speaking a little faster, and an edge had crept into his voice. It wasn't much, but it was enough to make Tim realise that Keeve, although he appeared calm, was teetering on the edge of frenzy, liable to spiral out of control at any moment.

'No, James, you were our *friend*,' Eric said, reiterating Jackie's words, his voice soothing as though speaking to a snarling, prowling animal. 'We *all* liked you. We always have.'

For an instant Tim thought that the shrill double-bleat was some kind of mad, inhuman sound of ridicule or disbelief that Keeve had made in response to his father's words, before realising it was the telephone. After the second pair of rings, Keeve rose from the armchair and crossed the room, lifted the telephone from its shelf and placed it on the floor next to Eric's head. Over its fourth pair of rings he said, 'You'll make them believe that everything's fine here, won't you, Eric?'

Eric nodded, and Keeve lifted the receiver and placed it to the side of Eric's head. 'Hello,' Eric said, managing to make his voice sound almost normal. He blinked and looked up at Keeve as if for approval, but Keeve seemed almost uninterested in the interruption now, gazing at Eric abstractedly as if trying to remember the whereabouts of something he'd misplaced.

After a short pause, during which the caller's voice sounded to Tim like an insect rustling in the hollow of the mouthpiece, Eric said, 'Er ... yes, we're fine, Mum. Look, can I call you back later? Things are a bit hectic just now.' He listened again, then said, 'All right, speak to you later. Look after yourself, Mum. Bye.

'My mother,' he said to Keeve, who replaced the receiver and carried the telephone back across the room. 'You remember her, don't you, James? She used to give you lemonade and biscuits when you came to our house. Always said what a nice young man you were.' He paused as though debating whether to add what was also in his mind, then said, 'She's in her seventies now. She was devastated when she heard what had happened to Chloe. Absolutely devastated. Chloe was her only granddaughter.'

However hard it had been for him to say that, he had managed to keep most of the waver out of his voice. Keeve, however, gave no indication of having even heard Eric. He put the telephone on its shelf, then walked back over to the armchair and sat down. For a few seconds he looked utterly vacant, as if he was in a deep trance, and then unexpectedly he said, 'She's dead now.'

Silence followed his words as if everyone was waiting for a punch-line, before Eric asked, 'Who, James?'

'My mother. She ... she died.' Just for a second Keeve's voice faltered, and Tim thought he was actually going to show some emotion. Then he recovered, smiled vaguely. 'But she's in a good place, I know it. She's gone where she deserved to go.'

'I'm sorry to hear that, 'Eric said. 'About her dying, I mean. You and she were always very close, weren't you?'

Again Keeve gave the impression he hadn't heard. As though eulogising, or about to, he said, 'She's floating now, somewhere above us. No cares, no pain, nothing.'

Like Chloe, Tim thought, but remained silent. Keeve seemed to him like a bomb that his dad was desperately trying to defuse. He didn't want to be the one who said the wrong thing and made the bomb go off.

'Is that why you're doing this, James?' Jackie asked. 'Because of your mother?'

Keeve stared at Jackie for a long moment. His gaze seemed to hum with potential. Then in a voice so flat it was terrifying, he said, 'What's she got to do with this?'

'We don't know, James,' Eric said levelly. 'You tell us.'

'Nothing,' Keeve said, shaking his head slowly from side to side. 'She's got nothing to do with this. She always looked after me, protected me. She'll be in a better place now, after all she's done.'

Tim couldn't help feeling that the exchange between his dad, Jackie and Keeve had suddenly slipped to a deeper, more fundamental level. Certainly his dad's voice was softer now, as though he was probing more cautiously.

'When we were children? Is that what you mean, James? She protected you when we were children?'

Keeve had become very still. His eyes seemed fixed, like a dead man's.

'Always,' he murmured. 'She always protected me. She was a good mother.'

'I'm sure she was,' Eric said. 'But what was she protecting you *from*, James?'

'Outside,' Keeve said.

'The outside world, you mean?'

Keeve seemed to consider the question. 'People.'

'What kind of people, James?'

Tim could almost believe that his dad was hypnotising Keeve, that eventually he would order Keeve to untie them and hand over the knife and Keeve would obey. And then Keeve said, 'Pretending you don't know won't help you.'

If Eric was taken aback, he didn't show it. 'I want to hear you say it, James. I want to hear you tell us.'

Keeve's eyes swivelled slowly to look at him. '*You* want it?' he said.

Eric licked his lips. Until now he had seemed calm, but all at once he looked nervous. 'That is ... of course ... if you wouldn't *mind* telling us,' he said contritely.

The silence that followed seemed to go on for ever. Even Annette had stopped wriggling by now, and both she and Jackie were watching Keeve with wide, wary eyes. Tim's leg and back were aching intolerably due to his confrontation with Mike Jordan, and the cut on his arm was a hot itch, and his hands were numb, but he dared not move.

Tim's fear had actually made him forget what his dad was hoping Keeve would tell them when Keeve said abruptly, 'People who might find out. People who you wanted to blame me for what we did.'

'People who might find out about the fire, you mean?' Eric coaxed.

'You know what I mean.'

'But we didn't tell anyone about the fire, James. None of us did. We agreed not to. Don't you remember?'

Keeve's voice didn't change, but there seemed to Tim to be a measure of contempt in it all the same. 'Don't think you'll confuse me, Eric.'

'I'm not trying to confuse you, James. I'm just trying to get at the truth.'

'I know the truth.'

'Then why don't you tell us what it is?'

'You know it too.'

Eric laid his head back on the carpet for a moment and stared up at the ceiling. Tim thought he looked like a man who had driven up a dead end road and wasn't sure of his route back. As if picking up where he had left off, Jackie said cautiously, 'You say your mother protected you from people who might find out about the fire?'

'You know that's what I said.'

'But doesn't that mean that she must have known about the fire herself? Doesn't it mean that someone must have told her?'

For a moment the room seemed so stretched with tension that Tim expected something to snap. But Keeve just sat there, holding the knife and saying nothing for so long that eventually Eric, who had raised his head again to gauge Keeve's reaction to Jackie's question, asked quietly, 'Did *you* tell her, James?'

Keeve's head rolled slowly back on his shoulders, as if he was growing weary of the conversation, or in need of sleep. He murmured, 'She knew what to do. She knew how to stop everyone from blaming me.'

'And how was that, James?'

'She looked after me.'

'And how did she do that?'

Keeve looked down again, head tilted almost coquettishly. 'By being cleverer than you. By keeping everyone away. She knew that if she kept everyone away, I'd be safe.'

'Safe from whom, James?'

'The people who you wanted to blame me.'

'But who *were* those people, James?'

'You know who they were. You hoped they'd take me away when they found out.'

'Is that what she told you, James?' said Jackie. 'That unless you stayed with her, people would find out about the fire and they'd blame you and take you away?'

For a moment Keeve stared at his two childhood friends as if he was uncertain, then stubbornly he said, 'She looked after me.'

'How often did she tell you this, James?' Jackie pushed. 'Every day?'

'She looked after me. She loved me.'

A screen seemed to have slid down behind Keeve's eyes. Tim thought, It's no good, he's not going to listen. He's only going to believe what he wants to believe.

Eric glanced at Jackie as if warning her to go easy, but she said, 'Every time you were late home from school or from work? Every time she saw you talking to someone? Did she tell you it was dangerous to make friends, James? That if you made friends, they'd find out? Did she drum it into your head, James, day after day? Did she make you so scared of being found out that you couldn't sleep at nights? Did you lie awake, unable to think of anything else except how important it was to stay with your mother so that she could look after you?'

A frown had appeared on Keeve's face and he raised a podgy hand slowly to his forehead. 'I don't think I want to talk any more,' he mumbled.

'Why not, James? Am I getting too close to the truth? Am I making you realise that all this time you've been blaming the wrong people for how your life's turned out?'

Keeve looked confused and betrayed, like a small child who had just been told that Santa Claus didn't exist. Abstractedly he said, 'Be quiet now, please. I've had enough.'

He lurched to his feet, making Jackie's eyes widen in fear that she might have gone too far, and causing Tim to jerk in his seat with a suddenness that sent a trident of pain shooting down his arms and back. The confusion on Keeve's face was already slipping into sullenness. In a voice that was almost whiny he said, 'I knew there'd be no point talking to Andrew, so I didn't even try, but I thought the two of you would be different. I thought there might be some shred of decency left in you somewhere. I thought you might at least admit to what you'd done and be sorry for it.'

'Would it have made a difference?' Eric asked cautiously.

'It would have made us all feel a lot better.'

'So what if we were to say sorry now? What if we were to say that we're deeply sorry for whatever you feel we've done to you?'

Keeve smiled almost coyly. 'That would be nice.'

'In that case, I'm sorry, James. Jackie and I are both deeply sorry. Aren't we, Jackie?'

Jackie licked her lips, looking nervous but a little indignant. Then she nodded and muttered, 'Yes.'

'You mean it?' said Keeve.

'Of course.'

'That *is* nice. That's *really* nice,' Keeve said. He stood in front of the armchair, swaying slightly, the knife in his hand.

'I'm glad you're pleased,' Eric said. He hesitated, then said tentatively, 'So look, James, why don't we call it quits, forget that all this ever happened? I mean, now that we're all friends again, there's no need to carry on with all this ... bad feeling, is there?'

Keeve smiled again, and Tim thought: My God, he's going to let us go!

Then Keeve said, 'Don't be silly, Eric. I can't do that, can I?'

He made it sound as though Eric had asked him an impossible favour. All the hope, all the resolve, drained from Eric's face, and suddenly he looked as scared as Tim felt.

'W-why not?' he said.

Keeve was still smiling, but now it seemed like a doll's grin, wide but vacuous. 'It wouldn't be right, would it? Not after all these years.'

Tim could see that his dad was at a loss. He'd cut what had seemed like all the right wires, but the timer was still ticking inexorably towards destruction. All the bitterness and fear and indignation that

Jackie had been holding back suddenly came flooding out of her.

'So what are you going to do?' she demanded. 'Kill us all in cold blood, just because you're too fucking inadequate to deal with life?'

Tim held his breath. For a few seconds Keeve simply stood there, the same empty smile attached to his face. When he did speak, his voice was eerily reasonable, almost compassionate; it was the voice a vet might use to explain to a child why it would be kinder to put their old, sick dog to sleep.

'I have to *make* you sorry for what you've done to me. Surely you can both see that? Just *saying* sorry isn't enough, is it? I'm not saying I don't appreciate it, but a few little words can't mend all those broken years, can they?'

'*But we haven't DONE anything!*' Jackie screamed at him. '*It's your mother you should have killed! She's the one who ruined your fucking life! We kept our side of the bargain!*'

Her words twisted off as if she had been strangled. She was trembling now with rage and fear. Keeve, however, still smiling faintly, seemed completely unmoved by her outburst. 'No, no, you didn't, you see,' he said. 'You all went away and left me.'

'We didn't leave you,' Eric said desperately. 'We made lives for ourselves, that's all. It's what people do. It's what *you* should have done.'

'How could I,' Keeve said bemusedly, 'after the trap you'd left for me?'

'There *was* no trap, James, or if there was it wasn't of our making. Can't you see that it *wasn't us?* We didn't do *anything*. It was your mother who held you back and threatened to tell, wasn't it? She was the only one who knew about the fire apart from us. And she used that information to terrify you, used it so effectively that you couldn't tell what was real and what wasn't. Why can't you see that, James? It was your mother who ruined your life!'

But Keeve just looked at him with something like pity, his bland smile still fixed to his face. 'No,' he said, 'she loved me.'

'Which is exactly why she did it! She loved you so much that she was prepared to do anything not to let you go!'

Keeve moved the knife from his right hand to his left and then back again. 'If you could only hear yourself. If you could only hear how ridiculous you sound, how much you're twisting the truth.'

'No, James, *you're* the one who's twisting the truth, and deep down I think you know it. We're innocent, James. Everyone you've killed is innocent. My daughter, Chloe, was innocent. Andrew's children were innocent. And what about the policeman in the kitchen? What has he ever done to hurt you?'

It was clear that Eric's pleas were falling on deaf ears. Keeve was looking around now as if seeking fresh entertainment, as if Eric was a toy which had lost its novelty.

His gaze fell on Tim, and Tim shuddered, then the gaze moved on. All at once, as if selecting a chocolate from a box, Keeve said, 'Annette first, I think.' He looked round, his smile finally slipping, face becoming deadpan once more. 'Eric and Jackie, I want you to watch. Tim, you can close your eyes if you like. I want to show you how frightened I've been, how much hurt I've had to put up with all these years.'

He walked to the settee, stepping over Eric and Jackie. Eric began thrashing about frantically, trying to loosen his bonds or otherwise stop Keeve in some way. Annette's eyes were bulging in terror, and she was making high-pitched, inarticulate noises behind her gag which made Tim think of the sounds a scared and injured dog might make. He himself was so seized by terror that his innards felt like cement; he couldn't move or speak, or even close his eyes as Keeve had suggested he should.

Eric was pleading now, and it was awful to hear, all faculties of reasoning stripped away, only the raw extremities of emotion left. '*No, James, please. Please don't hurt her. Think about what you're doing. Please, James. Please, don't.*'

But Keeve paid not the slightest attention. He clambered awkwardly on to the settee beside Annette, grabbed hold of her hair with one podgy, blood-stained hand, and dragged her, squealing, into a semi-upright position.

Eric was so white he looked as though he might pass out or even have a heart attack. He began babbling, half-sobbing, his words barely intelligible. Jackie joined in his pleas, though she seemed so profoundly terrified now that her body was actually vibrating.

Annette squeezed her eyes shut as Keeve brought his knife-hand round in front of her face. He turned his wrist so that the knife was pointing right at her face, then he placed the point of the blade almost gently on the soft flesh beneath her left eyeball. Slowly, slowly, he began to exert pressure, the knife-point breaking the skin, coaxing out a bead, and then a trickle, of blood. Tim's mouth opened wide as if to shout or vomit, but nothing emerged; even his breath seemed to have solidified in his gullet.

Keeve glanced round, grey eyes like marbles behind his spectacles. 'Are you watching, Eric?' he said. 'This is my pain.'

And then the room exploded.

Or at least, that was how it seemed to Tim. For suddenly there was a massive and directionless series of crashes, the shock of which made him feel as though he had been wrenched from his trussed body. He'd barely recovered before the room was flooding with people.

It took him perhaps three long seconds to realise that the newcomers were policemen. Policemen wearing what looked like riot gear and carrying rifles. He was too disorientated to tell how many of them there were, though they seemed to fill the room, to come from all directions, bulky figures in dark padded jackets and visored helmets. They surrounded Keeve and pointed their weapons at him. Tim wondered why they didn't just shoot him, but then he saw that in the few seconds it had taken for the policemen to enter the house and take up their positions, Keeve had dragged Annette round in front of him, and was now kneeling on the settee, using her as a shield to protect his body, pressing the knife against her throat. After the flurry of activity of a few moments before, the room suddenly seemed to become as still as a photograph. Then Tim saw Farrington. She too was wearing a black padded jacket, though unlike the others, she had neither a helmet nor a gun. She came forward slowly, holding up her hands, showing Keeve her empty palms.

'Mr Keeve,' she said, almost conversationally, 'I think it's over. So why don't you put down the knife and let the lady go?'

Keeve seemed to stare right through her. 'This is my pain,' he murmured.

Then with one swift motion of his arm, he cut Annette's throat.

63

It happened so quickly that Tim barely had time to register what Keeve had done, before his ears were ringing from the crack of a rifle that sounded in the confined space as though the house had split in two. With the echoes still drilling through his skull, he saw Keeve's head jerk backwards, yanking the rest of his body behind it, and thought for one ludicrous moment that he was attempting an audacious somersault over the settee.

Then Keeve rebounded from the back of the settee with such force that he was thrown forward, folding at the hips, and as he crumpled face-down on the floor, Tim saw his shattered head and the stuff that was leaking from it. There was startlingly red blood, and slimy clumps of pinkish-grey dough that he couldn't quite accept were brains. His stomach cramped violently, but when he saw Annette – her body convulsing, her bulging eyes full of an awful, crazed terror, her throat gaping like a mouth whose lips were spilling a thick crimson soup that had already soaked her to her waist – the urge to vomit was replaced by a sickening flood of darkness, and he passed out.

He was unconscious for what seemed like no time at all, but when he awoke it was to see Inspector Farrington sitting astride Annette's now limp body, hands round her slashed throat, strangling her. Both women were drenched with blood, and Tim was reminded fleetingly of a film about female mud wrestlers that he and Chloe had watched one night when their parents were out. Lots of people were shouting and running about, but Farrington was yelling the loudest, evidently trying to extract information from Annette, because she was shouting, 'For God's sake, tell me!' For a split-second Tim was appalled at the treatment Annette was receiving, before he realised what Farrington was really doing. She was trying to hold the lips of Annette's wound together with her fingers, and she hadn't said 'tell me' at all, she had said 'help me'.

A few of the men threw down their weapons and rushed forward, blocking Tim's view of the two women. However, although he could no longer see Annette, he could hear her, even with all the noise that was going on around him. She was trying to breathe, making an awful bubbling gurgle that sounded like sludge running down a drain. Tim found it hard to convince himself that he was listening to anything other than her life trickling away.

Farrington instructed her men to lift Annette gently, one at each limb, one supporting her head. They did so, now reminding Tim of pallbearers carrying a coffin. Carefully they shuffled from the room, each of them having to step over Keeve's body, the leaking skull of which was now hidden from view by a police jacket. Farrington went with them, fingers still pinching the lips of the wound together, which made it look as though the blood had set like red cement, fusing the Inspector's hands to Annette's throat.

Only now did Tim become aware that someone was pleading to be untied, and had been doing so for a while. He looked down to see his father, still lying on the floor beside Jackie, his body rocking to and fro as he tried frantically to sit up, his long, white, bare feet flecked with Keeve's blood. His voice was raw with frustration and panic. A nearby policeman removed his helmet, revealing a flushed face, laid down his rifle, and crouched beside Eric. 'All right, sir, just try to keep calm, and we'll have you out of this lot in a moment or two.' He began to pick at the knotted washing line around Eric's ankles with his fingers, but after a few seconds he shook his head. 'Hang on, I'll have to find something to cut this with.'

He looked around, started to reach for the blood-stained knife, then thought better of it and went into the kitchen. He returned moments later with a pair of scissors. They weren't very sharp, and he had to work at Eric's bonds for a while before they suddenly snapped free. The instant they did, Eric was on his feet and lurching in pursuit of the procession that had borne Annette from the room.

The policeman who had released Eric now crouched beside Jackie, who was still trembling, her mouth open wide with shock. 'You're all right, love, it's all over now,' he said, his voice surprisingly gentle. As he began to cut through the washing line with the scissors, Farrington re-entered the room, looking haggard, holding up hands that were gloved to the elbows with blood.

'Inspector,' Tim croaked, surprised at the voice which came out of his mouth. Farrington looked up, her face unreadable, made a gesture to indicate that she was going to wash her hands, then went into the kitchen.

Tim leaned back in the chair, the pain in his arms and back so deep-seated by now that it felt as though it had always been there. He felt sick and faint, but slightly spaced out, like when he'd had a pre-med before having his tonsils out when he was eight. He was cold, which he thought was a symptom of shock, though it could just as easily have been caused by the wind whistling through the open doors of the house. The policeman who had freed his dad had cut Jackie's bonds now and was sitting her up. Farrington came out of the kitchen, drying her hands on a blue and white checked tea towel, which she dropped on to the settee as she crossed to Tim.

'Are you all right?' she asked him, then perhaps realising how ridiculous a question it was, snatched up the scissors which the policeman had placed on the floor after cutting Jackie's bonds, and without waiting for a reply said, 'Let's have you out of there.'

As the blunt-bladed scissors gnawed at the washing line round his ankles, Tim asked, 'Where's Mum?'

What he had really wanted to ask was, 'How's Mum?' but had been too afraid of the answer.

Farrington seemed to interpret the real meaning of his question, however. 'They think she's going to be fine, Tim. Try not to worry. She's on her way to hospital now in one of the ambulances that I had standing by. Your dad's with her. I told him I'd look after you. I know there was a lot of blood, but Keeve didn't have time to cut deeply enough to do any permanent damage, and fortunately he missed your mum's jugular vein.'

Suddenly the washing line around Tim's ankles snapped, and his feet seemed to spring apart. 'Can you stand?' Farrington asked.

Tim tried, but his feet were fizzing with pins and needles. 'I'll be able to in a minute,' he told her.

'All right. You just try and stamp some feeling back into your feet while I get your hands free. You'll have to just lean over to the side a bit if you can. There, that's fine.'

A couple of minutes later, Tim's hands sprang apart with a spasm of pain that made him cry out. Gently Farrington helped him to his feet, then took her jacket off and draped it across his shoulders. With an arm around his waist, she helped him shuffle from the room, out of the house, and into a night that was bitingly cold.

There was a police van and a number of police cars parked on the street, an ambulance standing directly outside the house with its back doors open, and people milling about everywhere. Jackie was being helped into the back of the ambulance by a paramedic wearing a white jacket with yellow reflector strips on the back and sleeves. Neighbours were looking out of their windows, or silently standing at the doors or gates of their houses, which added to Tim's sense of unreality, made him feel oddly like a performer in a play.

'If you go in that ambulance with Miss Foster, it'll take you to the hospital where you can see your mum,' Farrington said.

Tim nodded, and allowed Farrington to lead him down the path and out on to the street.

Here the blur of voices, the crackle of police radios, the growling of the ambulance engine, all seemed to combine, to act as a cocoon of sound which wrapped itself around him, making him feel secure and blessedly insignificant. Fumes were pouring out of the ambulance's exhaust, turning orange under the street lamps like magician's smoke.

'Are you coming too?' Tim asked Farrington as a paramedic came forward to guide him into the ambulance.

'No, I've got things to do here. I'll see you later.'

'How did you know Keeve was in the house?' Tim said, as if it was a question he'd been meaning to ask for a long time, though in fact it had only just occurred to him.

'Mike Jordan told me that Keeve had a set of keys to your house. When I rang up to warn PC Cutler, your dad answered and talked as though he was speaking to his mother. I guessed at once what was happening.'

Tim nodded. 'Thanks,' he said.

'For what?'

'For ... for everything. For saving my mum's life.'

Farrington raised her eyebrows as if she was undeserving of such praise. 'You're welcome,' she said. 'See you later.'

Epilogue: Friday 9 December

'You're going then?' said Tim.

'Yes. As soon as the funeral's over. All the children are back with their parents now, and the police have said we can.'

'Where will you go?'

'I don't know. On to the next place. We don't plan a route, we just ... travel. Find somewhere we like, stop for a bit, then move on.'

Tim shook his head. 'I still don't really see the point of it.'

Oonagh smiled. 'I don't see the point of staying in one place when there are so many to explore.'

Tim sighed and looked around, hands stuffed into his pockets. He felt self-conscious in his dark suit and tie, self-conscious too about the haunted, hollow-eyed expression that he knew clung to him like a mask he couldn't remove. He'd hardly been sleeping since it all ended over a week ago, and when he did, all he had were nightmares. He'd wake up in a cold sweat, convinced that a squat, bulky figure was standing beside his bed. The aftermath of the terror he'd experienced was like a fever that he couldn't shake from his system. Sometimes, even in daylight with people around him, he'd feel a sense of panic overwhelming him, a panic so acute that he couldn't draw breath. He'd shock himself by bursting into tears at the slightest thing, and there had been days when he'd felt crushed under a depression so black that he couldn't see the point of carrying on.

He'd thought today, the day of Chloe's funeral, would be particularly bad; he'd thought there was going to be no way that he'd be able to get through it. But oddly it seemed as though his mind, faced with the ordeal, had rallied, providing him with a strength he hadn't known he possessed. Not that he felt strong – far from it – but he was at least coping, going with the flow.

His mum and dad were inside the church, staring at Chloe's coffin, which was so smothered with flowers that it seemed the mourners had been trying to disguise it. Tim had asked if he could wait outside for Oonagh, and his dad, pushing the wheelchair which the hospital had lent Annette so that she could attend the service, had distractedly given his assent. It was a cold, breezy day, but crisp and clear. At first Tim had fielded the sympathetic looks and mumbled condolences which arriving mourners had bestowed upon him, but when a minibus had pulled up outside the church gates containing a group of Chloe's teachers and school friends, he had run and hidden behind a gravestone like a truant.

Eventually Oonagh and her parents had appeared, Oonagh wearing a long black overcoat and a black velvet hat whose brim framed her face. Tim's emotions were so brittle that he had almost cried at seeing her, before clearing his throat, vacating his hiding place and walking towards them. If they had been surprised to see him rising from behind a tombstone they hadn't said so. Graeme had shaken his hand and Linda had given him a hug, then they had gone into the church, leaving Tim and Oonagh alone.

Although seeing Oonagh had been the only thing Tim had been looking forward to today, he had at once felt nervous and tongue-tied. 'Hi,' he had said, and she had said, 'Hi,' back. There had been a silence, and then he had said quietly, 'You look ... great.'

'Thanks,' she had said, smiling. 'You look terrible.'

That had made Tim smile too; he wasn't quite up to laughing. He had reached out and grasped her hand. 'It's really good to see you.'

'You too,' she replied, then had said quickly, 'Look, have we got time for a quick walk round the church? There's something I need to tell you.'

They had strolled along the path between the gravestones, hand in hand, both of them silent as if in mutual understanding that a certain point had to be reached before either of them could speak. Then Oonagh had said, 'I know this isn't a good time, Tim, but I had to tell you that after today I might not see you again.'

Tim had guessed she would be leaving at some stage, though he hadn't wanted to think about it. Now, after she had told him she didn't see the point of staying in one place when there were so many to explore, he sighed, unable to think of much else to say. He wanted to plead with her to stay, but he knew it was pointless and impractical. He wanted to ask her whether she'd stay if it was purely her decision, but he was too afraid of what her answer might be. He wanted to tell her he needed her, but he didn't think he'd be able to lay his soul so bare, and besides wouldn't that just be emotional blackmail? In the end it was Oonagh who spoke, gently, compassionately.

'We're very different, you and me.'

'We're not that different,' Tim protested.

'Yes we are. We have different lifestyles. We want different things.'

'Is this your way of chucking me?' Tim said.

Oonagh smiled and squeezed his hand. 'I didn't even know we were officially going out.'

A breeze lifted Tim's fringe and rearranged it. He squinted and said, 'If you weren't going away I'd ask you to go out with me.'

'Ask me anyway,' said Oonagh.

'What's the point?'

'Just ask me.'

Tim sighed. 'Will you—'

'Yes. But it'll have to be a long-distance relationship. I'll write to you. I'll even ring you from time to time.'

'Might I really never see you again?' said Tim.

'I don't know. I'll probably be back for Mike Jordan's trial. I'm a witness, aren't I? Maybe I'll see you there. Or maybe I'll come back for you one day.'

Tim tried to smile, but his heart wasn't in it. 'We'd better get in there. They'll be about to start.'

Oonagh nodded, but still they hovered, as if reluctant to break the moment. Then she said, 'Just one kiss then. For courage.'

She stood on tiptoes and kissed him on the lips.